C000154448

MY BEST FRIEND'S SECRET

DANIELLE RAMSAY

B

Boldwood

First published in Great Britain in 2023 by Boldwood Books Ltd.

Cover Design by 12 Orchards Ltd

Cover Photography: Shutterstock

A CIP catalogue record for this book is available from the British Library.

Paperback ISBN 978-1-83751-090-0

Large Print ISBN 978-1-83751-086-3

Hardback ISBN 978-1-83751-085-6

Ebook ISBN 978-1-83751-083-2

Kindle ISBN 978-1-83751-084-9

Audio CD ISBN 978-1-83751-091-7

MP3 CD ISBN 978-1-83751-088-7

Digital audio download ISBN 978-1-83751-082-5

Boldwood Books Ltd
23 Bowerdean Street
London SW6 3TN
www.boldwoodbooks.com

To my mother, Janette Whittet Ramsay

'In the end, we will remember not the words of our enemies, but the silence of our friends.'

— MARTIN LUTHER KING JR

'I've learned that people will forget what you said, people will forget what you did, but people will never forget how you made them feel.'

— MAYA ANGELOU

'Vengeance and retribution require a long time; it is the rule.'

— *A TALE OF TWO CITIES*: CHARLES DICKENS

1

THURSDAY

I glanced at Willow, Issie and Ava as they focused on the minister's reading of Psalm 23. It was unspoken, but each of us could feel this insidious rift between us – guilt. We were all plagued by the same question: how could we not know? One of us must have been able to prevent it. Worse still, which one of us was to blame?

The hornets' nest in the pit of my stomach stirred. I held my breath, hoping the waspish noise would abate. Instead, the frenzied swarm buzzed in all directions. As if reading my mind, my husband Jacob took hold of my hand and squeezed it.

I caught Willow quizzically looking at me. Heat flushed up my neck. I pretended to read the Order of Service in honour of Jasmine Donaldson, or Jaz as she was known to us. Thankfully, Willow turned her attention back to the elderly minister. The last thing I needed today was her questioning me. I watched, unable to stop myself from feeling a stab of jealousy as Charles put his arm around her delicate shoulders and pulled her into him. I could feel the tears pricking at my eyes again.

I pulled my hand from Jacob's suffocating hold. I breathed out and turned my attention to the people around me. Aside from

Willow, Issie and Ava, most were strangers, their long, mournful faces lost on me.

'And I will dwell in the house of the Lord forever,' the minister sombrely concluded, with a discernible quiver in his voice.

He had shared in his eulogy with the mourners that he had baptised Jaz as a baby in this very church thirty-three years ago. And now, here he was, tragically laying her to rest. I watched as he lowered his white, wispy-haired head as if in silent prayer. He then lifted his watery light-blue eyes and nodded at Jaz's father in the front row before stepping down from the imposing wooden pulpit.

I dropped my head as Jaz's father stood up. I waited a few moments before looking up to see his tall, black-suited, rigid figure approach the white-clothed table in front of the wooden pulpit. It was adorned with elaborate bouquets of cream roses and lilies – Jaz's favourite flowers – surrounding two large photographs of her. He stopped, his eyes resting on the beautiful black-and-white head-shot of his daughter as she confidently beamed out from the silver photo frame at him – at us. It was a recent black-and-white photo, unlike the other one, which was an old colour photograph of Jaz taken at Queen Victoria's School for Girls as a tall, striking eleven-year-old, full of life and dreams of the bright future ahead of her. He shook his head as if struggling, as I was, with the knowledge that he would never feel the warmth of Jaz's infectious smile again.

Stiffly, he turned his gaze to the elaborate solid walnut coffin positioned to the side of the pulpit. I watched as he walked towards it, his trembling, liver-spotted hand touching the polished lid before climbing his way up to the pulpit. Once there, his rheumy hot eyes sought out mine. My skin burned with shame. It should have been me up there telling the mourners about my friend. But I had declined Jaz's father's request to read out a tribute, too fearful that I would choke on my words. Instead, I had given it to him to read on my behalf. I had made the excuse that my grief was so overwhelming that I doubted I would be able to speak without becoming an inconsolable mess. But, in reality, it was guilt that silenced me. Not that I could tell him. Nor could I tell Willow, Issie or Ava. Jaz was the one person who knew, and she was the reason we were here.

How could I stand up there and pretend that I had no part in Jaz's death? I thought back to the texts and voicemail message I had left Jaz two weeks ago. I replayed them over and over again in my mind, drowning out her father's voice as he read my eulogy about his daughter – my oldest friend.

I watched as Willow crumpled into Charles, her body convulsing in silent sobs as Jaz's father read my words. Jacob sought my hand, gently touching it. I couldn't bring myself to look at Ava or Issie sitting ahead of me, holding one another's hands for support.

I squeezed my eyes shut as her father described his much-loved and only child to the mourners as I tormented myself with the 'what if' scenario. I scratched and tore at my last words to her, questioning what part they played in her death – *if any*. I needed to remind myself of that fact as I didn't know whether she had listened to my voicemail. However, I knew that she had read my WhatsApp messages by the double blue ticks. But her only response had been silence, prompting me to ring her. When she'd declined my calls, I had left a drunken voicemail message. Spiteful, unjust and accusatory. I'd made a point of reminding Jaz that I was always there for her. Or, at least, I thought that was the case. Jaz chose not to talk to me that night. Instead, she took her life.

When I woke up the following morning feeling miserable and hungover, Jaz was already gone. The reality that I could never take back those cruel last words to her tore me apart. Up until that moment, too caught up in my own maelstrom, I didn't even realise that Jaz was in trouble. Now that she had my full attention, it was too late. *I was too late...*

I had failed her.

Oh God... Jaz... I am so sorry.

I suddenly realised that Jaz's father had stopped speaking, and everyone was standing, singing. I stood up and looked down at the Order of Service, clutched in my hand, momentarily thrown by the photograph of Jaz on the cover, smiling up at me as if nothing was wrong. Hands shaking, I fumbled through the pages searching for the hymn as the voices soared around me:

> Be still, my soul: when dearest friends depart
> And all is darkened in the vale of tears...
> Be still, my soul....

The Order of Service in my hand became blurred as tears blinded me. I slowly breathed in as I tried to focus on keeping it together, but the tears continued to trail down my face.

Tears won't bring her back, Claudia!

I squeezed my eyes tight as I tried to silence the guilt-fuelled voice in my head.

If only...

I stopped myself.

The singing surrounding me was drowned out by my inner voice as it raged at me about my failure to help Jaz when she needed me the most.

'Claudia? Hey? Claudia?'

Jacob's concerned voice cut through my tortured thoughts.

I shakily breathed out as I opened my eyes and turned to look up at him. How long had I been standing with my head bowed and eyes closed?

Praying for what, Claudia? For Jaz? Or for yourself?

'Come on. We need to go,' he tenderly prompted.

It was then that I realised the funeral service had finished, and we were the last people left in the small, centuries-old stone-built church. The rows of worn wooden pews now empty.

I looked up at the front of the small kirk to the table with the lavish flowers adorning Jaz's photographs. She smiled at me, laughter in her eyes, as if mocking me for my grief.

I tried but failed to swallow back the tears.

'I know this is hard on you. We don't need to stay for the burial. They'll understand,' Jacob whispered as his dark brown, gentle eyes searched mine.

I turned away from him, looking for her – for Jaz. But her coffin was gone.

How did I miss them taking you?

But I had. Just as I had missed the signs that my best friend was suicidal.

Oh God, Jaz...

Jacob touched my face, moving a stray lock of hair that had fallen across my wet cheek.

I instinctively flinched.

I looked at him. The hurt in his eyes was unmistakable.

He sighed. 'I don't think staying will help. Let's give our apologies to Jaz's parents and go. Yes?'

I remained silent.

'Come on, I hate seeing you like this.'

'Claudia? We wondered where you were,' a voice interrupted.

I turned to see Issie standing in the church doorway.

'We think it's right that the four of us are together for...' She faltered, unable to say the unthinkable, shaking her head instead.

For the truth was, we were about to bury our old school friend. Nothing could make that fact bearable.

'I'm coming,' I somehow managed to answer.

Issie looked at me, then at Jacob. The strain between the three of us palpable. Embarrassed, she nodded, then left.

As I made my way out of the pew, Jacob grabbed my arm to stop me.

'Don't do this,' he said. 'Let's just go.'

I pulled myself free from his tight, smothering grip.

I couldn't believe the way he was looking at me. I wanted to scream at him that I had lost my best friend. That she and I had been inseparable from the age of eleven, until, that was, she decided to kill herself. But the words failed me.

Without answering, I turned and walked away.

'Claudia? Claudia!' Jacob's desperate voice echoed behind me.

* * *

I looked at Jacob. He briefly held my gaze, his beseeching eyes searching mine for some acknowledgement that we were going to be all right. I couldn't give it to him. Instead, I turned my attention back to the heavy silence that clung to the intimate gathering as they began lowering Jaz's coffin to her final resting place.

Issie grabbed my hand as Willow heaved a deep sob as the cold earth took our friend from us. Even Ava momentarily lost her composure.

I looked across at Jaz's mother, her noble, handsome face worryingly pale. Her elderly husband, twenty years her senior, was oblivious to her pain, stoically watching as his only child disappeared. I shifted my gaze, too guilt-ridden to look either of them in the eye. I looked beyond them to the backdrop of their tragedy, the bleak and rugged Scottish mountains which dominated this isolated part of the world. It felt as if the Isle of Skye's Cuillin Hills' oppressive shadow stretched out to us from across Loch Scavaig, up the shores of Elgol, to the small, intimate graveyard and the very soil I was standing on.

I suppressed the anger I felt at her burial place. Somewhere so remote from the city life that had liberated Jaz. She had found freedom hundreds of miles away from what had become a foreign land to her. The irony that she had ended up back here, to lie for eternity beneath these low grey skies, under the baleful watch of her ancestors, their headstones and tombs dominating the small iron-fenced graveyard, was not lost on me, or Issie, Willow and Ava. We all felt it – the inequity of our friend's abrupt death and her bitter end. It was as if we were schoolgirls again, but we weren't. We were four thirty-three-year-old women brought back together by the funeral of the one friend we all loved without question. For Jaz was our linchpin. And now that she was gone, I was in no doubt that our friendship would end up buried with her.

I turned towards the entrance to the family graveyard and was surprised to see a woman in her late twenties to early thirties watching me. She was alone beyond the centuries-old cast-iron bars separating the ancient graveyard from the narrow country road which led to the Donaldsons' old, large, detached ancestral property that had been in their family for over two hundred and fifty years. There was something about her that made me uncomfortable. Her eyes were hidden behind sunglasses. A coldness cut through me as she moved her attention to Issie, then Willow and finally Ava.

I squeezed Issie's hand.

'Are you all right?' Issie asked, turning to me.

'Look over there towards the gates. Can you see her?' I lowly whispered.

Issie followed my gaze. 'So?'

'Who do you think she is?'

'I don't know. Perhaps it's one of Jaz's colleagues from her law firm,' Issie suggested.

'Don't you think it's odd that she's standing alone out there watching us?'

'I don't think it's necessarily us she's watching. Maybe she is paying her respects without imposing on Jaz's family.'

Accepting Issie's explanation, I turned my attention back to the minister as he concluded the burial service.

'She's leaving,' Issie pointed out a few minutes later as the people around us started to disperse.

I looked back and watched as the woman with the long dark chestnut brown hair and sunglasses hurried away from the grave-yard towards the row of parked cars.

'Did you see her during the church service?' I asked.

'No. Did you?'

I shook my head.

'Why are you so bothered about her?' Issie asked.

'I swear she was watching us. It's as if she knew us.'

'How could she?'

I didn't have the answer. But for some reason, I couldn't dispel the unease I felt. I knew she was watching the four of us.

But the question was why.

2

Jacob caught my eye from across the room. I had promised that I would only stay an hour when we all returned to Jaz's parents' house. I could tell that he was unimpressed that I was now on my second glass of wine.

'How do you do it?' Issie longingly questioned, shaking her head. 'He still adores you after all this time.'

I broke away from Jacob and turned my attention back to my old school friends. I smiled at Issie, watching as long, blonde curls flounced around her head before taking a mouthful of wine, so I didn't disabuse her of that notion.

The five of us – Jaz, Issie, Willow, Ava and I – had shared a dormitory for seven years at Queen Victoria's School for Girls in the Surrey countryside. We couldn't have been more different if we tried, but despite that, we had remained friends with no secrets between us since the age of eleven.

At least, that is what I'd thought until Jaz decided to take her life.

Issie was the artist, living in a cottage in Kent and working out of her studio in the back garden. Willow, like Issie, had been drawn to the arts as a gallery manager for an art studio in Soho, whereas Jaz and Ava were dedicated lawyers. And I'd followed my passion for reading to become an associate professor at University College London. We all lived in London, or in Issie's case, within easy reach of it, apart from Jaz. She had chosen to practise law in Edinburgh.

Maybe if she had stayed in London, we wouldn't all be reunited here today.

'We're all still meeting at Barrafina in Soho, next Friday?' I asked, pushing away that thought.

Ava nodded, as did Willow, while Issie mumbled: 'Of course.'

It was Jaz's favourite tapas bar, and we had all agreed to have a meal and drinks in her honour and celebrate her life, just the four of us.

'So, tell us about the new man in your life, this Charles,' I said, turning to Willow, acutely aware that we were avoiding the elephant in the room – Jaz's shocking suicide. All we knew was that she had taken her life. But we didn't know how or why. That was the question that haunted us. Not that we had openly spoken about it.

'Oh... Charles is just so wonderful,' Willow enthused. 'I mean, he's not Jacob, but who is?'

I smiled at Willow, glancing back over at my husband. He was now deep in conversation with the elderly minister and a couple of Jaz's parents' friends. Jacob was a paediatric cardiologist at Great Ormond Street Hospital for Children. He had worked what felt like day and night to achieve that position and rightly deserved it. He was a year older than me, physically attractive, confident and...

I took a sip of wine, stopping myself from going there. Now wasn't the place or occasion.

'Is it serious?' Issie asked.

Willow's face flushed with joy as she nodded.

'How long have you known each other?' Ava asked, refraining from being her typical sceptical self.

'Oh... nine weeks now.'

Willow tended to fall in and out of love in keeping with the seasons. A trait that had not gone unnoticed by us. So, whether Charles would still be around in a few months was highly debatable.

Willow sadly shook her head, forcing her black tight coiled spirals to swish in protest at her grief. 'I wish Jaz could have met him.'

No one spoke.

Finding the sudden silence more awkward than the small talk, I found myself craving a cigarette even though I hadn't smoked one in years. I distracted myself with another sip of wine.

Ava turned to me. 'Have you spoken to Jaz's mother yet?'

I shook my head. 'I haven't found the right moment.'

'You're the one she will want to talk to since you spent all your school summer holidays here,' Ava pointedly stated.

I stared at her, questioning whether I detected an iciness in her tone or if it was my imagination.

'They're definitely sure it wasn't an accident?' Issie interjected.

I nodded, accepting it was wishful thinking on her part. Jaz's father had asked me to ring the others – Issie, Willow and Ava – to tell them about Jaz. So, the three of them knew it was suicide as Mr Donaldson had been clear on that fact.

I noticed Ava drop her gaze to the glass she was holding.

'Do you know something?'

Ava's uneasy silence condemned her.

'If you know something, you need to tell us,' I insisted. Though I had no idea how Ava could have possibly found out more than Mr Donaldson had told me. When Jaz's father had informed me that his daughter had taken her life, I'd accepted his unwillingness to elaborate and refrained from asking for any morbid details.

'I didn't want to say anything,' Ava began, her face reddening. 'At least, not today. I didn't want our last memory of Jaz to be...' Her voice trailed off.

Surprised, I waited, as did Issie and Willow.

'I... I rang Mr Donaldson,' Ava finally admitted.

I was shocked. As far as I knew, Ava didn't know Jaz's parents. At least, not well enough to ring them. 'When?'

'After you had called me.'

'I didn't know you had their telephone number.'

'Jaz came back here the weekend before she—' Ava abruptly stopped. She breathed in before continuing, 'The mobile reception is patchy up here, and so, she gave me her parents' landline number.'

'Why?' I asked.

I could see from Willow and Issie's reactions that they, like myself, had no idea that Ava and Jaz had become so close. Jaz and I had always been the inseparable ones in our group.

'Why did she want to talk to me?'

I couldn't help but notice the defensive tone in Ava's voice. I watched as she irritably pushed her long, sleek dark brown hair back from her pretty face.

'Of course not. Why ring Mr Donaldson?' I asked, refraining from asking the burning question of why Jaz chose to talk to her and not me. Not that I would give Ava the satisfaction of knowing that. That Jaz had omitted to tell me she had been back here the weekend before she died cut me to the core.

'Because I couldn't accept what you told me. I talked to Jaz that weekend and she seemed upbeat. You know? Like Jaz. So, the idea that she would take her own life jarred with me. I had to ring Mr

Donaldson to make sure that it wasn't some terrible accident. That maybe you had misheard him.'

'How could I mishear the words "Jaz has taken her life"?' I questioned, taken aback.

'I just had to be sure. You would have done the same,' Ava insisted.

My expression challenged her assumption.

'She seemed happy,' Ava stated in an attempt to justify herself. 'She had met someone, and she'd also had confirmation that she was going to make partner.'

Jaz had worked hard to achieve a partnership in her law firm, so the news wasn't such a shock. But the fact she had shared this with Ava while simultaneously pulling back from me stung.

'So, what did Mr Donaldson say?' Willow asked quietly.

Ava uneasily glanced over at Mr Donaldson.

As did I. But Jaz's father had his back to us, talking with some guests.

Lowering her voice, Ava continued, 'Jaz was due in court that Friday morning and didn't show or report in, which was unheard of for her. Her secretary contacted her parents, and when they couldn't reach Jaz either, they travelled down to her apartment in Edinburgh. It was Jaz's mother who found her first...' She paused, seemingly struggling to find the words. 'She... she was lying in the bath with her wrists slit. She had drunk a bottle of vodka first.' Ava shook her head, blinking back tears as she took a mouthful of wine.

I heard Willow gasp. 'Oh God... Why? Why did she do that?'

'Shh!' Ava hissed.

'It's just difficult to believe that Jaz would take her own life, let alone cutting her wrists. We all know that after—' Willow stopped herself as Ava glared at her.

I noted that something passed between them.

'After what?' I questioned, puzzled.

I turned to Ava, but she avoided my gaze.

'After what?' I repeated. 'Was Jaz in trouble?'

'No, of course not,' Willow uncomfortably replied.

She nervously dropped her eyes to the glass she was holding.

A voice cut through the awkward silence, sharp and authoritative: 'Claudia.'

I turned as Jaz's mother approached us.

'Could you help me carry these back to the kitchen?'

'Of course,' I automatically replied as I handed my wine glass to Issie and took one of the trays Mrs Donaldson was holding.

Inwardly cringing, I followed Jaz's mother's tall, slender figure out into the wide, oak-panelled hallway, now wishing I had listened to Jacob's suggestion to head directly home after the funeral service. If I had, then I wouldn't be trailing behind like an errant child about to be scolded. I had succeeded in avoiding her so far, until now, too embarrassed and guilt-ridden about my failure to help my best friend – her only child –when she most needed me. I had tried to call numerous times to pass on my condolences, but Mr Donaldson had always answered the phone, explaining that his wife wasn't up to talking.

Ahead of me, Mrs Donaldson walked into the immaculate, spacious kitchen. She placed the tray she was holding down on the kitchen island.

'Shut the door behind you, please.'

There was no mistaking the coolness in her voice.

I did as she instructed and waited.

'Claudia... I need to ask you something,' she began, still with her back to me.

'Yes?'

'Jasmine...'

I felt the sting of her name as Mrs Donaldson paused.

She spun around to face me.

Still holding the tray, I didn't move.

'I suppose that Ava girl told you what happened.' Her voice was as hard as her expression.

I nodded.

'Well?'

I looked at her, unsure of what she wanted.

'Claudia, I asked you a question,' she stated, her sharp tone cut through my stumbling thoughts.

'Ava told us that she spoke to Mr Donaldson,' I confessed.

'And?'

'That...' I faltered, not wanting to repeat it.

'I take it that she told you.'

I nodded. Despite being familiar with Mrs Donaldson's brusque manner, her words still cut through me.

'I never liked that Ava girl. Always too nosy for her own good. Why Jasmine tolerated her was beyond me. Or you, come to that,' she accused.

'Jasmine's father should never have answered her vile questions. If she had spoken to me instead of Edward, she would have received short shrift. How dare she ring this house and ask such insensitive questions!'

Despite her anger, I could feel the shame radiating from her. Whether she assumed she had failed as a mother, I couldn't say.

'Did you know?' she asked.

I looked at her, unsure of her question.

'Did you know that... that Jasmine was feeling that way?'

I shook my head. 'No, I didn't know.' It was an honest answer.

'That Ava girl,' she said, her voice dripping with disdain. 'Did she know?'

'No. None of us knew.'

'Jasmine left no explanation as to why she did it,' Mrs Donaldson shared.

I stared at her, surprised by this revelation. It seemed out of character for Jaz not to leave a note so we could make sense of her irrevocable decision. It was just as out of character as taking her life in the first place.

'Did she say anything to you? Whether she was troubled by something or someone?' she asked, searching my face for the reason why her daughter had made the tragic decision to end her life.

'No. She never said a word to me,' I quietly answered.

It was clear that she thought I was lying. All I wanted to do was turn and run out of the kitchen which I couldn't do.

'Why didn't you read your own tribute to Jasmine at the service? Why add to poor Edward's burden?'

I swallowed. 'I... I just...' I shook my head, unable to further justify why I had refused Mr Donaldson's request.

'Really? As a professor of literature, you're telling me you couldn't stand up and give a reading. You were her best friend. She deserved more from you.'

Her words tore through me.

'Please go. I don't need your help after all,' she declared.

'But—'

'Leave,' she ordered, not giving me the opportunity to reply.

My face flushed at her abrupt dismissal. 'I'm sorry.'

She stared at me with incredulity. 'Don't you dare say you are sorry!'

I didn't defend myself. Instead, I placed the tray on the kitchen worktop closest to me and turned to leave, wanting to put as much distance between myself and Jaz's mother as possible.

'Why?' she asked as I started to walk away.

I paused.

'Why weren't you there for her? You were so close – like sisters, the two of you would always say. You must have known what she was thinking. You must have known something.'

I shook my head as I turned back to her. 'I messaged, then rang Jasmine that night, but she didn't reply. If I had known what she was going through, I would have...' I faltered.

'You would have what?' she demanded.

'I would have stopped her.'

The disbelief in her eyes took me by surprise. 'You? You of all people would have stopped her?'

I remained silent.

'You say you rang Jasmine that night.'

I nodded, as my skin crawled with guilt.

'And you texted her as well.'

I forced myself to answer her, 'Yes.'

'You must have known something was wrong.'

I shook my head. 'I wish I had. But I didn't. I called because I needed her advice.'

'You're lying. I checked her mobile phone hoping to find an answer, and there were no missed calls or texts from you. How dare you stand there telling me that you tried to reach out to my daughter to assuage your feelings of guilt. How dare you!'

I was stunned. 'I swear that I messaged Jaz... Jasmine. When she didn't reply, I then rang her, a couple of times, but she didn't answer, and so I left her a voicemail.'

'You're lying!'

I could feel my cheeks smarting from the sting of her accusatory words.

'Show me, then,' she demanded, 'these messages you sent Jasmine the night she—' She stopped herself from saying the unimaginable.

I stared at her. 'I... I deleted them that night when she didn't respond,' I confessed.

I could see from her eyes that she didn't believe me.

'I was so angry and hurt that Jaz didn't respond when I needed her, that I deleted all our conversations on WhatsApp,' I admitted, ashamed.

'The police checked Jasmine's phone and there was nothing on it—'

'Jaz must have deleted my messages as well,' I interrupted.

She shook her head at me in disgust.

It was evident she didn't believe me. But then, why would she? I had no evidence of the WhatsApp messages. All I had was the guilt I carried with me. For I knew the drunken messages I sent were spiteful and unjust.

If only you hadn't deleted them in a drunken rage that night. Or, crucially, if only you hadn't sent them in the first instance.

'Please go,' Mrs Donaldson demanded.

I turned to leave, confused. Why would Jaz delete my messages?

Nothing was making any sense – the most nonsensical thing of all being Jaz's decision to take her own life.

Why Jaz? Why did you do it?

3

I headed to the first-floor bathroom and locked myself in. I leaned against the door and shakily breathed out. The tears that I had managed to hold in now cascaded down my face. I felt numb. I couldn't believe what had just happened in the kitchen. I wanted to leave. To get as far away from Mrs Donaldson's raging grief and Jaz as possible – for everywhere I looked, I could see her. Jacob had been right; I should never have come back to the house.

I moved to the sink and turned the cold tap on, bent over and splashed the cool water on my face. I needed to pull myself together. All I wanted right now was a drink to steady me. Just one more before the insufferable drive back to London. But I knew it wasn't worth it.

I opened the bathroom door and headed towards the stairs. I paused, caught off guard by the photographs covering the walls. I noted one of Jaz in our first year at Queen Victoria's School for Girls. Alongside it was a much older, black-and-white photograph of a group of equally young, eager-faced girls with the school's imposing manor house in the background. I recognised Rhona Donaldson in the front, shocked at how similar she and Jaz looked.

Family tradition had sent Jaz so far away from home. Her mother had attended the boarding school in Surrey, as had her mother.

Turning away, I walked back down towards the various muted conversations drifting from the living room. I couldn't see Jacob. Nor could I see Ava. Jacob had given up smoking a few years back, but I assumed he had joined Ava outside for a cigarette. As I approached the French doors, I noted that they weren't seated on the patio. I walked outside, folding my arms against the biting cold air. I heard their laughter first, eliciting a stab of insecurity within me. I headed around the side of the property. Jacob had his back to me and only realised something was wrong when Ava, who was facing in my direction, stopped talking.

'Hey, Claudia,' she greeted. 'Sorry, Jacob and I have just shared my last cigarette.'

'I just came to find Jacob,' I explained, feeling as if I had walked in on something. 'Time's getting on. We need to leave.'

Jacob straightened up and turned to me. He looked awkward as hell.

'Not great dealing with small talk,' he explained, gesturing with his head in the direction I had come. 'Ava offered me a smoke and...' He shrugged.

I simply nodded.

'Right. I'll go say my goodbyes and then bring the car round,' Jacob suggested.

Before I had a chance to respond, he was already heading back in.

As Ava followed him, I stopped her. 'Can I have a word?'

'I'm cold, Claudia. Can't we do this inside?' she suggested.

'No. I want to talk to you about Jaz.'

'I don't want to discuss her,' Ava stated.

'I do. I need to know if you had any idea what Jaz was thinking.'

'Why would I?' she asked.

'Because you were the only one that had talked to her recently.'

'I thought you were close to Jaz. Surely you must have known what she was thinking.'

There was no mistaking the accusatory tone in her voice.

'We hadn't spoken properly for a while,' I reluctantly admitted.

Ava remained silent.

'Did she say anything to you?' I asked, desperate for answers.

'About?'

I shrugged, not wanting to say the obvious – that she was suicidal.

'Did you talk to her that night or the days leading up to...' I stopped, unable to articulate it.

'I already told you that Jaz seemed happy with her life.'

'There was nothing in her tone that might have suggested that she wasn't coping?' I pushed.

'No. Don't you think I have scrutinised my conversations with her?'

'You said she was seeing someone,' I said.

'So?' Ava irritably questioned.

'Had you met them?' I pushed again, aware she was acting defensively, which wasn't like her.

'No. You know how private Jaz could be. All I knew was that she had recently started dating someone.'

'Did she give you a name?' I asked.

'No... And what difference would it make now? It's too late for us to do anything. We're too late, Claudia. Maybe if you hadn't—' Ava stopped herself.

She shook her head, then turned, her black heels clicking on the sandstone paving slabs as she walked away.

I felt physically winded. Had Jaz forwarded my texts and voice messages to Ava? I tried to recall what I had said in the voice message. But I was drunk and fuelled with vitriol. I knew I'd said some terrible things in both the voicemail and WhatsApp messages, but precisely what eluded me.

I could feel my face burning, despite the chilled air, at the thought that Ava might have heard what I had said. Or read my texts to Jaz.

Had my cruel, spiteful words contributed to your death, Jaz?

Is that what Ava thinks?

4

'I need a coffee. I've been driving for four hours straight.'

The tension in Jacob's voice forced me to look at him. We had driven in silence since leaving Skye.

'I offered to drive.'

He clenched his jaw in response.

'Christ! You begrudge me one drink at my best friend's funeral?'

'I saw the amount of wine in your glass,' he replied in a strained tone. 'And it wasn't just the one.'

'Fine. Now we've established that I'm an alcoholic and you're a —' I stopped myself.

'What am I?' he snapped, turning to me.

'Nothing. Let's just leave it.' The atmosphere between us was already bad enough without me making it worse – if that was possible.

'What were you going to say?'

'I said leave it. I've just witnessed my best friend being buried today.'

A few seconds later, I felt his hand on my knee. He gave it a gentle squeeze. 'I'm sorry. You know that, right?'

'Are you?' I asked, regretting the words as soon as I had spoken them.

He snatched his hand away, placing it back on the steering wheel. 'I'm trying! Can't you see that?'

A wave of heat engulfed my skin as my burning eyes simultaneously began to fill up. Hurt, I looked out of the passenger window.

'Claudia?'

I shook my head.

'Hey, I'm sorry. All right? I didn't mean to shout. It's just that...' His voice trailed off.

Tears silently slipped down my cheeks.

'Hey, Claudia. Come on. We'll get through this, you and I. Together. Like always.'

But I wasn't so sure.

'Claudia? Please. Look at me.'

Despite myself, I turned to him. His dark brown eyes bore into mine. The beguiling gentleness in them overwhelmed me. I could feel myself sinking into them, compelling me to believe him and forget my insecurities. There was something about Jacob's eyes that had seduced me from the first moment he had ever looked at me. I trusted them without question. I always had done.

A wave of nausea hit me. A reminder that he had betrayed me. I could feel the jealousy, toxic and poisonous, spreading throughout my body and taking me hostage. I despised myself for succumbing to it. But I couldn't help myself. There were still too many unanswered questions that burned within me. Questions that Jacob point-blank refused to answer.

Before I could stop myself, I found myself asking him: 'What were you and Ava talking about?'

'Sorry?'

'Outside in the garden?' I questioned.

'Christ! I don't know... How shit we felt about Jaz.'

'That's it?'

'What else do you want me to tell you?' he said, exasperated.

'Why the two of you were hiding out of view by the side of the house?'

'What?'

'Why not sit on the patio outside the French doors?'

'Are you for real?'

I didn't answer. I couldn't. I could feel the betrayal choking me, forcing the words to remain lodged at the back of my throat.

'Oh, come on. You're acting paranoid! This is Ava we're talking about.'

'Exactly!' I regretted it almost immediately.

'You can't seriously think I'm attracted to Ava?'

'Why not? She's pretty fit, if that's your type.'

'Well, she's not my type. All right?' he demanded wearily.

The problem wasn't Ava being Jacob's type. It was the fact that Jacob had always been Ava's type.

I watched as he indicated before pulling out to overtake another car, his brow knotted in concentration.

'Are you sure?' I continued, unable to stop.

Jacob swung the car back in. 'I am not fucking attracted to Ava! All right?'

'So, what were the two of you laughing about?'

'For fuck's sake! I can't remember. I was being nice! Okay?'

'Funny sort of nice!' I retaliated.

'When is this going to end?' He shook his head. 'I'm serious, Claudia. I can't keep going on like this.'

I could feel the knot in my stomach tighten. I couldn't stop myself from baiting him. I knew it was self-destructive, but something inside me couldn't let it go.

'What can I do to prove to you it won't happen again?' he questioned, turning to me.

'Tell me about her. This... Bex woman.' Thinking of her made me feel sick to my stomach, never mind saying her actual name out loud.

'We've been through this! There's nothing to tell,' he irritably reasserted, returning his attention to the road.

'Seriously?'

'I've already told you no one knew who she was or how she had joined our group. All I am guilty of is making sure she got home safely. She was ridiculously drunk. She came on to me, and I rejected her. Then she turned batshit crazy. How many times do I need to say it? Nothing happened!'

I wanted to scream: *No, it's not all right. I know you cheated on me.*

Instead, I repeatedly twisted my wedding ring to stop myself from howling out the tormented thoughts that consumed my waking hours.

I'd found out two weeks back – the same night Jaz killed herself – that Jacob had escorted some drunken woman home to her flat in Islington. I remembered Jacob acting odd when I returned from a two-day academic conference at Bristol University. But I soon caught sight of the scratches that covered his body, as if he'd had an entanglement with the She-Wolf from Jackson Pollack's 1943 painting.

He had assured me that nothing had happened. But during the days and nights that followed, I thought I was going insane as I veered between crying and wanting to scream and scream to lessen the pain. All I could do was obsess and pick away at the sores that festered in my mind. I couldn't eat or sleep, too caught up in the agony of his infidelity, cripplingly compounded by Jaz's sudden, shocking suicide. I had dragged, cajoled and bribed the details from him, piece by piece, but he refused to complete the painful, sordid events. I suspected he had slept with her. His body was a testament to that fact. Yet, he continued to claim that she had lashed out, scratching and biting him when he'd refused to accept her drunken advances. He also claimed she had attacked him in the doorway of her flat when he wouldn't follow her inside.

So why was his body covered in marks? Surely, that suggests he had no clothes on.

I had never doubted Jacob's fidelity or love for me and respect for our marriage. *Until now.*

'Does Ava remind you of her? This Bex woman?' I asked.

'Drop it, Claudia!'

I looked at him as he stared straight ahead at the A82, the whites of his knuckles prominent as he gripped the steering wheel.

'Does she?' I persisted.

'NO!'

I turned to the passenger window and stared out at the bleak, miserable, rain-drenched west coast scenery of Loch Lomond as dusk settled. It was early March, and the skeletal, limp, dripping trees shivered together against the backdrop of the harsh snow-covered Munros. Jacob and I had often talked about walking the West Highland Way. At this moment, I couldn't imagine spending the remaining seven hours' drive back to London to our cosy, two-bedroomed Victorian terrace in Kew Gardens with him, let alone the eight days it would take to complete the walk.

Jacob had insisted on driving to Scotland, disregarding my suggestion to fly. He believed the drive would give us time to reconnect and work through our issues. However, the insufferable reality was the antithesis of what I expected Jacob had envisioned.

I watched as the rain slid like tears down the glass, blurring the grey exterior.

'Why, Jacob?' I finally asked, looking back at him.

'Why what?'

'Why did you let her bite and scratch you?'

He narrowed his eyes in response.

'Jacob?'

'I have gone over this countless times already! She attacked me when I rejected her. Do you honestly think I would have sex with someone and let them bite and scratch my body?' he questioned, annoyed.

I looked at him, searching his face for some confirmation that he was lying to me. But all I could see was sincerity.

'I don't know. Did you?' I challenged.

'For fuck's sake! No. How many times have I told you that?'

I chewed my bottom lip again, this time tasting the sour, metallic taste of blood. All I wanted was Jacob to confess to having sex with her. The suppurating boil in my mind needed lancing before I could move on.

Can you move on, Claudia? That's the question.

'Clearly, you enjoyed it!' I retaliated.

'What? Being attacked by some crazy person? No, I didn't enjoy it, and I bitterly regret trying to help her!'

He suddenly braked and the car behind furiously beeped at us, as, tyres screeching, Jacob pulled off the A82 onto the A83.

'Where are you going?'

'There's a petrol station further on in Arrochar. We need fuel and I need a coffee.'

I swallowed back the compulsion to rage at him for his aggressive recklessness with our marriage. And now, with our lives.

We drove in screaming silence until he pulled into the petrol station.

Jacob killed the engine and turned to me. 'Don't you think I feel stupid as it is? You couldn't make me feel more humiliated than I already do. Clearly, I didn't read the signs. I just wanted to make sure she got home safely. She was so drunk, she could have ended up raped, or worse. I just did what was right.'

I didn't say a word. I understood Jacob's logic, but it didn't mean I felt comfortable with the scenario.

'I'm going to get a coffee. Do you want one?'

'Have you seen her again?'

He stared at me. 'Stop this, Claudia.'

I could feel the wetness on my cheeks as tears betrayed me.

'If you can't get past this, then...' Jacob shook his head.

My stomach lurched. 'Then what?'

He shrugged. 'I don't know.'

'I've just lost my best friend,' I stated.

'I know. Which is why I haven't done anything.'

'You,' I spluttered, incandescent. 'What do you mean by that? I'm the aggrieved party here, Jacob. Not fucking you!'

I watched as he licked his bottom lip as if deliberating what to say next.

'I know you don't believe me and there's nothing I can do to prove to you that nothing happened. You've only got my word...' He faltered and dropped his gaze.

I waited, feeling as if I was slowly suffocating.

'I've tried to make it right. But' – he raised his eyes to meet mine – 'your behaviour, Claudia has been... Well...' He shrugged. 'It's as if you desperately want to believe that I cheated on you. This whole drama that you are creating fits your theory of abandonment.'

I stared straight at him. 'Don't try to turn the tables on me, Jacob! You are the one who's in the wrong here. This isn't about me and my upbringing. How dare you!'

'They screwed you up by fucking off to another country when you were eleven years old,' he continued, on a roll. 'Worse, they promised to come back for you but never did. So, yes, I am bringing up the fact your parents messed you up because I am the one paying the price for what they did to you.'

I swallowed back the tsunami of cruel memories his words unleashed.

I shook my head. Now wasn't the time to psychoanalyse the fact my parents had relocated to another country without me. This situation was about Jacob, no matter how much he wanted to deflect.

'No!' I yelled. 'You don't get to make out that it's my problem!'

Jacob stared at me before lowly stating: 'I can't continue like this, Claudia. Nothing happened. You need to trust me on that.'

'And if I can't?' I questioned.

He didn't answer me. But the look in his eyes said it all.

'Jacob, I—'

'You have a choice,' he irritably interrupted. 'Either you accept that I wouldn't do anything to jeopardise losing you and we move forward. Or you allow it to poison everything we have together. The decision is yours. I love you more than you could ever know and the fact that you don't believe that is killing me inside.'

I didn't say anything. I couldn't.

'It's over with, Claudia. One way or another. You didn't lose me that night. But if you continue as you are, then...' He shook his head, unable to say it.

Without giving me a chance to answer, he got out of the car and slammed the door.

He then proceeded to fill the tank.

He had just given me a fait accompli. If I wanted him to stay, I had no other option but to accept his terms.

Numb, I buzzed down the window and shakily breathed in the damp, drizzling air. The surrounding atmospheric scenery of Loch Long and the dramatic snow-covered Arrochar Alps and evergreen forests failed to distract me.

Without Jaz, Jacob was all I had left. And he knew that.

What are you going to do, Claudia?

How can you stay with Jacob if you don't trust him?

5

FRIDAY

It was after 2 a.m., and we were relieved to be home after an excruciating twelve-hour drive from Skye to Kew. I couldn't bring myself to follow Jacob to bed. Instead, I poured myself a large glass of wine and joined Darcy, our large tabby cat, on the couch, relishing in his contented purring vibrating throughout his heavy body. I reached over with my free hand and picked up my wine glass from the antique wooden chest. I relaxed and allowed myself to luxuriate in not being made to feel guilty by Jacob. In the past two weeks, I had drunk more than usual. However, I had two good reasons why.

I swallowed a mouthful as I considered Jacob's threat. Either I contain my jealousy and fury and accept his word that nothing happened, or he would leave me. But I didn't want that, regardless of how betrayed and angry I felt. I knew I had no choice but to accept that nothing happened and that he'd acted out of concern for her welfare, which would be typical of Jacob. If I continued as I was, I would drive myself insane – and Jacob away.

I took another sip of wine. Unlike Jacob, I didn't have to be up early.

Placing the glass back on the chest, I nuzzled into Darcy, remembering when Jacob had bought him home as a ten-week-old kitten. We had been married for less than a month when Jacob had surprised me with him. My father's job meant that we'd moved every two years, so a pet was out of the question. Then, from the age of eleven, the only home I had known was Queen Victoria's School for Girls, where I'd boarded – until now. Jacob had promised that he would never abandon me, unlike my parents, which made him having an affair out of character. I realised then that I had my answer. I breathed out, releasing the tension I had held onto for the past two weeks. I knew deep down that Jacob would never lie to me. If he said he didn't sleep with her, then he was telling the truth.

I stroked Darcy, unable to imagine my life without him. Or Jacob.

I looked around at our living room and the comfortable life we had built together, thanks in part to my parents, who had gifted the substantial deposit, securing the two-bedroomed Victorian terrace in Windsor Road. I had refused their offer, seeing it as guilt money for their abandonment of me. However, Jacob had pragmatically accepted their wedding gift. It was the only thing that had ever divided us. Until recent events.

We had gutted the property, stripping the floorboards through-out. We had also knocked the dining room through into the long galley kitchen to make an open-plan space for entertaining. Bi-folding doors led out onto the small, secluded garden stocked with mature shrubs, plants, a cherry blossom tree and grass. The kitchen boasted an island with a Belfast sink and contemporary, sleek light-grey units with integrated appliances. When not at work, Jacob loved to cook, and so we'd installed a red Aga range cooker. An old, rustic dining-room table and chairs sat opposite the kitchen units, positioned under an extension we had built with a glass roof for maximum light. We'd also refurbished the bathroom with an original claw-foot Victorian bathtub, a walk-in shower and under-heated flooring. We had spent a small fortune making the place our home – making it perfect for the two of us.

Maybe the three of us... For we had been trying but failing to get pregnant for over a year.

I looked across at the two walls lined with handmade bookcases crammed full of books. Then, the eclectic pieces picked up on our travels. Jacob's prized Yamaha GC82C grand concert classical guitar stood in the corner of the room on display. The Madagascar rosewood guitar, with a solid American cedar top, had been handcrafted to perfection. My eyes finally rested on the large, framed oil painting that Jaz had given us above the original Victorian marble fireplace. It was by an unknown artist, dated 1912 and depicted a naked couple embracing. The woman was pale, with long, wavy auburn hair with an uncanny likeness to me, and the male was tall and dark, like Jacob, so she had felt compelled to buy it as a wedding gift.

Jaz's death suddenly hit me. Tears started to fill my eyes. The fact that Jaz would never sit with me here on this couch again, laughing hysterically at something that only she and I got, blindsided me. She was my person, and I had been hers. Or at least, I'd thought that had been the case until... Tears cascaded down my cheeks as a strangled sob escaped from my throat.

I sat upright, much to Darcy's outrage, deciding it was time to go to bed; otherwise, I would drive myself insane obsessing about Jaz and my future without her. I blindly groped around for my phone and realised it must have slipped down behind the scatter cushions. I reached down until I found it, but there was something else. Surprised, I pulled it out. It took me a moment to understand what I was holding – a vintage silver bangle. Its hallmark stated that it was a Georg Jensen.

Surprised, I stared at it, not recognising it as a piece of jewellery belonging to any of my friends. I questioned who else had been in the house. Could it have been a female friend of Jacob's? But I knew all his friends, and I couldn't remember the last time one of them had been in our home. Or could it have been when I was at a conference at Bristol University? Then it hit me. I tried to discount the thought. But the sickening feeling in the pit of my stomach worsened as I accepted that there was only one possible way the bracelet had ended up there. Numb, I stared at it.

Jacob had brought her back here. The She-Wolf.

He had lied. He had stated that he had made sure she had got back to her place safely. But the evidence was in my hand. While I had been away at an academic conference in Bristol, he had brought her to our home.

My home... Oh my God...

The ten years we had been together evaporated as I stared in horror at the evidence in my hand.

Had they had sex? On this couch? In our bed? Would Jacob really do that to me?

I didn't know any more.

I reached out and shakily picked up my glass. I gulped back some wine in an attempt to dislodge what felt like tiny shards of glass stuck in the back of my throat. The stranger lying sleeping upstairs wasn't the medical student I had fallen in love with or the person I'd later married. That man would never have slept with someone he had met in a bar, let alone bring her back to our home.

I clenched the bracelet tight in my trembling hand, fighting the temptation to run upstairs and scream at Jacob like a banshee. Ripping the sheets and comforter off him, yelling at him to tell me how often he had fucked her and where exactly. Demanding to know how he could have committed such a betrayal against me – against us. I wanted to hurt him. Scar him with my hatred for him.

To scratch, claw and hit him until the raging ache inside me lessened.

I breathed out, aware that my body was shaking. My chest felt heavy and tight. I drained what was left of my wine and finally went upstairs. I crept into the bedroom, avoiding the waxed floorboard that always creaked. Jacob was sleeping on his side with his back to the door. I tiptoed over to the bedside table and retrieved his mobile phone.

I held my breath, not daring to move as he stirred in his sleep. I didn't want him waking up to find me trying to open his phone. Regardless of my reason, it was an act he would never accept or forgive.

'Hey, babes...' he sleepily murmured as his eyes fluttered half-open.

I quickly replaced his phone as he suddenly rolled over.

I didn't answer. I couldn't without screaming.

Not that he noticed. I watched him as he drifted back off, unable to silence the piercing rage of betrayal.

Did you fuck her in our bed, Jacob? Did you? DID YOU?

Trembling, I turned and left the room.

As I lay in the guest bed with Darcy curled up with me, I couldn't stop torturing myself, going over the last ten years with Jacob, trying to figure out how we had ended up here. But I couldn't see a defining moment.

We had it all. Or so I had naively believed.

The tears glided down my face as I thought about the previous year spent trying to get pregnant.

* * *

I woke up with a start. I then realised the cause – my phone was ringing. I moaned as daylight stabbed through the partially open wooden shutters. Then my stomach lurched as it hit me.

The bracelet. Her bracelet...

I felt as if I was going to throw up. My head was pounding, and the continuous ringing wasn't helping. I stretched my arm out and blindly fumbled for my phone on the nearby bedside cabinet, knocking the bracelet onto the floor in the process. Seeing it was Jacob, I declined the call. I realised he must already be at work. I couldn't bring myself to talk to him, to pretend that everything was okay. It started ringing again and again. I rejected the call. He immediately called back.

I knew Jacob wouldn't give up, so I forced myself to answer.

'Hey,' I croaked.

'Are you okay?'

I could hear the fear in his voice. I wanted to scream at him that, no, I wasn't okay. How could I be okay after he had blatantly lied to me?

Instead, I swallowed back the rage, pretending that everything was all right. 'I just have a bad headache.'

'Is that why you didn't sleep in our bed?'

'Yeah. I couldn't sleep. So, rather than disturb you, I decided to go to the guest bedroom.'

When he first woke up, he would have initially assumed I was in the bathroom or downstairs making coffee before realising that my side of the bed was untouched. Even when I had woken up on that Friday morning two weeks ago feeling wretched and desperately hungover, I was still in our bed. But then, I was oblivious to the excruciatingly cruel and gut-wrenching fact that he had brought another woman back to our home – our bed.

'You sure it wasn't anything else?'

'Like what?' I questioned, trying to sound normal.

He didn't answer.

My eyes caught sight of the silver bangle now lying on the floor; evidence that he had brought this woman back to our home. That he had lied to me about escorting her back to her flat in Islington.

What else has he lied about?

I stared at the bracelet.

'Have you taken something for it?' he then asked.

'I will do.'

'Okay. I just wanted to check that you were all right. You had me worried for a moment.'

'I'm fine,' I said. But it couldn't have been further from the truth. 'Remember that I have drinks tonight with Helena and some of the others from the English department,' I added.

I heard Jacob exhale. 'I was hoping we could spend this evening together. I'll cook your favourite king prawn garlic and chilli linguine, and we could share a bottle of Sancerre.'

I knew he was trying to reach out to me.

You're too late, Jacob...

The thought caught me out.

'Claudia?'

'Uh-huh?'

'You'll cancel?'

'You really want me to?' I questioned. It wasn't like him. I realised he was feeling vulnerable. Worried that I might retaliate, for he had met this woman when he had gone out after work to celebrate a colleague's birthday.

'I just think we need some time together. Especially after Jaz's death and...' He faltered.

He left it unsaid. But my mind filled in the silence: *After you brought some random person you picked up in a bar back to our home.*

I tried to silence the opposing thoughts as my mind vacillated between wanting to believe Jacob and being crippled by jealous insecurity that maybe he did have sex with another woman.

'If it means that much to you, then I'll let Helena know I can't make it,' I suggested, accepting it might be the perfect opportunity to discuss whether Jacob had brought this Bex woman back to our home. And if he had, as I feared, lied to me.

'Thank you. I love you, Claudia. You know that, right?'

DO YOU?

I felt cold inside. All I could think about was the silver bracelet that I had found.

'Claudia, I love you,' he repeated.

Why did you bring someone back to our home and lie about it, then? WHY?

I forced myself to respond. 'Same.'

'We're going to be fine. You'll see.'

But I could hear the doubt in his voice.

Are we going to be fine? How? How could we possibly be fine after I discovered you brought some stranger back to our home and... You promised me you hadn't slept with her, but I have evidence you lied to me.

Oh God, Claudia. What else has he lied about?

6
_____

I checked my phone. It was 8.55 p.m. I had two missed calls and four texts. All from Jacob. I had switched my phone onto silent before joining Helena and five others from the English department for drinks. We had been out for the past two hours and were now in a cosy basement bar in the heart of Bloomsbury. It felt good to be distracted. The past two weeks had been unbearable. I had lost my two oldest best friends in one night – Jaz and Jacob.

'Something wrong?'

I looked up from my phone. It was Helena with our drinks.

'Just need to let Jacob know that I will be later than expected.'

'Everything all right with you two?' she asked, sitting down.

'Of course,' I lied, before texting him back.

Phone's been on silent. Helena insisted I came out for one drink. Lost track of time. Sorry. Will make it up to you x

I had to force myself to put an 'x' at the end of the text. I deliberated deleting it but accepted that Jacob would construe it as passive-aggressive. Which it would be.

I pressed send. Waited.

'Yesterday must have been difficult for you,' Helena sympathised.

I raised my head and looked at her. Helena's slow, dark eyes were filled with genuine concern. I nodded. 'It was unbelievably difficult. We had been friends since the age of eleven and... well, nothing in life prepares you for something like that.'

'You want to talk, I'm here. You know that, right?'

I nodded again.

We had known each other for five years and had both been appointed our roles within weeks of one another. We soon became united in our dislike of the internal politics that dominated the Arts and Humanities department. Helena was one of my closest colleagues, and yet, shame had prevented me from telling her about Jacob's infidelity. She had assumed that my distant behaviour was caused by Jaz's shocking death, not realising that I was dealing with a double whammy at the same time.

My phone screen lit up.

'Sorry. Jacob,' I apologised.

I read his reply.

I thought you agreed to give it a miss. Why didn't you let me know earlier? I've been really worried about you!

I typed:

Sorry.

His response was immediate.

Is Ethan Novak with you?

I stared at the text as I contemplated what to say.

Dr Ethan Novak had joined University College London's English department last year and had caused quite a stir amongst the students and staff members. He was in his late twenties, tall, dark, tattooed and edgy. His specialism was the American author Thomas Pynchon and mine was nineteenth- and twentieth-century African American and American literature. Subsequently, we found ourselves attending the British Association for American Studies conference, amongst others, together. I had foolishly mentioned to Jacob that Ethan had recently hit on me at an academic conference. Ethan and I had both had too much to drink, and so, I'd thought nothing of it. Neither of us had mentioned it the following morning. I took it for what it was – a drunken pass. Jacob had reacted by laughing about it – as I had done. However, it seemed that it had hit a nerve with him. Maybe it was because I had told Jacob that Ethan had gained a name for himself in his short time at University College London when it came to seducing colleagues.

Jacob fired off another text.

?

I understood that his unease was coming from guilt. Any pity I felt for Jacob quickly evaporated when the silver bangle came to mind.

Ignoring his question, I texted:

Don't wait up.

* * *

Sometime later and I could feel the effect of the countless glasses of wine I had drunk as I made my way to the toilets.

'Damn!' I muttered as the walls and floor of the toilet cubicle started tilting.

I collapsed onto the toilet seat and tried to compose myself. I had lost track of how much wine I had drunk. All I knew was that it was too much. But it had had the desired effect and had blotted out the past two weeks.

Someone banged on the cubicle door.

'Give me a minute,' I called out.

'Claudia? Are you all right in there?'

I recognised Helena's concerned voice.

'No... I mean yes. I'm fine,' I answered.

'You've been in there for ages.'

'I'll be out in a minute,' I assured, trying to sound sober.

I rummaged around my bag for my phone. Eventually, I found it. There were three texts: all from Jacob.

Claudia? When are you coming home? Worried!!!

I was surprised that it was already 12.19 a.m. Jacob had sent the first text two hours ago. I read the next two.

Call me. Please!!

FFS! I know you're angry. But this is pathetic!

I stared at the texts.

Fuck you, Jacob! Fuck you and your fucking lies!

'Claudia? Hey, you still alive in there?' Helena questioned.

Startled, I looked up. 'Yeah. Just coming,' I replied.

I heard someone walk into the toilets.

'I always suspected something was going on between those two! And she's married!'

I realised I recognised the high-pitched nasally voice: Rowena from our department.

Helena whispered something to her, before clearing her throat and shouting out: 'Hey, Claudia, are you nearly done in there?'

I hurriedly shoved my phone in my bag and stood up. I lost my balance for a moment, slamming against the cubicle wall.

I breathed in, unlocked the door and walked out.

Rowena was standing in front of the mirrors, checking her sleek, shoulder-length black hair. I caught her eye. She gave me a cold, hard look which confirmed my suspicion she was talking about Ethan and me to Helena, not realising I was in the cubicle.

Or maybe she did and wanted me to overhear her jibe. I stared back at her, furious at her insinuation that something was going on between Ethan and me. Worse, that I was cheating on my husband.

Without saying a word, she turned and walked out.

'How about we call it a night?' Helena suggested once Rowena had left.

I knew that Helena was right. It was time to go home before I did something reckless. Something that I knew I would regret in the morning. Something that would hurt Jacob as much as he had hurt me. But I waved my hand at her. 'Nope. I'm fine. Honest.'

Not that I felt fine. I was dangerously drunk and reeling from Jacob's betrayal and Jaz's death. Not a good combination.

'Don't say I didn't try,' Helena said, shaking her head at my reflection before resuming reapplying her lip gloss.

I stared at myself in the mirror, willing myself to not act on what I had been thinking about all night. I had a good reason not to – my husband. Jacob was waiting for me back at home, no doubt frantic with worry.

You're married, Claudia!

So?

I shakily breathed out. Tried to temper the temptation to deal Jacob with an equally crippling blow.

Fuck it! Did Jacob think about you when he took some random woman home? No!

* * *

Although it was a Friday night, soon eight of us dwindled to three, leaving Helena, myself and Ethan.

'Right, I'm going home,' Helena decided, standing up. 'Are you coming?'

I turned to her, surprised. 'You're not going now? Ethan and I are in the middle of a serious conversation about...' I faltered and looked at him for help. I was more drunk than I realised.

He grinned at me. 'Henry Louis Gates Jr's cameo in *Watchmen.*'

'That's why I'm going,' Helena said. 'Are you coming?'

'I'm going to stay for a bit longer,' I answered.

'It's after 2 a.m.'

'And it's a Friday night,' I retaliated.

'You're going to regret this in the morning,' she warned. 'And what about Jacob?'

'That's right, you're a married woman,' Ethan added, smiling at me.

'Yes, she is, with a husband waiting for her at home,' Helena pointedly stated as she stared at Ethan.

'I'll be fine,' I reassured her. 'Honestly, I'll get a cab home soon.'

It was evident that Helena didn't believe me.

'Can I have a word?' she asked.

'Sure.'

'In private,' she added.

I sighed as I pushed myself up, feeling myself wobble slightly. A reminder I'd drunk a little too much.

'Won't be long,' I said to Ethan before following Helena. 'What's wrong?' I asked her.

'You should go home.'

'Seriously?' I questioned, annoyed at her tone. 'You were the one who convinced me to come out in the first place!'

'Look, I care about you. Okay? I don't want you doing something that you'll regret,' Helena explained. She glanced back towards Ethan. 'And he isn't the answer. You know he's got a reputation for sleeping around. And he clearly doesn't give a damn that you're married. I mean, why the hell's he entertaining the idea—'

'I'm not planning on sleeping with him,' I argued, cutting her off. 'All I'm doing is having a good time. Is that too much to ask after I had to watch my school friend buried yesterday morning?'

Helena didn't reply.

'What?'

'As I said, you're making a mistake. Go home and sort out whatever is going on between you and Jacob.' Before I had a chance to deny anything was wrong between Jacob and me, Helena raised her hand. 'I don't want to hear any more bullshit. I hope you don't wake up tomorrow filled with regret.'

'Meaning?'

But I knew exactly what she meant.

'You and Ethan. Don't go there, Claudia. You're better than that.'

With that parting shot, she hugged me, then left.

I watched as she disappeared as one thought hurtled through my mind:

What the hell are you doing, Claudia?

7

SATURDAY

I tried to open my eyes, but my head threatened to explode from the nauseating pressure inside my skull. I could feel the heat of Jacob's bare skin against my own. Then his hardness as he pulled my naked body into him.

'Mm...' I moaned, feeling too ill to contemplate anything other than lying perfectly still. Even breathing was proving to be debilitating.

Then fragments of the night before started to assail me. A memory of being with Helena. Drinking shots late into the night. Snapshots of moments leading up to... I stopped. The flashbacks were too much. Too soon. I tried to swallow but couldn't. My mouth was unbearably dry. Desperate for a drink, I blindly reached out, groping for a bottle of water. Instead, my fingers touched a small foil packet. I forced my eyes open, wincing in pain as I tried to focus on what my fingers had felt – a red Durex packet. I could feel the heat spreading up from my neck, engulfing my face as I realised what it meant. Sudden frenzied snippets assaulted me. I had come back to Ethan's apartment. We had drunk Jack Daniel's and then...

No... no... SHIT!

Panic overwhelmed me as fleeting images of Ethan on top of me, then I on top of him flashed through my mind.

My fingers squeezed the condom packet. It was empty. Not that I needed that confirmation to know that we had sex. I already knew it. I could taste it. Feel it. Remembered enjoying it.

Oh God! But did we use a condom? An empty durex packet means nothing.

'Are you okay?' he questioned. His voice was deep. Seductive.

'I need to go.'

'Sure,' he replied.

'God! What time is it? Jacob will be frantic,' I said, panicking as I pulled the covers back and sat up.

'It's late. Just before eleven,' Ethan answered.

'Shit!' I muttered, as I bent down, scooping my abandoned clothes up off the deep-pile cream carpet. I caught sight of another condom packet on the floor. I picked it up. It was empty.

The feeling of nausea overwhelmed me.

I sat back up and breathed in and out, trying to quell the over-riding desire to be sick. But the need to get out of Ethan's apartment was more pressing than the need to lie down and ride it out.

Neither of us spoke as I pulled my top on and then my panties, jeans and boots.

'My jacket and bag?'

'Living room,' he casually said.

It was evident he didn't share my guilt or embarrassment. Then again, he wasn't the one who was married.

'Right.'

'You need me to get you a cab?'

'No, I'll be fine,' I said, standing up. I felt shaky, but reality had kicked in and I just wanted to get out as fast as possible.

I hurriedly grabbed my jacket and bag and left.

* * *

I sat in the taxi fighting the urge not to succumb to panic as I looked at the countless missed calls from Jacob. There was also one from Helena. It was now 11.11 a.m. Helena had called me at 9.33 a.m. When she couldn't get me, she had texted:

You all right? Wanted to make sure you got home safe xx

I pressed call.

'Hey,' she answered after the first couple of rings. 'I've been worried about you.'

'No need,' I assured her.

'Where are you?'

I realised she could hear the traffic.

'In a cab.'

'Tell me you didn't go back to Ethan's after I left you.'

A wave of shame hit me.

'Claudia?'

My silence condemned me.

'Oh shit! You did, didn't you?'

'I just went back for a couple of drinks,' I answered.

'Save it for Jacob. It's me you're talking to!'

'All right, I slept with him...' I muttered.

'Shit! Claudia! You haven't been home yet?'

'Literally just woken up at his place and jumped into a cab.'

'Where does he live?'

'I don't know exactly. It's one of those new apartment buildings in Poplar overlooking the canals.'

'Shit! It'll take you at least another hour to get home.'

I remained silent, acutely aware of this fact.

'How did you leave it with Ethan?'

'I didn't. I just bailed,' I confessed. 'He's the least of my problems.'

'What have you said to Jacob?' she questioned.

'Well... that's why I called you.'

I heard her sigh.

'I wouldn't ask, but... I need a cover story,' I admitted as a wave of guilt coursed through me.

'Shit, Claudia! I don't like this.'

'Please. I fucked up. I admit it. I... I just needed to blow off some steam after what happened to Jaz, and I went too far,' I explained. But the words sounded hollow.

I waited.

'All right. Just this once,' Helena reluctantly conceded.

'Thanks. I owe you.'

'You want to tell me what's going on with you and Jacob?'

I didn't reply. I didn't have the strength to go there. All I wanted to do was crawl into our bed and forget everything – particularly last night. I couldn't believe I had slept with Ethan. If I could have turned back time and left with Helena rather than tempting fate, I would have done.

'Claudia, this isn't like you.'

'I know. I...' I faltered, feeling my cheeks burn with the sting of Helena's words. Because she was right, this wasn't like me.

'Let's talk later. Yeah?' Helena concluded.

'Sure,' I answered before hanging up.

I then texted Jacob:

Sorry. Drank too much and ended up back at Helena's. On way home x

My phone pinged.

It wasn't Jacob – it was Ethan.

Hey, hope everything's okay when you get back.

I felt sick. I just wanted last night to have never happened. For Ethan to disappear.

I looked out of the taxi as we passed Canary Wharf heading for Limehouse. It was a beautiful, crisp March late morning. Not that I could appreciate it. I thought about Ethan. I had no idea how I was going to face him at work on Monday. But before then, I had to survive the weekend with Jacob. I sighed, closing my eyes against the intrusive, chastising glare of the sun, and rested my head back in the cab as I tried to psych myself up for what awaited me at home.

* * *

'I don't believe you!' Jacob shouted as he stood in the doorway of the bathroom with his arms folded.

Ignoring him, I switched off the water and stepped out of the walk-in shower cubicle. I picked up a large bath towel and wrapped it around my body. I could see Jacob's furious gaze watching my every move in the large bathroom mirror as I dried my hair with a smaller towel.

'For fuck's sake, Claudia! Did you hear what I said? Or are you just going to ignore me?'

'Can't this wait until I've had some sleep? I can't even have a shower without you interrogating me,' I snapped, shaking my hair loose and throwing the towel in the laundry bin before pushing past him. As soon as I had walked into the house, he had pounced on me, demanding to know exactly where I had spent the night.

'Do you know how worried I was about you? How close I came to calling the police,' Jacob demanded, following me down the hallway into the bedroom.

I picked up an oversized baggy T-shirt from the pile of clean laundry on the chest of drawers and pulled it over my head, letting the bath towel fall. I was too exhausted to answer him. Nor did I feel like I had the right to defend myself.

'Do you? For fuck's sake, Claudia! At least look at me.'

I spun around. 'I'm tired, and my head is pounding. Let me sleep, and then we'll talk.'

'I've been up all night worried about where the fuck you had gone to, and you think it's acceptable to ask me to wait! I deserve the truth, Claudia. Not some crap that you made up on the way home. In the five years we've lived in Kew, when have you ever crashed at Helena's? It doesn't make sense.'

Helena lived a few miles further out from us in Richmond in an enviable first-floor flat overlooking The Green. Jacob was right; staying at hers made no sense. The cab would have to pass through Kew to get there, so why wouldn't I just come home?

'Ring her if you don't believe me,' I defiantly suggested, feeling cornered.

'Why? To hear her repeat what you've told her to say.'

'Whatever!'

'That's it? That's all you've got to say after you spent the night out with Ethan Novak.'

I stared at Jacob. His hands were clenched in anger as his dark eyes blazed with jealousy.

'You want me to tell you what happened?' I dared him.

'Yes. You owe me that.'

'I owe you nothing,' I threw back.

'At least I was honest with you,' he retaliated.

I wanted to scream at him: *Stop lying to me! I know! I know you brought her back here!*

Instead, I shook my head in disbelief. 'Honest? You? You only told me because you had no choice. Did you think I wouldn't notice the bite marks and scratches?' I demanded.

He didn't respond.

'And what about the silver bangle lodged down the back of the cushions on our couch?'

'What?' he questioned.

I stared at him. 'You know exactly what I'm talking about.'

I marched out to the guest bedroom and grabbed the bracelet from the bedside cabinet where I had left it.

'HERE!' I screamed at Jacob when I returned to our bedroom, throwing it at him to elicit some reaction.

It fell to the floor by his feet.

'So, tell me, what exactly happened that night with some random woman whose only detail you can remember is that she was called Bex?'

He didn't answer.

'Where did you fuck her? In here?' I yelled.

'Lower your voice. The neighbours will hear you.'

'I'm sure they already know all about it. They no doubt heard the two of you fucking!'

He didn't reply.

His silence was confirmation of his guilt. Rage coursed through me, dangerously fuelled by righteousness, spurring me on.

'So, did you fuck her in our bed?'

I waited as Jacob licked his bottom lip, contemplating his response. There was no mistaking the desperate panic in his eyes. 'I didn't sleep with her. She wanted me to, but I didn't. That's why she attacked me.'

'You expect me to believe that? You lied to me about taking her home, Jacob! In reality, you brought her back here.'

He didn't say anything.

'Bastard!' I shouted. 'Why? Why would you do that to me?'

'I swear, I didn't sleep with her,' he nervously pleaded with me.

'But you brought her back here. To our home, and you didn't think I had a right to know about it?'

He shook his head. 'I'm sorry...'

'Fuck sorry! Sorry doesn't even come close. You lied to me!'

I stared at him as a tumult of emotions raced through me. I wanted to hurt him so badly.

'She was so drunk that she had no idea where she lived,' Jacob began, with desperation in his voice. 'When it came to closing time, we didn't know what to do. No one had any idea who she was, and she didn't have a phone on her, so it's not as if we could have rung someone in her contacts. So, we agreed that someone would have to let her crash at theirs until she sobered up in the morning. Somehow, it ended up being me. That's the truth, Claudia. I brought her back, and she crashed on the couch; she was too drunk to make it up the stairs to the guest bedroom. That must be how the bracelet got there.'

'What about the scratches and bite marks? When did that happen?' I demanded, not believing him.

Uncomfortable, Jacob shook his head. 'I... I woke up to find her climbing into bed.'

'What?' I spluttered. I stared at him, wide-eyed, trying to comprehend what he had just admitted.

'I know. It's weird. I jumped up and asked her to leave, and that's when she went ballistic and started clawing and trying to bite me. Then, before I knew it, she was gone. I heard the front door slamming behind her. I went out after her, but there was no sign of her.'

I couldn't believe what I was hearing. Blinding rage coursed through me.

'I know... I know. It all sounds crazy.'

I didn't reply. I couldn't. Too paralysed by Jacob's sudden admission to formulate any words.

'Please, Claudia. I swear that's what happened.'

When I didn't respond, he started to walk out of the room.

'Where are you going? I thought you wanted to know if I had fucked Ethan Novak,' I yelled after him.

Jacob stopped, slowly turned around and looked me straight in the eye. 'Don't do this.'

'Do what? Tell you the truth. Just like you swore you told me the truth.'

'Please... don't do this.'

'What? Be honest?'

He didn't say a word, but the terror in his eyes said it all.

We both knew if I crossed the line, there would be no coming back from this. But I couldn't stop. Not now. I had lost all rationale at the thought of Jacob with some woman in our bed. Rage and vengefulness had me by the throat.

'Yes, I fucked Ethan. I FUCKED ETHAN NOVAK!' I screamed at him.

The wounded sadness in his eyes took me by surprise.

He swallowed, then shook his head. 'For what it's worth, I never slept with her. Yes, I lied about bringing her back here because I didn't know how you would react. But... I—' He faltered. 'I would never cheat on you. No matter what.' With that, he turned and walked away. He paused by the door, and without turning back to look at me, he asked, 'Tell me you used protection.'

I thought back to the empty Durex wrapper on the bedside cabinet and the other used packet on the carpet.

'I... I... Yes,' I mumbled. The all-consuming rage had burned itself out, replaced by shame radiating through my skin.

He then walked out of the room.

I wanted to run after him and tell him I was sorry, that I didn't mean to hurt him, that I wanted to take it back. But I couldn't admit that what I had done was spiteful and callous.

Trembling, I climbed into our super king-size bed and curled up in a foetal position as hot, salty tears glided down my face. Darcy sprang up from nowhere and nestled into me, purring.

'Oh Darcy,' I pathetically sobbed.

I was the guilty party now – not Jacob. All my seething anger had dissipated, replaced by fear. I was the one who had potentially ended our marriage. It took me throwing the fact that I'd slept with my colleague in his face for me to seriously doubt that he had slept with that woman. The crippling pain in his eyes caused by my betrayal compelled me to believe him.

Maybe he had been telling me the truth?

But now it was too late. There was no way of undoing what I had done or said.

* * *

I lay there as the sunlight gradually disappeared and darkness crept through the wooden shutters on the two Victorian sash bedroom windows. Still, Jacob didn't come back upstairs. A terrifying sense of foreboding accompanied the darkness that sneaked into the room. Jacob typically played rugby on a Saturday afternoon. But I knew he hadn't gone since his rugby bag was lying in the corner of the bedroom. However, the house was eerily silent.

I must have finally drifted off because when I woke with a start, night had taken over. I reached out, expecting Jacob to be in bed next to me, but his side was empty. A knot of panic unfurled in my stomach. I checked the time on my phone: 2.03 a.m.

I got up.

'Jacob?' I tentatively called out in the darkness.

No reply. Not even from Darcy.

I tried to quell my rising panic as I headed along the landing towards the stairs, flicking the lights on, checking the guest bedroom as I passed. It was empty.

I crept down the stairs, assuming he must have fallen asleep on the couch. I opened the living-room door. The room was shrouded in darkness. It took my eyes a moment to register Jacob sat in the leather armchair.

'Hey,' I greeted.

No reply. My stomach lurched.

'You had me worried.'

Still, he ignored me.

'Jacob?' I questioned, panicking.

He continued staring straight ahead as if he hadn't heard me.

Fear held me hostage as I stood there, not knowing how to undo what I had said to him. Worse – what I had done.

Oh my God, Claudia... Will he ever forgive you?

8

SUNDAY

'Jacob?' I repeated.

No response.

I forced myself to walk across to him, despite my legs feeling as if they were going to give way. I tentatively crouched down in front of him.

'Hey,' I said, placing my hand on his leg. 'It didn't mean anything.'

His body stiffened against my touch.

I quickly pulled my hand away, swallowing back the hurt tears that threatened to fall.

Oh Jacob... I am so sorry.

'I don't know what to say,' I admitted.

'There's nothing you can say,' he answered, his voice thick with reproach. 'Go back to bed, Claudia.'

'Not without you,' I answered, staring up at him, willing him to look at me.

He shook his head. 'I'm not tired.'

'I won't be able to sleep without you.'

Jacob's mute reaction to my admission cut through me like a knife.

I knelt there in pained silence for what felt like an eternity waiting for him to say something – *anything*. But he didn't.

Terror gripped me. The thought of losing him was too much to contemplate. I felt as if he was all I had, more so with Jaz gone. I couldn't silence the feeling that I was clinging on by my fingertips to a sheer rockface, and any second, I would lose my hold and plummet into the dark abyss below.

'Please, come to bed,' I whispered, piercing the suffocating silence.

He heavily sighed.

'Please, Jacob. Let's sleep on it,' I suggested, my voice filled with desperation.

'You really think I can fall asleep after what you told me?' he threw back at me.

'I'm sorry,' I mumbled. 'If... If I could take it back, I would.'

'Take back not telling me?' Jacob questioned, still refusing to look at me.

'No,' I slowly answered. 'Take all of it back.'

'What? Sex with Ethan Novak. You want to take that back?'

Burning tears escaped down my face at his acerbic tone. But I knew I deserved it.

'Yes. Of course, I want to take that back. I wish it had never happened,' I replied, my voice filled with regret.

'Really?' he muttered.

I could feel the panic rising inside me in reaction to Jacob's coldness. He felt like a stranger to me. Then again, I was sure he felt the same about me. More tears slid silently down my face at the acknowledgement that maybe this was it. But I knew I couldn't cope on my own. Not without Jacob.

'I only did it out of revenge because I thought you had slept with this Bex woman. You've got to believe me,' I pleaded.

'Do I?'

'Yes.'

'Why?' he questioned.

'Because I love you. I did something out of hurt. Out of spite. And I'm sorry. I am so sorry. If you hadn't lied to me—'

More tears escaped down my face as I watched him, waiting for him to let me in.

He didn't say a word, but his clenched jaw and narrowed eyes were enough for me to know that I had pushed him too far. Too hard.

'Please, Jacob,' I whispered. 'Don't do this to me. Please... just look at me.'

I wanted to scream at him to stop punishing me. That I couldn't cope with any more guilt, not after what had happened to Jaz. I was accountable for not knowing that she wanted to kill herself. Responsible for not being there when Jaz needed me the most. I had lost my best friend and now... I choked back the strangled sob in my throat. Now, I was on the verge of losing my husband – my marriage.

'I can't,' he answered.

'What?' I questioned as his words tore through me. 'You can't even look at me?'

He shook his head.

More hot, salty tears fell. I hated myself enough for what I had done without Jacob hating me too.

'What can I do?' I asked, trying to control the terror inside me at the acknowledgement that my world was evaporating in front of me.

'Go back to bed,' he repeated.

'Not without you,' I replied. 'Please. I don't want to be on my own.' I needed to be close to him, to feel him next to me. To know that even though I had screwed up, he still wanted me. I accepted that it was selfish, but I didn't care.

'You can always go to Ethan's place,' he suggested caustically.

'Don't do this,' I begged, his behaviour scaring me as more tears glided down my cheeks. This wasn't like him. Jacob was always the one who tried to make things right between us.

'Do what? I didn't do anything. You're the one who slept with your colleague,' Jacob lowly stated.

'Only because I thought you had sex with that woman!' I retaliated.

'I told you I hadn't. My word should have been enough. You've known me for ten years, Claudia. When have I ever given you a reason to doubt me? Doubt us?'

I wanted to scream at him that he had still lied to me. He had brought her back to our home.

YOU WERE COVERED IN SCRATCHES AND BITE MARKS.

'You've repeatedly lied to me!' I heard myself saying. 'I mean... God! How can your word be enough when you keep changing the narrative?' I demanded, raising my voice. 'And yet, I'm the one who's in the wrong here. We both fucked up! What part aren't you getting? We both need to take responsibility for this... this shitshow!'

I waited for him to answer, wiping the tears away with my hands, then drying them on my baggy T-shirt.

'Why him, Claudia?' he mumbled. 'Of all the men you could have had sex with, you chose him.'

I was momentarily at a loss.

'Did you hear what I asked you?'

'Yes,' I mumbled.

'So, why him?'

'It meant nothing,' I whispered into the darkness.

'That's not what I asked.'

'I was drunk and angry. Ethan was there. That's all there is to it,' I answered, wanting him to stop, to just come to bed. For it to all be all right again. To pretend that it had never happened.

'It's not though, is it?' Jacob pointed out, looking at me.

'I promise, it is,' I assured him as I stared up at his dark, distrustful eyes.

'You're lying to me and, worse still, to yourself,' Jacob bitterly replied.

'I'm not,' I retaliated.

Disgust filled his eyes, forcing him to turn away from me.

'I've been waiting for this moment.'

'What?' I questioned, terrified by his tone.

'You and Ethan,' he flatly stated.

'I don't understand.'

'It was so transparent that you wanted him. You did nothing to hide it.'

'No... No, that's not true,' I stuttered, feeling as if I was going to be sick.

'Stop treating me like an idiot, Claudia! You've flirted with the idea of sleeping with Novak for the past year! You know it, and I know it.'

'No...' I repeated. His chilling tone scared me. 'That's not true...' But my words sounded hollow because I knew Jacob was right. I just didn't want to hear it.

'You always found an excuse to talk about him. Your face would light up at the mere mention of his name. That's how I knew.'

I didn't respond. Didn't know how to respond.

'Then, when you told me he hit on you at that conference at Bristol University, I knew it was only a matter of time.'

'Jacob, you're wrong—'

He cut me off: 'Don't patronise me!'

Neither of us said anything for what felt like hours as each second dragged, but in reality, it was only a few minutes. I tried to convince myself that everything would be all right. That Jacob just needed to rant against me and that I needed to give him the space to do that. Then he would forgive me, and we would forget about it – eventually – and our lives would return to some semblance of normality. However, without Jaz, I was unsure as to whether that would ever be possible. Raw grief forcefully hit me at the realisation that she was gone – forever. There was no going back from her decision.

'Jacob?' I questioned, my voice quivering.

He slowly turned to me.

'We can get past this. Right? I... I can't go on without you. Not with what happened to Jaz.'

His lack of response filled me with dread.

'I mean... We've renovated this house and... We've been trying for a baby for the past year and...' My voice faltered as I registered his incredulous expression.

His eyes blazed with resentment as he shook his head. 'You don't get it. Do you?'

'Get what?'

'This,' he said, gesturing around him with his hands. 'It's all fake, all some act. As are you and I. We're one big fucking lie.'

I recoiled in reaction to his words. I didn't understand why he was saying such things.

'No... No! That's not true!' I argued, desperate for him to stop before he said something that could never be unsaid.

'It is,' he wearily replied, the fight gone from him.

'But? But the baby? That was your idea.'

He nodded. 'I thought that it would give us some focus. Keep us together. But I was wrong. You and I are wrong.'

I sat for a moment, struggling to find the words to persuade him otherwise. But they failed to materialise. I had been restless for some time now. Jacob had sensed it. He had tried his utmost to pull me back to him. But I had become bored with Jacob. With us. It had felt stale. Too safe. Too predictable. I couldn't imagine spending another eight years married to him. Paradoxically, I now couldn't contemplate not being with Jacob. It had taken the knowledge of Jacob potentially sleeping with someone else to wake me up, gasping and spluttering, from the marital stupor that had taken hold. Now I was drowning, desperately thrashing around, trying to grab hold of something from the wreckage to keep me afloat.

'We were too young. You know that,' Jacob flatly stated.

I shook my head as more tears came. 'No,' I mumbled.

'Yes,' Jacob asserted. 'We should never have got married. If it wasn't for your parents…'

I stared at him, waiting for him to finish. But he was too cowardly to say it.

'What about my parents?' I dared him.

'It doesn't matter.'

'If you've got something to say about my parents, then say it!'

'They just took over. If it wasn't for them, we wouldn't have got married so soon. If at all.'

'You mean you, don't you? Because I, for one, wanted to marry you.'

Jacob shrugged.

I couldn't believe he was acting so cruelly. I knew his words came from anger which stemmed from betrayal, but I couldn't stop myself from reeling from this spiteful revelation.

'And this house. Are you blaming them for that as well?'

He frowned as he looked straight at me. 'They paid a substantial deposit so we could afford to buy it. I mean, you're talking hundreds of thousands, Claudia.'

'I know what they paid, and if you remember, I refused it. You were the one who accepted it without my knowledge,' I retaliated, feeling the heat of indignation rise up my neck.

'I felt coerced into it,' he stated.

'Which one?' I demanded. 'The wedding or the house?'

Jacob remained silent for a moment.

'Both,' he finally admitted.

I involuntarily gasped. It took me a moment, but I somehow managed to stagger to my feet.

'There are some things you can't take back. You know that, right?' I hoarsely whispered.

Jacob's words had destroyed my world – our world.

'Yeah. And there are some acts that can't be undone, either,' he pointedly stated.

Trembling, I shook my head at him. 'If you wanted to hurt me, then you've succeeded.'

'No...' Jacob mumbled. 'It wasn't about that.'

'What was it about, then?' I asked as hot, angry tears slid down my face.

'I've sat here for hours and hours going over our life together to try to understand why you would do that to me. To us. And then, I realised that if we hadn't married, then I doubt we would be together now.'

Stunned, I shook my head. 'How can you even say that?'

'Because it's the truth. You would have left me, Claudia. You know it. I've known it for some time now, but I just refused to accept it.'

'That's not true. If you hadn't lied to me about bringing some stranger back here, then I would never have slept with Ethan. We were fine up until then!' My body ached with despair. It felt as if Jacob was looking for a reason to end our marriage. 'Why can't we give each other another chance? I made one mistake. You made a mistake. We've been together ten years, surely that means something to you,' I begged, swiping at the desperate tears that continued to fall. 'Christ, Jacob! Can't we just try to move on from this?'

He didn't respond.

'Jacob? Please.'

'I don't even know who you are any more.'

I shook my head. 'Don't say that.'

'Jaz said she didn't know who you were any more.'

'Jaz?' I questioned, taken aback.

'Yes, Jaz. You claim you don't know why she pulled back from you before she killed herself.'

'You know I don't know!' I fired back at him.

'By all accounts, Jaz wasn't good enough for you either, and you let her know in no uncertain terms.'

'What?' I spluttered. 'Did Jaz say that?'

'Ava told me at the funeral that you hurt Jaz. Badly,' Jacob replied.

'What? When you were sharing a secret cigarette with her?'

'Before then. When you disappeared with Jaz's mother.'

'Did Ava say what I had done?' I asked, suddenly feeling nauseous.

He stared straight at me. 'Only that you did something that crossed a line. Enough to destroy your friendship.'

'And you've kept that from me, until now?'

The betrayal I felt was crushing. Jacob and I had always shared everything. Or so I believed.

My mind went into a tailspin. I could feel my face burning as shame radiated from every pore of my body. It had to be the voicemail message I had left on Jaz's phone the night she killed herself. She must have shared it with Ava. Or maybe forwarded the WhatsApp messages. But for the life of me, I had no idea what I had said, only that it was spiteful and vitriolic, spoken out of hurt and anger.

Nothing more. But I knew it wasn't enough to destroy our friendship.

I then remembered that I had asked Ava if she had spoken to Jaz that night – the night she'd killed herself – or the days leading up to her death. But she had avoided answering, by simply saying that Jaz seemed happy with her life.

Why? Why didn't she answer your question?

And if she was so happy, why did Jaz kill herself?

9

After Jacob's accusation that I had failed Jaz, I had fled upstairs, leaving him to contemplate what remained of our marriage. I had then lain in our bed staring up at the ceiling as dawn snuck in, stealing the darkness, while I tried to recall what I had said to Jaz the night she died. Hours later, and I still couldn't remember, but I knew it wouldn't have been bad enough for Jaz to believe our friendship was over.

Or was it?

Frustrated, I'd turned and looked at the space where Jacob should have been lying, unable to rid myself of the crippling guilt that consumed my body and terrorised my mind.

* * *

'Do you want some coffee?' I asked, trying to act normal as Jacob stepped down into the long, open-plan kitchen. I uneasily noted he was still wearing the same pale blue shirt and jeans from the previous day, suggesting he had spent all night sitting in the armchair.

He shook his head. Bleary-eyed, he headed for the cupboard where we kept the medical supplies. I watched, expecting him to take out painkillers after noting the empty bottle of Au Vodka on the kitchen worktop. I was surprised when, instead, he pulled out his emergency packet of cigarettes and lighter. He had given up two years back and had placed them at the back of the cupboard. Apart from sharing a cigarette with Ava at Jaz's funeral, he hadn't needed one – until now.

'Jacob?'

'Don't,' he darkly muttered.

I watched as, shoulders slumped, he headed to the bi-folding doors and out into the garden.

I felt sick. Whatever hope I had that the conversation last night with Jacob wasn't as devastating as I recalled, immediately evaporated.

I poured myself a strong, black coffee before following him out. I closed the bi-folding door behind myself to prevent Darcy from escaping and joined Jacob in the small garden.

'Did you get any sleep?' I asked.

Jacob didn't answer.

Shivering as the cold air embraced me, I watched as he dragged heavily on the cigarette. The feeling that I was drowning engulfed me.

'I know you're angry with me. You have every right to be. But you can't keep on ignoring me,' I said, desperate to get him to talk to me. To prevent this from escalating to a point where neither of us could back down. 'Seriously?' I said, when he still failed to respond. 'I'm sorry. All right? I'm sorry! If I could undo it, I would.'

I waited while he studied the dreary, gunmetal grey sky.

'Jacob?' I finally questioned out of frustration.

I could feel the anger radiating off him, accompanied by the sour stench of alcohol.

I watched as he continued smoking, struggling with whether to bring up what he had said to me last night.

I shook my head as I found myself asking Jacob, 'Did Ava really say that to you, about Jaz and me, at the funeral?'

Again, he didn't answer.

'Maybe I should ring Ava and ask her,' I threatened.

Jacob turned and looked me straight in the eye. 'Maybe you should. Why don't you tell her about sleeping with Novak while you're at it!'

'Screw you!' I muttered. I spun around and headed back to the bi-folding door.

Without waiting for a reply, I shut the door behind me.

Jacob avoided me for the rest of the morning, as did I with him. We were both too raw, too riled, to be civil to one another, let alone be in the same room. Or house. I spent the morning curled up on the couch with my journal, trying to document everything that had happened since Jaz's funeral. Unsurprisingly, I was left feeling even more raw. I had hoped that Jacob would have come looking for me. But he didn't, making it transparent that he was beyond talking.

I slowly breathed out when I heard the front door banging closed. I walked over and looked out of the living-room window to see Jacob heading to his car. I had no idea where he was going, and that was his intention. I watched as he threw a holdall into the boot.

For a moment, I feared that he'd packed some clothes and left without saying a word. But I knew he wouldn't do that.

Would he?

I sat back down on the couch and braced myself. My eyes drifted over to the mantelpiece to where I had left Bex's bracelet for Jacob to do whatever he wanted to with it.

I breathed in, steeling myself as I picked up my phone.

'Ava,' I greeted, trying to sound normal when she finally picked up my call.

'I haven't got time to talk right now,' she stated.

'Oh... Sure. Can I call you back later?'

I heard her sigh before replying, 'I'm busy. Horrendous workload as usual.'

'This can't wait,' I uncomfortably insisted.

'It will have to wait.'

'It's about Jaz.'

She sighed again. 'Save it for when we all meet on Friday at Barrafina.'

'No,' I replied, anger rising at her refusal to talk after discussing me with my husband. 'You said something to Jacob at the funeral.'

She didn't reply.

'It was about Jaz and me,' I persisted.

'And?'

'What have I done for you to be so cold with me?' I demanded, unable to rise above the hurt I felt.

'I don't know what you expected would happen. The stuff you said was unforgivable and beyond disgusting! Even I struggled to believe you would do that!' Ava caustically replied. 'I should have said something at Jaz's funeral, but I didn't want to make it any worse for her parents.'

My body recoiled from her damming tone – and words. While, simultaneously, my mind went into freefall at this revelation.

'You heard the voice message I left Jaz,' I mumbled.

'What?' Ava snapped. 'For God's sake, Claudia! If you're not going to admit what you did, then I'm not going to bother talking to you! In fact, after what you did, I don't even know why I answered your call!'

'No! Wait! What am I supposed to have done?' I questioned.

What else could it be if this wasn't about the WhatsApp messages or voicemail that I had left Jaz?

'You're the reason that Jaz did what she did! You!' she hissed lowly, vitriol dripping from her words.

Shocked, my breath caught at the back of my throat.

Before I had a chance to respond, the line went dead. Trembling, I immediately rang her back. But she declined my call. Again, and again.

Frantic, I messaged her:

I have no idea what you're talking about.

Heart thundering, I waited. Hot, terrified tears filled my eyes as I stared at my phone, willing Ava to answer me, to absolve me of my guilt, but she didn't reply.

Panicking, I thought about who I could talk to about Ava – and Jaz. I mentally went through who was still at the funeral after Jacob and I had left. I then remembered that Issie was still there. If anyone knew what Ava was referring to, it would be Issie.

When she answered, I somehow managed to croak through the tears, 'Issie?'

'Claudia?'

'Yeah,' I pathetically mumbled.

'What's happened?'

'Ava,' I answered.

'Oh...'

'You knew?' I asked, surprised.

'No... Well... I knew something was up with Ava.'

Still reeling from Ava's vociferous attack, I remained silent.

'Claudia? Are you there?'

I nodded. 'Ahuh.'

'What did she say to you?'

I shakily breathed out, unsure whether I could actually repeat it.

'Claudia?' Issie questioned.

'She... she said that I was to blame for Jaz's death.'

'She said what?' spluttered Issie. 'Are you sure?'

'Yes.'

'No... No, you must have got it wrong. We all know what Ava is like and how direct and unthinking she can be. I'm sure she didn't mean that.'

'She did,' I assured her as more hot tears fell.

'Oh Claudia, I'm sure she didn't.'

'She did,' I repeated.

'Look, we're all feeling racked with guilt over Jaz. All that Ava was doing was lashing out. I think she feels it more than the rest of us because she was talking to Jaz the days leading up to her... to her death.'

'I don't know...' I muttered, unconvinced. 'Ava was adamant I was to blame.'

'But why?' Issie asked, confused.

'I... I messaged and tried calling Jaz that night. The night she...' I faltered.

'What?' Issie replied, confused. 'I thought you said you hadn't talked to Jaz in weeks?'

'I hadn't.'

'I'm lost.'

'For some reason, Jaz was ignoring me. And before you ask, I have no idea why, so I tried to get in touch with her that night,' I explained.

'What did Jaz say to you that night?'

'She didn't answer my calls or messages,' I replied, my voice quivering as tears glided down my cheeks. 'Maybe if she had talked to me, then...' I faltered, choking on the words.

'Listen, we have to accept that Jaz was in a really bad place. Yeah? I'm not sure that any one of us could have prevented her from doing what she did,' Issie said, attempting to ease my guilt.

It failed. More tears came at the acknowledgement that I should have known that something was wrong. That if I had, then I could have stopped Jaz. But that was the point; I didn't know. I had assumed that everything in her life was perfect. While, simultaneously, mine had been falling apart.

'I had no idea she was feeling so low,' I quietly admitted. My skin prickled with shame, for I should have known. But Jaz had ghosted me. 'Did you know or even have an inkling that something wasn't right?'

'No,' Issie answered, the sadness in her voice palpable.

'And, according to Ava, she was happy,' I stated. 'She made partner in her law firm, and she had started seeing someone. Does that sound like someone wanting to end their life? It just doesn't add up.'

'I know,' agreed Issie. 'But I don't think we're ever going to find out why Jaz did it.'

'I miss her, Issie,' I confessed as more tears cascaded down my cheeks. 'I miss her so much. I have this constant ache deep inside, and there's nothing that takes the pain away. I think about her all the time, and I can't stop myself from going over and over why Jaz chose to do what she did. I wish she had let me in. Let me know what she was going to do, so I could stop her. I can't bear the fact that she's gone.'

'Oh, Claudia,' Issie sympathised. 'It's hard enough for us, but I can't imagine how difficult this must be for you.'

'So why does Ava blame me?'

'Like I said, she'll just be lashing out. She's been off with me as well,' Issie assured me.

'She hasn't blamed you for Jaz's death, though, has she?'

Issie was silent for a moment.

'You said you messaged Jaz. What did you say?' she asked.

'I... I asked Jaz what was going on,' I began. 'And why she was ignoring me.'

Issie waited for me to continue.

'When she didn't respond, I left a voicemail message,' I continued. 'I was fuelled by too much drink, and...' I faltered. I didn't have the energy to discuss Jacob's decision to bring a drunken woman back to our home for the night. Then lie about it. Or the scratches and bites she had left on his body. For that was the reason I had reached out to Jaz. I had desperately needed her, and she chose to ignore me.

My eyes drifted back up to her bracelet – Bex's bracelet – evidence that some strange woman had been in my home while I was at a conference.

'And?' Issie gently prompted.

'And anger. Anger that Jaz wouldn't talk to me, that she wouldn't tell me what I had done wrong. So, I ranted at her about what a shitty friend she was and... left messages to that effect.' I stopped, unable to continue as the tears fell again. 'And... and then, very drunk and equally angry, I deleted them, along with all of Jaz's messages. Our conversations all wiped out. You know? Stupid photos and GIFS we'd send one another. All gone...' I could feel the tears burning my eyes that I couldn't pick up my phone and scroll through to find a silly or happy photo of the two of us together messing around. I had unwittingly deleted Jaz from my mobile, unaware she was dramatically ending our relationship by taking her life.

'Oh Claudia...' Issie consoled. 'I just think Jaz was in a bad place and shut you out. That happens when people get really depressed. They isolate themselves.'

'But she didn't. Did she? Jaz was talking to Ava. Why, Issie? Jaz was never close to Ava.'

I heard Issie slowly breathe out.

'Do you know something?' I asked as a knot of panic twisted in my stomach.

'No...'

'Are you sure?' I questioned, not believing her.

'Ava has asked to meet up with me to talk about Jaz.'

'When?' I asked, surprised. I then realised it must be the get-together the four of us had agreed. 'You mean when we all meet up on Friday?'

'I'm sure that's what she must have meant,' Issie replied.

I had the distinct feeling that she was lying to me.

'You would tell me if something was going on?'

'Of course I would,' Issie quickly assured me.

'Did Ava tell you whether she talked to Jaz that night?'

'She didn't. At least, that's what she told me. Why?' questioned Issie.

'Because Ava told Jacob at the funeral that I had crossed a line with Jaz. That I had done something which had really hurt her.'

'Ava said that to Jacob?'

I could hear the shock in her voice.

'Do you think Ava knew about the voice message you left Jaz?' Issie suggested.

'That's what I thought. But when I asked Ava if it was the voice message, she acted as if she didn't know what I was talking about.'

'Oh...'

'Did Jaz say anything to you about me?' I questioned.

'Like what?'

I could hear the unease in Issie's voice as if I had touched a nerve. Or maybe I was imagining it.

'Whether I had hurt her somehow.'

'No,' Issie answered. 'What makes you think you hurt her?'

'I don't know.'

'Look, I'm sure Ava didn't mean what she said. You know what she's like. Why don't I talk to her?' Issie offered.

'Will you?' I asked, relieved. I couldn't cope with the idea that Ava believed that I was capable of hurting Jaz. Worse, that I had done something that would make Jaz want to end her life. Even though I knew I hadn't, I couldn't silence the doubts that Ava's words had seeded in my mind.

'Of course, I will.'

'And you'll let me know what it is that I'm supposed to have done to Jaz?'

'Listen, silly, you haven't done anything! All right? So, get that ridiculous idea out of your head.'

'Thanks, Issie. For a moment there, I was starting to believe that I was responsible for Jaz...' I stopped myself.

'Claudia, what happened to Jaz is unbearable. But you did nothing wrong.'

'Or maybe that's the point, I did nothing.'

'Then, we're all to blame. Not just you.'

Neither of us spoke for a few beats.

'Look, I need to go. But as soon as I've talked to Ava, I'll let you know. I'm sure she'll message you with an apology later.'

I wasn't convinced but let it go. There was something else that was bothering me – the inexplicable feeling that they were excluding me.

'The three of you wouldn't keep anything from me, would you?'

'Like what?' Issie questioned.

I hesitated. 'To do with Jaz.'

'Of course not. Why would you ask?'

I considered how to answer her. There was something Willow had said, or, crucially, hadn't said at Jaz's funeral. Willow had started to question the way Jaz had taken her life and then abruptly stopped. A look had passed between her and Ava. Then Mrs Donaldson had conveniently interrupted us.

'Claudia?' Issie questioned in reaction to my silence.

I forced myself to speak. 'At the funeral, Willow was about to say something about Jaz...' I hesitated, struggling to say the words. 'She seemed to imply that she thought it odd that Jaz had chosen to cut her wrists. Then I swear Ava gave Willow this look to silence her. But before I had a chance to question what Willow meant, Jaz's mother came over.'

Issie paused before replying, 'Did she?'

'Yes.'

'Oh... I can't remember, Claudia,' Issie said. 'It was such a challenging day. Maybe it's worth asking Willow herself on Friday.'

I didn't respond.

'You know there's no secrets between us,' Issie assured me.

'I know,' I mumbled.

But I couldn't silence the feeling that Issie, like Ava, was holding something back from me – something connected to Jaz's death.

But what could they possibly know?

Then it hit me: did they know why Jaz decided to kill herself?

10

SATURDAY, ONE WEEK LATER

It felt like I had sleepwalked through the past week. I barely ate, slept, did anything, aside from work, where I somehow managed to keep it together, given the fact that Jacob had avoided me. He stayed out until late, and when he did come home, it was only to sleep, which he did in the guest room. If he intended to punish me, he was succeeding. I had tried talking to him, but he just gave me the silent treatment. So, I resorted to giving him space, hoping he would eventually calm down.

It was now Saturday evening, a week on from when I'd sabotaged my marriage. I was at home with Darcy snuggled up on my lap, unable to do anything other than obsess about Jacob's whereabouts. I had heard him come in last night after midnight, slamming the front door behind him before stomping down the hallway to the kitchen, where he'd proceeded to clatter around. Whether he was drunk or trying to get a reaction from me, I couldn't say. Or maybe it was both. I'd resisted the temptation to get up out of bed and have a go at him for making so much noise, accepting that was what he wanted – a fight. I was too emotionally exhausted to argue with him. When I had awoken this morning, Jacob was already gone. Whatever hope I had that Jacob would quickly come round had long since dissipated.

I checked my phone for the umpteenth time, but there was nothing from Jacob. I had messaged him, asking if we could talk. However, he had ignored it. But Jacob wasn't the only person avoiding me.

I had sent Ava two more messages at the beginning of the week, asking to talk, but to no avail as she didn't reply. I had then contacted Issie to see whether she had chatted to Ava. However, Issie had said she hadn't had the chance. I had been hoping to see Ava in person yesterday evening, but she had posted on the WhatsApp group chat that she couldn't make it. Then Willow had bailed, forcing Issie to suggest that we meet up the following Friday at the tapas bar. I couldn't silence the feeling that they were pulling back from me. I put it down to paranoia. After all, we had all lost our childhood school friend. I was sure that the others were equally struggling to accept Jaz's decision to end her life. But still, I couldn't silence the fear that there was more to their withdrawal than Jaz's death.

I took a sip of wine and tried to relax. But I couldn't switch my mind off. I put my book down, too distracted to focus. Jacob and I had always spent Saturday evenings together. Whether as a couple with friends or on our own, but it was our night. Or, it used to be.

I heard the front door open, then close.

'Jacob?' I called out. 'Is that you?'

No answer.

I gently moved Darcy onto the throw and jumped up off the couch and headed out to the hallway.

'Didn't you hear me?'

'No,' Jacob answered as he shut the vestibule door behind him.

'Did you get my text?' I questioned.

He raised his head and looked at me. I was taken aback by the haunted look in his eyes.

'Jacob?' I mumbled as an uneasy sense of foreboding descended on me.

'That's why I'm here,' he dispassionately answered.

I noticed the holdall in his hand.

'Do you want a glass of wine?'

'I'm not staying.'

I could feel the terror building inside me.

'Please, Jacob. Don't do this,' I pleaded.

He dropped his gaze to his feet. 'I can't continue like this.'

'We need more time. That's all,' I insisted.

He didn't respond.

'Jacob? This is fixable. You know that, right?' I pleaded. The fear of losing him had made me realise how much I needed him and how badly I wanted our marriage to work. I couldn't imagine my life without him.

Jacob didn't reply.

'What about counselling? Because if that's what it takes to get us back on track, I'll do it. I'll do whatever's required to make this work.'

His silence screamed at me that it was already too late for counselling.

'Jacob?' I questioned, trying to hold it together. 'Sara and Richard spent six months in therapy, and they couldn't be happier now.'

'We're not Sara and Richard,' Jacob pointed out.

'No,' I agreed, 'but it's the same principle. I'm sure we could get a lot out of therapy together.'

Jacob shook his head as he looked me straight in the eye. 'I can't do it. Not right now. I need time.'

'Okay. Take as much time as you need,' I suggested.

He broke away from my gaze. 'I need time away.'

'Away?' I numbly repeated.

'From you,' he clarified.

'No...' I mumbled. 'Please, don't do this to us,' I begged.

'That's why I need to leave. Otherwise, our marriage won't stand a chance.'

'I don't understand. I haven't made any demands on you, have I? I've let you have your own space. So why do you need to move out?' I questioned, hating myself for sounding so desperate.

'It's not enough,' he stated. 'I need time on my own to work through this.'

'Work through what?' I whispered.

'You having sex with Novak,' he answered.

I stepped back, winded. The lack of fight in his voice threw me. The jealousy and rage that had fired him up were gone, replaced by what sounded like defeat.

He had given up on us – on me.

Despite my mute reaction, I was screaming on the inside. I wiped away the tears that had started to trail down my cheeks with my other hand. I swallowed. Then shook my head.

He waited, watching me as if gauging whether to tell me.

'Someone at work has gone to the States for three months,' he cautiously began. 'Their flat is available for the duration, and it's a five-minute walk from the hospital.'

'Why are you telling me this?' I asked. But I knew why.

'I've signed a contract for a short-term lease,' he admitted.

Shocked, I stared at him, not recognising the man standing in front of me. 'Why?'

'I need some time. That's all,' he answered.

'When?' I somehow managed to ask, despite feeling as if my mouth was full of grains of sun-scorched sand.

Jacob didn't need to speak for me to know the answer. I could see the unease in his eyes.

'So, you waited until moving out to tell me,' I said, incredulous.

I could feel raw, hurt tears gliding down my cheeks to my chin. I swiped at them, annoyed at myself for crying.

'I didn't know how to tell you.'

I didn't answer him. I couldn't.

'I'm going to pack a few things now and then I'll come back in the week and get the rest,' Jacob said, raising the holdall in his hand.

I felt detached from my body. Jacob was leaving me, and yet, it was as if it was happening to someone else.

He walked past me and headed up the stairs.

One crucial factor replaced the initial shock of Jacob's sudden revelation – money.

'How can we afford this?' I suddenly questioned.

Jacob stopped. He looked back down the stairs at me. 'I don't know. I just know I need some space.'

'But space costs. How can we afford to pay for a flat for three months on top of the mortgage payments?'

He shrugged. 'I haven't given it much thought.'

'Don't you think you should have done before signing a lease for three months?'

He didn't reply.

'Jacob,' I demanded. 'We're struggling as it is to meet the mortgage payments, on top of the countless loans we took out to refurbish this house. Then there's the lease for your car.'

Again, he shrugged. 'We'll figure out a way.'

'How?' I asked, trying to temper my rising anger at his recklessness.

'Why don't you ask your parents to help out?' he suggested. 'You know they would.'

'Are you serious?' I demanded. 'Is that your way of telling me that you're not going to make any payments towards the mortgage for the next three months? It's your credit rating that will be affected as well as mine.'

'Your parents won't let that happen,' he pointed out.

'Fuck you!' I cursed. 'I never thought of you as selfish! Or someone who lacked self-respect.'

He stared me straight in the eye. 'Yeah? I never thought my wife would throw in my face that she had fucked her colleague.'

With that, Jacob continued up the stairs and along the hallway to our bedroom. Whatever rage he had held in, he now unleashed above me as he threw open the wardrobe and pulled out drawers as he collected his clothes.

Shocked, I stared up the stairs, letting the tears slide down my face.

Was Jacob really leaving me?

11

SUNDAY

I lay in bed unable to move, despite the fact it now had to be mid-afternoon, paralysed by one continuous thought: *Jacob's left you. He's really gone...*

The house was achingly silent as if it too mourned the loss of Jacob.

I turned over in bed, sighing heavily.

Don't go there... Not again, Claudia. It's masochistic to keep reliving it. To keep scrutinising each moment as if you could change things.

But I couldn't stop myself from repeatedly reliving the night I'd returned from a two-day academic conference at Bristol University to discover Jacob covered in scratches and bite marks on his chest and back. Enraged by jealousy and betrayal and fuelled by alcohol, I had interrogated Jacob until he had had enough and stormed out. Unable to cope with the crippling knowledge alone, I had texted, then rung Jaz, needing her reassurance that my world had not ended. But she had added to my desperation by ghosting me.

When I had woken up the next day with my head feeling as if it was going to explode and my mouth so parched that I was sure that my organs would shut down from dehydration, I had no idea that the nightmare was only beginning. Piece by piece, the jigsaw puzzle had gradually come together as I remembered Jacob's betrayal. Suspecting Jacob had cheated on me was horrific. But the worst was yet to come. At that point, Jaz was already dead. Not that anyone knew – not yet. It took Jaz's secretary alerting her parents that something was wrong, then their drive down to Edinburgh. It wasn't until mid-afternoon that the police had arrived at Jaz's apartment. By then, Jaz had lain in the bath, undiscovered, and alone, for hours. They were too late. When I'd found out that night, I was too late.

Wincing, I squinted my eyes to check the time on my phone. It was 4.33 p.m.; I had squandered the day, revelling in self-pity, despite having a first-year lecture to finish off and scripts to mark for tomorrow, but I still couldn't bring myself to crawl out of bed. I had hidden under the comforter since last night, unable to accept the painful reality that Jacob had left me, and there was no Jaz to talk to about it. She was dead, and there was nothing that could change that brutal fact.

I noted a missed call from Issie on my screen. I couldn't cope with talking to her or anyone else. I just wanted to be left alone to blot out the fact that my life was now in fragments.

I pulled the comforter over my head and squeezed my eyes shut against what had become of my world.

'No... Darcy. Not now...' I moaned as he started screeching at me to get up.

He jumped on the bed and persisted in wailing and clawing at the comforter in an attempt to rouse me.

'Okay,' I muttered, accepting defeat. 'Okay!'

* * *

After feeding Darcy with his favourite cat gourmet salmon pâté, I ground some coffee beans and made a pot of strong black coffee. I then picked up the Sunday papers from the doormat and headed back upstairs. I sat in bed, gingerly sipping my coffee while I blankly stared at the newspapers laid out in front of me. I noticed my journal lying open on the bed from earlier. I reached across and picked it up, resisting the masochistic urge to scavage over the bones of my misery detailed in my most recent entries. Instead, I closed it and put it back on my bedside cabinet along with my pen.

My phone started to vibrate. I grabbed it. What hope I had that it would be Jacob instantly evaporated. Nor was it Helena or Ethan: the only two people who persistently messaged. Helena was worried about me. Understandably so. Even I could see that I was a mess, both physically and emotionally. As for Ethan, he had been trying to talk to me since that Saturday morning. Not that I wanted to talk to him. I just wanted to forget that it had ever happened.

I stared at the text:

Tried calling earlier. Need to chat x

It was from Issie. I contemplated what to do. I didn't want to talk to her for fear of inadvertently confessing that my marriage could be over. Let alone the part I had played in its destruction. I was still holding out that Jacob would come to his senses within the next few days. Nor did I want Issie repeating Jacob's departure to Ava.

It suddenly dawned on me that Issie might have talked to Ava. I pressed call.

'Hey,' I said, trying to sound upbeat when Issie answered.

'Thank God you rang me, I've been going out of my mind,' Issie blurted.

'Did you talk to Ava?' I immediately questioned, noting the urgency in her voice.

Issie hesitated. 'No.'

'Oh, why not?'

I heard Issie sigh.

'Issie?'

'She's caught up with work. I'll talk to her this week. I promise.'

'Is she still on for this Friday evening?' I asked.

I needed Issie to talk to Ava first before we all met up.

'It's two weeks this Friday,' she corrected.

'I'm sure it was this Friday.'

'Check the group chat. Ava realised she can't do this Friday either, so asked to push it back.'

'Oh right, I haven't seen it.'

I had been too preoccupied to check the WhatsApp group chat. Although, I was quietly relieved that Ava had postponed it again, giving me some much-needed time to get my head together. The last thing I wanted was Ava, Willow or Issie knowing what had happened between Jacob and me – especially Ava. I still hadn't managed to reconcile catching her flirting with Jacob at Jaz's funeral. Under any other circumstances, I would have dismissed it, but given her behaviour towards me, I doubted it was harmless. It felt too predatory, too personal.

'If you can't make two weeks on Friday, we can figure something out.'

'No, that should be fine,' I answered. 'You'll talk to Ava before then?'

'Of course,' Issie assured me. 'I'm sure it's all just a misunderstanding, though.'

I didn't share the sentiment. Ava blamed me for Jaz's death. I wasn't imagining it. She'd said I was responsible. But why, was still beyond me.

'Is everything all right?' I asked. Issie rarely rang without reason. So, if she hadn't managed to talk to Ava, then why was she calling?

'I just found out that Sebastian has got engaged,' Issie replied.

'Seriously?' I questioned, shocked.

'And she's only twenty-six,' Issie added.

'Oh, Issie, I'm sorry.'

Issie had never gotten over Sebastian. Or the fact that he had left her without an explanation the week before their wedding. Unable to accept that it was over, her wedding dress had remained hanging in her spare bedroom for months afterwards. Issie had been a wreck, so much so, Jaz and I had taken it in turns to stay with her, fearful that she would do something stupid. That had happened two summers ago, and while Sebastian had moved on, Issie was still stuck in a past that no longer existed. She'd had three dates since then, all of which had been disasters for one reason or another. Until Issie truly accepted that Sebastian wasn't coming back, I doubted that any other man stood a chance. Maybe Sebastian getting engaged might finally make Issie let go.

I spent the following couple of hours on the phone with Issie while she tried to find out what she could about Sebastian's new fiancée on social media. It distracted me from dwelling on Jacob and what he was up to. When Issie had exhausted her masochistic compulsion, she assured me that she didn't need me to drive over to hers to spend the night. However, I needed convincing that she wouldn't do anything foolish, bordering on bunny-boiler behaviour; since Issie had succeeded in ascertaining an alarming number of facts about Sebastian and his new fiancée, including her address.

I didn't feel like leaving the house, let alone making my way to Issie's place in Kent. But if I needed to, I would have done it without question. But Issie was certain that she would be fine and equally adamant that she wouldn't do anything crazy. After multiple promises from Issie that she was all right, I hung up.

I padded downstairs, followed by a meowing Darcy, to get some fresh water.

'Seriously?' I questioned as Darcy screeched up at me. 'I fed you not that long ago, buddy.'

I bent down and picked him up and carried him through to the kitchen.

'Are you missing your dad? Eh?' I cooed.

He pathetically wailed in response.

I realised I had retreated from the world to my bed, ignoring everything and everyone, which wasn't like me. Nor was it like me to leave dirty plates and mugs lying around, instead of loading them into the dishwasher, or piles of dirty laundry in the bathroom and bedroom. As I looked around the kitchen, I realised that during these past couple of weeks, chaos had taken over. I had been too distraught by Jacob's behaviour towards me to notice, and he had avoided being around me, so was rarely home, and now he had moved out.

But he'll come back.

What if he doesn't, Claudia? What then?

I blocked out the terrifying thought and busied myself with filling a bowl with some dry food for Darcy. I filled my water bottle and took it back upstairs, deciding to tidy the house tomorrow after work. I didn't have the strength or inclination to tackle the mess of the past couple of weeks. Not without Jacob.

I lay down on the bed and curled up in a foetal position, desperate for sleep to take me away from the aching emptiness that consumed me. The fact that Jacob hadn't even reached out to make sure Darcy and I were all right struck me as cruel and selfish. Traits that I would never have attributed to Jacob. Then again, I would never have believed that he could have lied to me. And so convincingly. I tried to block out the torturous thoughts of Jacob's deceit, the catalyst for our lives falling apart, desperately wanting to drift off into oblivion and forget.

12

FRIDAY

I had managed to keep it together for the past week at work, or so I believed. Helena had since disabused me of that notion. Knowing something was very wrong, Helena insisted we go for a quick drink and something to eat after my last seminar late Friday afternoon. She suggested the walk-in Michelin-starred authentic Spanish tapas bar, Barrafina, in Dean Street, Soho – Jaz's favourite haunt and where I was supposed to meet Issie, Ava and Willow until Ava had postponed it for another week because of yet more work commitments. It was a fifteen-minute walk from my office at University College London in Foster Court, Bloomsbury. And refusing to take no for an answer, I had no choice but to join her.

'Are you okay?' Helena asked as concern etched her face.

We were both sat at the bar, on bar stools, sharing a bottle of cava and small plates of food. I had no appetite. Something that hadn't gone unnoticed by Helena as she delighted in the delicate bites we were being served.

I had just explained everything to Helena, starting with Jacob bringing some random woman back to our home, our bed, to the finale with him walking out on Saturday evening.

I was hoping that sharing what had happened with someone would make me feel better. It didn't. After watching Helena's visibly shocked reaction, I felt worse, if that was possible. Admitting that Jacob had left me made it real and also made me feel pathetic and a failure.

'I honestly don't know what to say,' Helena remarked.

I attempted a smile. Failed. 'There's nothing you can say.'

I took another sip of wine, aware of Helena's awkward silence.

'Jaz loved it here,' I suddenly shared. 'She was a real foodie, you know? And this place...' I shrugged as I looked around the vibrant setting. It was already buzzing. 'It was a piece of heaven for her.'

I regretted the words when I saw Helena's reaction.

'Oh Claudia, I am so sorry! Christ! Here I am trying to help, and I bring you here of all places! I'm such an idiot!'

I shook my head. 'You're not. I appreciate the fact that you brought me here. Otherwise, I would be at home alone dwelling on Jacob and whether or not he was with someone.'

Helena gave me a sympathetic look.

I took another sip of cava.

'So, when did you last see him?' Helena asked.

I looked at her and sighed. 'That's the point. Jacob won't see me.'

'Seriously?'

'He won't return my calls. I haven't seen him since last Saturday evening.'

'But that's what?'

'Six days.'

'And he's not contacted you at all?'

'No,' I reluctantly admitted.

'Oh, Claudia...'

'When I rang him, he declined my call.'

Helena shook her head in disbelief before taking a mouthful of cava.

'Then, I came home from work yesterday to discover that he had been back and taken his guitar, vinyls and the record player, amongst other items.'

'Shit!' muttered Helena. 'That's crap. Funny how he has forgotten that he was the one who lied to you in the first instance about bringing some random, drunken woman back to your home because he somehow felt responsible for her. Fucking men! Bastards all of them!'

Helena was cynical where men were concerned. When her ex-partner of twelve years was offered a coveted professorship at Oxford, he had faithfully commuted back to their home every weekend for the first year until his affair with one of his colleagues finally took precedence. That was a year and a half back, and she still hadn't gotten over him leaving her on the wrong side of forty, or his choice of a woman who was half her age, and size.

'Sorry... I'm just so furious,' she apologised, noting my embarrassment. 'I mean, what the fuck is Jacob playing at?'

I didn't answer her. I couldn't.

'What happens now?' she asked, pouring the remainder of the bottle of cava into my glass and then her own.

'I don't know,' I answered honestly. 'I wait.'

I was quietly hoping that Jacob would come to his senses and come back home.

'Can you afford to wait?'

It was a good question and one that I didn't want to contemplate.

'You know what a horrible time I went through when Seamus left me. The worst part was nearly losing the flat. Not that he gave a damn. The shite!' Helena added.

I sympathetically nodded.

'So,' she continued, 'back to Jacob, where's he staying?'

'He's signed for a flat for three months next to the hospital.'

'Oh... Claudia...'

I shrugged. I had assumed that the worst-case scenario would be Jacob staying at his friend Zain's place for a week or so to cool off. So, the revelation on Saturday evening that he had a three-month lease on a flat had thrown me. I was acutely aware that a lot could happen in three months. In the space of weeks, my best friend had taken her life, and my husband had left me.

'How are you going to afford to pay for the house?' Helena asked.

'No idea, to be honest.'

'What has Jacob said?'

I swallowed another mouthful of dry cava, preparing myself for Helena's explosive response. 'That I can't expect him to contribute his share of the mortgage when he now has rent to pay.'

'Bastard!' cursed Helena. 'Typical! Leaves it all to you to sort out while he gets himself a bloody shag pad. Defaulting on the mortgage payments will surely affect him as well.'

I nodded as I took another sip of cava.

'Christ!' muttered Helena in disgust. 'Isn't he a paediatric cardiologist now at Great Ormond Street? Surely his salary will stretch to his share of the mortgage and paying rent on this flat he's found.'

'Remember, he works for the NHS...'

'So? He'll still be earning a lot more than you as an associate professor,' Helena pointed out.

I shrugged. I knew she was right. Not that I wanted to admit it. Jacob's salary was easily double my earnings. And yet, he was prepared to let me struggle financially.

Why?

But I knew why.

He's pissed at you, Claudia. Too angry to realise the financial implications of his spiteful actions: for it was his name on the mortgage as well.

'Why has Jacob reacted like this?' she questioned, picking up on my reticence to discuss our finances.

'Because I slept with Ethan,' I reminded her.

She looked at me as if I had lost my mind. 'Seriously, Claudia? He lied to you. Wake up!'

Wounded, I sat back.

'Look, I'm sorry. I know you think I am being hard on you, but I want you to consider the full picture here.'

I inwardly sighed. It wasn't what I wanted to hear. However, I should have anticipated Helena's reaction.

'Say Jacob has been seeing this woman for some time, and it wasn't just a one-night stand,' Helena posited.

I vehemently shook my head. 'Not possible. Jacob wouldn't do that. And he didn't have sex with her—'

Helena cut me off. 'Get with the programme, Claudia. He's already lied to you and probably had sex with her in your home.'

'No... I know he didn't.'

'How can you be so certain?' Helena sceptically asked.

'You forget that I've been with him for ten years. I know everything there is to know about Jacob and vice versa,' I argued. 'And he had nothing to lose after finding out I slept with Ethan. That was the perfect opportunity for him to hurt me by throwing in my face he slept with her. But he didn't, Helena. And the reason he didn't admit it is because he didn't have sex with her.'

I had spent enough hours mulling over the fact that Jacob had the perfect opportunity to retaliate and lash out at me for sleeping with Ethan. But he didn't. Instead, he cut me to the core by telling me he felt forced into marrying me and buying our house.

Helena sighed. 'Okay. Have it your way. I just want you to start thinking objectively here. For your sake. What about your parents?'

'What about them?'

'Can they help you financially for the time being?'

'No. I don't want my parents to know what's happened.'

'Why? Surely if it means they can help you out, it would be worth the embarrassment.'

'No,' I repeated, even though my parents had ample funds to pay the entire mortgage off. I didn't want them interfering, or worse, saying that they had told me it wouldn't work, that we had been too young and, consequently, too impulsive. Also, I was painfully aware that my mother would blame me for Jacob leaving. For whatever reason, I was always in the wrong where she was concerned. Nothing met her impossibly high standards, including me as her daughter. As for my father, he typically sided with my mother. In his defence, he had to live with her – I didn't.

'Okay. Well...' Helena faltered, as if unsure whether to propose it. 'You might have to consider what I had to do until I got myself turned around...'

'I couldn't cope with a total stranger living in my house,' I immediately fired back.

'Even if it's a temporary measure to cover your mortgage payments?'

'I know you're trying to help, but—'

'You only need someone short-term until you and Jacob sort out what's happening,' she interrupted.

'Yes. But I don't want anyone.'

'What you do or don't want is irrelevant here. Simple maths, you don't earn enough to pay your mortgage single-handedly and you don't want to involve your parents. Right?'

I nodded. I didn't want to add to our debt, but I didn't see an alternative if I wanted to make the mortgage payments for the next three months.

What happens after that, Claudia? What if Jacob doesn't come back?

I pushed the disruptive thought away and took another sip of cava.

'I might have the answer to your problems. Riley Harrison. She's just transferred. She had a few personal problems and wanted a fresh start. We had a meeting yesterday to discuss her PhD and she was saying that she is looking for a room for a few months or so until she gets herself sorted.'

I shook my head. 'Nope. Not interested.'

'Hear me out, will you?' Helena insisted. 'You'd be helping her out. She has to get out of her apartment by Sunday, and she still hasn't found anywhere. She's desperate, Claudia.'

'I feel sorry for her,' I sympathised. 'But I don't want some young twenty-something in my home. It just wouldn't work.'

'That's where you're wrong. Riley's a mature PhD student. If I recall, she said she's thirty-three. It's only temporary as well. She has somewhere else lined up but can't move in until the beginning of the summer. You're only talking three months.'

'Hasn't she got any family or friends that can help her out until the beginning of summer?' I questioned, not wanting to be guilt-tripped into taking in a lodger. I was still holding out that Jacob and I would sort things out, and he would return home soon.

Helena shook her head. 'Nope. No family. As for friends, she didn't mention any. She seems very quiet. I don't think you would even know she was living with you. And, it's only short-term. It means that you wouldn't have to worry about how you pay for the mortgage. Then she moves out, and Jacob moves back in. It's perfect. She's perfect!'

I took another mouthful of cava as I contemplated Helena's proposal. It did seem tempting. More so, if, as Helena said, I wouldn't even know that she was there.

'What's her name again?'

'Riley Harrison,' Helena repeated. 'You'll love her, I promise.'

'And she's definitely quiet? Not someone who is going to be

bringing people back at all hours. I mean, what do you really know about her?'

'Good question, and full transparency, I've just met her. But she seems very introspective and shy. All she needs is a bedroom to sleep in and study, that's it. Her words. I'd be surprised if you see much of her.'

I raised my eyebrows at this statement.

'I'm serious! She's not looking for anything more than to rent a room for three months.'

'You think it would work?' I questioned, unsure. Not that I wanted to rent out my guest bedroom, but I accepted it would solve my money worries.

'I wouldn't have suggested it if I didn't think so.'

'And she's not crazy?'

Helena laughed at me.

'I'm serious,' I replied. 'This is a stranger you want me to take into my home.'

'She's my research student,' Helena pointed out.

I watched as she got her phone out.

'I'll send you Riley's number.'

'I'm not promising,' I warned. But it was an option.

'For all I know, she's already found somewhere,' Helena stated. 'She had to be out by Sunday.'

'I'll give her a call when I get home,' I suggested. 'And if I do take this Riley Harrison in, I'll be holding you accountable.'

Helena shook her head, smiling at me. 'You'll be thanking me soon enough.'

Will I? Or will I regret taking some stranger into my home?

13

I stared at my reflection in the bar's bathroom mirror as I considered Helena's proposal to my financial problem. I thought about Jacob and whether I should let him know I was considering a lodger. Then again, he hadn't returned my call. Nor had he reached out to make sure I was all right. Our finances weren't great, as he was well aware. He knew that without my parents' help, I would be unable to pay the mortgage for the next three months single-handedly. His behaviour was the antithesis of the man I had fallen in love with and married. The Jacob I knew would never have behaved in such a callous manner.

Maybe Jacob thinks the same about you? After all, you had revenge sex with a colleague and couldn't wait to throw it in his face. You pushed him so hard that he had no other choice but to run from you. What did you expect, Claudia? What the fuck did you think would happen?

I didn't recognise myself. If Jaz were still here, none of this would have happened. She would have stopped me and talked me down from revenge fucking Ethan Novak.

But she's not! She's gone. Now Jacob's gone too. And you're to blame. No one else.

I shakily breathed out and held onto the sink. I had only drunk half a bottle of cava, yet I felt woozy. I realised I hadn't eaten all day. Helena had other plans for the evening. Otherwise, we would have shared another bottle. She had dashed off to meet up with a friend for further drinks. I had contemplated staying for another drink on my own but discounted it. I couldn't put off the inevitable – going home. The weekend loomed ahead of me like some dark, ghostly spectre. I was facing forty-eight hours alone, desperately wondering whether Jacob was with someone.

I straightened myself up and finished reapplying my lipstick. I then picked up my bag and walked out of the toilets, heading through the busy tapas bar for the exit. I froze when I recognised her voice, cutting through the air. I could feel my stomach contract. I didn't know whether I had the strength to face her. Not now. Not alone.

Then I heard another familiar voice.

No!

I should have continued walking. Instead, I found myself compelled to turn in the direction of their voices. I gasped when I saw the three of them together sat at the bar – without me.

Maybe I had got it wrong. Otherwise, why would they be meeting up without me? It was 8 p.m., the time we'd agreed at the *venue* we'd agreed.

I tried to swallow, but my mouth was too dry. I stood there paralysed, doubting what was in front of me – Ava, Issie and Willow ordering drinks.

But Ava had postponed it for another week. Hadn't she? That was what Issie had said to me on Sunday on the phone. Or had she?

Jacob leaving me had thrown me into a frantic tailspin, and so, it would be no wonder that I had misheard her.

I took out my phone and opened the WhatsApp group chat to check whether I had made a mistake about tonight. My heart accelerated as I read through the conversation thread. Ava had posted that she couldn't make it this evening, followed by Willow suggesting they rearrange for the following week. Issie and Ava had agreed with the new date – next Friday. Willow had then posted a message asking me if I could make it. But there was no other post about tonight. Nothing.

How did I not know that tonight was still going ahead? Maybe I didn't get the message. Or....

Numb, I stared at my phone as I absorbed the shattering truth. There was no message about tonight because I wasn't supposed to be here. If it hadn't been for Helena spontaneously dragging me here after work, I wouldn't have caught them together – without me. I deeply breathed in, feeling unsteady as their betrayal hit me.

Before I had a chance to compose myself, or leave, Issie, as if sensing my presence, turned around. Her stunned expression turned to horror when she saw me. It was enough for me to know that they had intentionally uninvited me.

Issie's reaction alerted Ava that something was wrong. She looked at Issie, then followed her gaze to my awkward figure. The coldness in Ava's eyes tore straight through me. I stared back at her, searching her face for some acknowledgement of shame or remorse. But there was nothing.

How could you, Ava? How could you want to hurt me like this?

My head was screaming at me to run, to get as far away from them and their treachery. But I somehow kept it together and managed to walk towards the exit.

'Claudia? Wait!' Willow suddenly called out, climbing down off the bar stool.

Ignoring her, I continued walking.

Willow caught up with me as I reached the door. 'Please, Claudia.'

I turned around, tears burning my eyes.

Willow looked confused. 'Is something wrong? Are you all right? Oh, Claudia...' Her voice trailed off at the tears now gliding down my face. 'What's happened? Is it too soon after Jaz?'

I stiffly shook my head.

I could see in her startled eyes that she had no idea what was going on.

'Claudia?' she questioned, her voice trembling.

'I wasn't invited,' I flatly replied.

'What? Ava said you couldn't make it.'

'Seriously? And you believed her?' I threw back at her.

Willow looked stunned. 'Why wouldn't I? She... She said you were ill.'

I dug my fingernails into my palms, not believing what I was hearing. I couldn't even bring myself to look over at Ava.

'Do I look ill?' I retaliated.

'I don't understand,' Willow said, confused.

I could see the hurt in her eyes at my abruptness. But I wasn't angry with her.

'That makes two of us.'

'Join us, so we can talk this through. I am sure it is all just a misunderstanding,' pleaded Willow.

'I can assure you it's not. I talked to Issie on Sunday, and she said tonight wasn't happening. It was postponed because Ava couldn't make it,' I pointed out, trying to keep the anger that was raging through my body out of my voice.

'That's correct. But then, this morning, Ava rang me and said she could make it and that she urgently needed to talk to us. All of us,' she insisted.

'Well, she didn't ring me.'

'Oh...' mumbled Willow. 'I... I don't know why.'

'Neither do I. I suggest you ask Ava.'

'Claudia,' Issie said as she uneasily approached us.

I turned to her. She looked alarmed. I assumed it was because she had been caught out.

I shook my head. 'How could you? After all, we've been through. I was the one, along with Jaz, who stayed with you after Sebastian broke off the wedding. And you do this to me?' I incredulously demanded, gesturing with my hand over to the bar where Ava was still seated.

Lost for words, Issie stared at me.

I pushed the door open and walked out, not giving Issie the chance to reply. For there was nothing that she could say that could make this right.

'Claudia? Come back. Please,' Issie shouted after me.

I continued walking away before I did or said something I would later regret.

Why? Why would they meet up without me?

The question scorched through my mind. But I couldn't come up with an answer. Then it hit me.

Ava blames you.

That was why they had met up without me, for Ava to discuss what part I'd played in Jaz's decision to end her life.

* * *

Once home, I got inside, locked the door and stood there trembling. Darcy raced up to me, meowing at my distress. I scooped him up and blindly walked through to the kitchen. He struggled in my arms, forcing me to let him go. Realising that all he wanted was food, I dished up his favourite gourmet salmon pâté, then grabbed a glass and a bottle of Chablis from the fridge and headed to the living room. I threw my bag down and collapsed on the couch.

Still trembling, I opened the bottle and poured myself a large glass. I gulped back a mouthful. The knowledge that my school friends were in Barrafina in Soho, without me, was too much to bear.

I felt hurt and humiliated. I was angry at myself for not calling them out. I should have marched over to where they were seated and demanded to know why they hadn't invited me. But I hadn't. Instead, I had run away, unable to confront whatever it was that Ava believed she had on me.

Maybe she did have something on you? Perhaps she had listened to the drunken voice message you left Jaz the night she died?

I still couldn't remember what I had said to her. But I was sure that it wasn't bad enough for Jaz to take her life. *Or was it?*

No matter how hard I tried, I couldn't get rid of the terrifying feeling that Ava was right and I was responsible for my best friend's suicide. I took another glug of wine in a bid to wash away the sour taste of guilt from my mouth and lessen the shame pricking my skin.

Oh God... What had I done?

I could feel the grief that had dragged me down into the darkest, loneliest waters of despair in the days following Jaz's death, threatening to return, to hold me down, overriding my instinct to survive, until I took my last breath. There was no Jacob to pull me up out of the cold, black abyss. Or Issie. Or Willow. I was completely alone.

I thought about calling Jacob. But what would I say? More to the point, would he answer?

I drained my glass and, with a shaking hand, poured myself another.

My phone rang. I assumed it was either Issie again or Willow. I had declined Issie's repeated calls on the cab journey home. I couldn't bring myself to talk to her. To listen to her fumbling lies as she attempted to absolve herself of her guilt at my exclusion. For Issie had lied to me. I recalled the look of shock, then horror when she saw me in the tapas bar.

However, the one person who wasn't in the least perturbed was Ava. Nor did she call or text me to assure me it was a mistake, because it wasn't an oversight. Ava knew what she was doing and why.

As for Willow, she had looked as confused and lost as I had felt. It was obvious from her reaction that she had believed what Ava had told her – that I couldn't make it.

I reached inside my bag and pulled out my phone to turn it to silent. But when I looked at the screen, I was surprised to see it was Helena calling me.

'Hi,' I answered attempting to disguise the fact I was upset.

'Are you all right? You don't sound so good,' Helena immediately replied.

'I'm fine,' I lied, unable to tell her what had just happened, for the shame that I must have done something unforgiveable still clung to my skin.

'Riley rang me. She's desperate, Claudia. She still hasn't found anywhere,' she began.

I inwardly sighed. 'Aren't you meant to be having drinks with a friend?'

'I am, but when I saw it was Riley calling, I couldn't not answer.'

My silence forced Helena to continue.

'She could stay with you,' Helena enthused.

'Oh, come on, Helena! I haven't agreed to anything, let alone talked to her.'

I preferred to take things at my own pace. I hadn't had chance to come to a conclusive decision yet about a lodger. Seeing Issie, Willow and Ava at the tapas bar as I was leaving had completely thrown me, and sharing my home with a total stranger was the last thing on my mind.

'Did something happen when I left you?'

'No,' I lied again.

'Claudia?' Helena questioned, not believing me.

'Look, I hate being railroaded into something,' I replied.

'I've been where you are, Claudia. It's shit! It's hard enough dragging yourself out of bed every morning without the added pressure of figuring out how you're going to keep the roof over your head. You're my friend, and I'm trying to help you! Also, I think having someone else in the house will be good for you. You need a distraction to stop you thinking about Jacob all the time,' Helena insisted.

'Okay... Okay,' I conceded, knowing from past experience that once Helena had an idea it was virtually impossible to persuade her otherwise.

I also accepted that there was an element of truth in what she had said. The next three months would be unbearable here on my own. Maybe a lodger would distract me from the aching emptiness that filled the house with Jacob gone. It would also force me to get my shit together. I had been too absorbed in self-pity to care about tidying up, so it may be the motivation I needed to get me back on track.

'Good. So, what do I tell Riley?'

I sighed. 'I don't know.'

'Well, I'm going to give her your number and get her to call you. Talk to her and then you can decide. Yeah?'

'Okay... Okay, I'll do it,' I replied in an attempt to appease her.

'That's great news!'

'No, wait! Helena, that's not what I meant.'

'Look, I've got to get back to my friend, but I'll message Riley and let her know to ring you to finalise it,' Helena stated, either not hearing or choosing not to hear what I had just said. 'Remember that she's shy, more so on the phone, so don't be put off. But I promise you that you won't regret giving her a chance,' Helena assured me before hanging up.

I sat back against the scatter cushions and breathed out, not sure what had just happened. Typically, Helena had gotten carried away being the good Samaritan.

It suddenly hit me:

What the hell have you done? You've just been coerced into having a stranger move into your home.

14

SATURDAY

The following day, much to Helena's delight and my somewhat consternation, Riley Harrison moved in. She would be renting the guest room for the next few months until she could move into her new accommodation. I reassured myself that Helena was right. It was a win-win situation for me; I could meet the mortgage payments, without the need to alert my parents that Jacob had moved out, and it would help keep me distracted until he came back.

If he comes back...

I swallowed, forcing the thought to the back of my mind.

I tentatively knocked on the guest bedroom door. 'Hey, how are you doing in there?'

Riley had been in there for hours. I had already ascertained that she was exceptionally timid. I had offered to help her move when I'd talked to her last night, but she had politely declined. Her responses to my questions had been painfully monosyllabic. I had assumed that she was perhaps uncomfortable speaking on the phone. But when she arrived late this afternoon in a black cab, travelling with simply a leather suitcase and a matching holdall, I knew after an awkward introduction that it was more than that.

I had first taken Riley to her room so she could dump her bags. I had expected to show her around the house, but she had closed the door on me and hadn't ventured out since.

Now, I waited for a response, but she didn't answer me.

I knocked on the door again, louder this time. 'Riley?'

A few moments later, the door opened barely wide enough for her to peek out.

I noted that she had changed into grey sweatpants and a matching long-sleeved top. She had also pulled her thick long blonde hair back into a loose knot.

She was tall, slim and naturally pretty, but I had a distinct feeling that Riley didn't realise how attractive she was. I couldn't help wondering who she was and why she had found herself temporarily homeless. However, whatever the reason, it was to my benefit, and I was just grateful she didn't look like she was going to cause trouble.

'Hey,' I greeted, smiling. 'Would you like a glass of wine?' I breezily questioned, acutely aware of her discomfort at my presence.

'Do you mind if I pass?' she quietly asked, her wide intelligent grey eyes filled with unease.

'Sure,' I answered, despite feeling disappointed that she didn't want to spend her first night getting to know me.

'Sorry. I have an early start tomorrow,' she explained as if reading my mind.

'Hey, I understand,' I answered.

'I transferred three months' rent into your account,' she added, her cheeks suddenly flushing crimson.

'One month upfront would have been sufficient. You might change your mind after a week,' I light-heartedly replied. I didn't like the feeling of being obligated to her. Not that I wasn't grateful for the money upfront, but I felt uneasy. What if I didn't get on with her?

'I'd rather pay you for the three months, regardless.'

'Okay,' I answered, not knowing how else to reply.

She turned and looked behind her at her room as if desperate to get away from me.

'Well, if you change your mind, you're welcome to join me,' I added.

She awkwardly nodded.

I remembered that Helena had said that Riley was quiet, so much so I wouldn't even know she was living with me. I suspected that this was more than simple shyness and that Riley might have social anxiety. I was the personal tutor for one postgraduate student who had social phobia and found interaction with others on the course excruciating and at times impossible. I wondered whether this was the case with Riley. I realised that this must be equally challenging, if not more so, for her to find herself sharing a house with a stranger.

'Well, if you need anything, I'll be downstairs,' I concluded, accepting that my attempt at making her feel at ease was having the converse effect. 'Remember that this is as much your home as mine, now.'

I could see that she was politely waiting for me to leave her alone.

I gave her a smile and then turned to leave.

'Oh, I nearly forgot,' I said as Darcy sidled up to me. I bent down and picked him up and turned back to Riley before she had a chance to close the door. 'There is only one house rule, and that concerns Mr Darcy, here. He's a housecat. So it means that you have to be careful when you're going out of the front door or going into the back garden.'

I watched as her grey eyes cautiously studied him purring contentedly in my arms.

'You don't mind cats, do you?' I questioned when she didn't coo over him, which was most people's response when introduced to Darcy.

She shook her head.

'Cool,' I replied.

Before I had a chance to say anything else, Riley closed the bedroom door.

I stood there for a moment, accepting that whatever expectations I had of my new lodger distracting me from my marriage falling apart weren't going to materialise. At least, not any time soon. But at least my financial worries were over.

'Come on then, Mr Darcy,' I whispered, nuzzling my face into his fur as he purred even louder. 'Looks like you and I are watching something on Netflix together.'

I grabbed a bottle of chilled wine and a glass from the kitchen and headed to the living room, where I poured myself a liberal drink. I then sat down on the four-seater couch and picked up my mobile from the wooden chest. There were countless calls and texts from Issie. None of which I had answered. I had no idea when I would be able to bring myself to listen to whatever lies she and Ava had concocted together. The hurt I felt at their betrayal was still too raw for me to process.

I couldn't help feeling disappointed that there was nothing from Jacob. I resisted the compulsion that had been driving me to distraction since last night to text or call him. I had the excuse – Riley Harrison. Notifying him of the fact that I had brought a lodger into our home was reasonable. But I knew that I was using it as a means of reminding him that I existed. For it was evident from his radio silence that he had forgotten about me. Worse, forgotten he was still married.

Who are you with tonight, Jacob?

I took a drink of wine to distract myself from the jealous thoughts that played over and over in my head. It scratched and tore at me, driving me insane.

For fuck's sake, Claudia! Get a grip!

My phone screen then lit up. Suddenly hopeful, I looked at it. My heart sank. It was a text from Helena.

How's it going with Riley?

I typed back:

Quiet!

Helena immediately replied:

Told you!

I typed back:

She won't even come out of her room for a glass of wine.

I waited as Helena typed her response.

I said she would stay in her room. That's what you wanted.

She was right. That was what I had wanted. But I also wanted someone to distract me from compulsively thinking about Jacob.

I took another sip of wine before conceding:

I know.

Helena quickly replied:

She's the perfect lodger. Didn't I say?

Before I had a chance to respond, the doorbell rang. I wasn't expecting anyone and wondered whether it was someone for Riley, which I presumed unlikely unless it was a delivery of more of her belongings.

The doorbell rang again. This time longer and with more urgency.

I put my phone and glass of wine down and headed out to the hallway. I looked up the stairs for Riley, but there was no movement.

The bell rang for a third time.

'Hang on,' I called as I made my way to the door to unlock it.

I opened the door and, startled, stared speechless at the person standing in front of me.

'What are you doing here?' I demanded.

Issie uneasily looked at me. 'We need to speak.'

'Maybe I don't want to listen to your lies again.'

'It's not like that,' Issie replied, her voice quivering. 'You've known me long enough to know that I wouldn't lie to you.'

'Have I?' I said, folding my arms.

Issie didn't answer. I noted her car parked further down the street.

'So, what are you doing here? I assume you stayed with Ava last night.'

She looked dreadful. Her spirally curly blonde hair was an unruly mess, and her bare face was ashen, made worse by the black smudges of mascara beneath her puffy eyes. If it wasn't for her standing, shivering in black leggings, trainers and a long, baggy jumper instead of the dress she was wearing at the tapas bar, I would have said she had stayed out all night.

'No. I got the train back home,' Issie answered.

'So, you drove all the way from Kent for what?'

'To see you,' Issie quietly replied.

I tried to ignore the tears glistening in her eyes. I was the one who had been hurt here, not her. She didn't have the right to be upset.

'I've been going out of my mind with worry. I didn't sleep last night thinking about you,' she explained.

I shrugged.

'Can I come in?'

I didn't move.

'Please? I don't want to do this out here.'

Despite the compulsion to slam the door in her face, I moved back to let her in.

'Thanks,' Issie mumbled stepping inside.

I waited for Issie to speak, watching as she furtively took in the gaps in the living room that had once been filled with Jacob's eclectic possessions. Some pieces were obvious in their absence, some not so much. But it was his missing prized guitar and stand that were the giveaway.

Issie didn't articulate what she was thinking, but I could see in her eyes that she knew something was wrong.

Very wrong...

'You can sit down,' I offered. Not that the tone of my voice supported my words.

Issie looked at me, hesitant, before nodding. 'Thanks.'

I needed a drink to stop myself from exploding at whatever lies Issie was about to spin.

'Do you want a glass of wine?' I found myself asking as Issie sat on the edge of the couch.

'Please,' she answered.

I nodded and then went to the kitchen to get her a wine glass, leaving her to prepare whatever words she had rehearsed on her drive from Kent. I still couldn't believe that she had just shown up.

Come on, Claudia! What choice did she have if you wouldn't answer her calls or texts?

I conceded that if the roles were reversed, I would have done the same. I felt a flush of hot guilt rise up my neck at the fact I had not only ignored Issie's calls and texts, but also Willow's countless, frantic messages. I accepted that Jaz's death had made us all nervous.

Not all of us.

Ava was the exception. She still hadn't reached out to me.

I returned to the living room. Without speaking, I poured Issie some wine, handed it to her and then refilled my glass. The silence was unbearable. Even Darcy had taken refuge somewhere else.

I sat down at the other end of the couch from Issie and waited.

She took a nervous sip of wine first before speaking.

'I... I didn't know that you weren't invited last night. Neither did Willow.'

Not believing a word, I simply stared back at her.

She looked flustered. 'I mean it, Claudia.'

Again, I said nothing.

'When I talked to you on Sunday, the arrangements were for us all to meet up in two weeks. You know that?' she nervously questioned.

I took a mouthful of wine to silence the betrayal I felt inside as Issie floundered for more words.

'I... I... Stop looking at me like that!' Issie suddenly said.

I raised my eyebrows at her.

'Please, Claudia. I didn't do anything wrong here.'

I choked back the words that wanted to spew out from me.

'Please. I didn't know that Ava hadn't included you. She... she rang me yesterday morning and said that she could now make it that evening. That she was ringing everyone to make sure they were free as well. Same time and location. I just assumed that she had talked to you. She said it was urgent and that we needed to be there. I swear, I didn't know that you weren't supposed to be there.'

'So why did you look so shocked to see me?' I demanded.

Issie shook her head. 'It was in reaction to you. You looked aghast when you saw us. As if we weren't supposed to be there. Then, instead of joining us, you rushed out. Your actions didn't make any sense.'

I could feel my skin prickling at her words.

'Claudia, you have to believe me,' Issie begged. 'Seriously? Do you really believe I would do that to you?' she continued in response to my silence.

But you did!

I took a sip of wine to stop myself from blurting out exactly what I thought.

'Look, Ava's pissed with you right now. That's why she didn't ring you,' Issie explained in an attempt to justify what had happened.

I raised my eyebrows. 'Which is why I asked you to talk to her on my behalf.'

Issie uncomfortably broke away from my scrutinising gaze. I watched as she took a sip from her glass.

'You're admitting you knew that she excluded me?'

Issie dragged her eyes up to meet mine. She shook her head. 'No. Not until you had left.'

'Really?'

'Yes, really! Come on, Claudia. What's got into you? It's not like you to be so paranoid.'

'Maybe having a friend you've known for twenty-two years tell you that you're responsible for your other friend's suicide does that to you,' I heatedly retaliated.

'Oh Claudia,' Issie exclaimed. 'Ava doesn't think that!'

'Doesn't she?'

'No,' Issie assured me.

I stopped myself arguing with her.

'So, you tell me why she didn't want me there,' I fired back.

Issie sighed. 'I asked that question when I returned to the table after you'd gone. Ava explained that it was a sensitive matter involving Jaz. That she needed to talk to Willow and me first.'

I felt sick. It had to be the messages I had left Jaz the night of her death.

'I said to Ava that you had a right to be there. That we wouldn't discuss anything to do with Jaz without you,' Issie added.

'And how did Ava respond to that?' I cynically questioned. I doubted that would have made any difference to Ava. She had always acted as if she was accountable to no one. Nor had she ever considered anyone's feelings but her own.

'She agreed to wait until all of us meet up again next Friday.'

'Ava agreed to that?' I questioned, shocked.

Issie nodded, her eyes filled with sincerity.

'Did she mention the messages I had left for Jaz the night she...?' I stopped myself.

'No.'

'What do you think Ava wants to discuss?'

Issie uneasily took another sip of wine.

'Issie?' I demanded, staring at her.

'Ava began to say there was a letter...' She faltered, dropping her gaze.

'A letter?' I spluttered. 'Who to?'

'To Jaz,' Issie answered.

I sat back, stunned by this news. It took me a moment to process it.

Why would Ava not want me to know? It made no sense.

'Did it have something to do with Jaz's decision to...' I stopped myself from saying the unthinkable, that my best friend had taken her life.

'Ava seems to think so.'

'Who sent it?' I questioned.

'I don't know.'

'What did it say?'

'Again, I don't know,' Issie frustratedly answered.

'How can you not know?' I demanded, sitting forward.

'Because Willow and I had a full-blown argument with Ava about her exclusion of you. That's how. We said we didn't want to know unless she shared whatever she had with you as well.'

I slowly breathed out, absorbing the magnitude of the situation.

Did it mean I wasn't responsible for Jaz's decision to take her life that night? If not, who was culpable? Who had sent her a letter and what did it say?

And why didn't Ava want me there to discuss it?

'Why are we waiting another week if Ava has something that could explain to us why Jaz chose to make that decision?' I asked.

Issie took another mouthful of wine as she shook her head. 'Ava's in LA for the next week with work. She flew out early this morning. But obviously, whatever she knows was troubling her and she wanted to get it off her chest before she left.'

It made sense. Ava was a ruthless and consequently successful entertainments lawyer who worked for one of the most sought-after firms, with offices in London, NYC and LA. I assumed she would have been called out to the LA office to broker the terms for some project for one of the firm's clients.

'And just so I've got this straight, someone sent Jaz a letter, but you have no idea who or why.'

Issie nodded.

'Christ!' I heavily exhaled.

'I know, right?' Issie agreed.

'Does Ava know who sent it?'

Issie drained what was left of her wine first before answering me. 'She didn't say. She only had twenty minutes and most of that was taken up with Willow and I arguing with her about you. Then her cab arrived and she left.'

I leaned over and poured Issie some more wine.

'Thanks,' Issie said.

'When did Jaz get the letter?' I asked her as I topped my glass up.

'Ava said Jaz got it days before she...' Issie faltered and looked at me as tears filled her eyes.

I found myself adding in my head: *Before she killed herself.*

'Does Ava have a copy of the letter?'

'I don't know whether Jaz sent her a copy or read it out to her.' She looked dreadful.

'Issie? What is it?'

'Nothing... Just shocked. I mean, did someone threaten Jaz?'

'With what?'

Issie shook her head. 'I don't know.'

I narrowed my eyes as I watched Issie drop her uneasy gaze. I was certain that she knew something. Issie had always been terrible at lying.

What are you hiding from me?

15

'When did Jacob move out?' Issie gently asked as I returned from the kitchen with another bottle of wine.

'We were talking about the letter that Jaz received, Issie. Not my personal life,' I defensively replied.

Issie's acknowledgement that Jacob had left me had blindsided me and I could feel hot, salty tears threatening to fall. Avoiding her concerned gaze, I sat down and topped her wine glass up and then my own. I realised my hand was trembling.

'Hey, it's okay,' Issie soothingly reassured as tears slid down my cheek.

I wanted to scream at her that it wasn't. That none of it was okay. Not Jaz dying. That wasn't okay. Nor was Jacob leaving me after my best friend had died.

None of it was okay! NONE OF IT!

More mute tears fell as, inside, I screamed and screamed at the injustice of it all.

Issie gently rubbed my hand and waited.

'Do you want to talk about it?' she asked.

I brought my teary gaze up to meet hers.

She sympathetically smiled and then reached for my wine glass, offering it to me.

'Thanks,' I mumbled, taking it from her.

I took a much-needed gulp to prepare myself.

Once I found the words, they poured out. I shared everything, from Jacob bringing this Bex woman back to our home; to my revenge sex with Ethan Novak, resulting in Jacob moving out for three months to get his head together – or whatever crap he was telling himself.

Issie, who had remained silent, slowly exhaled.

'Oh, Claudia...' she sympathised.

'I know,' I replied at a loss as to what else to say.

I then heard footsteps in the hallway. We both did.

Issie looked at me, confused. 'I thought you said Jacob had moved out.'

I nodded, swallowing back another mouthful of wine. I had temporarily forgotten I had taken in a lodger, obscured by the breakdown of my marriage.

'Riley Harrison,' I said. 'My lodger,' I added.

'You've got a lodger?' exclaimed Issie.

'Shh!' I hissed. 'She'll hear you.'

'Sorry,' apologised Issie. 'But, still! A lodger? Since when?'

'This afternoon,' I whispered.

'Today?' she spluttered.

I nodded and took another drink.

'Why?'

'I need the money,' I explained.

'What? With your parents? Christ, Claudia! They could buy this place outright no problem.'

I waited, straining to hear Riley, but there was no sound coming from the hallway.

'For sure they'd help me out financially, but it would come at a high price. My mother would never let me forget it. No, they can't find out,' I stated.

'And Jacob?'

'He doesn't give a damn. His attitude is he's paying rent on the flat for three months at some exorbitant rate which absolves him from contributing to our mortgage. He thinks the bank of mummy and daddy will cover it. Not his parents, mine, can I add.'

'That sucks,' Issie consoled. 'I'm surprised at Jacob though.'

'You and I both!'

I breathed out, trying to let go of the anger that I felt at his abandonment of me – and Darcy.

I picked up the bottle of wine to top Issie's glass and my own.

Issie shook her head. 'No more for me,' she replied, adding, 'I need to drive home later.'

'You're welcome to stay the night,' I suggested.

Issie hesitated. 'Are you sure?'

'Of course, I am,' I assured her.

Once Issie explained that she didn't know Ava had excluded me last night, my anger towards her dissipated. And she had been so worried when I declined her calls that she had driven a couple of hours from her home in Kent to see me. As for Ava, I hadn't heard anything from her. No apology – nothing.

'Thanks,' Issie said as she offered me her glass.

'So, can I meet her? This mystery lodger?' Issie excitedly asked.

'Nope,' I answered.

'Why not? Surely there's no harm in asking if she wants a glass of wine?'

'I already asked her before you turned up, and the answer was no. Anyway, you can meet her in the morning.'

'Where am I sleeping? I assumed I'd be crashing in the guestroom, but that will be her room?'

'Yup. So either you sleep on the couch or share my bed?' I suggested.

'I'll share your bed,' Issie replied. She looked towards the living-room door which I had left ajar. 'I mean, you've got a stranger living in your house.'

I burst out laughing. 'Seriously? You live in the middle of nowhere and always forget to lock your front door, and you're scared of my lodger.'

'Well, what exactly do you know about her?'

I took another drink as I thought about exactly what I knew about Riley Harrison.

I shook my head. 'Not a lot. But enough,' I added in response to Issie's concerned expression.

'So, who is she?' Issie questioned.

'She's Helena's research student. She's moving out at the beginning of the summer when the accommodation she's leased becomes available.'

'And?' Issie prompted. 'There has to be more.'

I cracked a smile. 'You don't give up, do you?'

Issie raised an eyebrow at me.

'And she's quiet. Studious might be the better word.'

'What early twenties postgrad is studious and quiet?' Issie sceptically questioned. 'Christ! Claudia, she could have people back at all hours. Loud music. Worse, loud sex!'

I choked on a mouthful of wine. It took a moment of spluttering and coughing while Issie laughed at my predicament before I could answer her.

'She's a mature student in her early thirties.'

'Even more intriguing. What's her past?'

I shook my head, smiling at Issie's barrage of questions. 'I don't know. And I don't care. As long as I can pay the mortgage, that's all that concerns me. That, and she's not a sex addict!'

'Do you think she is?' Issie asked in a mock-horrified tone.

'No!' I replied. 'I was joking! She's the least likely person to be on some hook-up app. You'll see when you meet her tomorrow. She's sweet.'

'That's what you think now. Wait a few weeks and we'll see if you still feel the same way.'

I shook my head at her.

'If she's our age, let's look her up on Facebook and Instagram,' suggested Issie as she picked up her phone.

'I'm not sure.' I hesitated, not certain it felt right checking up on her.

'She's living in your home, Claudia! It's the first thing I would have done before even letting her walk through the door,' Issie asserted, already searching on Facebook. 'Oh...' mumbled Issie, frowning.

'What?'

'There aren't a lot of female Riley Harrisons. And none in London. Or even the UK.'

'Are you sure?' I questioned, surprised.

'Yep.' Issie looked up at me. 'She's definitely called Riley Harrison?'

I nodded.

'Nope, I can't find her,' Issie said.

'Maybe she's not on social media,' I suggested.

'Who's not on social media at our age?'

I shrugged. 'She keeps herself to herself. Maybe she hasn't got any friends and so there's no reason to be on Facebook.'

'Or maybe there's a reason she doesn't want to be found,' Issie ventured.

'Don't!' I replied, suddenly feeling uneasy. 'She's living in my home.'

I had naively trusted Helena and hadn't thought to check out

Riley on social media. How could I have been so foolish?

'I know!'

'Issie, don't! Maybe she's just a very private person.'

'Yup. You keep telling yourself that.' Issie laughed.

She abruptly stopped laughing. 'Claudia?'

'What?' I irritably asked.

'What if she's hiding from someone or something? That's why there's no trace of her on social media.'

I sighed. 'Seriously?'

Issie didn't say a word, but her expression told me she was deadly serious.

'Moving on,' I suggested, wanting to steer Issie away from catastrophising about my new lodger's lack of social media activity. I didn't need her making me feel unsettled about my decision. 'What do I do about Ethan Novak?'

'Meaning? You've already fucked him,' Issie answered with a wicked grin. 'What was he like? And, more to the point, I need to see a photo.'

'I haven't got one and I can't remember,' I quickly replied. 'And shh! Not so loud! Riley's in the same department as me. She'll know who we're talking about!'

'Ethan Novak's the first person you've had sex with apart from Jacob in what, ten years. Of course, you can remember what he was like in bed!' Issie replied, ignoring my request to keep her voice down.

'I was drunk. Ridiculously, shamefully drunk!'

'Which tells me you had hot, lustful, explosive sex!'

'How have you come to that wild conclusion?' I asked, incredulous.

'You, Claudia Harper, used the words "shamefully drunk", which tells me you can remember but you're ashamed to admit it because you loved every second of it!'

I threw a scatter cushion at Issie.

'Ouch! Yup, you're acting defensive because I'm right.' She laughed.

'Tell me why I don't make you sleep down here, tonight,' I demanded.

'Because you love me, and you don't want to wake up to me, murdered by your lodger in the night,' she playfully answered.

'Shh! Seriously, Issie? She'll hear you! You'll feel so bad when you meet her!'

Issie shrugged. 'So, has he been in touch?'

'Who? Ethan?' I asked.

'You know exactly who I mean,' answered Issie.

'Well... Yes. He's called and he's texted me countless times.'

'And?'

'And, I've declined his calls and ignored his texts.'

'Why?' demanded Issie.

'Because—' I faltered.

'Christ! You're heartless! Imagine if he did that to you?'

'Men ghost women all the time after they've slept with them,' I pointed out.

'Doesn't make it right, though. Does it?' replied Issie.

A few hours later, and we made our way upstairs to my bedroom. I repeatedly had to tell Issie to keep her voice down for fear of disturbing Riley. Not that either of us had seen or heard from her all evening.

By the time I crawled into bed after using the bathroom, Issie was sprawled on my side, passed out. I lay there for a moment, trying to comprehend how life could change so quickly. A week ago, Jacob and I were still together. A month back, Jaz was still alive. And now, here I was with the two people who knew me better than anyone, both gone and I now had a lodger. Something I would never have contemplated until Helena had coerced me into it.

I thought of Jaz. I wondered what she would have made of Riley Harrison. But if Jaz had still been alive, I would never have met Riley. For Jaz would have talked me down, and the domino effect of me revenge-fucking Ethan Novak, causing Jacob to bail on me, would never have happened.

I suddenly remembered Issie's revelation.

The letter... What the hell was in the letter? And who had sent it to Jaz and why?

I stared at the ceiling as I thought about the fact it had been sent to Jaz only days before she decided to take her own life. Ava surely believed there was a connection, otherwise she would never have mentioned it to Willow and Issie.

But why exclude me? And how did Ava know about the letter? Had Jaz told her?

Pain, cold and cutting, tore through me at the acknowledgement that it wasn't only Ava who had excluded me. Jaz had cut me from her life in the weeks leading up to her death.

What was going on in Jaz's life that she couldn't share with me – her best friend?

16

SATURDAY, ONE WEEK LATER

'What do you think?' I asked Issie. 'And be honest.'

Needing reassurance, I had FaceTimed her so she could give me her opinion on what I was wearing.

'Put the phone down and move back so I can get a better look,' Issie suggested.

I positioned the phone on the Victorian cream and beige marble mantlepiece in my bedroom and stepped backwards.

'Can you see the dress?' I asked.

'Step further back,' Issie instructed.

I did as she asked.

The past week since Issie had surprised me by turning up had passed in a blur. She had called me every other day to make sure I was coping without Jacob. I would catch myself laughing at something crazy Issie had said or done, only to be plagued by guilt at the thought that I wouldn't be able to share it with Jaz. Then there would be an awkward lull in the conversation, both of us feeling Jaz's absence. We had more questions than answers about Jaz's decision to end her life and inevitably ended up going around in circles. I was grateful we had each other to talk to about Jaz. Otherwise, I would be driving myself insane going over and over what had happened. If anything, Jaz's death had brought Issie and me closer together.

Issie had suggested that instead of torturing ourselves, we wait until Ava returned from LA to discuss the letter. Ava was held up in LA, and consequently, we hadn't met up last night as planned. Maybe when we finally did, we would have the answers we so desperately needed to find acceptance.

Not that I ever believed I could come to terms with Jaz's choice. It didn't resonate with the friend I had known most of my life. We had become inseparable on our first day as eleven-year-olds at Queen Victoria's School for Girls boarding school and were, until recently.

But was I misremembering those perfect, halcyon days of our past? If it was so perfect, then why had Jaz pulled back from me? Worse, why had she taken her life without reaching out to me for help?

'The dress is beautiful!' Issie interrupted, bringing me back to the present moment.

'You think?' I doubtfully questioned as I glanced across at my reflection in the large bedroom mirror.

I was wearing a low-cut, slinky black dress, accompanied by black heels. I had chosen a seductive red lipstick to accentuate the deep red tones in my auburn hair. I had also loosely tied it up, with curls cascading down. I was aware that Jacob loved it like that, and it was his eye I wanted to catch.

'Jacob won't be able to keep his hands off you! Claudia, you look gorgeous!'

'I just hope he's there.'

'Of course Jacob will be there. It's his best friend's birthday!'

'You really don't think it's too much?'

'For the hundredth time, no! What does Riley think?' she asked.

I shook my head. 'Haven't seen her.'

It was like living with a ghost. Riley was rarely here. Then, occasionally, I would hear footsteps in the hallway or on the stairs, or the creak of her door or bed, reminding me I shared my home with someone.

A stranger.

I had planned to introduce Riley to the delights of living in Kew last Sunday morning with Issie, but Riley had already left, returning late that evening after I was in bed. Instead, Issie and I had brunch without her at The Kew Greenhouse Café on Station Parade. We had both sat outside enjoying the glorious Sunday, bright, late-March sun surrounded by plants and vibrant, flower-filled hanging baskets, watching the locals and visitors milling around. Issie had joked while we drank our coffee and observed the world passing by that my lodger was either imagined or a ghost.

We then took a stroll around Kew Village Market. It was something that Jacob and I would ordinarily do together, indulging in not only the divine macaroons and brownies from one of our favourite stalls but also the intimate village feel of Kew with its leafy, tree-lined streets and the Royal Botanic Gardens nearby, all of the reasons why we wanted to live here, including The Tap on the Line, a traditional station pub where we often met up after work for a drink before walking home.

However, we now both aspired for a property on The Green in Richmond, where Helena lived, but it came at an astronomical price. We often spent a Saturday or Sunday in Richmond, coveting the lifestyle and the properties. Our favourite haunt was The Cricketers, overlooking The Green, one of the oldest and quaintest pubs in Richmond. In the summer months, it was so popular that we, like other customers, would take our drinks and sit on The Green, enjoying the ambience of the outdoors. Or we would have lunch or dinner in the back garden of The Britannia, a gastropub steeped in hundreds of years of history with old wooden floors, tucked just off The Green down a narrow, old-world, charming, cobbled alleyway. It was easy to miss, which was part of its allure.

There was something magical about the place, and I could identify with the lyrics of the bluesy song 'Richmond', by the band The Faces, yearning to be back home in Richmond instead of the rainy city of New York.

On other weekends, Jacob and I would either cycle or jog through Richmond Park, enjoying the deer and other wildlife in the national nature reserve. If the weather permitted, we would take a picnic to share under one of the centuries-old trees where we would imagine our future lives.

Now we had refurbished our house, which had taken over five years, we wanted to move on, aspiring to Richmond for the next stage of our life – becoming parents.

But whether it would happen now was debatable. Because the crucial question was whether Jacob would actually come back to me.

Stopping myself from spiralling, I walked back over to my phone and picked it up.

'Are you sure this Riley's not a figment of your imagination?' Issie teased with a playful smile when I held the screen up to my face. 'I mean, I only have your word she exists. I still can't find any trace of her on social media. And believe me, I have tried!'

'You are so obsessive!' I laughed, shaking my head at her. 'She just likes to keep herself to herself.'

Riley Harrison, as Helena had stated, was the perfect lodger. She spent most of her waking hours at the uni; I assumed mainly in the library as I hadn't seen her in the department. When she did return home, it wasn't until late in the evening. She was so quiet, I would never hear her come in and would only realise she was back from the glow of the desk lamp seeping out from under her door when I passed her room on my way to bed. I accepted that all Riley wanted was a place to stay. She was renting my guestroom. That was it. I couldn't help but notice that she didn't use the rest of the house, aside from the bathroom. I presumed that she ate out or brought food back to her room. Any ideas I had of sharing a bottle of wine or two over a meal had long since evaporated. She didn't want a friendship. And that was okay.

Of course, it's okay. She's a lodger for Christ sakes! You're not at Queen Victoria's School for Girls! She doesn't have to be your friend!

My phone suddenly buzzed.

'Who is it?' Issie asked. 'Tell me it's Jacob,' she added, hopeful.

I had spent the past week expecting a call or even a text from Jacob asking whether I was going to Zain's birthday drinks – Zain was Jacob's best friend and best man at our wedding. But it had never happened and, before I knew it, Saturday had arrived. I was acutely aware that Jacob had walked out on me two weeks ago to this night. The question that was plaguing me was whether he would use this evening to prove something to me. That our marriage was over and he was never coming back. We should have been going to the party together. I didn't want to go to the party on my own. But I had no choice if I wanted to see Jacob.

My eyes were starting to prick at the acknowledgement that Jacob might have checked out emotionally as well as physically.

I checked the message. 'Nope. Ethan,' I replied, unable to keep the disappointment out of my voice.

'Again?'

I nodded.

I stared at his message:

We need to talk. Please?

'What is it? Three weeks since you slept with him?' Issie questioned.

'Just over three weeks.'

'Why don't you just talk to him? Or at least answer his texts?'

'I will,' I replied. 'Just not now.'

'Christ, Claudia! He must like you. I would have sacked you off weeks back,' Issie pointed out. 'I thought you said he had a reputation for sleeping around and not wanting to get involved with anyone. Why is he persisting with you?'

'We're in the same department. I imagine he wants to clear the air so there's no awkward vibe between us. So far, I've been avoiding him at work, but I can't keep that up.'

I felt bad for Ethan. He didn't deserve the silent treatment. I had ignored his texts and phone calls, not having the emotional energy to deal with him. I just wanted it – him – to go away as if it had never happened.

But it has happened, Claudia. You need to face reality.

I dismissed the thought and focused back on Issie. Trying to sound breezy, I asked her, 'Are you sure I look all right?'

'You look more than all right! You look beautiful. I promise you that Jacob won't be able to take his eyes off you!'

'I wish you were coming with me,' I said, nervous at the prospect of turning up on my own.

'You'll be fine! Stick to what we discussed. Now go!' Issie instructed, blowing me a kiss before disconnecting the call.

I nodded. Not that I felt fine. I didn't want to go, but it was Zain's thirty-fifth birthday, combined with his passing a gruelling eighteen months accelerated programme to become a detective inspector with the Metropolitan Police. Consequently, I felt duty-bound to make an appearance. I planned to stay for two drinks and then make my apologies and leave.

* * *

I got on the District line at Kew Gardens to Whitechapel. Fifty-five minutes later, I left the underground for Whitechapel Road and the Victorian East End pub, The Blind Beggar, infamous for its connection to East End gangsters, the Kray twins. In March 1966, Ronnie Kray had shot and murdered George Cornell, an associate of a rival gang, as he was sitting at the bar. The Krays weren't the first to bring infamy to the East End. The unsolved murders of eleven women, known as the Whitechapel murders, committed between 1888 and 1891, were attributed to the unidentified serial killer, Jack the Ripper, who had stalked the streets of the East End. However, Zain's chosen venue had nothing to do with its dark, murderous past and his interest in solving crimes but with logistics. He had recently moved into a fifth-floor, two-bedroom apartment in the Silk District, literally a three-minute walk to The Blind Beggar, now his local.

Reaching Zain's chosen venue, I watched as two women came out of the pub, bringing with them a sudden burst of lively chatter from inside. I took a deep breath, pushed the door open and walked in. I made my way to the bar and waited to catch the attention of one of the bartenders.

'A double Jack on the rocks,' I ordered.

I then looked around for Jacob. The place was packed, but he was nowhere to be seen. I spotted Zain at the other end of the bar, surrounded by a group of people, none of whom I recognised. I expected that most of them would be Zain's colleagues.

'That's nine pounds twenty.'

I turned back to the bartender and flashed my bank card at the small device he was holding. I then picked up my drink and took a welcome mouthful, savouring the burning sensation as it hit my mouth and slowly worked its way down the back of my throat.

'Hey? Claudia?'

Recognising Zain's scratchy Scottish voice, I spun around. 'Happy Birthday,' I said, hugging him.

'You look beautiful!'

I laughed. 'You don't have to compliment me to get a drink. What are you having?'

'I'm good for now.'

'Are you sure?'

'I have too many lined up as it is,' he assured me.

'Okay. Well, this is for you,' I said, offering Zain the gift bag.

I watched as he took the boxed bottle out.

'You shouldn't have,' he said, admiring the thirty-three-year-old Balvenie single malt whisky. 'Shit, this is too much!'

'You deserve it.'

'I doubt that!'

'Congrats by the way. So now you're a detective inspector?'

'Thanks.' He grinned. 'Yup. I worked my balls off for it! Sacrificed what personal life I had to achieve it.'

'You'll be able to focus on settling down now.'

'As my Glaswegian granny would say: what's for you will not go by you.'

'I'm sure that philosophy will work for you as a DI.'

He laughed.

'So, the beard. Is that a conditional part of the job, or are you involved in some covert police operation?'

He stroked the thick, black hair on his chin. 'Nothing that exciting, I'm just going for the more mature look.'

'That's one word for it,' I mocked.

Someone shouted out Zain's name. He turned in the direction of the voice and raised his hand in acknowledgement. He turned back to me. 'Let's join them. I promise it won't all be shop talk.'

'I'll get another drink, and then I'll come over.'

Leaning in and kissing me on the cheek, he whispered, 'Talk to Jacob when he gets here. He's not been the same since the two of you split up.'

Before I could ask him what he meant, Zain released me and headed over to his friends. Surprised at this revelation, I drained my drink. I caught the same bartender's eye and raised my empty glass. I turned back around, and just as I did, Jacob walked into the bar – with a pretty twenty-something woman. My heart stopped.

Jacob looked equally taken aback to see me. I watched as he said something to the petite blonde with the pixie haircut, who giggled in response. She then looked over in my direction, her eyes sparkling. I turned away as a wave of heat flushed my cheeks. I could feel the humiliation radiating from me.

Shit! Shit! Shit! You should never have come! What the hell were you expecting? Just go! Go before he proves a point that he has moved on by introducing her to you.

Needing a distraction, I took out my phone just as Helena called me. I stared at it, unsure what to do. Helena would hear the background noise and start asking questions. She wouldn't be impressed if she knew I was here in the hope of seeing Jacob.

Damn it!

I slowly breathed out. I was mindful that I hadn't properly spoken to Helena since Riley had moved in last Saturday.

Then Issie texted:

So? x

I would ring Helena tomorrow and make some excuse up for not taking her call.

I furiously typed back to Issie:

Jacob here with a size-0 blonde! Wtf! x

I pressed send.

She immediately replied:

You look beautiful! Remember that! Just breathe and be you x

I typed back:

I can't! I want to go home!

I waited as Issie typed a response.

Unleash your inner goddess! You've got this! Love you! x

It was a typical Issie response.

I slowly breathed out. If I left, then Jacob would know that he had got to me. I didn't want that. Conversely, I didn't want to remain here and be humiliated.

The bartender came over and placed my drink down. I paid for it and then took a much-needed mouthful.

You can do this, Claudia! It will be over with soon, and you can curl up on the couch with Darcy and a glass of wine and forgot about Jacob and his ridiculously young, size-zero blonde. Show him that he hasn't got to you.

* * *

Fifty minutes later, and I had surprised myself. I had spent the time socialising with Zain and his friends and was now talking with one of Zain's colleagues from the Met. Jacob had kept his distance, but I couldn't help notice him watching me. I questioned whether it was out of jealousy, as for the past twenty minutes, Ronan, another DI, had been chatting to me and was now waiting at the crowded bar to get us drinks.

'Hey, how are you?'

The voice was deep, husky and very familiar. A bolt of electricity scorched through my body.

The excitement quickly evaporated to be replaced by trepidation.

Had he brought her over to punish me? To throw it in my face that he was sleeping with her. For hadn't I done that to Jacob when I had attacked him with the fact that I had spent the night fucking Ethan Novak?

I knocked back the dregs of my drink before turning around to find Jacob standing next to me. Without the size-zero blonde.

'Good,' I lied, noting with relief that he had left his date with Zain.

Jacob nodded. 'You look amazing.'

'Thanks.'

Neither of us spoke.

'How's the flat?' I asked in a bid to break the awkward silence.

'Great.'

I nodded.

'How's work?' Jacob then asked.

'Busy,' I answered.

I looked down at my empty glass, longing for a drink. I had drunk typically more than usual, but it still didn't feel enough.

'Can I get you another?'

I shook my head. 'Thanks, but Ronan has just gone to get me a drink.'

'Right,' answered Jacob as he looked across at him. 'Wouldn't have said he was your type?'

'I could say the same about you.'

'Natasha's a colleague from work.'

'Since when?'

'For a while,' he stated.

'She doesn't look old enough to have graduated from medical school.'

'She's older than she looks.'

'I'll take your word for it,' I answered.

I desperately wanted to ask why he had brought her, but I refused to humiliate myself.

'You're jealous of her?' Jacob questioned as if reading my mind.

'Should I be?'

My heart raced as Jacob held my gaze. Neither of us spoke for a few beats.

It was Jacob who broke the silence first. 'Let's get out of here. We need to talk.'

I raised my eyebrow at this assumption.

'I need to talk. All right? I knee-jerked and...' He shrugged.

I hesitated. 'Why?' I asked.

'Why what?'

'Why talk now? You've ignored me for the past two weeks,' I said, trying to hide my hurt.

'I'm trying to make things right between us,' Jacob replied. 'I needed time to process what had happened and now...' He faltered and shook his head, not taking his eyes off mine. I could see the fear in them.

Fear of rejection?

I couldn't say.

'I'm sorry,' he added. 'I know I could have handled it better. If it had been anyone other than Novak, then...' Jacob stopped and dropped his gaze.

Again, neither of us spoke.

I was conflicted. I wanted to go somewhere else with Jacob. No Natasha. No Ronan. Someplace where maybe we could work it out.

But I was scared of what he wanted to say to me. For what if we couldn't work it out? Or worse, what if Jacob didn't want to come back to me? Maybe, now he had tasted it, he liked being single and dating someone like Natasha.

Come on, Claudia! Jacob wants to be with you, on your own. If you don't go, then you'll never know what he wants. And Jacob will go home with Natasha. Not you.

'Let's go. Before either Zain or your date notice,' I heard myself saying.

I looked across at the bar to catch Ronan's eye, but he had his back to me. I felt bad for leaving without saying anything, but it was just a drink. I was sure Zain would explain the score to him.

17

We sat in the back of the cab in silence. The tension between us was electric. I didn't even notice where we were going. I tried to steady my breathing, but the intoxicating, heady scent of Jacob's aftershave, Guerlain's Royal Extract II, which was my favourite, blindsided me. My body felt as if it was on fire with the anticipation of what was to come.

The minutes passed in a blur, and before I knew it, I recognised where we were – the Bloomsbury district in the West End of London. The leafy squares lined with Georgian mansions were a giveaway, as were the university colleges, various hospitals and impressive hotels. Both our workplaces were based in Bloomsbury and many of the impressive mansions surrounding us now functioned as places for researching and administering healthcare rather than residential premises.

'Great Ormond Street,' informed the driver as he pulled over.

I followed Jacob out of the cab.

'You've brought me to work?' I questioned, surprised.

Jacob shook his head and gestured to the impressive Georgian property in front of us.

'Perfect location for work,' I dryly commented.

Jacob had everything he needed here: the hospital directly opposite the apartment and within proximity to Russell Square tube station providing access to the Piccadilly line. For a moment, I questioned whether he would want to come back home to Kew when he had all this and more, in particular, his freedom.

'Where's the car?' I asked.

'Secure underground parking at the Imperial Hotel by Russell Square,' Jacob explained, heading towards the black railings and gate.

'How much does that cost a day?'

Jacob shrugged. 'Paying for it monthly.'

I raised my eyebrows at this statement, acutely aware of how tight money was, at least for me, as the one left paying our mortgage.

'It's worth it for the convenience. And it's only for three months,' he defensively added.

I followed him through the gate and down the stone steps leading to the basement flat. I expectantly waited as Jacob searched his pockets.

'Damn it!' he cursed. 'I've left my keys at Zain's. I dropped his birthday gift off before meeting Natasha.'

I was relieved. For a moment, I had assumed he had left them at Natasha's place.

'Do you want to go back to the bar?'

He shook his head.

I watched as he bent down and lifted one of the many potted plants in the small courtyard, removing a spare key.

As Jacob unlocked the door, I ignored the voice in my head, questioning what the hell I was doing here. Instead, I followed him into the deceptively spacious open-plan living space.

Jacob flicked on the lamps and then headed to the kitchen area.

I looked around at the minimalist, Scandinavian-style furniture. I noted the unopened boxes stacked against the back wall – the only personal items that Jacob had unpacked were his beloved classical guitar, a record player and a few favourite vinyls.

'Why don't you put something on?' Jacob suggested as he headed to the kitchen.

I placed my coat and bag down on the couch and walked over to the record player. I looked over at Jacob, about to ask him what he was in the mood for, but he was preoccupied with pouring a liberal measure of Jack Daniel's into two glasses. I found 'Kind of Blue' by Miles Davis and put it on the record player.

'Excellent choice,' Jacob noted as the 1959 session recorded in just a few hours with minimal rehearsal began to play.

I walked over to him, luxuriating in the ethereal sounds of tenor saxophonist John Coltrane, alto saxophonist Julian 'Cannonball' Adderley, pianists Bill Evans and Wynton Kelly, bassist Paul Chambers, drummer Jimmy Cobb and, of course, trumpeter extraordinaire, Miles Davis.

'Thanks,' I said as Jacob handed me my drink, his dark, suggestive eyes never leaving mine.

I could feel my heart accelerating. The first time I had gazed up into those gentle, searching eyes, I knew that Jacob was the one. It was that simple, that cliched.

My breath caught at the back of my throat as my body tingled at the prospect of him touching me. There was something inexplicably sexy about Jacob. Even after all these years, I still physically craved him.

I dropped my gaze to the thick scar across his top lip as I took a mouthful. Even now, looking at him, I couldn't get rid of the feeling that he would always be the one.

Without question, I let him lead me out of the open-plan living space, down the hallway towards the master bedroom.

* * *

I looked at my watch: it was 6.03 a.m. I closed my eyes, relishing the feel of Jacob's skin against mine as I lay on his black hairy chest. I had missed his flesh against mine, the heat of his powerful, muscular body as he held me tight.

A dull, throbbing pain in my bladder reminded me why I had stirred. I gently lifted Jacob's arm from around my shoulder and crept out of bed. I tiptoed to the large, contemporary four-piece bathroom. Flicking the light switch on, I looked around. It was immaculate. I checked the bathroom cabinet for signs that another woman had been there, but there was nothing. I searched in the bin and the laundry basket. Again, no tell-tale signs.

Stop looking for something that isn't there, Claudia! He told you he hadn't brought anyone back to the flat. That he hasn't had sex with anyone. That he couldn't because he loved you – wanted only you. Didn't he prove that to you last night? So, trust him.

For some reason, I couldn't. I was terrified that it was all a lie, and all of Jacob's whispered promises in the dark of us getting back together would come crashing down around me like a house of cards. Consequently, I was looking for evidence of another woman. It was a constant fear that refused to be silenced.

Annoyed with myself, I used the toilet, then washed my hands. I flicked off the light and walked down the wooden-floored hallway to the large open-plan living space, heading to the fridge for a bottle of water. I took one out, and as I untwisted the top, I noticed Jacob's phone light up. He had left it next to his car keys, spare house key and wallet on the kitchen counter. It was a text. I should have ignored it and headed back to the bedroom. But I couldn't.

I picked up his phone, and as I read the words, I felt light-headed.

Can't wait to fuck you again tonight.

Another message flashed up on the locked screen: the same number.

Getting wet at the thought!

I felt numb. I realised my hand was trembling. I watched as the phone fell onto the worktop.

I couldn't believe that he had lied to me – again. I felt so betrayed. Jacob had reassured me only hours before that he hadn't slept with anyone else while we had been apart, and nor had he slept with the woman he had brought back to our home.

However, the texts proved that wasn't the case.

I threw the water bottle down and headed back to the bedroom to grab my clothes.

'Hey, wondered where you'd got to,' Jacob groggily greeted.

I couldn't bring myself to speak.

Shaking with betrayal, I bent down, scooped up my dress and proceeded to put it on.

'Claudia?'

I picked up one of my shoes. Its partner was missing. I crouched down and looked under the bed, assuming it had fallen under there. I was right. I reached under and grabbed it.

'What's going on? Why aren't you talking to me?'

I turned my back on Jacob as I proceeded to force my shoes on.

I felt humiliated. I had trusted Jacob. I thought of the twenty-something size-zero blonde with the pixie haircut whose eyes had been filled with amusement when they'd met my gaze.

Was that because she was sleeping with my husband?

Fuck!

I felt sick at the thought.

Jacob pushed himself onto his elbows, staring at me in confusion. 'What have I done?'

I spun around to face him, unable to help myself. 'You've got two texts from whoever it is you're currently fucking.'

'What? Are you mad?'

It was taking all my willpower not to scream at him.

'Claudia? Seriously? You're acting crazy. Please come back to bed.'

'How could I have been with you for ten years and yet not even know you?'

He stared at me, incredulous. 'What the hell is that supposed to mean?'

I didn't reply.

He threw the duvet back and jumped out of bed. 'For Christ's sake, I thought we were past all this, Claudia. What was last night about?'

'You tell me?' I fired back. 'I'm not the one who's fucking around.'

He stood there naked, with a look of disbelief on his face. 'I told you I haven't slept with anyone. We've been through this.'

'The texts that came through on your phone while I was getting a drink of water suggested otherwise. Is it her?'

'Who?'

'The date you were babysitting. Natasha.'

'What the fuck? Come on, Claudia.'

'Check your phone if you don't believe me!' I hissed.

He stared at me as if I had lost my mind.

'Check your fucking phone!' I repeated, raising my voice.

I watched as he stormed out of the bedroom. I then looked around for my bag and coat before remembering that I had thrown them onto the couch.

I walked through into the open-plan living space to see Jacob standing by the kitchen counter with his back to me. Hearing me come through, he turned around.

'I don't know who this is,' he said, bewildered.

STOP LYING TO ME!

I shook my head, swallowed back the rage that was lodged at the back of my throat. Even when confronted with evidence of his own lies, he couldn't stop himself.

'How can you say that?' I somehow managed to whisper.

'Because it's the truth.'

'Why would someone text saying they can't wait to fuck you tonight?' I questioned, my voice quivering with fury.

'How the hell would I know? It's no doubt a mistake.'

Just stop lying to me!

I stared at him, willing him to tell me the truth. To admit that he was fucking someone else.

'Prove it,' I said.

'How?'

'Reply.'

'Saying what?'

'That they've got the wrong number.'

'Are you serious?'

'If you want to convince me that it's a wrong number, then do it,' I stated.

Accepting that I wasn't going to back down, he wearily sighed, but he did it.

'Now what?'

'We wait,' I replied.

I watched as his phone screen lit up.

'What did she say?'

But I could tell by the way the colour drained from his face that it wasn't the response he was expecting.

'Jacob?'

'It doesn't make sense. I...' He faltered.

'Let me see what Natasha said,' I demanded.

'It's not Natasha,' he flatly answered.

I stared at him.

'If it's not Natasha, who is it?'

He looked nervous. 'Claudia... It's not what you think. Honestly. I don't understand how she has my number...'

I held my hand out for the phone. I read the reply.

Wtf Jacob? Remember to bring the bracelet I left this time. C u later.

I gasped, then looked up at Jacob.

I threw the phone back at him. 'Fuck you!'

'I don't know what's going on here. I promise you,' Jacob implored, his eyes despairing.

'She's asking for the bracelet back that she left down the back of our couch!' I screamed.

'It can't be her. I didn't give her my number. You've got to believe me, Claudia. Please,' he begged, looking as frantic as he sounded. 'She didn't have a phone on her. And why text me after all this time? I mean, that was weeks ago.'

'Christ! You can't stop lying, can you?'

Jacob shook his head. 'Honestly, I didn't give her my number. This is crazy! Someone is fucking with me! I haven't seen or heard from her since that night. She upped and left after acting all crazy. I have no idea who she is or where she lives. You've got to believe me, Claudia. Please?'

I stared at him. 'The fact that you can lie so convincingly to my face scares me. I don't know who you are any more. I doubt I ever did.'

I turned and headed for the door.

Jacob dashed forward and grabbed my arm. 'No! Please? Claudia? There has to be some rational explanation. I swear on my life that I'm telling the truth.'

I yanked my arm from his grip.

'I fucked up. I admit that. I should have told you I brought her back to our home to sober up. But this...' He faltered as he shook his head, his eyes wild with fear.

'Screw you and whoever you're fucking! I'm through with your lies!' I spat.

'I'm not sleeping with anyone. Don't you get it? I love you.'

STOP LYING TO ME!

I could feel the hot tears spilling down my face. I had believed Jacob last night when he had whispered that he loved me. He had convinced me that he hadn't had sex with anyone else. But it was all a lie. The texts on his phone said as much. I grabbed my coat and bag off the couch and headed for the door.

'Claudia, wait!'

I rushed out, slamming the door behind me.

All I could think about was that my marriage was over.

How are you going to survive on your own, Claudia?

18

SUNDAY

I closed the heavy front door behind me and made my way into the kitchen. I fumbled around until I found them hidden at the back. I threw my bag on the rustic wooden dining table, and clutching my phone and Jacob's contraband, I opened the bi-folding door and went outside.

Shivering, I huddled over the cigarette I was trying to light. Finally, succeeding, I deeply inhaled, coughing as the heat caught at the back of my throat. I folded my arms across my chest and stared up at the new dawn as angry hot tears slid down my cheeks.

My phone started to ring for the umpteenth time. I looked at it to see Jacob was calling again. I pressed decline.

Instead, I rang Issie. I waited as it rang and rang. Finally, it went to voicemail.

Fuck!

Agitated, I cut the call and immediately rang again.

I stared at my phone, willing her to answer. *Pick up! PLEASE!*

I dragged on the cigarette again, held it, then slowly blew out as it rang and rang.

Where the hell are you?

Finally, Issie answered after my fourth attempt at calling her.

'You know what time it is?'

'Issie... He's fucking that woman,' I mumbled, wiping away the tears.

Silence.

I blew out smoke before agitatedly demanding, 'Did you hear me?'

'Are you smoking?' Issie questioned, surprised.

What the hell?

'Yes, I'm smoking because I don't know what the fuck else to do!' I retaliated, pacing up and down. I hadn't smoked in ten years, but rather that than drown in a bottle of vodka.

I thought of Jaz and how she had drunk a bottle of vodka before slitting her wrists in the bath. Grief, coupled with guilt, surged through my body. Familiar emotions that still had the power to blindside me.

How could you have not known that Jaz was so desperate?

'What woman?' Issie questioned.

'Her! Bex! The one he brought back here!'

'Do you want to tell me what happened last night?' Issie calmly suggested.

I paused, before blowing out the smoke as I went over in my mind the evening's events which had led me into Jacob's bed.

You're an idiot! How could you believe he hadn't slept with her? She covered him in bites and scratches, for fuck's sake! How could you be so gullible? How?

'Claudia?' Issie prompted.

'Sorry,' I answered. 'I'm still trying to process it.'

'Is she the blonde that Jacob brought to Zain's party?'

'No. That was Natasha. She's a colleague. But he's no doubt screwing her as well!' I spat.

'So how do you know he's still sleeping with this other woman?' Issie asked.

'Because she texted him at six this morning about their next hook-up tonight. She was quite explicit.'

'Oh...' mumbled Issie. 'Yeah, that's shite!'

'I know, right?' I agreed, feeling sorry for myself.

'I take it he spent the night with you?'

'No. I mean yes... I stayed at his flat,' I explained.

'Oh, Claudia...' Issie sympathised.

I then went into detail about how I had stayed the night with him, believing that we were getting back together, only to discover that he had lied to me all along. Issie listened to me and occasionally commented or added a word or two of sympathy or support. By the time I'd finished, the rage I had felt had abated and was replaced by a cold numbness.

'You need to get some legal advice,' Issie suddenly advised me.

'Why?' I asked. 'This is Jacob, Issie.'

'I know. But you've just told me how you found out he's sleeping with this Bex woman.'

I remained silent as Issie's softly spoken words hit me. My marriage was over. It was really over. Oh God... How? How had it come to this?

I shakily lit another cigarette and drew heavily upon it. I held in the smoke, before slowly exhaling as tears glided down my cheeks.

'People change, Claudia. I know that better than anyone. Look at Sebastian.'

Jacob's not like Sebastian. Jacob was one of the good ones.

More tears fell as I realised the operative word there: 'was'.

'You need legal advice regarding your house. Okay? You've paid in substantially more than Jacob and you need to protect that.'

'No, it was my parents,' I argued.

'Same difference,' Issie replied.

I breathed out, reining in the compulsion to scream at her to stop. I didn't want my marriage to be over. Worse, Issie was telling me it was over. She wasn't supposed to do that.

'It's only just happened,' I mumbled, shocked by her unwarranted advice.

I heard Issie let out a low sigh. 'Have you heard yourself?'

Issie's sharp words cut through my panic-stricken and nonsensical thoughts.

'You've just told me you have evidence that he's sleeping with another woman and he blatantly denied it, even when confronted with her texts. He's also signed a lease for a flat, Claudia.'

'Only for three months,' I retaliated.

'That's what he's told you!'

I didn't respond.

'Have you seen the lease?' Issie questioned in response to my reluctant silence.

'No,' I muttered.

'You need to talk to Ava,' Issie suggested.

'She's an entertainment lawyer.'

'And she's one of the best. She'll know someone in family law.'

'She's not speaking to me,' I pointedly replied.

'She is. Or she will be when she hears this,' Issie answered.

'No! Please, don't tell her.' The last thing I wanted was Ava finding out that Jacob had cheated on me. Worse, he had left me.

'You can trust Ava! If anyone can help you, it will be her,' Issie replied. 'I just don't want you losing your home.'

'Jacob wouldn't do that to me.'

'Wouldn't he?' Issie questioned.

Her words hurt more than I wanted to admit because there was an element of truth to them. But I couldn't reconcile myself with Jacob forcing the sale of our home. I knew Jacob better than Issie, and I knew he would never do that to me.

But he's moved out, Claudia! And he's sleeping with the woman he brought back to your home.

The reality that I might actually lose my home hit me. I turned around and looked back at the house. I froze. My heart suddenly stopped.

Shit! Darcy!

The bi-folding door was open.

How could it be open? Oh my God!

I dropped the cigarette I was holding.

'I'll call you back!'

I ran towards the door. I went inside and closed it. Breathing shallowly, I frantically looked around the kitchen for Darcy, but there was no sign of him.

I suddenly felt as if I was going to throw up.

'Darcy!' I called out, trying to ignore my thundering heart, which felt as if it was going to explode. 'Darcy? Darcy?' I yelled.

I headed out into the hallway, then ran into the living room. Followed by the dining room. Still no Darcy.

He has to be upstairs! Of course, he'll be asleep on my bed.

I sprinted up the stairs to my bedroom.

'Darcy?'

I stopped. He wasn't on the bed.

Fuck!

I tried to breathe. To stop myself from freefalling. I collapsed down onto my knees and looked under the bed.

No! Oh God! Darcy, where are you?

I stumbled up and frantically pulled the scatter cushions, pillows and comforter back from the bed, hoping he had buried himself underneath. He wasn't there either.

I could hear the blood pounding in my ears.

Where could he be? He had to be in the house. He had to be!

'Darcy!' I frantically yelled.

I waited to hear the familiar thud of his portly body hitting the floor.

Nothing.

I got up and headed towards Riley's bedroom.

The guestroom was one of Darcy's favourite sleeping places before Riley had moved in.

I knocked on her door. Waited. There was no response.

I knocked again. 'Riley?'

Again, there was no reply.

Fuck! Fuck! Fuck!

'Riley,' I called out, louder this time.

Silence. Foreboding and suffocating.

Holding my breath, I placed my hand on the round doorknob and twisted it. I knew I shouldn't go in without her permission, but this was an emergency.

'Riley?' I tentatively pushed the door open, expecting her to be asleep.

But she wasn't there. The bed was already made up with the scatter cushions, pillows and throw in the same manner as I had prepared it for her. The room looked as if she had never moved in. I glanced over at the study desk. No books. No laptop. Nothing. I then noted that the large leather bag she carried her laptop and books in was missing. She must have headed out while I was out in the garden talking with Issie.

'Darcy,' I called out. 'Hey, Darcy!' I repeated.

I already knew he wasn't in the room, but I felt compelled to check under the bed. As expected, there was nothing there, aside from random fluff bunnies.

I shakily breathed out.

Where the fuck are you, Darcy? Where?

I rushed downstairs and checked all the rooms again. There was no sign of him.

I felt nauseous. I knew it was my fault. That I had left the kitchen bi-folds open, and Darcy must have ventured out while I was distracted.

I headed back into the garden and searched in the bushes and amongst the plants. I then looked over the fences into the neighbours' gardens on either side, but there was no sign of him.

'DARCY?' I yelled.

Nothing.

My mind went through every scenario but always concluded with me leaving the kitchen door open.

How could you have done that? How? In the eight years with Darcy, you have never made that mistake!

I thought of Jacob. It was all his fault.

Bastard! I fucking hate you for this!

I then thought of Riley.

Maybe she knows where he is?

I got Riley's number up on my phone. Pressed call. Waited. It went to voicemail.

Fuck!

A few seconds later, she texted me.

Is everything OK?

I breathed in. Replied:

Did you see Darcy this morning?

I waited as she typed back.

Yes. As I left.

I immediately typed back:

Where?

She responded:

Sat on the living-room windowsill.

I ran back into the kitchen.

'Darcy?' I called out as I headed towards the hallway. 'Darcy?' I repeated, reaching the living room.

It was shrouded in silence.

Trying to ignore the fear in the pit of my stomach, I headed over to the bay window.

I pulled back the heavy curtains, expecting to find Darcy obliviously asleep behind them. But the wide, waxed wooden windowsill was empty.

I gasped as panic took hold. I had already lost Jaz, then Jacob and now Darcy.

Oh God... Not Darcy! Please... Where are you?

19

I spent the entire day and early evening searching for Darcy. But there was no sign of him. I had first alerted my neighbours, who searched their houses and gardens for him, but to no avail. I had then printed flyers with a photograph of Darcy and my contact details, which I had posted through countless doors and tied to lampposts and trees. Finally, I had registered his disappearance with the local police, vets and animal rescue charities. He had never been out and consequently would have no bearings.

I took a drink of wine as I glanced again at my phone, willing it to ring. I was desperate for someone to report finding Darcy. To tell me that he was safe and well, waiting for me to collect him. But my phone didn't ring. Nor did anyone knock at the door. I was alone, nursing a bottle of wine, trying to stop myself from becoming a hysterical hot mess. It felt that all I had done since I'd returned from my academic conference over five weeks ago to the discovery of Jacob's suspected infidelity was cry. It seemed as if it had been one life-altering event after another.

Issie, who was shocked at the news that Darcy was missing

when I rang her back after cutting her off, suggested she come over, but I had resisted, aware she had to prepare for an upcoming showing of her paintings at a small art gallery. She had suggested I call Willow, who lived in Kensington, and ask her to help. Which I did, only to discover that Willow was in France, visiting her parents with Charles.

I had contemplated calling Jacob but quickly discounted the idea. I had even considered asking Riley to help me hand out flyers but rejected it. She wasn't my friend, only my lodger. Nothing more. Darcy meant nothing to her.

And why would he?

Exhausted, I emptied the remnants of my wine down the sink before heading for bed. I passed Riley's room, noting the light wasn't on. I hadn't heard her come in either, so I assumed she was still out. I decided to text her about Darcy. It would save her the discomfort of me telling her in person.

Sighing, I climbed into bed and checked my phone one last time. Nothing. Aside from another text from Jacob. I swiped delete without reading it. I couldn't be bothered with any more of his lies. However, I desperately wished that I could call him. To have Jacob reassure me that Darcy would be found. To unburden the guilt that I felt.

I picked up my journal and pen and sat staring at my last entry: Friday evening. I reread my scrawled handwriting full of hope and promise of winning Jacob back the following evening. But it had all gone wrong. What hope I had of Jacob and I reconciling was irrevocably shattered. And now, Darcy was missing. It was a domino effect. If I hadn't seen the texts on Jacob's phone confirming his infidelity, then I would never have stupidly had a cigarette in the garden, and I wouldn't have left the bi-folding door open behind me.

I looked down as the ink blurred and the words bled into one another. I swiped at the tears, but they wouldn't stop.

I had lost everything...

* * *

I'd left the house early on Monday morning to look for Darcy. I'd spent an hour searching before calling it quits and heading into work.

It was now mid-afternoon, and I had a seminar in thirty minutes. Once that was over, I planned on going home and resuming the search as there was still no word about his whereabouts.

There was a light rap on my door. I paused and looked up from my computer as Helena popped her head around my office door.

'Still no word about Darcy?'

I shook my head.

She paused as if debating what to do, her dark eyes troubled. 'Look, there's something I need to discuss with you.'

I nodded.

She came in and closed the door, then looked at me, frowning. 'You haven't heard?'

'Heard what?'

'People are talking about Ethan and you,' she answered, concerned.

Fuck! No! That's not possible. No one knows about us.

'Who?' I questioned, aware of the slight tremor in my voice.

'Cassie Williams,' Helena answered.

I recognised the name. She was a postgraduate student.

'What is she saying?' I asked as I felt a flame of terror ignite in me.

Sighing, Helena walked over and sat down opposite me. She looked me in the eye, 'The last thing I want to do is add to everything that you've had to deal with lately. But I think you need to be aware of this.'

I nodded, feeling dazed. I waited for Helena to say the unthinkable.

'Cassie Williams knows you and Ethan had sex.'

I found myself gasping. 'How? How could she possibly know that?'

Helena shrugged. 'Ethan told her?'

I shook my head. 'No. Ethan wouldn't do that.'

Helena didn't look convinced.

'Who else was there that night?' I asked her. 'No, not Rowena?'

Helena's visible discomfort confirmed my suspicion.

'But I thought she left just before you.'

'She did,' Helena answered uneasily.

Rowena was a fellow associate professor in contemporary poetry, and Cassie Williams was one of Rowena's acolytes. It all made sense. I had always suspected that she had a thing for Ethan and was jealous, but I was shocked to think that she would act so vindictively.

FUCK! But who told her that I didn't leave with Helena, that I stayed on alone with Ethan?

'Did you tell Rowena?' I asked, unable to stop myself.

'Of course, I didn't!' retaliated Helena.

'So, how would she know? I'm assuming Rowena told her postgrad student. How else would Cassie Williams know?'

'Maybe Ethan said something to Rowena,' Helena defensively suggested.

'Why would Ethan tell someone?' I asked her, unconvinced that he would speak about what happened that night.

'To get back at you?'

'For what? Having sex with him?' I asked, incredulous.

'No. For leaving it the way you did.'

'He's avoided me as much as I have him,' I argued.

'Come on, Claudia. You know that's not true.'

'Seriously?'

Helena shifted in her seat, unable to hide her exasperation. 'You work together, Claudia! People have started to notice that you are avoiding him. I imagine he feels used.'

'This is coming from the self-proclaimed misandrist. Since when did you feel anything aside from contempt for the opposite sex?' I couldn't stop myself feeling irritated at her statement. Ironically, I had ignored Ethan to avoid being the topic of gossip amongst my students, and worse, my colleagues.

'That's below the belt!' Helena stated, squaring her shoulders. 'You know what I went through when Seamus—' She shook her head, unable to say it.

'I'm sorry. That was uncalled for,' I quickly apologised. 'I'm just going through a shitty time.'

'What's going on, Claudia? This isn't like you.'

I frowned as I looked her in the eye. 'What isn't like me?'

'Sleeping with Ethan and...' She faltered.

'And what?' I questioned. I needed Helena's support right now, not condemnation.

She shrugged. But she was holding something back.

'Say it.'

'Well, I rang you on Saturday night and you never got back to me. It just feels very one-way with you.'

Her words stung.

'Seriously? I... I never got back to you because I was busy. I planned on ringing you on Sunday, but...' I stopped myself, and shook my head at the thought of Darcy.

'What were you doing on Saturday night that was so important that you couldn't even send me a text to acknowledge my call?' she continued.

I stared at her, surprised at her insecurity. 'Really?'

She held my gaze, waiting for me to answer her question.

'I was out for drinks celebrating a friend's birthday. I had too much to drink and didn't realise you'd called until the following morning, at which point Darcy escaped.'

I could see from the look in her eyes that she didn't believe me.

'Surely, if it was so important, you could have left a voice message or texted me to call back ASAP.'

'It doesn't matter now.'

'What's wrong?' I asked, realising that there was more to this than Helena simply feeling ignored.

I watched as she struggled to speak.

'Helena?'

'My mother had another stroke on Saturday afternoon,' she quietly answered.

'Oh God! I am so sorry,' I replied, shocked. 'Is she all right?' I suddenly felt dreadful. I hadn't returned Helena's call until this morning on my way into work. And even then, I had left a garbled voicemail message about Darcy's disappearance.

She was right. I was completely self-absorbed.

Helena shook her head as she broke away from my questioning gaze. 'The doctors don't know yet what the long-term effects will be. It's her age and...' She stopped herself.

'Oh Helena, I am so, so sorry.'

She didn't reply.

Neither of us spoke for a few moments.

It was Helena who broke the silence first. 'I thought I had done something to upset you.' she said, looking back at me.

I raised my eyebrow at this statement. 'You? Like what?'

'I assumed you had heard the rumours and thought I was responsible.'

'No! You're one of my closest friends.'

'So why don't I feel it? You've been so remote, lately.'

'I am trying my damnedest to keep it together! I've lost my best friend, husband and now Darcy in the space of a few weeks. My life seems to be evaporating in front of me.' I leaned back and breathed out.

'I'm sorry,' Helena said. 'You've got a lot to deal with right now. I should have known better.'

'No, Helena! Don't say that. I'm always here for you. Okay?' I assured her.

Helena stood up.

'Why don't we have a drink after work this week?' I suggested.

'I can't,' she answered.

'Oh, of course. Your mother.'

She gave me a weak smile. 'Maybe when she gets out of hospital?'

'Sure,' I answered.

But from Helena's demeanour, I doubted that would be any time soon.

She went to leave, then stopped and turned back to me. 'As for the rumours, I'm refuting them, but you need to get to the source.'

'I will do. And I'm sorry about your mother. Keep me posted. Yeah?'

I waited until Helena closed my office door before exhaling.

I was so swept up in my own drama that I had forgotten about Helena's mother. I should have realised when she had rung me that something was wrong.

Poor Helena! You simply assumed she wanted to check in on how things were going in your life. You hadn't even considered the possibility that something could be wrong with her life.

And yet, Helena still came to warn me about the rumours about Ethan and me.

Then it hit me. Other people knew and were talking about it.

But who had started the rumours? And why?

20

I took a sip of wine and let the babbling conversational snippets float over me as I waited for Ethan. I had chosen the Grade II listed former underground Victorian water closet, WC Wine and Charcuterie Bloomsbury, situated on a traffic island on Guildford Place opposite Coram's Fields, to meet to avoid seeing any students or colleagues.

I watched as Ethan's tall, dark figure walked into the place. He looked as awkward as I felt. I raised my hand so he could see me sat in one of the intimate booths. He caught my eye, but it was a cold, hard look.

I inwardly recoiled.

What did you expect, Claudia? He's got every right to be pissed with you!

'Hey,' I greeted, smiling as he walked over to me.

'Hi,' he coolly returned. He gestured to my drink.

'No, I'm good, thanks.'

He nodded before turning and heading to the long bar.

Ethan came back a few minutes later with a bottle of Mexican beer. He pulled out a chair and sat down opposite me. 'So?' His voice emotionless, matching his expression. As he waited for my reply, he took a long glug of beer, his narrowed eyes never leaving mine.

I tucked a long, wavy strand of hair behind my ear as I inwardly took a deep breath. 'Yeah... Look, I'm sorry that I haven't been in touch since...' I dropped my gaze. 'You know?'

He didn't respond.

'Anyway, I wanted to apologise for disappearing on you like that,' I said, looking back at him. If I was hoping for redemption, I had come to the wrong person. 'You knew I was married and that it couldn't go anywhere,' I continued.

'I wasn't expecting it to,' he darkly threw back at me.

The coldness in his voice cut deep.

I could feel the heat radiating from my cheeks.

'Why did you come?' I ventured.

I had texted Ethan, asking to meet up to clear the air and apologise. However, he hadn't replied. I'd texted again, which prompted a terse, reluctant response.

'Curious to hear what excuse you came up with for ghosting me.'

He held my gaze.

'Look, I'm sorry. All right? It was a crap thing to do.'

'Yup,' Ethan agreed, raising his bottle at my statement before taking another glug.

What the fuck did he expect would happen? You're married. You made that clear to him from the first time he hit on you.

'What can I do to make things right between us?' I asked.

'You tell me?' he threw back.

'I don't know. I just want to go back to the way it was between us.'

He didn't react.

I thought back to Helena and the student she had overheard.

Was it Ethan who had started the rumours? If so, why? Unless it was, as Helena had said, to get back at me for acting as if he didn't exist.

'Claudia, what's going on here?' Ethan suddenly questioned.

'What do you mean?'

'This,' he said, gesturing with his hands at me. 'You. Me. Sat here.'

'I wanted to apologise and make things right.'

'That's bullshit, and you know it!'

'It's true,' I defended.

He scowled at me. 'What? What do you want from me? Forgiveness for being such a bitch? For thinking that I don't have any feelings. That I don't deserve an explanation?'

I numbly shook my head. 'It's not like that.'

'Keep telling yourself that same lie. But it doesn't wash with me.'

'We were both drunk. It should never have happened. I was embarrassed and dealt with it the only way I could. I had just lost my best friend, then my husband...' I faltered.

'I heard. I also heard that your husband cheated on you first.'

I was shocked that he knew that.

Before I had a chance to ask him who had told him, he continued: 'You wanted to get one over on your husband, and that's where I came in.'

'No,' I replied, holding his furious glare. 'I had no intention of sleeping with you.'

'Bullshit! You were coming on to me all night,' he said, lowering his voice as someone walked by.

'If that's the way you want to remember it, then go ahead,' I retaliated.

'It's a fact. You knew what you were doing that night. You had every intention of having sex with me. I wasn't the only one who noticed you hitting on me.'

Rowena. I recalled her making a snide remark about me and Ethan, insinuating that something was going on between us. If she had heard that Ethan and I were the last ones at the bar, she might have put two and two together.

'Has someone said something to you about that night?'

Ethan stared at me. 'Does it matter?'

'Yes,' I answered. 'If someone started rumours about us, I have a right to know.'

He shrugged. 'You should have thought about that before you hit on me.'

'Will you stop saying that?'

'Why? Does it hit a nerve?' he asked, a facetious smile playing at the corner of his mouth.

'You were the one who came onto me from the first day,' I pointed out.

'Maybe,' he said, staring straight at me. 'But you made it clear that nothing could happen between us. So, I repeat my point, you hit on me that evening, and you did it intending to sleep with me.'

It wasn't going to plan. Not that I had a plan, but I hadn't expected Ethan to be so intractable.

What the hell did you expect would happen if you fucked him to get back at Jacob? Seriously, Claudia?

I deeply breathed in as I deliberated my next move.

'Look, all I want is to stop the rumours. Surely you don't want your personal life being the topic of student gossip?' I questioned.

I could see from his eyes that my attempt at reasoning had failed.

'Be honest. You couldn't give a shit about me. It's your reputation that you're trying to salvage here,' he stated.

'You're a dick. Do you know that?'

Ethan gave a bitter laugh. 'Yeah? Maybe I am. The difference between us is that I'm not bothered by what people think about me.'

'Are you being serious?' I asked, astounded by his callousness.

'I'm simply pointing out that treating me like a piece of shit doesn't quite fit in with the self-sacrificing image that you've created for yourself.'

'Fuck you, Ethan!'

I jumped up and snatched my bag and coat from the bench.

I looked at him. 'I believed we were friends. You know that?'

'So, did I. The sad part of all of this is you're only concerned about yourself. If you hadn't heard the rumours about us, who knows when you would have spoken to me?'

'It's not like that,' I replied.

He shook his head at me. 'It's exactly like that. I was foolish enough to think you actually cared about me.'

I had heard enough. I started walking away.

'Hey, Claudia,' he called out after me.

I spun around.

'Maybe you should question who your friends are?'

'What the hell is that supposed to mean?' I fired back.

'Who do you think started those rumours?'

'Why don't you tell me?'

Ethan held my gaze. 'Give me one good reason why I should.'

I shook my head. I'd had enough of his games.

I turned and left as one questioned tormented me: Who would want to publicly humiliate and hurt me?

21

'Hi,' I greeted, answering my mobile.

'Hey, how are you coping?' Issie gently questioned.

'I'm not,' I admitted, collapsing onto my bed. 'No sign of Darcy. Not even one response to all my flyers and posters. I even made him wear a collar with an ID disc just in case something like this happened. He hated needles, and there was no way Darcy would let the vet microchip him. And he was a house cat, so I didn't see the need,' I explained, my voice filled with regret.

I lay there looking up at the gloomy shadows cast on the white ceiling from the bedside lamps. The house was eerily silent. I assumed that Riley was still out or in bed as there was no noise coming from her room, and there had been no light coming from under her door when I'd passed it. What hopes I'd had of a lodger distracting me from Jacob moving out had been shattered by the reality. I ached for things to be as they once were when Jacob's presence seemed to fill the entire place. I thought of Darcy and how he would follow me everywhere, so much so, Jacob would joke that Darcy had abandonment issues. Without Darcy, the house now felt so empty.

I choked back a sob. At least attempted to and failed.

'Oh, Claudia...' Issie sympathised.

Sad, lonely tears escaped from the corners of my eyes, trickling down to my ears. I roughly swiped at them, berating myself for being so pathetic.

I seemed to be plagued by 'what if' scenarios.

What if Jaz had talked to me the days, even weeks, leading up to her death?

What if I hadn't had revenge sex with Ethan Novak?

Or if I hadn't slept with Jacob and then seen those texts on his phone, resulting in me being so distraught that I had a cigarette in the garden, leaving the kitchen door ajar without thinking?

I knew the outcome of each scenario could have been so different. *If only...*

I sighed heavily before continuing, 'And as if things aren't bad enough, Helena came by my office this afternoon. She said that she overheard a research student discussing Ethan and myself, and the fact that we...' I faltered.

'Oh fuck! Seriously?'

'Seriously.' The knot in my stomach tightened. 'For all I know it's around the entire department.'

'Shit!' Issie was quiet for a moment before continuing, 'What are you going to do?'

'There's not much I can do. Helena said she was refuting the rumours. All I can do is hope that works.'

'Who do you think started the rumours?' asked Issie.

I had repeatedly asked myself that from the moment I had found out. I still couldn't discount the source being Rowena. But the crucial question was who had told her?

'Helena believes that Ethan told either a colleague or this research student,' I replied.

'Why would he do that to you?'

'For ghosting him,' I answered.

'Are you going to talk to him and get to the bottom of the rumours?'

'I already did,' I answered. 'I met up with him after work.'

'So?' Issie prompted at my failure to elaborate. 'What did Ethan say?'

'Not a lot, but enough for me to know he didn't start the rumour,' I replied.

'Who do you think it was then?'

I took a deep breath.

'Claudia?'

'I would have said this other colleague, Rowena, who was there that night when we were having drinks, but I don't know. Ethan said something odd. He implied that I couldn't trust my friends.'

'Seriously?'

'That's what he said. And Rowena's not a friend.'

'Who else did you tell?'

'No one,' I answered. 'Just Helena. Maybe he's just psyching me out.'

'Maybe,' Issie agreed. 'Or maybe Helena said something to this other colleague?'

'To Rowena?'

It was a question I had already considered.

'Is it possible?' Issie asked.

'Anything's possible. But Helena has known me for five years. She would never betray my confidence.'

'Is she friends with this Rowena?'

'Yes.'

'Have you done anything that would give Helena cause to feel aggrieved?' Issie asked.

I hesitated. 'No.'

'You don't sound so sure.'

I thought back to her phone call that I didn't answer on Saturday evening when her mother had suffered a second stroke. But that wouldn't be enough cause for her to tell Rowena about Ethan and me.

Or would it?

'Oh, I nearly forgot, this Saturday's cancelled,' Issie uneasily announced.

'What? Why?'

'Ava can't make it.'

'Why?'

It was the third time Ava had cancelled.

'Ava's got to go back out to LA. They're having some major problems with this deal and the client will only work with her.'

'So, when are we meeting up?'

'I don't know,' answered Issie. 'We have to wait until Ava's back.'

'And that would be?'

'I honestly have no idea. Her workload is crazy right now.'

I could feel the panic rising inside me at the thought that Issie could be lying to me. That they didn't want me there. That, whatever information Ava had, she wasn't going to share it with me.

But why?

Because she blames you for Jaz's death. She said as much.

'Tell me the three of you aren't meeting up again without me.'

'Of course not!' Issie replied, incredulous that I would suggest such a thing. 'We've gone over this already. It was a mistake. Yeah?'

'On your and Willow's part, yes,' I agreed. 'But Ava knew what she was doing.'

'Claudia! Seriously? You need to get over it.'

'Maybe when Ava apologises to me...'

'And I am sure she will when we next see her,' Issie reassured me.

'And the letter?'

'What about it?' questioned Issie.

'Has Ava said any more to you about who sent it and the contents?'

'Don't you think I would tell you if she had? Stop being so paranoid, Claudia!'

I didn't reply.

'Seriously, you'll find out, as will I, when we meet with Ava. Okay?'

'Okay.'

But why was I struggling to believe her?

I thought back to the funeral and the look that had passed between Willow and Ava. I was sure that they were withholding something from me connected to Jaz's death. What that could be, I had no idea. And now there was the discovery that someone had sent Jaz a letter days before she chose to take her life. Could the letter and her suicide be connected? It had to be...

I inwardly sighed. There were too many questions, and Ava was the one calling the shots. I had no other option but to wait until we were all together to get the answers I needed.

'I've got to go, but as soon as I get a date to meet up from Ava, I'll let you know,' Issie assured me.

I cut the call and breathed out. I still couldn't fathom Ava out. If she had crucial information about Jaz's decision to take her life, why wasn't she sharing it with us? And why wasn't Issie bothered about Ava withholding it from us for so long? It felt as if Issie was protecting Ava for some reason.

Why?

My phone buzzed. It was another text from Jacob. Without reading it, I put my phone down. I had enough to deal with without him. I deliberated contacting Helena to tell her about meeting up with Ethan. But then Ethan's words came back to me:

Maybe you should question who your friends are.
I thought of Helena: *Would you really do that to me?*

22

THURSDAY, LATE APRIL

I couldn't stop my body from shaking.

I was on the bathroom floor with my knees pulled into my chest, contemplating how I had ended up in this situation.

Fuck! Fuck! Fuck!

Three weeks on from Helena's revelation that rumours were flying around the department about Ethan and me having sex, and I had found myself alienated at work. Issie had argued that I was being paranoid. However, I knew it wasn't my imagination when I caught students looking at me and whispering in lectures and seminars. Worse, colleagues were awkward around me, some even going out of their way to avoid me. Nor could I fail to notice that Helena had pulled back. Her mother was still in hospital, and so I put her remoteness down to that. Recently, a few colleagues, including Helena, had got together for drinks after work without me. The fact they hadn't invited me was hurtful, and I knew it was pathetic, but I felt excluded.

Then there was Issie, Willow and Ava. We still hadn't met up despite my attempts. Nor had Ava disclosed any details regarding the letter sent to Jaz. Over the past three weeks, I had rung and texted Ava, but she still hadn't returned my calls or responded to my messages. Issie had reassured me that Ava was extraordinarily busy and that it wasn't personal. But we both knew that wasn't the case.

I knew that with Willow, she was preoccupied with her new relationship with Charles. I was happy for Willow, more so after the loss of Jaz. Out of the five of us, Willow had always been the sensitive one, and without Charles, she would have struggled to deal with Jaz's death.

But I missed Willow. And, at a push, even Ava.

It was as if my close friends and colleagues were withdrawing from me, and I had no idea why.

Or was I disappearing?

The anxiety I felt was athazagoraphobia. The dread that I was fading into oblivion.

Come on, Claudia! Stop procrastinating! You need to get showered and get into work! Just look at it!

But I couldn't look. It would be too final. I thought of the paradox of Schrödinger's cat, both, as Schrödinger explained, 'living and dead... in equal parts' until observed. It was the same principle. Once I looked, it would be definite. And what if I were? Cold dread coursed through me at the thought.

I breathed in, and with a trembling hand, I picked up the white pregnancy stick. Shocked, I stared at the small window. There was no mistaking that one blue word: *pregnant.*

I tried to swallow, but my mouth was too dry. I thought of Jacob. What would he say? We had tried for so long and failed. Then Ethan Novak came along...

Shit! Shit! Shit!

I stared at the pregnancy stick, hoping that it had been a mistake. That it would now say 'not pregnant'. But it hadn't changed. My period was two weeks late, something I had attributed to stress. However, combined with the past couple of days of nausea that I had initially dismissed as a stomach bug, the signs couldn't have been more obvious. I could feel my throat constrict at the sight of that one life-changing word, a word that, ironically, I had craved month after month with Jacob. And yet, here I was, paralysed with dread.

Oh my God... My parents. How would they react to the news that they were going to be grandparents? My mother as a grand-mother... It wasn't worth contemplating.

I felt as if my world was suddenly spinning out of control.

Being pregnant was all you wanted.

Yes, with Jacob. Together, not alone.

Jacob had tried to reach out to me, but I had ignored all his attempts. Finally, he'd accepted my silence, and I hadn't heard from him in over a week. Would Jacob believe it was his?

It had to be Jacob's. The alternative didn't bear thinking about.

Ethan and I had used protection. I had seen the empty condom wrappers. I reassured myself with the knowledge that Jacob and I had sex over three and a half weeks ago, long enough for there to be detectable levels of the pregnancy hormone in my body.

Then it hit me: *What if Jacob wants nothing to do with you or the pregnancy?*

I let out a strangled sob.

How will you cope as a working single parent when you can't even manage the mortgage now? How will you afford childcare for a baby?

I knew my parents would help financially, but at what price?

I could feel my life imploding at the prospect of the exploding life inside me.

I forced myself to get up off the floor, hiding the positive preg-nancy stick at the back of the bathroom cabinet before turning the shower on. I needed to pull myself together and go into work. Ordi-narily, I loved my role as an associate professor in American literature. I had fought hard to get that much-sought-after position. But, recently, I dreaded going in, feeling as if colleagues were gossiping about me.

Or maybe it was guilt that was driving me into a paranoid frenzy? I despised myself for the way I'd treated Ethan. I didn't recognise myself. I would never have envisioned cheating on Jacob with a colleague, one I had cruelly ignored, wanting to pretend that fateful night had never happened. Maybe if Jaz had never died, then—

But it did happen... And Jaz did take her life.

* * *

'Helena?' I called, spotting her as I came out of my small, first-floor office.

She didn't react.

'Helena?' I repeated.

I threw my leather bag over my shoulder and ran to catch her up.

'Hey,' I greeted.

It was evident that Helena was avoiding me.

Why?

'Oh... Hi,' Helena uncomfortably answered.

'Do you have time for a quick coffee? It feels like forever since we had a catch-up.'

'I already have plans. Sorry,' she said with a forced apologetic smile.

'What about tomorrow?'

'I can't. Another time?'

'When?' I asked, wanting a definitive answer.

I wasn't ordinarily combative, but if something was wrong, I would rather she told me.

Helena reached her office door, then heavily sighed before turning and looking at me. 'Not sure right now. Let me get back to you. I'm running late. I need to grab a few things from my office and then head off to the hospital.'

'Helena?'

'What?'

I couldn't fail to be stung by the exasperation in her voice.

'What's going on?'

Without answering, she unlocked her door and opened it.

'Have I done something to upset you?' I asked, floundering.

Helena turned to me, her eyes narrowed. 'I felt sorry for you,' she lowly hissed. 'When those rumours started about you and Ethan, I tried my damnedest to discredit them. I did it because you were my friend. A close friend whom I trusted.'

I felt winded. Helena's words were delivered with such anger that it took me a moment to respond.

'And you can still trust me,' I stated, trying to keep my voice level.

'I told you my worst fear was Seamus sleeping with someone I knew. That I wouldn't be able to get over that kind of betrayal.'

I remained silent, unsure of why she was mentioning her ex-partner, who was a narcissistic dick. She was better off without him.

'You know I have always struggled with my weight. Seamus would go on at me all the time. I mean, when I stand next to you, I'm invisible. I'm just some obese, middle-aged woman.'

I frowned. I was aware that Helena felt she had a weight problem. But to compare herself to me. This wasn't like Helena.

'Hey, what's going on?' I questioned, reaching out to touch her arm.

'Don't! Don't you dare!' she hissed, pulling her arm away as a flash of anger crossed her dark eyes.

I took a step back, shocked. 'I have no idea—'

'Don't!' she cut in. 'Don't even dare to pretend that you don't know what I'm talking about.'

'Helena, please. I have no idea what this is about.'

'I trusted you, Claudia. I thought you were my friend!'

Before I could defend myself, she shut the door on me.

What the fuck?

I stood there for a moment, not sure what had just happened. I knocked on the door before opening it. 'Helena?'

She ignored me, furiously muttering to herself as she picked up some papers and stuffed them into her bag.

I couldn't figure out why she was behaving in such a manner towards me. Then I realised – Seamus had hit on me two years back at their New Year's Eve party. I knew not to mention anything while they were still together, so I had waited until he had left her for his colleague, before confessing what had happened. She had been angry with Seamus, not me, at the time. So what had changed?

'Is this over Seamus making that drunken pass at me?'

Helena spun around to face me as her dark eyes flashed with fury. 'But it wasn't just a drunken pass, was it?'

'What?' I asked, incredulous. 'I told you what happened. Seamus followed me when I was going to the bathroom and forced his way in after me. He proceeded to attempt to come on to me and I asked him to get out. That was it.'

'Did you though? I never minded the fact that you're so beautiful, whereas I'm...' Helena looked down at herself and shrugged. 'Well... I'm just ordinary and overweight.'

'You're beautiful!'

'Come on, Claudia! Even for you, that's a stretch too far.'

I was about to argue with her, but she raised her hand, cutting me off.

'Don't! As I was saying, I never felt threatened as your friend because I never thought you would even entertain the idea of

Seamus, not when you had Jacob. But it turns out that you lied to me about that night. That more happened than you admitted.'

Numb, I shook my head, not believing what I was hearing. 'No—'

'Don't act all innocent with me. Remember, I watched you that night with Ethan. You wanted to get even with Jacob, and Ethan was just collateral damage. Other people noticed as well.'

'What? Rowena?' I scoffed.

'But as for Seamus,' she continued, ignoring my remark. 'Why? What did you get out of it? The knowledge that it would destroy me?'

'For fuck's sake, Helena! Nothing happened. He grabbed hold of me and tried to kiss me, all right?' I revealed, exasperated.

I stared in horror at her expression. I had never told her Seamus had tried to kiss me. I had only said he had made a pass. At the time, she was reeling from his affair. I believed the less she knew, the better.

'You told me nothing had happened. Now you're telling me he kissed you.'

'I never told you because I thought it would hurt you. Yes, Seamus tried to kiss me, but I slapped him.'

I could see from her expression that she didn't believe me.

'For Christ's sake, Helena! This is ridiculous! It happened two years ago. You're bringing it up now. Why? In fact, why don't you ask Seamus?' I suggested. It then hit me. 'I assume you must have done,' I stated, 'and he's lied to you about me for some reason. Maybe it's all a mindfuck on his part? Who knows the motives of a narcissist? What I don't understand is why you would be digging up events from two years ago. It smacks of a witch hunt, Helena. Not very feminist of you!'

'Just leave!' she demanded in a raised voice.

'That's it?' I questioned. 'You expect me to leave after you've accused me of...' I faltered, narrowing my eyes at her. 'What exactly are you accusing me of here? Fucking your partner two years back in your bathroom? Is that it?'

She remained silent, but her eyes said it all.

'Woah!' I spluttered. 'You really think that lowly of me?'

'You explain to me why the two of you were gone for so long. Rowena commented that night on the fact that the two of you had disappeared.'

I inwardly recoiled at the mention of Rowena. I should have known that she would be responsible in besmirching my character. 'I'm lost. Has Rowena said something? And if so, why now?'

'Rowena shared something with me that she had kept quiet for fear of upsetting me at the time.'

'What did she say?' I questioned, feeling sick.

I knew that whatever Helena was going to share would be a vicious lie.

'Rowena said that she needed the bathroom and had waited for ages outside. She ended up so desperate, she banged on the door until Seamus opened it. She said she saw you behind him looking guilty pulling your dress back down.'

It took me a moment to absorb Helena's words. It explained why she had been so off with me lately. But Rowena? I assumed this was all to do with Ethan Novak and the fact I had slept with him. That conniving backstabbing bitch!

'And you believe her?' I asked, incredulous.

'You can't explain where you were for so long, can you?' she continued, ignoring my question.

'I was so upset by it that I went outside for some fresh air,' I began. 'I needed to calm down before I re-joined the party. I didn't want you knowing something was wrong, or Jacob, come to that. Maybe I should have said something. Forgive me for not wanting to ruin your New Year's Eve party. And as for Seamus. I have no idea where he disappeared afterwards. I kicked him out of the bathroom, and that was the last time I spoke to him. All right?'

She didn't say anything.

'Seriously, Helena?'

Her silence condemned me.

'You can't see that Rowena is demonising me?' I demanded. 'Rowena is jealous of me because of what happened with Ethan. You know that she has always had a thing for him. That, and she's never liked me. But what I don't understand is why you're listening to her.'

Helena didn't answer me.

I shook my head. 'Why condemn me without allowing me to defend myself? I thought of you as one of my closest friends.'

She still didn't answer me.

Stunned and deeply wounded by the fact that she believed such hateful lies against me, I turned and left her office. I blindly pushed my way past students in the corridor trying to hold back the threatening tears.

All I could think was, who else had Rowena repeated this slanderous lie to? The administration staff? Fellow professors? Her PhD research students who were notoriously interested in gossip about their and their peers' supervisors? If you wanted to know about the personal lives of your fellow colleagues in the department, you just had to eavesdrop on the PhD students in the cafeteria. Aside from gossiping, and researching their chosen speciality for their 80,000-word doctorate thesis, PhD research students were required to give lectures and seminars to first-year tutees. Maybe my students were whispering about me because one of Rowena's PhD students had badmouthed me to their tutees about having sex with my colleague. Worse still, now also the husband of another colleague.

Humiliation crippled me, overshadowing my internal guilt. I

could feel the scathing judgement of others, scorching me in shame.

Could that be why everywhere I turned, I felt like a modern-day Hester Prynne from *The Scarlet Letter*, condemned to publicly wear the letter 'A' for adultery?

23

I was struggling to concentrate. I couldn't stop thinking about Helena and her accusation based on unsubstantiated lies. She knew that Rowena had never liked me, so why would she believe something Rowena claimed to have witnessed over two years ago? Surely, Helena could see that Rowena was capitalising on the rumours about Ethan and I having sex.

And who started those rumours, Claudia?

I forced myself to focus on the lecture I was giving and not my problems. I could see from most of the third-year students' fatigued expressions that their interest was rapidly waning. It was no surprise they were struggling to concentrate. The lecture theatre was unbearably warm, combined with the fact that it was the end of a long day.

'Consequently,' I pushed on, 'it is Bentham's prison that is now widely associated with the word "panopticon". However, Bentham never saw a panopticon prison built during his lifetime. It wasn't until the 1920s that it became actualised in the form of Presidio Modelo prison in Cuba. Now abandoned, it was infamous in its time for corruption and cruelty,' I explained, scanning their faces.

A jolt of shock coursed through my body as I stared up at the back row. Riley was sitting there, looking straight at me.

Maybe she had attended because she was interested in the lecture. Unless she wanted to see me about something afterwards?

I cleared my throat and continued, 'Can you imagine architecture and geometry alone creating within an individual's mind a form of self-surveillance? The French philosopher Michel Foucault kindled interest in Bentham's panopticon in his 1975 book *Discipline and Punish* by using the panopticon as a way of demonstrating how authoritarian societies are predisposed to control their citizens. "He is seen, but he does not see; he is an object of information, never a subject in communication."' I paused to take a sip of water. 'Subsequently, the inmates have no other choice then but to police themselves for fear of punishment.'

I looked up at the back row again. There was no sign of Riley. The seat was empty. I wondered if something was wrong with her.

Or maybe Helena had said something to her about me.

No... That's not possible. Why would she?

Then Helena's accusation came back to me. Maybe she had said something to Riley to spite me because she felt I had betrayed her.

I shakily breathed out, noticing some of the students start whispering to one another. Furtive glances at me only compounded the mounting paranoia that had besieged me. It felt as if they were waiting for me to fall apart.

Oh God... I can't do this.

'I'm going to finish early,' I heard myself saying.

Their response only increased my paranoia as the muttering became louder as they glanced questioningly at me.

'We'll discuss the idea of the panopticon in context with American slavery further in our next seminar,' I concluded, trying to keep my voice level.

I hurriedly closed my laptop, forced it into my bag and left the lecture theatre as quickly as possible to avoid any questions. I kept telling myself I needed to catch up with Riley to check she was all right. To accept the truth that I was fleeing because I couldn't cope only intensified the suffocating panic.

I dashed out into the hallway. There was no sign of Riley. I quickly headed out of the American Literature department building, following four students engaged in a heated debate as they spilt out onto the paved-over courtyard of Foster Court.

The day had disappeared, replaced by the warm glow of lights illuminating the courtyard, warding off the predatory darkness of the coming night. I turned, and thought I spotted Riley's long blonde hair, the black beanie hat and the oversized cream cable knit Aran jumper in the opposite direction.

I hurried down Malet Place towards the black wrought-iron gates and railings that led out onto Torrington Place, chasing her elusive figure. Losing sight of her, I dodged across the busy road as rush-hour traffic honked at me in annoyance, passing the large Waterstones on the corner of Malet Street. I had planned on browsing the pregnancy section in the bookstore after work, but the need to find Riley was more pressing.

I hurried along the wide, lamp-lit path with its mature trees on either side, forming an archway over the road. A few minutes later, I reached the London School of Hygiene and Tropical Medicine, with my favourite detail: the gilded, deadly, poisonous and disease-carrying wildlife on the black railings. I abruptly stopped at the corner of Keppel Street and looked at the building directly opposite – Senate House Library. I assumed this was Riley's destination.

It was an awe-inspiring mid-30s art deco architectural statement with relatively small windows that made it look bigger and even more imposing. The Ministry of Information had used the building during the Second World War, and unsurprisingly, given its striking appearance, the building had appeared in numerous films.

Famously, the Ministry of Truth, in George Orwell's novel *Nineteen Eighty-Four*, was inspired by Senate House, where his first wife worked for the Censorship Department of the Ministry of Information.

Senate House Library was a beautiful sanctuary and one of my favourite haunts. The lure of the warm, seductive glow of the lights from inside the multitude of small windows beckoned to me as I shivered, as the cold, early-evening air wrapped itself around me. I hesitated, unsure of whether I should go in or if I was acting irrationally.

Of course, you are!

After all, by all counts, I should have still been delivering my lecture.

Damn it, Claudia! What are you thinking? Quitting early to, what? Stalk your lodger?

I turned back, keeping my head down, not wanting to bump into any of my students, as I retraced my steps along Malet Street, back to Torrington Place, then onto Gower Street, for my usual route home via Warren Street and the underground for the Victoria line. Not that I registered the crowds of people around me on the Tube platform or even changing at Victoria for the District line. Nor did I recall coming out of Kew Gardens station, passing the station bar, the village shops, and onto the tree-lined North Road for the ten-minute walk home.

Reaching our road, I appreciated it had everything Jacob and I wanted, a village lifestyle, close to the Victoria Gate entrance for the Royal Botanical Gardens in a quiet residential cul-de-sac. But we wanted more bedrooms for starting a family. That was why we had shifted our covetous gaze to Richmond.

The thought suddenly struck me that I was pregnant.

You'll need a nursery, Claudia. Or you'll have to use the guest bedroom. But how could you afford the mortgage without a lodger?

I had grown accustomed in this short time to Riley's rent. But she would be gone soon. If Jacob didn't return home, how would I cope?

Then the conversation with Helena came to mind. I had played it over and over again in my head as I walked back from the station. I couldn't understand what had happened or why. Her unfounded accusation that I had sex with Seamus at their New Year's Eve party was preposterous. How she could believe that I was capable of doing that was beyond me.

As I was unlocking the front door, it hit me that Darcy wouldn't come running down the hallway, screeching at me that I had left him alone all day.

My phone started to ring. I fumbled around in my bag to get it and saw it was Issie.

'Hey,' I answered. 'Please tell me tomorrow's still on with Ava and Willow. It's taken forever to pin everyone down.'

'Of course, it is,' Issie dismissively replied. 'And? What's this news you said you were desperate to share? I've been waiting in anticipation all day!'

'I'm pregnant!'

'What?' exclaimed Issie.

'Let me get in and I'll call you back in five minutes. All right?'

I locked the door, then, flicking the lights on, headed towards the kitchen. I needed a cup of chamomile tea to calm me down. I dumped my bag and coat on the dining-room chair first before switching the kettle on.

Carrying my cup of tea, I made my way upstairs to my bedroom. All I wanted to do was strip out of my work clothes and curl up in bed. As I passed Riley's room, I hesitated. The light from the bedside lamp seeped out from under the door. But before I had a chance to decide whether to knock, she switched the lamp off. I stood there for a moment, deliberating what to do. I assured myself that if she wanted to talk, she would have come out when she heard me come home. Shrugging her attendance in my lecture off as simple academic interest, I continued to my bedroom.

Now sat in a baggy T-shirt, I leaned back against the countless pillows and scatter cushions on my bed and slowly breathed out. It had been the worst day I had ever experienced at work. I was mentally and physically exhausted.

I reached out and picked up my cup of chamomile tea. I took a sip as I pressed call.

'You're definitely pregnant?' Issie immediately questioned on speaker. 'I mean... you're certain?'

'One hundred per cent,' I answered glancing over at my bedroom door which was slightly ajar.

'Oh fuck!' Issie muttered. 'Are you going to tell Ethan?'

I realised that she must have assumed it was Ethan's because Jacob and I had tried for so long and failed. Then, when we weren't trying, it had happened. What were the odds?

'It can't be Ethan's. We used protection.'

'Oh right. Who else knows?' she asked.

'Only you,' I answered.

Ordinarily, I would have confided in Helena. And there was still Ava and Willow to tell. Of course, if Jaz had still been alive, she would have been the first to know. But she wasn't.

If only...

I stopped myself. No matter how many times I revisited the past, it would never bring her back.

'You haven't told Jacob? Oh, Claudia, you have to tell him!'

'Do I? Remember I found those texts on his phone. He still won't admit that he's cheated. I mean, can you believe that?'

Issie was silent for a moment.

'Please don't breathe a word of this tomorrow night.'

'Of course, I won't,' Issie assured me, before adding, 'Ava has something she wants to tell you.'

'What?' A sense of dread coursed through me. 'Is this about Jaz?'

'Yes and...' Issie stopped herself.

'Is this to do with the letter that Jaz received?'

Issie didn't answer me.

'Is it?' I demanded as anger started to build.

'Yes. In part,' she confessed.

'Seriously? Does Willow know?'

Again, Issie's awkward silence confirmed my suspicion.

'Fucking hell!' I snapped.

'Claudia! Please it's not what you think.'

'No! You don't get to tell me what I think! You've just admitted that the three of you know something about Jaz's death. Something that you've all kept from me. How could you do that to me? You of all people, Issie.'

'Look, you'll understand when Ava tells you why I couldn't say anything. Okay?'

'No, it's not okay. None of this is okay,' I argued, swiping at the tears that had started to fall. My chest felt tight. 'Why don't you just tell me, now? Huh? Why make me wait?'

'I can't, Claudia. Please. It will all make sense in person. We all need to be there to discuss it. To decide what we need to do.'

I tried to breathe in, but couldn't catch my breath.

What did she know? No... what did they *know about Jaz's death?*

24

FRIDAY

I checked under the hallway table, then the kitchen for my laptop bag. I couldn't remember where I had dumped it when I came in last night.

'Damn!' I muttered.

I was running late and should have left ten minutes ago.

I headed back into the living room. That was when I spotted it lying on my study desk in the alcove.

Relief coursed through me as I grabbed it and headed out to work.

* * *

I sat down at my office desk and took my laptop out and signed in. I froze; the desktop was empty.

What the hell?

All my files were gone.

Trying not to overreact, I closed the laptop down to reboot it, hoping it was only a glitch. I waited a few seconds before switching it back on. I stared again in horror; the files were still missing. I could feel my heart rate accelerating. All my work had disappeared.

'Shit,' I cursed.

I tried rebooting it again. It was still blank. My research, lecture and seminar notes had all been erased.

'Shit! Shit! Shit!'

I stared at the blank screen not knowing what to do.

Jacob came to mind. He had always been my go-to tech person, but I didn't want to call him. I couldn't. I hadn't spoken to him since that Sunday morning at his flat, despite him denying any knowledge of who had texted him. But there was no way of explaining away the obvious – that he was having sex with another woman. Not just any woman, the same one he had brought back to our home when I was away at a conference.

I was getting riled again and now wasn't the time.

I stared at the blank desktop. It had to be a glitch. That's all.

I then remembered that everything would be backed up on the cloud. I hurriedly signed in and then stared in disbelief. The account was empty. Everything was gone.

I could feel heat rising up my neck towards my face.

Think, Claudia! Don't panic. Think!

I knew it wouldn't be a virus as it was a Mac. Maybe I had inadvertently wiped it myself last night when I'd hurriedly shut it down after the lecture?

How the hell would you do that? You're a Luddite as it is, so how could you possibly wipe all your documents and files?

Then I remembered that Jacob had insisted I use Dropbox. I recalled exporting a lot of my work material to the account, which meant it still had to be there.

Not daring to breathe, I signed in to Dropbox.

Thank God!

All my uploaded files were intact.

I picked up the bottle of water on my desk, unscrewed the cap and took a much-needed long glug as relief flooded through me. I had a first-year lecture in less than thirty minutes, followed by a second-year one this afternoon. Thankfully, I now had the lecture notes. Otherwise, I would have had to wing it as it was too late to cancel at such short notice. The last thing I wanted was students and colleagues questioning my professional capability. More so when my personal life was under scrutiny. It wouldn't take much for gossip to spread like wildfire that I was falling apart.

Are you falling apart, Claudia? I mean, how the hell did you wipe all your files? Even last night, you abruptly ended the lecture early. People are already talking about you. The last thing you need is students complaining that you're not up to the job.

I shook off the doubt. I was starting to become paranoid. I swilled back another mouthful of water as I tried to drown out the neurotic thoughts attacking me. It wasn't like me. But then, my world had radically shifted, and it felt as if I was in freefall.

* * *

Friday morning and early afternoon passed in a blur. I had successfully restored the files on my laptop from Dropbox and delivered both lectures. Now I was playing catch-up with a pile of unmarked scripts. But I was struggling to concentrate. I was meeting up with Issie, Willow and Ava later, and I couldn't stop thinking about whatever it was that Ava was going to reveal to us, or, to be precise, me. For it was evident from my conversation with Issie last night that she and Willow were already in the know. I was sure that the letter must have some bearing on Jaz's death; otherwise, why would Ava want to discuss it? And what else were they going to disclose?

It still hurt that they were withholding something from me. I had known Issie, Willow and Ava most of my life, and yet, they had closed ranks against me. Something didn't feel right, and I couldn't silence the feeling that I would be walking into a trap.

I slowly breathed out as I massaged my forehead. I could feel a stress headache building. Then I realised it could be hormonal. Of course...

You're pregnant!

It still took me by surprise. I then felt a wave of terror flare up inside me at the prospect of being on my own. It wasn't the life I had planned. I was in no doubt that my parents would throw money at my situation, but there would be no emotional or physical support. They had a life together in Japan, one that didn't include me. Even as a young child, my parents had barely anything to do with me. As soon as I was old enough, they'd sent me to board at my mother's old school – Queen Victoria's School for Girls in the Surrey countryside. When I was eleven, I'd urgently needed an appendectomy and was in the hospital critically ill, and still they didn't return from Japan.

I knew it was more my mother than my father. She was possessively jealous of my father, and, in time, I realised that she perceived me as a threat to their relationship. She wanted my father all to herself, and so she chose to exile me. My mother was an exquisitely beautiful, charming, intelligent and profoundly selfish woman. She was someone who should never have had children, which was why I had no siblings. As for me, she had often remarked that she never wanted me and that my father was the only reason she went ahead with the pregnancy as he wanted a child. However, my mother had since done everything within her power to thwart his relationship with me. So much so, they had spent most of my life living on a different continent from me.

A knock at my office door thankfully pulled me back to the present.

'Come in,' I called out.

I watched as Sakura, my research student, sheepishly walked in. She was a petite young woman in her early twenties but could easily be mistaken for a first-year degree student.

'We're not scheduled to meet until next week. Unless I've got my dates wrong.'

Sakura nodded as her cheeks flushed crimson. 'Yes, it's next Tuesday. But this isn't about my thesis. I wanted to talk to you about something personal.'

'Sure,' I replied. 'Is it urgent or can it wait?'

She looked uncomfortable. 'It's kind of urgent. It's not about me, it's about Riley. Riley Harrison.'

'Oh,' I answered, not quite able to conceal my surprise. 'Come in and take a seat.'

She closed my office door, walked over and pulled out the chair across from my desk.

I could feel a flush of shame scorch through me at the acknowledgement that Sakura – and Riley – must have heard the gossip about Ethan and me.

'You do know that Riley is Dr Ramirez's student, not mine,' I stated.

She nervously looked at me through her razor-sharp black fringe. 'I didn't know who to talk to about it, and then I recalled Riley saying that she lives with you.'

I nodded. 'Yes, Riley shares my house.'

I waited as Sakura gathered her thoughts. She seemed to be at odds as to whether to tell me.

'I'm sorry,' she said, 'this isn't something I would normally do. It's as if I'm betraying her.'

'Listen, if it doesn't feel right, don't tell me,' I advised her. 'To be honest, you might be better discussing your concerns with Dr Ramirez.'

I was sure that whatever concerns Sakura had regarding Riley, that Helena, as her PhD supervisor, would be the most appropriate person.

Sakura gazed down at her small, delicate hands as she weighed up what to do. Conflicted, she anxiously looked back up at me. 'It's nothing to do with her research. It's kind of personal. Whatever I tell you is confidential, right?'

'Of course,' I assured her. 'Anything you tell me stays within my office. Unless, that is, you tell me that someone is at high risk of harming themselves or others.'

Sakura stared at me. 'Do you already know?'

'Sorry?' I was starting to feel uncomfortable. I knew nothing about Riley and I wasn't sure that I wanted to hear whatever it was that Sakura wanted to disclose.

'About Riley? About the...' Sakura faltered. She looked scared. 'You won't repeat this, will you? And you won't tell Riley I told you?'

'Of course not,' I assured her.

I waited for Sakura to tell me why she was here, but she seemed conflicted.

'What's troubling you, Sakura?' It was clear that she was oscillating between confiding in me or keeping whatever was concerning her to herself.

She sighed. 'I was in the library, yesterday afternoon. When Riley saw me approach her, she quickly shut down whatever she was working on, grabbed her laptop, phone and bag and got up to leave.'

I waited.

Sakura's cheeks flushed an even deeper crimson. 'As she put her stuff in her bag, her sleeve got caught on the buckle and pulled up, exposing her wrist.'

I narrowed my eyes. 'I'm not sure I understand what you are getting at.'

'Her wrist was covered in scars. I mean, it was bad.'

I was shocked. 'Are you sure?'

She nodded.

'Did Riley say anything to you?'

Sakura shook her head. 'No. She acted as if nothing had happened. But she witnessed my reaction. She left so quickly that I didn't have a chance to talk to her. I'm worried about her. You know, in case she's self-harming,' Sakura stated.

'Do you think she's self-harming?' I asked.

Sakura nodded her head. 'Why else would her wrist and lower arms be covered in scars?'

'I don't know. Maybe Riley was involved in an accident?' I suggested, trying to downplay it.

'I don't think so. The scars looked to be caused by a knife or a razor blade.'

'Did they look recent?'

Sakura shook her head. 'I don't think so. But I only caught a glimpse, so I can't say for definite.'

'Has Riley ever mentioned her past to you?' I asked, knowing nothing of it myself.

'No,' answered Sakura. 'I don't really know her.'

'When did you first see her?'

Sakura shrugged. 'About three months back.'

'Three months ago?' I repeated, surprised.

As far as I knew, she had only transferred from Bristol a month or so back. Maybe Sakura had got it wrong. Or perhaps Riley had visited a couple of times to see whether she wanted to transfer here.

'Yes. I recognised her from around the department and in some lectures. I thought she might have been a newly appointed lecturer because of her age.'

I thought back to yesterday evening when I had seen Riley in my third-year lecture. Then, as soon as I had spotted her, she had disappeared.

'Maybe I shouldn't have said anything?' Sakura uneasily questioned in response to my silence.

'No, you've done the right thing by coming to me,' I assured her.

Not that I felt it was my place to talk to her. Helena was Riley's supervisor, but after yesterday, I was reluctant to ask for her intervention. But, given what Sakura had just confided, I had no choice. Helena would be the best person to disclose this information to concerning Riley. However, Riley was a mature student, in her early thirties, not in her late teens or early twenties. It was a difficult situation, but one that I knew Helena would handle with discretion and compassion.

Sakura suddenly looked anxious. 'You won't mention to her that I've been to see you?'

'No, of course not. I will have to mention it to Helena, as she is Riley's supervisor. All right?'

Sakura nodded. 'It's not as if she's a friend or anything. But after what I saw, it made me worry. I know she's older than me, but still...' She faltered.

'Of course, you're worried. Thanks, Sakura. You did the right thing.'

She stood up. 'I hope so.'

I watched as she left my office and went over what Sakura had said. Riley always wore long-sleeved clothes, despite the warmer weather. Maybe Sakura was right, and Riley was self-harming.

Or maybe she has tried to take her life.

Jaz came to mind. If I had no idea that my oldest and closest friend was suicidal, what chances did I have with someone who barely talked to me? But then, Jaz had stopped talking to me the weeks leading to her death. I thought about this evening with Issie,

Willow and Ava, and whether I would find out why Jaz had killed herself.

And the reason why they haven't you told you until now.

* * *

I looked at my phone; it was 6.45 p.m. The four of us were meeting at 7 p.m.

Filled with anticipation about the letter sent to Jaz, I had arrived early at The Queen Charlotte, on the corner of Goodge Street and Charlotte Street in Fitzrovia. The place was already busy, and I had been lucky to grab the last four seats outside. The late April weather was unseasonably warm and balmy, prompting people to sit outside and enjoy the sun's last rays.

I had requested a mineral water for myself, deciding to wait for the others rather than ordering for them. It was a beautiful little pub with an olde-worlde feel, furnished with rich dark wood panelling, wooden flooring and wooden and leather seats. The place may have specialised in speciality craft beers and beers from across the world, but their cocktails were exceptional.

I realised I would have to think up some excuse as to why I wasn't drinking alcohol as I didn't want Ava and Willow to know about the pregnancy, at least not yet.

My phone pinged. It was Issie. She had sent a message on the group WhatsApp chat:

Won't make tonight. At the emergency vets with Jasper. I think he's been poisoned x

I stared at the message.
Oh God... Poor Issie. Poor Jasper.
Jasper was her father's old cat. Issie's mother had died of

secondary breast cancer after fighting it for nine years when Issie was sixteen. With no other family, it had only been her and her father. Then he was diagnosed with prostate cancer three years back, but it was a late diagnosis and consequently had rapidly spread. So, all Issie had left was Jasper.

And all you have is Darcy, Claudia, and—

My eyes started to burn from the stinging sensation of threatening tears. The body-wrenching ache I felt at his loss was always beneath the surface, waiting to blindside me at the most unexpected moments. I had heard nothing regarding his disappearance nearly four weeks ago. No one had answered my flyers or posters. Nor had he been handed to a veterinary practice or one of the cat charities or animal shelters.

I slowly breathed out, refocusing on poor Issie's message.

Before I had a chance to reply to her, Willow rang.

'Hi, you. I'll be there in two secs,' Willow breezily greeted.

'Where are you?' I questioned, looking for her.

'Waving straight at you, silly.' Willow giggled.

I then spotted Willow standing on the edge of the opposite pavement, frantically waving as she waited to cross the road to join me.

'I'm ordering us a bottle of champagne,' she gushed, sounding giddy.

I broke into a grin. 'I take it from the sound of your voice that you've got some exciting news that you want to share.'

'Can you tell?'

I laughed. 'You always were terrible at keeping secrets.'

'Oh, Claudia, I don't think I have ever been so happy. I know tonight's maybe not the right time, what with this being about Jaz. But I knew I wouldn't be able to contain myself. So, I thought, why not? I know Jaz would have been thrilled for me.'

'If this is what I think it is, I am so happy for you! And Charles, of course.'

'Thank you,' Willow said. 'Don't breathe a word to the others until I announce it. Promise?'

'Promise,' I agreed, delighted for her.

I beamed at her as she darted out into the road between a gap in the traffic. Before I had a chance to react, a dark silver Range Rover sped towards her, coming out of nowhere. I watched, unable to do anything as it hit her, flipping her petite figure up into the air. She crashed down onto the car bonnet before being thrown into the road directly in front of me. A car screeched as it braked, swerving to avoid her lifeless body.

'WILLOW!' I screamed, jumping up, knocking my mineral water over.

Oh my God... Oh my God... WILLOW!

25

'WILLOW!' I yelled, shoving past the bystanders who had gathered from nowhere. 'MOVE!' I screeched. 'Move out the way!'

Pushing my way through, I managed to reach her. Collapsing to my knees, I bent over her. I stared in terror. Her eyes were closed, and her dark skin had turned a sickening sallow shade. Her nose was bleeding, and I could see blood trickling out from her right ear.

'Willow?' I cried out, my voice filled with desperation. 'Oh God, please be all right. Willow? Someone call 999,' I yelled up at the shocked, faceless gawkers circling us. 'NOW!' I barked at their lack of response.

I looked back down at Willow, conscious of the people gaping at her. Her floaty white dress had risen above her pierced navel. I pulled the dress down. The biker-style leather jacket she was wearing would have protected her arms from cuts and deep abrasions, unlike her bare legs. I blocked out the sight of the white bone protruding through her left lower leg as it lay twisted at a sickening irregular angle.

I noted that her chest wasn't moving. I put my ear to her mouth to see if she was breathing. Terrified, I then placed my right index and middle fingers under her neck, just beside her windpipe, to check her pulse.

'Is she still alive?' someone questioned.

I looked up at the cyclist now crouching down beside me.

'I can feel a pulse, but she's not breathing,' I answered.

'We need to move her into the recovery position to open up her airways,' the cyclist suggested.

'No! Don't. She might have spinal injuries,' I insisted.

'But...' He faltered, shaking his head, not knowing whether to listen to me or just proceed. He looked at me. 'She's not breathing. She'll die if we do nothing.'

'I'm serious. Don't touch her!'

'Are you a doctor?' he questioned.

Ignoring him, I moved to behind Willow's head and pulled back her tight curly black hair from her unresponsive face. I then rested my hands on either side of her cheeks.

'What are you doing? I thought you said not to move her?' the cyclist asked.

'Please!' I hissed. 'She's in respiratory arrest, and I need to concentrate.'

I breathed in. I needed to make sure my hands were steady. I placed my fingers at the bottom of her jawbone and my thumbs at the side of her cheekbones. Breathing out, I pressed down with my thumbs and simultaneously lifted forward and up with my fingers to open her airways.

Succeeding, I finally exhaled.

I looked at the cyclist. 'It's called the jaw thrust manoeuvre. It's used to clear the airways when an injury to the spine is suspected.'

'Has it worked?' he asked, noticing that I hadn't let go of her head.

I nodded as her chest rose. 'I need to keep my hands either side of her cheeks to prevent any movement until the paramedics take over.'

'How did you know to do that?'

'First-aid training.'

He frowned at me. 'Most people would freeze even with training.'

I swallowed. Tried to focus on his words and not the blood pooling beneath Willow's head.

She's going to be all right, Claudia. You've got her...

I dragged my gaze back up to the cyclist's. 'I... I witnessed a school friend have a terrible horse-riding accident. We were eleven, and she was competing. She... she hit the ground and she wasn't breathing. No one was able to save her. Not our teacher, or the judge. She died that day from acute respiratory and cardiac failure,' I explained.

'Oh... I'm sorry,' he awkwardly replied.

'Thanks,' I mumbled. 'I promised myself that I would get training so if I ever witnessed anything like that again, I would know what to do,' I added.

Embarrassed, I broke away from his sympathetic gaze. I then noticed Willow's black Givenchy bag. It had opened, and all her items, including her wallet, were scattered across the road.

'Could you get her bag, please?' I asked.

'Sure,' he replied, getting up.

'And her phone. She was on her phone when...' I faltered. I shook my head as I glanced around, but I couldn't see it. I could feel panic rising at the thought that I didn't know where her phone had gone. Willow was always on her phone; she wouldn't know what to do without it.

Oh God! Oh God! What if she—

I stopped myself. I couldn't go there.

'Don't worry. I'll find it,' he assured, seeing my distress.

The wail of sirens filled the evening air, signalling the nearing ambulances and police cars.

'Won't be long now, Willow. I promise,' I whispered to her. 'I promise that you're going to be okay. You hear me? You're going to be okay.'

I didn't let myself think about the alternative.

'I think I found everything,' the cyclist said as he placed Willow's bag next to me. 'I put her phone in her bag. Miraculously, it's not smashed up.'

I looked up at him. 'Thank you.'

'You know her?' he asked.

I hadn't expected that question. I looked down at Willow, noticing how young and fragile she looked. Out of the four of us, how could she, of all people, be lying here? Willow had never hurt anyone in her life. She exuded love and trust, even when it wasn't deserving.

I realised I was crying when my tears landed on her serene face.

I sniffed as I nodded, unable to take my eyes off her. 'Yes. I've known her most of my life.'

'Oh, Christ! I'm so sorry,' he sympathised.

I shook my head as tears continued to fall.

'She's going to be fine. I know she will,' I replied, not wanting to accept any other possibility.

* * *

I checked my phone, but there was no connection. I had called Charles on my way to the hospital and explained what had happened to Willow. I then rang Issie and Ava. Neither had answered, and so, I had left garbled voice messages about the accident. I then followed up with texts, letting them know where the ambulance had taken Willow. I was desperately hoping that they would get here soon.

I realised my hands were trembling as I lowered them, keeping hold of my phone as I waited. I didn't know what else to do. My mind was in freefall. I picked up the lukewarm paper cup of water on the Ikea-style table beside me and took a tentative sip as I focused on the internal window of the small light turquoise-coloured room. Someone had ushered me in here to wait for news of Willow. The blinds were open and, I could see a surgeon in blue scrubs walking in my direction. I expectantly looked at the door, but they continued to walk on. I accepted that not enough time had passed for someone to come and update me.

Willow had been examined by the emergency team when first admitted into hospital and then taken to theatre. That had been fifty-five long, painful minutes ago.

Suddenly, the door burst open.

'Charles,' I cried, stumbling to my feet as he walked into the room.

'Claudia? I... I... Oh God...'

'I know,' I mumbled as I hugged him, relieved that someone else was now here.

Finally, we released each other. I stepped back. It was odd, I barely knew Charles, but at that moment, it felt like we had always known each other. It was as if we were the only two people in the world. Our connection was the shared, cruel pain of not knowing whether the woman we both loved would live.

'What happened?' Charles asked.

I looked into his haunted eyes as they searched mine for answers. Before I had a chance to reply, there was a polite knock before two police officers walked in.

'Claudia Harper?' one of the officers asked.

'Yes,' I replied. I had already given my details to the officers who had turned up at the scene and then to the hospital staff.

'And you are?' he questioned, looking at Charles.

'I'm Willow's fiancé,' answered Charles. 'Charles. Charles Fernsby. I've... I've just arrived.'

I sat down. Charles did the same.

'I'm James, and this is Lauren,' the male officer said, introducing his female partner as they sat down opposite us. 'I understand that...' He paused for a moment and looked at the screen of the device he was holding. 'You were there when it happened, Claudia? When your friend was knocked down. Is that right?'

I nodded. 'I was waiting for Willow. We were meeting at The Queen Charlotte.'

I watched as the female officer took a note of it.

'Did you witness what happened?' he asked.

I tried to swallow, but my mouth was too dry. I picked up the paper cup of water and took a sip. I had replayed the scene of the car hitting Willow over in my head for the past fifty-five minutes. The noise of the impact of Willow's body slamming against the bonnet of the Range Rover, then the horrific screeching of braking tyres as she catapulted into the road of an oncoming vehicle. How they didn't run over her was beyond me.

'I... I was on the phone with Willow when it happened,' I replied, shaking my head as I recalled seeing her waving at me. 'She was on the opposite pavement. She then walked into the road heading towards me and...' I faltered. Again, I could hear the sickening sound of her body against the bonnet. Then the furious screeching of tyres as her body was thrown into the road.

I could feel my eyes smarting. I willed myself not to cry. Not here. Not now.

Focus, Claudia! Tell him what happened.

'This car came out of nowhere and hit her,' I recalled, wiping at the tears now falling.

'The car, can you tell me anything about it?' the male officer asked.

'It was a dark silver Range Rover.'

'Did you notice the driver?' he continued.

'I think it was a woman. It's a blur, if I'm honest with you.'

'This happened at approximately 6.48 p.m. It would still be light.'

I looked at him and nodded. It explained why the driver was wearing—

'Sunglasses. The driver was wearing sunglasses.'

The female officer shot her partner a look before making a note of it.

'Age?' he continued.

I shook my head. 'I don't know.'

'Hair colour?' he questioned.

'Dark, I think.'

The female officer recorded that detail.

'But I'm not sure. It happened so quickly. I was more focused on Willow.'

The male officer nodded. 'I understand. Would you be willing to help a police artist compile a sketch of the driver?'

'Sure. But, as I said, it's vague.'

'Who knew that Willow was meeting you this evening?' continued the male.

'What?' I said, thrown by the question. 'What are you suggest-ing? That it was deliberate?'

'All we're trying to do is establish the facts,' he calmly answered.

'Charles?' I asked, turning to him.

Shocked, he shook his head. 'No one,' he mumbled.

'Aside from the friends we were meeting tonight,' I answered.

'Who are they?' the male officer questioned.

'Ava Jefferson, Isabella Richardson-Willoughby and myself,' I explained.

I watched, alarmed, as the female officer took down their names.

'Were they with you?'

'I don't understand,' I said, staring at the officers.

'Please answer the question. Were they with you?' the male officer repeated.

'No... Issie had...' I recalled her WhatsApp message. 'Issie had an emergency and cancelled and Ava didn't turn up. I don't know why.'

If she had done, she would have witnessed Willow being attended to by the paramedics. Or, if she arrived late, the area would have been cordoned off as a crime scene.

'Have you heard from either of them?' he asked.

'No. But there's no mobile signal in here. I expect Ava will be here soon. But Issie lives in Kent, and her cat is ill...' I broke off, realising I wasn't making any sense.

Willow might die, Claudia! And you're talking about Issie's cat.

'I see,' noted the female officer. 'And why were you meeting up?'

'It was to commemorate our school friend, Jaz. She died nearly two months back, and we were getting together to—' I stopped myself.

The letter, Claudia. You were getting together to find out about this letter someone sent Jaz days before she died. Tell them that! That Ava had this letter: that the three of them knew something about Jaz's death. They knew something and kept it back from you.

Then it hit me: *Oh my God... Was Jaz's death really a suicide?*

I pushed the terrifying thought away.

'Who arranged it?' the female officer questioned.

'I suppose it was Issie – Isabella.'

She nodded.

'I don't understand. Are you insinuating that either one of them would want to hurt Willow? I mean, that is crazy! We've all been friends since the age of eleven. We boarded together, shared a dormitory for years. It isn't even possible to consider that either of them would do anything to... to Willow.'

'As we said, we are simply trying to establish the facts.'

No one spoke as the horrifying insinuation hung in the stale air.

'You're certain this wasn't just a terrible accident?' I asked, unable to reconcile myself with the alternative.

Another look passed between the two officers.

'Please? If you know something, we have a right to be told,' I stated.

The male officer sighed. 'We have three witnesses at the scene who said that the vehicle that hit Willow had been idling further down the road. That as soon as Willow stepped out onto the road, it pulled out and sped towards her. We don't believe that's a coincidence.'

The door suddenly opened as a doctor entered the claustrophobic room. She nodded at the two police officers before expectantly turning to Charles.

Charles jumped up. 'Willow?'

'She is still in surgery,' she explained. 'But we wanted to update you.'

'How is she?' Charles questioned, unable to keep the fear out of his voice.

'She has sustained various broken bones, and she has a punctured lung and damaged kidney. But it is the blunt trauma to her head that concerns us. She has suffered a traumatic brain injury. But we're doing everything we can for her.'

I watched as Charles dragged a shaky hand back through his hair as he absorbed this information.

'The next few hours are critical. I suggest you contact Willow's immediate family,' she gently advised.

'Her parents live in France. I talked to them about fifteen minutes ago, and they're making plans to get back to the UK.'

'I suggest they do it ASAP.'

Charles took a step back, momentarily losing his balance.

'As soon as I have an update, I'll be in touch,' the doctor said, giving him a sympathetic nod.

At a loss for words, Charles watched as she turned and left.

'Hey,' I said to Charles, reaching my hand up to touch his arm.

He looked back down at me.

'Willow may be petite, but she's one hell of a fighter. She'll get through this, Charles. I promise,' I assured him.

He nodded, but I could see the doubt in his eyes.

The two police officers stood up.

'If you remember anything about the driver, let us know,' the male officer said as he handed me his card.

'Of course,' I replied.

'We'll be in touch if we need you to help our police artist compose a sketch of the driver,' the female officer advised before following her partner out of the room.

I watched as Charles collapsed back down on the chair.

All I could think was, why Willow?

Why would someone want to hurt her, of all people?

And if it was intentional, who knew we were meeting at The Queen Charlotte?

26

SATURDAY

I walked outside, relishing the feel of the cool late April spring night air brushing against my clammy skin. The irony of the season hit me. It brought with it the promise of regeneration, of new beginnings and yet... for Willow, it had abruptly halted her life, while her fate was decided.

I pulled my long hair back, tying it up. I was exhausted, but adrenaline – *fear* – refused to let me acknowledge it.

Anxious, I checked my phone. No response from Issie or Ava.

Nothing!

I then remembered that Issie had taken Jasper to the vets.

Oh God... Jasper.

Issie's silence didn't bode well.

I thought of Ava and what her excuse could be. Could she still be angry with me over the messages I had sent Jaz the night she died?

How can you be so sure that she's seen them, Claudia?

I conceded I wasn't.

And now Willow was in a medically induced coma, and her next few hours were critical.

Where the fuck are you, Ava?

There was no point calling or messaging either of them again. I had left both a barrage of frantic voicemails and WhatsApp messages. All I could do was wait.

I prepared myself for my next call – Jacob. It was only right that he heard from me about Willow.

'Hey...' I awkwardly mumbled when he finally picked up.

'Yeah?' he groggily muttered.

'Jacob...' I began, struggling to find the words.

'Are you all right?' he asked, suddenly alert.

'Yes, I'm fine,' I replied. 'It's...' I faltered, trying not to cry.

'What's wrong? You know it's after one thirty in the morning.'

I nodded as tears silently escaped.

'Claudia? You're scaring me. Are you sure you are all right?'

For some reason, hearing his voice made the tears glide more freely down my cheeks.

'I'm here,' he said softly.

'It's Willow...' I began. 'She was knocked down by a car and is in a medically induced coma.'

'Oh, Christ! Where is she?'

'UCH,' I numbly answered. 'I've just come outside. I've been waiting with Charles while she was in theatre.'

'Is she out of surgery?'

'Yes. But no one's allowed to see her. Willow's brother, Eli, is here with Charles, so he's not on his own.'

'Are you going back in to join them?'

'No. Charles insisted that I go home and rest. I... I saw it happen, Jacob. I witnessed the car hit Willow, and then...' My voice cracked as the memory of Willow hit by the Range Rover assaulted me. The sickening thud of impact. Her floaty white dress billowing in the air before crashing down, her body limp, her limbs twisted, broken.

'I'm coming to get you,' Jacob stated. 'All right?'

'No...' I mumbled. 'I... I just want to go home.'

'I'll take you home,' Jacob insisted.

'No,' I repeated, not wanting to see anyone right now. 'There's a cab right here.'

'I'm worried about you being in shock,' he pointed out.

'I'll be fine. Look. I'll call you in the morning when I know more about Willow.'

'Promise?'

'I promise,' I replied.

'I love you, Claudia.'

Jacob's words caught me by surprise. Conflicted emotions choked me.

All I wanted was to have Jacob hold me. To take me to bed and make love to me. I yearned to feel a physical connection with him to remind myself that I was still alive, to override the coldness that had taken hold. To have Jacob take away the pain inside me, the knowledge that life was arbitrary, to stop the horror of that life-altering event from replaying again and again in my head.

Without thinking, I whispered back, 'I love you.'

I cut the call, not sure whether he heard me. Not sure whether I wanted him to have heard.

* * *

I unlocked the front door and quietly crept into the house. It felt like a mausoleum. The dark air sought me out, clinging to my body. Laughter and the promise of the future once filled this two-bedroomed Victorian house, which now creaked and groaned as if sighing with regret and sadness. There was no overweight furball of a Darcy to greet me, screeching at my absence, wanting me to pick him up and reassure him I would never leave again. And I wanted the same from Jacob, the man I still loved. I needed him, more than ever, to hold me and tell me that everything would be all right.

How could it ever be all right, Claudia?

They were both gone. As was Jaz. Now Willow...

It was after 3 a.m. and I didn't want to disturb Riley. Still wired and needing to try to unwind and process everything, I headed to the kitchen to make myself a drink.

I found myself sitting at the rustic wooden dining-room table in the open-plan kitchen blankly staring out into the blackness of the small, secluded garden, cradling lukewarm tea. I couldn't bring myself to drink it. Nor could I go upstairs to bed. I knew that as soon as I closed my eyes, the horrifying image of Willow's body being thrown into the air and then landing with a sickening thud on the road in front of me would haunt me.

Numb, I waited. For what, I wasn't sure. But that was all I could do. Wait for this nightmare to end. Wait for Charles to call and tell me that Willow would survive. For Issie to ring me and tell me she was on her way so we could be together. Anything rather than acknowledge that I was sat here on my own, waiting for one of my oldest school friends not to die.

I was on the verge of calling Jacob and asking him to come over when my phone suddenly rang. I snatched it up from the table, assuming it would be Charles with news about Willow. Or Issie.

I was surprised to see that it was Zain calling me.

'Zain?' I hesitantly replied.

'Look, I'm sorry to be calling you at this hour. But I assumed you would still be awake. I heard about Willow.'

'How?' I asked, puzzled. 'Did Jacob call you?'

'No, Jacob hasn't rung me. I've been assigned to investigate the incident.'

'Sorry?' I questioned, thrown.

'I'm heading the investigation,' he repeated. 'I just wanted you to know.'

I shakily breathed out. None of this was making sense.

Someone targeted Willow. They tried to kill her. Why?

'The vehicle that hit Willow,' Zain began.

I could hear the tension in his words.

'A witness was able to give us a partial registration, but we have accessed CCTV footage showing the vehicle's full registration,' he explained.

'Okay. That's good, isn't it?' I asked, unsure as to why he sounded so reticent.

'The Range Rover Velar...' He hesitated.

I waited.

'It's registered to Ava Jefferson.'

It took me a moment to absorb what he had just said.

'Ava? My Ava? No. You must have made a mistake,' I said, stunned.

'I'm sorry,' Jacob replied. 'There's no mistake.'

'No. That doesn't make any sense. Ava would never hurt anyone, let alone Willow.'

'I'm sorry. I wish it wasn't the case, but...' Zain faltered.

I hesitated, struggling to absorb what he had just told me. It was nonsensical.

'Someone must have stolen her car,' I reasoned. It was the only logical explanation.

He didn't respond.

'Zain? Did you hear me?'

'Yes, I heard you. Her car wasn't stolen.'

'How do you know?' I demanded.

'Ava is in custody, Claudia.'

'What?' I questioned, shocked.

'I'm sorry, Claudia. Really, I am.'

'No. You must have made a mistake. You've arrested the wrong person. Someone must have stolen Ava's car, Zain. I mean...' I found myself lost for words.

'There is impact damage to the bonnet of her Range Rover in keeping with the hit-and-run,' Zain quietly explained.

'But...' I faltered. 'But that doesn't mean that Ava was driving the car.'

'The CCTV footage shows a driver who matches Ava's appearance. The same with the three witness statements. A woman in her late twenties to early thirties with long, dark chestnut brown hair wearing sunglasses,' Zain informed me.

I suddenly felt nauseous.

'The footage also shows the vehicle speeding up as it approaches Willow after she stepped out onto the road,' Zain added in response to my silence.

'No...' I mumbled. 'This has to be a mistake. Someone who looked like Ava must have stolen her car and—'

'We picked the vehicle up outside Ava's property in Fulham,' Zain explained, cutting me off. 'So far, the only fingerprints recovered from inside the vehicle are Ava's. Also, the sunglasses worn by the driver were inside the vehicle.'

I felt faint. I bent my head down, and shakily breathed in, then out.

'Are you all right?' Zain asked.

No! You've just told me that Ava has tried to kill Willow! How can I be all right?

'I'm sorry for calling you so late with this, Claudia. I appreciate it must come as a shock. But I wanted to personally let you know, rather than you hearing about it second hand from someone else or in the news,' Zain continued, filling in the silence.

Then it struck me: What about Charles? Did he know?

'Willow's fiancé. Has he been informed?'

'Yes, I've told him that we have a suspect in custody who we are about to charge.'

Oh my God! He's talking about Ava! AVA!

I suddenly felt nauseous.

I cut the call and ran upstairs. I knelt on the floor next to the toilet until the urge to vomit again abated. I wasn't sure whether it was the pregnancy or the shock that had forced me to my knees.

Satisfied that it had passed, I shakily stood up, sloshed my mouth out with mouthwash and then headed for my bedroom, creeping past Riley's closed door.

Once in bed, I picked up my phone. I understood now why Ava had not answered my voice message. But Issie's silence was disturbing. I needed to talk to her. I still couldn't accept that Ava was responsible for the hit-and-run. It wasn't possible. Ava may have been guilty of acting coolly towards me lately, but I knew she would never hurt anyone, especially Willow. I was sure that Issie would be able to make sense of what was happening.

I called her. Again, it cut to voicemail.

Shit, Issie! Answer your goddamned phone, will you.

It struck me that maybe something terrible had happened to Jasper. It would explain her silence. I imagined that she wouldn't even think to look at her phone. That was if she even had it switched on.

'Hey, I'm worried that I haven't heard from you. Please call me ASAP. Please?'

I hung up. I then sent a follow-up text:

Call me! This is urgent!! x

I stared at my screen, waiting for a reply – nothing.

I couldn't quell the disquiet I felt that something was wrong. That Issie was in danger. I tried to talk myself down. That there would be a rational explanation for her silence, such as Jasper hadn't pulled through at the vets. Then it struck me that something had happened to my remaining three childhood friends the night we were supposed to discuss Jaz's suicide. Issie was atypically incommunicado, and Willow was currently critically ill in a medically induced coma after a hit-and-run. Worse, the police believed Ava to be responsible for this heinous act. Significantly, Ava was the linchpin. She was the one who knew the contents of the letter and its connection to Jaz's decision to take her life.

What was in that letter and why had they withheld it from me?

I tried calling Issie again. I needed answers. It cut straight to voicemail.

Maybe she was asleep?

Or maybe, something had happened to her as well?

I wrestled in my mind, oscillating between believing that I was overreacting to fearing that ignoring my gut feeling, which was screaming at me that something was wrong with Issie, could lead to her life being in jeopardy.

I decided to call Zain back.

He immediately answered: 'Claudia? Are you okay?'

'Yeah. Sorry, I cut you off before. I wasn't feeling so good,' I explained.

'Understandable,' Zain sympathised. 'You've already had a rough night, and my call was a lot to take in.'

'Zain?'

'Yeah?'

'I know I'm going to sound crazy here, but I'm worried about Issie,' I confided.

'How so?'

'Well, you know that the four of us were supposed to be meeting up for drinks.'

'Sure,' he answered.

'Issie arranged it all.' I paused, trying to find the right words.

'And?' questioned Zain.

'Issie messaged our group chat to say she couldn't meet us as she had to take her cat to the emergency vet. But I have messaged and left voicemails with her about Willow since it happened, but no reply.'

'Maybe she's lost her phone. Or something came up.'

'She has access to her messages on her laptop. So, why would she not answer me? This isn't like her.'

'Listen, I'm sure there is a rational explanation. You've been through a lot—'

'Something's wrong. Issie has never ignored me before!' I argued, cutting him off.

'As I said, I'm sure there's a rational explanation. Maybe she's heard about Willow and doesn't feel up to talking.'

I sighed. I wasn't buying it.

'You want my advice? Get some sleep. She'll no doubt contact you when she wakes up. I imagine she's asleep as we speak.'

'I don't know. There is something about Issie's silence which scares me,' I confessed. 'I'm tempted to drive to Kent and check on her.'

'Why don't you wait until I finish here? I can be at yours about eight, and I'll drive to Issie's with you.'

'Are you sure?'

'Yeah. But I'm certain by then Issie will have reached out to you.'

'I hope so.'

'Promise me you won't do anything stupid and that you will wait for me. You're tired and in shock.'

'I'll wait for you,' I assured him.

'Good. Now try to get some sleep,' Zain suggested before cutting the call.

Feeling marginally relieved, I switched the bedside lamp off and lay down. Maybe Zain was right, and Issie was reeling from the shock of what had happened to Willow.

I turned over onto my side, staring into the shadows, willing my unruly mind to be still. I lay there, struggling to fall asleep for what felt like hours. I rolled over and checked my phone. It was now 4.03 a.m., and still nothing from Issie.

Frustrated, I leaned up on my elbow and punched my pillow, then lay down again. I slowly breathed out, trying to ignore the relentless thoughts hurtling through my head. But it was pointless. I couldn't silence the questions that kept coming at me. None of what had happened made any sense.

Why would Ava hurt Willow?

I closed my eyes, but all I could see was the dark silver Range Rover hitting Willow. I tried to focus on the driver, but her features were still too hazy, obscured behind sunglasses.

Irritated and flooded with heart-exploding adrenaline, I heavily breathed out.

If I could see the person driving, then I could testify to the police that it wasn't Ava, that it was someone else.

It had to be. But, who?

And were they targeting my friends?

Issie immediately came to mind. Something was wrong. I could feel it. She would never ignore the messages I had left her. Not when Willow was fighting for her life in hospital.

I recalled the book *The Gift of Fear: Survival Signals That Protect Us from Violence* by Gavin de Becker; it had struck a chord with me at the time, so much so, the impact of his words had stayed with me. He espoused how every individual, particularly women and girls, should listen and learn to trust the 'gift' of their gut feeling: that dismissing or downplaying a hunch could severely cost you – ultimately your life.

Every fibre of my being was screaming at me that Issie was in danger.

I didn't have time – Issie didn't have time – to wait for Zain to finish his shift.

I thought of gentle, kind Willow fighting for her life in the hospital. Then beautiful, brilliant Jaz, her cold body, confined to spend eternity buried alongside her Scottish Highland ancestors under the baleful shadow of the Cuillins.

What if someone had also targeted Issie? Just as they had Willow.

And Jaz.

Was Jaz's death really a suicide?

27

I took a glug of water as I drove past a turn-off for the next village. I glanced at Google Maps, connected to my car from my iPhone. I would soon be at Issie's cottage. It was hidden down a dirt track roughly a mile outside of Waltham and seven miles from Canterbury. The two hours and twenty minutes it had taken to drive from West London had passed in a blur. All I recalled was that the roads had been deathly quiet. I couldn't even remember the handover of the black abyss of the night to the furious scarlet dawn, focused entirely on getting to Issie as fast as possible.

The ominous blood-red sunrise had added to my unease about Issie, evoking the words of Shakespeare's poem, 'Venus and Adonis':

> *Like a red morn, that ever yet betoken'd,*
> *Wreck to the seaman, tempest to the field,*
> *Sorrow to the shepherds, woe unto the birds.*
> *Gust and foul flaws to herdmen and to herds.*

I knew I was behaving irrationally, but I couldn't shake the disquiet that had taken me hostage. That had led me to drive like a maniac to Issie's to rid myself of the tight knot of fear that had taken up residence in the pit of my stomach.

But Issie lived alone, in the middle of nowhere. What if something had happened to her and she couldn't reach her phone to ring for help? Or she had been burgled and left tied up? I could taste the bitter, metallic taste of blood from continuously biting my bottom lip as my unruly mind threw terrifying scenarios at me.

I then thought of Zain. I hadn't told him that I was driving – alone – to Issie's. But I couldn't just sit around and wait until he finished his shift. I would call him when I arrived to let him know.

I glanced out at the Kent countryside to break away from the torturous thoughts driving me to distraction. But its glorious spring lushness and the explosion of pink sakura cherry blossom trees were lost on me as I sped past, driven by fear and blinded by panic.

Where the hell are you, Issie?

She still hadn't returned my messages or calls.

It was now 6.45 a.m.

What if someone has hurt her? She's all alone and—

Stop it! Stop going down that dark, treacherous rabbit hole.

I shakily breathed out, trying to stop myself from going over the possible 'what if' scenarios.

I forced myself to concentrate. I needed to keep an eye out for the turning coming up on that would lead me to Issie – at least, I prayed it would.

Spotting it, I pulled off onto the dense tree-lined country lane. Issie's property was tucked away a half of a mile or so from the road. It wasn't long before I reached the row of centuries-old stone cottages. I drove past her neighbours' properties before pulling up outside Issie's.

I noted her white 1958 Austin Healey Sprite, once her father's, parked on the track that led down the side of her property. I looked up at the dormer leaded window. Her curtains were closed, suggesting she was still in bed. Maybe Zain was right, and Issie was reeling from the news about Willow. I suddenly felt foolish driving all this way to find out that her radio silence was because she didn't want to see anyone. I would call Zain and tell him I was here once I had been in the cottage and found Issie to be okay. However, I now needed to desperately pee.

Aside from squatting behind a tree and getting caught by one of Issie's neighbours, I had no choice but to wake her up. I grabbed my mobile, threw it in my bag and climbed out of the car.

I opened the gate, wincing as it creaked objectionably, and walked up the winding path that led to the heavy, old wooden door. I raised my hand to knock on it when I realised it was open ever so slightly. I could feel the panic rising in me.

I pushed the door open. 'Issie? It's Claudia,' I tentatively called out.

I waited. There was no reply.

'Issie?'

Again, no response.

'Issie?'

Silence.

I questioned whether, in a state of shock, Issie had left the door open after hearing the news about Willow.

I stepped anxiously inside. The front door led straight into the living room. Nothing looked out of place.

Drawn to the impressive stone inglenook with the large, wood-burning stove which dominated the room, I noted the crocheted blanket and book discarded on the battered old leather armchair beside it. I cast my eye over the matching two-seater leather couch facing the inglenook, noting the large scatter cushions discarded on the rug, along with the throw.

'Issie?' I called as I walked through the living room, heading into the kitchen.

There was no sign of her.

I glanced around, noticing the wine glass containing dregs of red wine standing in the Belfast sink and the empty wine bottle on the marble worktop. I turned to the racing-green AGA, expecting the kettle to be simmering on the right-hand hotplate. Issie was a confessed coffee addict, and she couldn't think straight without copious amounts first thing in the morning. However, the kettle wasn't on the hotplate, nor was Issie's cafetière and favourite mug out in preparation. Maybe she was still in bed. It was a Saturday morning, after all. But why would she leave the front door open? However, Issie had often extolled how safe she felt out here compared to when she had lived in London, but I still found it odd.

'Issie?' I called out again, hearing the tremor in my voice.

I waited for a response.

Again, silence.

I looked out of the kitchen window at the back garden to see if Issie was outside or in the studio. I couldn't see any sign of her, and the studio was too far away to say whether anyone was inside. It wasn't unusual for Issie to work all night or get up early to work on a painting.

I decided to check upstairs first before going out to her art studio. I couldn't hold off the urge to pee for much longer. As I turned back around, I slipped.

'Christ!' I cursed as I regained my balance.

Inspecting the old stone floor, I found a small pool of liquid. Feeling something cold hit my head, I looked up. A splash of water simultaneously fell onto my forehead.

'What the hell?' I muttered to myself at the spreading dark yellow water stain on the ceiling above me.

Another drip of water leaked through the cracking plaster and landed on me, trickling down my face. As I wiped it from my cheek, I heard a faint noise above.

'Issie?' I shouted out.

Again, another muffled sound.

I ran out of the kitchen to the open-plan oak staircase in the lounge.

'Issie?' I cried out as I climbed the stairs two at a time.

I reached the top of the staircase and turned onto the landing.

'ISSIE?' I screamed out, dropping my bag when I saw her. 'Oh my God! Oh God!'

It took my brain a moment to register. Issie was lying prone on the floor. Her body was naked. I swallowed, trying to digest the scene in front of me, which made no sense.

My legs felt as if they were going to give way. I somehow managed to stumble forwards.

'Oh my God! Issie? Issie?' I collapsed next to her.

It was then that I noticed the blood. A deep crimson was spreading out from beneath her body, discolouring the rustic white wool carpet.

'Oh shit! Shit! Issie? What happened?' I questioned, noticing a trail of blood leading from her bedroom. At that moment, I understood that she must have dragged herself along the hallway when she'd heard me downstairs. 'Issie?' I cried, pulling her long, wild blonde spirals back from her sickeningly ashen, clammy face.

I didn't know what to do. I was frozen with panic.

COME ON! ACT!

I could hear the words screaming at me in my head to do something. Anything. But I couldn't move.

DO SOMETHING! FOR FUCK'S SAKE, CLAUDIA! SHE'S DYING IN FRONT OF YOU!

I shakily breathed out the air I had been holding in. I needed to act.

'Issie?' I tremulously questioned. 'Issie? Can you hear me?'

When she didn't respond, I gently placed my right index and middle fingers on the side of her neck in the hollow area beside her larynx. Her pulse was rapid – dangerously so.

'Come on...' I frantically muttered. 'Come on, Issie!'

Fuck! Fuck! Fuck!

Her lips were tinged blue as she laboured for breath. I had no idea how long it would take paramedics to get here, but my gut feeling told me too long. I needed to try to stop her from bleeding out before calling 999.

I staggered up and ran to the bathroom for towels to press against whatever trauma was causing the blood loss. I could already hear the water flowing before I pushed open the door. I stared in disbelief. The cold-water tap was pouring out water over the full Victorian claw-foot bathtub onto the flooded floor. I splashed through the pooling water on the floor and turned the tap off. I didn't have time to question why or who had left it running.

I grabbed a handful of towels and dashed back to Issie.

'I'm here, Issie,' I said, kneeling back down next to her. 'I need to move you, all right?' I warned before carefully rolling her onto her side. 'I'm sorry, Issie,' I cried as her eyelids fluttered as she moaned in reaction to the movement.

I gagged at the visceral sight.

'Oh God! Issie? What happened?'

Blood was seeping out from a deep five-inch incision below her navel.

'Shit! Shit!' I cursed.

I held my breath as I checked that nothing was protruding out, like glass or some other sharp object, before firmly pressing a towel against the gaping wound to stem the flow of blood. I kept it there while trying to reach for my bag with my other hand. Managing to grab it, I pulled it over to me and searched for my mobile. I dialled 999 and waited. I watched, terrified as the white towel started to turn red.

Frantic, I listened as the emergency call handler answered.

'I need an ambulance,' I hurriedly explained. 'My friend, she's... she's bleeding from her stomach. It's deep. Really deep. Please... Please you need to get someone here quickly. Her pulse is faint. I... don't know how long she's been lying here...'

'Firstly, I need you to slow down. All right?' a female voice calmly advised.

'Okay,' I answered, shakily breathing out.

'Your name?'

'It's my friend who's hurt,' I hurriedly answered in frustration.

'Your name and then your friend's name and your address,' she continued.

'Claudia, my name is Claudia Harper,' I fired.

'Good. Now your friend's name?'

'Isabella... Isabella Richardson-Willoughby. Her address is 1 Rose Cottage. It's a mile or so outside of Waltham. That's where I am. Where she's...' I faltered as I stared at Issie.

'Okay, Claudia.'

'Claudia,' she repeated. 'Can you hear me?'

'Yes,' I mumbled, unable to comprehend how Issie had been so badly hurt.

'I need you to tell me exactly what's happened,' the call handler stated.

'I don't know what happened. I think... I think...' I paused as the horrifying thought struck me. 'Someone's stabbed her.'

Fear coursed through me at the idea that whoever had stabbed

Issie might also hurt me. Could that person still be in the cottage? I looked over my shoulder, expecting someone to be coming up the stairs. But there was no one there.

I spun my head back to Issie as she let out a low moan.

'Oh God... Please. You've got to help me. I...I...' I stopped, staring in panic at the now saturated hand towel. 'I need help. Issie needs help. She's lost a lot of blood.'

'Claudia, can you see where the blood is coming from?'

'Yes. Yes... Her stomach...She's been stabbed,' I found myself repeating.

'I need you to try and stop the bleeding by pressing something against the wound,' she instructed.

'I'm doing that. I'm trying to stem the bleeding with towels,' I replied, distracted, as I cradled the phone against my shoulder as I reached for another towel.

'That's good, Claudia. Continue doing that until the paramedics arrive. An ambulance is on its way. I'll stay on the line with you until they get there. Okay?'

Issie suddenly vomited.

'Oh God, Issie.' I automatically used the towel I had grabbed to wipe her mouth and chin. 'Shit!' I cursed, realising that I had relaxed the pressure on her injury.

I reapplied the now blood-drenched towel and another one on top of it. As I did, I recoiled in horror at what I had somehow missed on her stomach. I lost my grip on my phone as it fell, bouncing on the carpet.

'Issie?' I mumbled, shocked.

There were deep lacerations on the right side of her stomach above the main wound. It took me a moment to make out that these weren't random slashes but letters.

Someone had etched 'R' and 'S' above her navel.

'Fuck! Fuck! Fuck!' I muttered, filled with panic. I blocked out the distant voice of the emergency call handler calling out from the phone lying on the floor. 'Oh fuck, Issie? Why would someone want to do this to you?' I cried as I pressed the fresh towel against the wound.

I watched as her eyelids started to open.

'Issie? Issie? I'm here with you,' I said, stroking her face with my other hand.

Her lips started to move, but no words were coming out.

'Issie? What is it?' I asked, crouching close to her mouth so I could hear her.

I watched as her lips started to move again as her eyes filled with terror.

'I can't hear what you're saying.'

'Re...' she attempted, struggling to breathe. 'Re... Bec...'

I felt sick as I watched her agitation as she tried to continue speaking.

'Ca...'

'Issie... Shh...' I murmured, trying to calm her down.

'Sss... Spencer,' she gasped.

I stroked her face. 'Issie... I don't understand... Rebecca? Rebecca Spencer? Who is she?'

I watched as she tried to swallow. Failed. Her dry lips opened and then closed again as she struggled for breath.

'Issie?'

But she stared straight past at me as her shallow breathing became even more erratic.

'Issie? Issie?' I frantically questioned as her eyelids fluttered before finally closing. 'No! Issie, stay with me. You've got to keep awake! ISSIE!'

Her skin had suddenly become cold and sticky.

No! No! NO!

I yanked my oversized baggy wool jumper with one hand while

somehow managing to keep the towels pressed against her abdomen. I covered her with it and then pulled her into me to keep her warm until the paramedics arrived.

'You're going to get through this. Do you hear me? You've just got to stay with me, Issie. Yeah?' I muttered as I held her face against mine, trying not to panic as her breathing became more and more irregular. 'Don't do this to me! Don't you dare! You hear me? You can't leave me!' I sobbed through hot, angry tears. 'I can't lose you like Jaz. Please... Please.'

I realised that I couldn't feel her laboured breath on me any more.

'ISSIE?' I screamed as her head lolled backwards. 'No... No!' I hoarsely sobbed.

My mind went into a blind panic. I didn't know what to do.

Oh God... Oh God... Please don't let her die. Please, God. Not Issie!

I heard myself cry out in anguish.

Do something! Claudia! Do something! DON'T LET HER DIE!

The words managed to drown out my wails of despair, forcing me into action. I felt for a pulse, but I couldn't find one. I scrambled onto my knees and laid Issie down on her back. I then opened her airways. I checked to see whether she was breathing.

She had stopped.

'Issie? Come on. Please,' I desperately muttered to myself.

I placed my hands over Issie's heart and began thirty hard, deep compressions on her chest. By the tenth count, I heard a sickening crunch as one of her ribs broke from the force of the impact. Reaching thirty, I stopped and bent over her lips and breathed twice into her mouth before resuming the chest compressions. Beads of sweat rolled down my forehead into my eyes from the exertion of keeping the oxygenated blood flowing to her brain. Sometime later, I heard sirens, followed by someone yelling something from downstairs.

I continued CPR as multiple footsteps thundered up the wooden stairs.

'Hey, love. How about we take over now?'

Blinded by furious tears, I allowed the paramedics to pull me back. I collapsed against the wall and stared at the two letters – 'R' and 'S' – on her lifeless blood-soaked body.

Who did this to you, Issie? Who would hate you so much as to want to mutilate and kill you? And why?

28

I leaned out of the car door and vomited.

I kept my head between my knees, waiting for the retching to pass.

'Here you go.'

I reached out with a shaking hand and grabbed the open bottle of water from the police officer. I took a glug and swilled it around my mouth before spitting it out. Then repeated the same action.

Finally, sure that I wasn't going to vomit again, I straightened up and handed the water bottle back to the officer. I shook my head, unable to speak. I then turned away from him, retreating into the rear of the car. I closed my watering eyes against the chaos around me. People were asking questions – questions I couldn't answer. I just wanted to be back home in my bed, curled up in a foetal position, pretending that none of this had happened.

I tried to block everything out around me, but the relentless ringing of a phone pierced the air. It took me a few minutes to absorb the fact that the intrusion was coming from my bag. I couldn't remember picking my bag up or even being led down the stairs or out of the cottage to the police car. I blindly groped for my bag, wanting to silence the shrill. I pulled my phone out and forced myself to look at who was calling.

I pressed decline.

Zain immediately called back.

I was about to switch my phone off, but then I remembered Willow – and Ava. Maybe this was about them.

I answered. Waited.

'Claudia? Where are you?'

'I...' But I couldn't get the words out.

Just hearing a familiar voice made the tears fall even harder.

'Claudia? What's going on?'

'I... Issie...' I sobbed, choking on the words.

'You didn't? Didn't I tell you to wait for me? I'm outside your place now. I mean, what possessed you to go on your own?'

I bit down on my bottom lip to stop myself from sobbing uncontrollably. 'Issie...' I somehow managed to repeat.

'What's happened?'

I couldn't say it.

'Claudia? Tell me what's happened.'

'Claudia? Talk to me. CLAUDIA!'

I turned to the police officer by the side of the open rear passenger door. I stretched my trembling hand out, handing the phone to him as I shook my head.

He took my phone. 'This is PC Gareth Huntingdon.'

Numb, I let his words drift over me, unable to accept that one of my oldest school friends was dead. Worse, murdered.

I closed my eyes, not wanting to know any more, willing the blackness to come to stop the pain.

* * *

'Claudia?'

I ignored the voice.

'Claudia? We're here.'

I forced myself to open my eyes. I realised the car had stopped moving.

Struggling to understand what was happening, I turned my head in the direction of the voice.

A female police officer was patiently holding the rear passenger door open for me.

'Where am I?'

'Canterbury police station,' she answered.

'My car?'

'It's safe.'

'I... I... just want to go home.'

'Of course you do. But first, we need a statement from you. Then we'll get someone to take you home.'

Numb, I looked down at my trembling hands. Issie's blood covered them.

'I... I... I,' I stuttered, unable to continue. Or move. Unable to stop them, I could feel the tears escaping down my cheeks.

The officer gently helped me out of the car, and guided me into the police station.

I waited, numb, while she and her colleague talked to the custody sergeant.

They both then led me to a small interview room with four seats and a small table. I sank into one of the seats as I tried to rationalise what was happening to me. But it was all a blur. All I knew for certain was Issie was dead.

* * *

I had no idea how much time had passed. At some point, I'd asked to go to the toilet. I had told the police every detail of last night, from Willow's hit-and-run with Ava's car to Issie cancelling because of an emergency visit to the vet with a suspected poisoned Jasper. Then her deathly silence. All of which had led me to Issie's cottage.

'Take your time,' the female officer kindly advised.

I nodded, as I tried to swallow, but failed. It felt as if something was stuck at the back of my throat. I picked up the paper cup of water in front of me and took a sip. Unable to stop my hands from trembling, some of the water spilt on the table as I placed it back down.

'Sorry,' I mumbled.

'It's okay,' she reassured.

I looked from her to her older male colleague.

'Issie's cat, Jasper?' I suddenly questioned. 'Can you find out what happened to him? I... I need to know if he's all right. Issie has no next of kin, so...' I faltered. 'Willow, Ava and me, we're all Issie has...' I shook my head, tried to swallow back the tears. 'Had...'

'Of course,' the female officer answered, sympathetically nodding.

I wanted to curl up in bed and forget. Forget everything that had happened to—

Then it hit me with such force, I gasped for breath.

Issie was dead...

I needed to get out of this small, suffocating room. The walls seemed to be closing in on me, and I couldn't breathe. The pungent air was stale, heavy with the sour smell of blood and acrid sweat. Feeling claustrophobic, I shakily pushed my chair back and stood up, I couldn't breathe. I gasped, panicking, unable to get any air into my constricted lungs.

I can't breathe... Oh God... I can't breathe.

29

'Claudia?'

I opened my eyes. I lifted my head off the table and looked up to see the female officer enter the small, windowless room. She handed me a mug of steaming liquid.

'Tea with three sachets of sugar in it. I made it for you rather than the insipid stuff you get out of the vending machines here.'

I nodded, giving her a weak smile.

'You gave us quite a scare,' she said, joining her male colleague as she took the seat opposite me.

I took a tentative sip. It was hot and sweet and strong: the perfect combination.

'How are you feeling now?'

'Better,' I lied. I still felt shaky, and my head was pounding. I had briefly blacked out. I assumed it was pregnancy hormones, low sugar levels and shock. The last thing I remembered was pushing my chair back and standing up.

'Your friend Zain's called. I explained that we still need to go through a few final details as you're a crucial witness. He's understandably concerned about you.'

I wanted it to have been Jacob who had rung about me, not Zain. For him to drive here and take me home. To have him hold me and reassure me that it was all a bad dream and that he wouldn't let anything happen to me. But he wasn't here. And why would he be? Jacob had no idea what had happened to Issie.

One school friend had been murdered, and I had no understanding why, and the other was lying in ICU.

What are the odds?

I was certain that was what the police were trying to establish.

'Did Zain mention how Willow was?'

'Yes, he said she's still in a critical condition.'

I nodded, then dropped my gaze to my hands. I couldn't stop them from trembling, nor could I block out the image of the blood that had covered them – *Issie's blood.*

'Do you feel up to continuing?' she asked.

I met her concerned gaze and nodded. I was tired and nauseous, but the sooner I answered their questions, the sooner I could leave.

'Did you see any vehicles when you drove down the lane towards Issie's cottage?' she asked.

'I... I don't know. Yes... I must have done, but I can't remember.' I shook my head. Everything was a blur. All I could recall was shaking Issie's unresponsive body, begging her to come back to me, not to leave me, holding onto her so hard, willing her to live.

I closed my eyes for a moment, trying to block out my desperate attempt to save my childhood friend's life.

Then it came to me.

'There was a silver Jaguar,' I stated, suddenly remembering passing it.

'Where?'

'Parked opposite Issie's neighbour. I pulled in front of it.'

She turned to her colleague. Something passed between them.

'What is it?' I asked.

She looked back at me. 'Issie's neighbour mentioned in their statement that when he had let his dog out around midnight, he noticed someone had parked opposite his property, blocking his black BMW in. He assumed that your friend had a guest, as he heard two raised voices coming from her cottage, one of whom he identified as your friend. He thought it was odd that the guest didn't park outside Issie's property. It was still there at 6.55 a.m. when he opened his bedroom curtains. He also noted your car parked outside your friend's cottage. But the silver Jaguar was gone by the time the ambulance and police arrived,' she explained.

I sat back and shakily breathed out.

'Did you notice the licence plate?' she questioned.

But all I could think about was that the murderer must have been in the house when I arrived. The police had found the murder weapon – one of Issie's kitchen knives – in the old-fashioned walk-in pantry in the kitchen. They must have been hiding behind the door while I was calling out for Issie.

Oh God... They could have killed you as well...

My mouth was suddenly dry. I shakily picked up the paper cup of water and took a sip as tears continued to slide down my face.

'Claudia?'

I shook my head as I looked at the officer. 'It was new, I think. But I didn't see the year or any other registration details.'

The officer nodded and made a note.

'Claudia?' interrupted her colleague.

I turned to him.

'I need to ask you this, do you have any idea who would want to kill your friend?'

I shook my head.

'And the two letters on Issie's body? Do you have any idea why someone would do that to her?' he quietly questioned.

I shook my head again as more tears blinded me as the image of

Issie's stomach with those ugly, brutal letters etched into her skin came to mind.

Then I remembered Issie's last words to me: Rebecca Spencer.

Who the hell was Rebecca Spencer?

I swiped at the hot, salty tears as I stared, wide-eyed, at the male officer.

'I've just remembered Issie's last words to me: "Rebecca Spencer".'

'"R" and "S",' he mumbled to himself as he took note. He looked back up at me. 'Do you know a Rebecca Spencer?'

I shook my head.

'Had Issie ever mentioned her before?'

'No,' I mumbled. 'Never.'

'What about your other friends, Willow and Ava?' he pressed.

'No.'

'Are you sure?'

I nodded.

I watched as he scribbled something else down.

'Do you think someone's targeting my friends?' I asked, unable to disguise the fear in my voice.

'We don't know at this point,' he said, looking back at me. 'But what we do know is that Ava appears to have been set up.'

'What?' I spluttered. 'I knew she would never hurt Willow! I said as much to Zain. Who? Who would do that?'

'That's what we're trying to establish,' he tried to reassure me.

If someone – this Rebecca Spencer – was targeting my friends, why?

And could I be next?

30

I gripped the steering wheel as I focused on overtaking the lorry. It was raining heavily, and the spray of water from the vehicle's wheels temporarily obscured my visibility.

'Shit! Shit! Shit!' I muttered under my breath.

'Are you okay?' questioned the voice on the hands-free call.

'Yeah,' I replied, breathing out now I was safely past the lorry.

The sky was a dangerous gunmetal grey. It was now after 5 p.m., but the oppressive dark clouds overhead made it feel much later. Even though I was an emotional wreck, I wanted to get back home where I could try to piece together what had happened to Issie – to me.

Oh God... Issie!

'Look, why don't you call Jacob and see if he can get a train over and drive you back,' Zain suggested. 'I would, but I'm busy here.'

'Too late,' I answered. 'I'm already on the M2 heading home. If you had called me ten minutes earlier, then maybe.'

'Shit! Claudia. The police let you drive after what you've been through?'

'An officer was going to drive me back to London, but I insisted that I wanted to drive myself home. So they brought my car to the station,' I answered. 'I was there for hours giving my statement and then going over it. I just wanted to be alone to...' Lost for words, my voice trailed off.

Zain was silent.

I waited.

'Claudia, I need to ask you this, and I'm sure the police asked you already, but do you have any idea who could have wanted to hurt Issie?'

'No. I've been thinking about it non-stop, and I have no idea. The last words Issie said to me were "Rebecca Spencer", but I have no idea who she could be.'

I sighed heavily. I had been wracking my brains as soon as I realised that the initials carved into Issie's stomach were the same name. But no matter how hard I tried, I had no memory of anyone ever mentioning a Rebecca Spencer to me: in particular, Issie.

'Sure. Well, we'll be running checks to find out who she could be. I recommend that you stay vigilant. All right?' he advised.

'What do you mean?' I asked as an icy chill ran down my back.

'What I say. Someone killed Issie, Claudia! And we're still investigating Willow's hit-and-run. Both your friends have been targeted within hours of one another. I've said the same to Ava. She needs to be careful. You both do.'

I gripped the steering wheel hard enough that my knuckles turned white.

'Don't you think I know that? Fucking hell, Zain!'

'Look, I'm just worried for your safety. Whoever killed Issie was still in the cottage when you were there. Do you think they saw you?'

'I don't know,' I quietly replied.

It was a question that I had repeatedly turned over and over in my mind, and I still didn't have an answer, but the thought unsettled me.

'How's Ava doing?'

'Not so good. You should call her,' Zain suggested. 'Her parents collected her. She's staying with them until... Well, until we figure out what's going on.'

Ava's parents owned a substantial gated property in Cornwall. I understood why she would have retreated there. I would have done the same.

Your parents don't even know what's happening, Claudia.

'Do you know if she visited Willow before she went back home with her parents?'

'The hospital was the first place she went after she was released.'

'And Willow?'

'No change, unfortunately.'

'Oh,' I heard myself mumble.

'Does Ava know about Issie?'

'Yes. Like I said, she's not holding up so well.'

I didn't reply.

I heard Zain clear his throat.

'I think you should spend the next few days with Jacob. Maybe at his place or ask him to come back to yours.'

'Jacob slept with someone, Zain!' I argued. 'Or have you forgotten?'

'You know, Jacob is insistent that he didn't have sex with her. That she acted all weird and crazy on him.'

I was surprised to hear Zain say that. I was even more surprised that Jacob had disclosed as much to him. Why? Why lie to Zain?

Unless Jacob was telling you the truth?

'He told you that?' I heard myself asking him.

'Yeah. And for what it's worth, I believe him,' Zain stated.

'You didn't see the texts from her, then?'

'Actually, he showed me them. He has no idea who sent them.'

I was startled by this revelation.

Maybe Jacob was telling the truth after all? That he didn't know who had sent those messages. But the texter knew about the bracelet that I had found behind the scatter cushions on the couch. How was that possible?

I pushed Jacob to the back of my mind. I had more pressing concerns.

'Anyway, I have a lodger, Riley.'

'Oh yeah, Jacob mentioned something about a lodger. Just make sure you lock your doors and windows. Yeah? And keep your phone with you at all times. Understand?'

'Yes,' I mumbled. I had already had the same reassuring conversation with the police before I left for London. 'Zain?'

'Ahuh?'

'Do you think whoever killed Issie wants to hurt me?' I asked, fearing the answer.

He hesitated before replying. 'I don't know. That's what's worrying me.'

I didn't respond, the prospect that Issie's killer could be coming after me too terrifying to contemplate.

Or Ava...

For there were only the two of us left.

Jaz and Issie were now gone and Willow...

Oh God, Willow...

I swallowed back the reality of what was happening. Someone was targeting my friends, one by one.

'Do you think Issie's murder and Willow's hit-and-run are connected?' I asked.

Zain heavily sighed. 'I can't say at this stage, but...'

'But what?'

'Look, something's just come in, and I need to go. Drive carefully, all right? And call Jacob and Ava,' he advised before cutting the call.

I got Jacob's number up on Bluetooth. I pressed call and waited. It went to voicemail. I cut the call.

And Ava?

I would call her when I got home and arrange to go to her parents' place in Cornwall to make sure she was all right. I needed her. However, I doubted the feeling would be reciprocal, given Ava's coldness towards me over the past couple of months.

But maybe Ava would know why this was happening. Why they had been targeted.

Jaz came to mind. It was two months since her funeral and so much had happened – gone wrong.

Tears blindsided me as I shakily breathed out. It still hurt, and I didn't know when it would end, if ever.

And now Issie...

I felt compelled to call Jaz's mother and inform her of what had happened out of respect for Jaz. Not that I knew what to expect from Rhona Donaldson, but I conceded it was the right thing to do. I would rather she heard it from me than on the news.

Or was it simply that I wanted to talk to someone who had known Issie as long as I had known her? I accepted that this was more about me than Mrs Donaldson.

I scrolled through my contacts on Bluetooth, then clicked call.

I took a deep intake of breath, steeling myself as I nervously waited while it rang. Just before I was about to cancel, a breathless Rhona Donaldson answered.

'The Donaldson residence.'

'Hello, Mrs Donaldson,' I nervously began.

'Whatever you're selling or surveying, I am not interested!' she forcefully answered.

'No! Wait! Please, it's... it's Claudia,' I uncomfortably declared, remembering that the Donaldsons had preferred to stay in the early twentieth century with their 1930s black Bakelite phones. Consequently, she had no caller ID and obviously didn't recognise my voice. 'Claudia Harper.'

I heard her hiss in annoyance at the mere mention of my name.

'What is it you want?'

Whatever hope I was feebly grasping onto that her hurtful words after Jaz's funeral were fuelled by pain and anger at the loss of her only child quickly evaporated.

'I need to tell you something...' I hesitated.

'Well? What is it? Is it about Jasmine?'

'No. It's nothing to do with Jaz. It's bad news, I'm afraid.'

Her silence added to my nervousness.

'It's Isabella,' I said.

'Isabella?' she repeated.

I could hear the unmistakable tremor in her voice.

'She...' I faltered, struggling to find the words.

'She what? For goodness' sake! Spit it out!' she ordered.

'She died this morning,' I quietly explained.

I waited a beat, allowing her to absorb the information.

'Was it some kind of accident?' she finally questioned.

I swallowed. 'No. She was... she was murdered.'

'What? Is this some ridiculous prank?'

'No,' I answered. 'No, it's not.'

'How? What happened?'

'Someone stabbed her... I found her this morning in her cottage. But... I couldn't save her. She had lost too much blood.'

Rhona Donaldson remained silent.

'I... just thought you should know, rather than hearing about it or seeing it on the news.'

'Have the police caught whoever did it?'

'No,' I answered, surprised by the hint of unease in her voice.

'Do they have any idea?'

'No.'

'Oh...' she muttered. 'Why would someone want to... to kill Isabella?'

'I don't know. I can't get my head around it.'

Again, she remained silent.

'And...' I hesitated. But she had a right to know. After all, she had known Willow and Ava from our time at boarding school. 'Willow is in a medically induced coma after a hit-and-run. The police believe that Ava appears to have been set up.'

'What?' she exclaimed.

I remained silent.

'Oh, poor Willow!' mumbled Rhona Donaldson. 'And you say Issie is...' She faltered.

'Yes, she's...' I also stopped myself from saying the unthinkable. 'The murderer etched two letters into Issie's stomach,' I heard myself saying.

'Two letters?' she repeated. 'Oh... Oh my goodness...'

'I'm sorry for upsetting you,' I apologised, realising I should never have mentioned it.

'No... No, you haven't upset me. It's just that...' She broke off.

I waited for her to continue, but she didn't.

'Just what?' I forced myself to ask her.

'Jasmine,' she replied in a conspiratorial tone.

'What about Jaz?'

'She... Before she... she took her life, she used a razor blade to carve a letter and a number above her navel.'

'What?' I questioned unsure I heard her correctly. 'A letter and a number?' My mouth was unbearably dry and my hands felt sweaty. I knew this wasn't a coincidence.

'Yes... The letter "R" and the number "5".'

Before I knew what was happening, I lost control and skidded, swerving across into the outside lane, nearly taking out another vehicle. The other driver furiously beeped his horn as he simultaneously gave me the finger.

'SHIT!' I swore, shaken.

'Claudia? What's happening?'

'I... I nearly had an accident.'

'Are you driving?' she asked accusatorily.

'Yes, but I'm on a hands-free call. Wait, I'm just going to pull over,' I said.

I breathed out, trying to slow my heart rate down as I pulled into a layby.

I was trembling from the shock. I had nearly killed myself and potentially another driver.

You momentarily lost it, Claudia! You should have waited for Jacob.

I scorned myself for thinking of him.

'You mentioned it was the number "5",' I said, recalling the reason why I had nearly crashed. 'But could it be the letter "S" instead?'

Rhona Donaldson took a moment before answering. 'I suppose it could be. It just looked like a five because it was so angular.'

'But if a razor blade was used, it would be difficult to make it curved,' I suggested.

'Why does it matter?'

I took a deep intake of breath. 'Because Issie had the letters "R" and "S" carved above her navel.'

'Oh...' she mumbled.

I watched my windscreen wipers furiously swish backwards and forwards at the relentless rain, psyching myself up to ask a question that had haunted me.

'Mrs Donaldson. Can I ask if Jasmine said anything to you or left even the slightest clue as to why she did what she did?'

She didn't answer me.

'Please,' I said, although, at the funeral, she had told me that Jaz hadn't left a suicide note. But I couldn't shake off the feeling Rhona Donaldson was hiding something from me.

'She left a printed note.'

I found myself inwardly gasping at this revelation.

'What did it say?'

I listened as she slowly exhaled. 'I... I don't see the relevance.'

'Please, Mrs Donaldson. Issie's death might be in some way connected to Jasmine's. And Willow's hit-and-run.'

'But Jasmine killed herself,' she stated, her voice thick with pain. 'The procurator fiscal ruled her suicide as unsuspicious.'

'Please,' I repeated.

'Very well,' she reluctantly conceded. '"I am not what I am."'

'Is that all she said?'

'Yes. She summed her reason for taking her life in just six words.'

I didn't feel there was anything I could add.

'Why? Why would she leave us that? Why an inversion of God's line, "I am what I am," from Exodus? Why mock us?' The sadness in Jaz's mother's voice took me by surprise.

'She wasn't mocking your faith,' I found myself explaining, 'Jasmine was quoting from *Othello*. Iago says to Roderigo, "I am not what I am."'

'I don't understand.'

'Iago is cryptically suggesting he isn't what he appears to be and that his motives are in alignment with the devil rather than God.'

'Oh...' muttered Rhona Donaldson.

I understood too well why Jaz would leave that quote for her parents to find since they had no idea about her. For their sakes, she masqueraded as the daughter they wanted: perfect – too perfect.

'What do the letters "R" and "S" mean?' Rhona Donaldson asked suddenly.

I closed my eyes.

You know what they mean. Issie told you.

For the 'R' and 'S' carved into her skin were the initials of her killer.

I could see her bluish lips as she used her last breath to tell me the name of her murderer – Rebecca Spencer.

Or was she also trying to warn you, Claudia?

31

'CLAUDIA?'

The sharp voice cut through my thoughts. My mind had gone into a tailspin at the recollection of Issie's last words. 'Yes... Sorry?'

'What does that quote have to do with the letters "R" and "S"?' Rhona Donaldson repeated.

'I don't know,' I lied. I planned on informing Zain, and letting the police contact Rhona Donaldson.

'I don't understand. Why would Jasmine do that to herself?'

I didn't answer her. My gut feeling was telling me that Jaz didn't do that to herself – someone else had carved those initials into her flesh.

The question was, why?

Why, Rebecca Spencer? What did they do for you to hurt them? To... To kill them? And, crucially, what connects you to my friends? Do I know you? If so, why can't I remember you?

'Do you think Issie marked herself with those letters as well? I mean, was this some kind of pact?' Mrs Donaldson questioned when I didn't reply.

'No,' I answered. 'I don't believe so.'

'You knew about Jasmine, didn't you?' she suddenly asked.

I hadn't anticipated the question.

'Claudia?'

Shit!

I didn't want to be having this conversation with Jaz's mother.

'Yes,' I quietly answered.

'How long?'

'She first confided in me when she was thirteen.'

'I see...' Rhona Donaldson muttered.

'When did you find out?' I heard myself asking.

'The weekend before she took her life,' she replied in a strained voice.

'She kept it from us for all these years,' she continued, more to herself than me.

I was surprised that Jaz had told them. For Rhona Donaldson was a God-fearing Scottish Presbyterian, as was her elderly husband, who made no apologies for his support of aversion therapy. Jaz had always known how they would react, and so had chosen to keep her sexuality from them.

Until a week before her death.

Why, Jaz?

It didn't make any sense.

'Why did she tell you?' I asked. I had nothing to lose. I seriously doubted I would ever speak to Rhona Donaldson again after this phone call.

She didn't answer me.

Her silence affirmed my suspicion that something or someone had forced Jaz's hand.

'Mrs Donaldson?' I prompted.

'She didn't. Someone sent us a letter telling us about Jasmine... About her... Her life choices.'

'Oh...' I muttered, shocked. 'Who sent it?'

'It was signed "An old school friend".'

I realised this must be the letter that Ava had referred to, the one she had wanted to discuss with Issie, Willow and me.

But now that would never happen...

I stopped myself. Swallowed. I tried to blink back the saltwater nipping my eyes.

I thought of the initials 'R' and 'S' carved into both Jaz's and Issie's skin. Could this Rebecca Spencer be an old school friend? I tried to recall someone of that name during the eight years I had spent at our boarding school.

Then it hit me.

I now understood why I hadn't immediately remembered her. There had been a Rebecca Spencer, but she had left after only a few weeks in the first year. Her departure had been sudden and unexpected, and her removal was obscured by a tragic death at the school.

Yet, why would a student who disappeared from school when we were all eleven years old be responsible for what had happened to Issie and maybe Jaz? It was illogical.

'Did you write it?' Jaz's mother suddenly challenged.

I gasped. 'Sorry?'

'You heard me. Did you send us that letter?'

'Why would I do something so heinous to Jasmine?' I questioned. I had kept Jaz's secret for two decades and would have continued to do so.

She didn't answer, but it explained why she was so hostile to me at the funeral.

One question hit me hard: *Why didn't Jaz call you? It was her worst fear realised, and yet, you knew nothing about it – until now.*

'Jasmine mooted that it might have been you,' Rhona Donaldson viciously threw at me as if sensing my vulnerability.

I held my breath as her words hit me. That wasn't possible. Jaz would know I would never send a letter outing her. Why would I? She was my best friend.

'Do you still have the letter?' I asked, trying, but failing, to keep my voice steady.

'No. Jasmine took it. I searched her flat for it and couldn't find it. I assume that she destroyed it.'

'I don't understand. What was in the letter that would make Jasmine think I had written it?'

'Why can't you just accept what I say?' wearily snapped Mrs Donaldson.

'Because I didn't send it. That's why!' I fired back.

She didn't reply.

'Please, Mrs Donaldson. I need to know,' I begged.

'She didn't exactly say it to me, personally,' she finally conceded. 'I overheard her on a phone call to Ava. She couldn't get a signal on her mobile and asked to use the phone in the study. I was passing by in the hallway outside and accidentally overheard her.'

'What exactly did Jasmine say to her?' I asked.

'Something along the lines that she immediately recognised the handwriting as yours. It was identical to the distinctive writing on the birthday card you recently sent her. I heard her say she compared it.'

I couldn't speak. I was at a loss as to who would want to out Jaz to her parents. Let alone, why – or how – they would copy my handwriting.

Fuck!

I understood now why Jaz declined my calls and refused to answer my texts and Ava's sudden and cold behaviour towards me, why she held me accountable for Jaz's death. Ava believed I had outed Jaz to her elderly, homophobic parents, consequently leading Jaz to take her life.

I felt light-headed. I was struggling to accept that they believed that I would actually want to hurt Jaz.

'If you hadn't sent that... that letter, then Jasmine would still be alive!'

Rhona Donaldson's vengeful words brought me back.

I realised that it was easier to blame me than question what part she had played in her daughter's choice to end her life. I could easily imagine Jaz's parents horrified and equally hostile reaction to the revelation in the letter about their daughter's sexuality.

Stunned by her vicious accusation, it took me a moment to find my voice.

'You said Jasmine had called Ava from your house. When was that?'

'Why?'

'Please, I need to know.'

'The weekend before Jasmine took her life,' reluctantly answered Mrs Donaldson. 'We received that letter on Saturday morning, and Jasmine drove straight up when we...' She faltered and cleared her voice. 'When I... I rang her about it.'

'What exactly happened when Jasmine arrived home?'

'I'm sorry?' replied Mrs Donaldson, caught off guard.

'What happened?' I repeated.

I waited as she contemplated whether to respond.

'We... we had words. Her father struggled to understand her lifestyle choice and... well, it turned rather unpleasant. Jasmine left, threatening that it would be the last time we would ever see her. I had no idea that her words would come true. I... I...'

I realised that she was crying. It took me by surprise.

'I'm sorry,' I awkwardly apologised.

'Why are you sorry?' she sniffed.

'For upsetting you,' I answered.

'I'm upset with myself for the words I said. I... I will never have the chance to tell Jasmine I didn't mean them,' she confessed.

'I'm not so sure Jasmine killed herself,' I blurted out, feeling compelled to ease her guilt.

'Sorry?' she said, startled.

'The letters on her abdomen. I think someone else did that to Jasmine. If they did, then they would have been present at the time she allegedly killed herself.'

I waited for her to say something, but she didn't.

'Mrs Donaldson?'

'But the procurator fiscal recorded Jasmine's suicide as unsuspicious.'

'Didn't the police or procurator fiscal find the letters carved into her skin odd?'

'Yes. But I had to explain that Jasmine's father and I had quarrelled with Jasmine before her death. They wanted to know what it was about, and I had no choice but to disclose why we had words. So, they assumed that was the reason Jasmine had...' She stopped, unable to say it.

'The letters. What was their explanation?'

'Oh, they just presumed it was some form of self-harming.'

'But Jasmine has never self-harmed—'

'Jasmine used the razor blade that she cut her wrists with, Claudia. There was no evidence to suggest someone else was involved,' Mrs Donaldson admitted wearily.

'Ava mentioned to me at the funeral that Jasmine had started seeing someone. Did you know about her?' I continued, not accepting that Jaz had acted alone – if at all.

I waited as Rhona Donaldson considered my question.

'Do you think she might have been the reason for Jasmine's decision?' she finally asked.

'I have no idea,' I answered. 'I just wondered how serious it was and whether she had been in touch or if you found anything in Jasmine's apartment from her.'

'No. I knew nothing about Jasmine's personal relationships.'

'She didn't mention anything to you that Saturday? Or mention anyone by the name of Rebecca Spencer?'

'No,' she replied. 'Nor did I find anything at her flat or on her phone which suggested she was in a relationship.'

'Oh...' I muttered, disappointed. I then recalled the woman with long, dark chestnut hair and sunglasses standing at a distance at the burial service, watching Ava, Willow, Issie and me.

Could that have been Rebecca Spencer?

'You asked about a Rebecca Spencer?' Rhona Donaldson suddenly questioned. 'Why?'

'They were Issie's last words to me,' I decided to share.

'Do you think Jasmine's death and Issie's murder are connected?'

'Yes,' I answered. 'And I don't think Jasmine killed herself. Nor do I believe she cut those letters into her skin. I think the person who sent the letter killed Jasmine and staged it to look like a suicide.'

'Why? Why would someone do that to Jasmine? I don't understand.'

'Neither do I.'

It was an honest answer.

'What happens now?' Rhona Donaldson asked me.

'I expect the police investigating Issie's murder might contact you regarding Jasmine's death. I will have to inform them about the letters cut into Jasmine's stomach.'

'Yes... Yes, of course,' she replied. 'And you honestly believe that Jasmine didn't take her own life?'

There was a desperation in Rhona Donaldson's voice. A need for absolution. I could easily imagine the cruel, toxic words she had thrown at her daughter. Words I assumed she believed contributed to her daughter's decision to end her life.

'Yes. I am certain that Jasmine didn't kill herself,' I assured her.

'Thank you,' she quietly said.

I didn't reply. There was nothing left for either of us to say. I listened as Mrs Donaldson cut the line.

I sat for a moment staring out through the blurred windscreen as the wipers futilely swiped at the torrential rain. Tears silently glided down my cheeks. I had lost two of my oldest friends, and I had no understanding why. All I knew was that Rebecca Spencer, a fellow student who had vanished from school when we were all eleven, was involved somehow. How that was possible, I had no idea. But it was her initials carved into Issie's and Jaz's skin.

Why?

I shivered as a coldness slithered its way down my spine as I questioned whether this Rebecca Spencer had sent that letter to Jaz's parents pretending to be me.

If so, why? She was no one to me.

32

I locked the car and headed towards the front door. My hand was shaking so much that I was struggling to get the key into the lock. Finally succeeding, I pushed the heavy, wooden door open. For a split second, I again expected to be confronted by Darcy, meowing in outrage that I had dared to leave him for so long. I tensed up as the pain of his loss ripped through me. I had never felt so alone. I could feel myself on the verge of crying as silence greeted me.

I headed into the kitchen, filled a glass with water and then walked to the bi-folding doors and stared out into the back garden. My mind threw me back to the phone call with Jaz's mother and the revelation that the letters 'R' and 'S' had also been cut into Jaz's abdomen – identical to Issie.

After I had ended the call with Mrs Donaldson, I'd sat in the car processing what she had told me. I had then rung Zain, who had instructed me to inform the police about the letters. I also gave the police what little I had recalled of Rebecca Spencer, which was vague, to say the least, given that it was twenty-two years since I had last seen her. And even then, it had only been a matter of weeks. I couldn't even say I counted her as a friend. All I could remember of her was that she was a painfully thin, shy girl with long mousy blonde hair who desperately wanted to fit in. The only remarkable quality about her was her sudden departure from school. I had no idea why she would hurt Issie and Jaz. And Willow.

It felt as if my world had imploded, shattering into unrecognisable fragments. I swiped at the tears silently slipping down my cheeks.

Sometime later, my phone rang and rang and rang. I slowly reached for it in my pocket.

'Hello,' I mumbled, barely audible.

I was surprised to see that the garden had been taken over by darkness. I had no memory of when the dusk became night. Blackness had swept over my world without me realising, blinding me.

'Hey, are you okay? This is the fourth time I've tried calling,' Zain replied.

I realised I hadn't switched any lights on. It was 10.03 p.m., and two hours had slipped by as I'd stared out into the garden holding a glass of water.

'Claudia?' Zain questioned, concern filling his voice.

The fear in his voice prompted me to reply.

'I'm here,' I whispered.

'Have you called Jacob yet? You clearly shouldn't be on your own.'

'I... I called him earlier. But he didn't answer,' I replied.

It hurt to talk. My head was pounding, and my mouth felt as if it was full of dusty, dry, brittle bones blocking my words.

'What about Ava?'

'Not yet. I'll call in the morning,' I replied. I had so many questions I needed answering, but I was too tired to speak to Ava. I imagined she was equally exhausted after her ordeal.

'Maybe you could stay with her and her parents in Cornwall for the time being. Just get out of London and—'

'And what? Hide? Why? I haven't done anything!' I demanded, frustrated that I should be the one to go into hiding when I hadn't done anything. Nor was I ready to see Ava. The letter to Jaz bothered me. It was the fact that Jaz and Ava had believed I could be behind outing Jaz to her parents. It cut me to the core.

How could they have thought that of me?

Before he had a chance to reply, I continued, 'I have work on Monday. What do you expect me to do? Call in and say that someone is targeting my friends and that I might be next. I haven't done anything, Zain! She could have—' I abruptly stopped, unable to articulate the thought.

She murdered Issie, and she could have killed you at the same time.

'I'm coming over,' Zain firmly stated.

'No.'

'Claudia, you shouldn't be there by yourself,' he reasoned.

'I'm not. My lodger's here.'

Not that I had heard her. But then, time had passed by without me noticing.

'Okay. But I'm worried about you.'

'Don't be,' I found myself replying as I stared back at my ghostly reflection. It was as if I was looking in at myself through the glass as my doppelganger talked on the phone. Nothing felt real any more.

I could hear Zain speaking, but it was just noise. The words weren't reaching me. They couldn't because I was trapped outside, watching as someone else impersonated me.

'I need to go,' I mumbled.

'Did you hear anything of what I said to you?' Zain questioned.

'I'll call you later,' I concluded, cutting the call.

I somehow managed to finally drag myself away from the pull that the blackness outside had over me. I checked all the doors and windows were locked before forcing myself to head upstairs. The police had reassured me that if Issie's murderer was going to kill me, they'd had the perfect opportunity when I had entered Issie's cottage. But I couldn't silence the unease I felt that whoever had killed Issie hadn't finished.

But why would they want to hurt you? What possible reason could there be?

But then, why would someone do that to Issie?

Maybe it was random.

But I was fooling myself.

I shuddered as the visceral image of the letters 'R' and 'S' etched into Issie's abdomen came to mind. The same letters cut into Jaz's abdomen. It wasn't a random attack.

I wanted to climb into bed and forget everything. But the pungent smell of death that followed me, clinging to my hair and skin, forced me to take a shower. Numb, I stripped out of the jogging bottoms and sweatshirt the police had given me as my clothes were soaked in Issie's blood.

Sometime later, I emerged from the steamy sanctuary of the bathroom. I'd stood under a hot shower for as long as it took to block out the terror on Issie's face as she uttered her last, desperate words to me and for my tears to stop. I passed Riley's room on the way to my bedroom. The door was closed. It was late, but I still wanted to knock and ask if she would sit with me tonight. But I had to remind myself that she was my lodger, nothing more. It wasn't her job to console me or keep me company. Tears pricked at my swollen, bloodshot eyes at the realisation that I had no one.

There's always Jacob.

I pushed the thought away. Jacob hadn't returned my earlier call, which hurt. He knew what had happened to Willow, and that should have been incentive enough to get back to me. But, evidently, it wasn't.

And Issie?

I was certain Zain would have told him.

So why isn't he with you?

Wounded by his callousness, I pulled back the comforter and sheet, crawled into bed and closed my eyes. I hadn't slept for over twenty-four hours. I knew I wouldn't fall asleep, but I just needed to lie perfectly still and block everything out. To pretend that the past twenty-four hours hadn't happened. For if I didn't, I was terrified I wouldn't be able to stop the dark pain that was slowly and surely choking me.

* * *

It was my phone ringing that dragged me away from the respite that was sleep. It then hit me hard and fast – Issie was dead. I gasped, curling my body into a foetal position as the painful reality coursed through me. I lay there ignoring my phone's constant ringing as the events of the past twenty-four hours came flooding back. Finally, I forced myself to open my eyes and answer my phone.

I squinted at the dusty stabs of daylight streaming through the wooden shutters on the two Victorian sash windows as I shakily stretched out my hand and fumbled around for my phone on the bedside cabinet. I was praying it was Jacob.

Disappointment surged through me when I saw it was Zain calling me – again. I had six missed calls and a text from him. I felt a wave of nauseating panic when I noted that there was nothing from Jacob. Or Ava.

Why haven't you called me back, Jacob? How could you ignore me?

I reluctantly clicked answer.

'Christ! Claudia? Are you okay?'

'Yes,' I groggily answered.

'You know it's after eleven?' he questioned.

'Oh...' I muttered. I was surprised that I had even managed to sleep.

'I've been trying to reach you for the past couple of hours,' he stated. 'If you hadn't answered just now, I would have come round.'

'Why?' I replied, confused. 'Has something happened to Willow or Ava?'

'No,' Zain replied. 'It's to do with Rebecca Spencer. I received an update from the Kent police earlier.'

'Have they arrested her?' I questioned, pushing myself up.

'No. They're not treating her as a suspect.'

'Seriously?' I questioned, shocked.

'Yes,' Zain replied.

'Why?'

'She's not resident in the UK,' he explained.

'I don't understand.'

'She was removed from your boarding school before the end of the first year.'

'Yes, that's correct,' I answered. 'At least, all I was aware of was that she left. No one knew why or where she had gone. She just vanished.'

'Her mother relocated to New York with her when she was eleven.'

'Oh...' I mumbled. 'So, did the police track her down?' I questioned, hopeful.

'No,' Zain replied. 'She has no living relatives in the UK, and both her parents are deceased. Her mother died recently and was still residing in New York at the time. Her biological father died some years back here in the UK, but her parents divorced when she was eight.'

'So, exactly where is she?' I asked.

'They don't know. But, as I said, Rebecca Spencer's not being considered a suspect.'

'But she could be here in London?'

'The police checked her British passport, and it's fifteen years out of date. Rebecca Spencer hasn't been in the UK since she was eleven years old.'

'She must be,' I argued. 'Issie named Rebecca Spencer.'

'Maybe it's a different Rebecca Spencer and not the one you remembered at your old boarding school,' suggested Zain.

'No. It has to be her.'

'Maybe you misheard,' Zain suggested. 'It's understandable, considering the stress you would have been under.'

'I didn't mishear. And her initials—'

'If they are initials,' Zain pointed out.

'But... Issie—'

Before I had a chance to continue, Zain cut me off. 'Claudia, you found one of your oldest friends dying from a stab wound, is it any wonder that you might have misheard her after witnessing such a traumatic event? Or that you unconsciously wanted to make sense of the letters and grabbed onto a fellow student with those initials to be able to help the police?'

'That isn't the case,' I argued. 'Issie said her name!'

'Rebecca Spencer was taken to New York to start a new life with her mother when she was eleven. That's a fact,' Zain calmly pointed out. 'She couldn't have committed Issie's murder or cut her initials into her stomach without returning to the UK.'

'But—' I began.

'Claudia, there is no record of her ever coming back to the UK. Not even for a visit.'

'Issie's last words were her name. I wouldn't imagine that,' I reasoned.

'Okay. What about motive?'

'Sorry?'

'Tell me Rebecca Spencer's motive for killing Issie,' Zain said.

There had to be a reason why Rebecca Spencer had killed Issie. It was something I had tried to figure out on the drive back to

London. But no matter how hard I tried, the motive for murdering Issie and maybe, Jaz, eluded me.

'What about Ava?' I suddenly questioned. 'Does she remember Rebecca Spencer? She might know why this is happening.'

'She vaguely recalls her. But she also said she had no idea if it was her.'

'Oh,' I muttered. I was certain that Ava would have all the answers; I was wrong.

'Look, you've had a traumatic thirty-six hours, Claudia. It's no surprise that your brain is trying to make sense of everything that's happened. It's perfectly normal. I suggest you rest up today. If I hear anything else, I'll be in touch. And make sure that your doors are locked and that you have your phone with you at all times. All right?'

'Sure,' I mumbled. 'Zain?'

'Yeah?'

'Have you heard from Jacob?'

'No.'

'He hasn't returned my call from yesterday.'

'He would have been playing rugby yesterday afternoon.'

'True,' I answered.

'I imagine he went to the pub afterwards with the team and got carried away,' Zain reassured me. 'Give him a call. He'll want to know what's happened.'

'You haven't told him?'

'No. I tried to catch him yesterday, but he didn't answer. And then, I've been caught up with this investigation.'

'Of course.'

'I'll call you when I hear something. Okay?'

With that, he hung up.

I stared in disbelief at my phone. I was sure that Issie had said the name Rebecca Spencer. The only Rebecca Spencer that either of us knew was from our first year at boarding school. But after the police findings, it made no sense.

I was scared that I was losing everyone close to me, one by one. And, I was equally terrified I was losing my mind.

Could I be mistaken about Issie saying Rebecca Spencer's name?

33

SUNDAY

I really need to talk to you.

I pressed send and waited, hoping Jacob would immediately read it and reply. He didn't.

I had called him, but he didn't answer, and so I'd sent him a text hoping it would prompt him to contact me. I couldn't allow myself to think that he could be spending Sunday with another woman.

But he said he loved you, Claudia. Remember?

But that was in the early hours of yesterday morning; a lot had changed since then. But I had a choice; I could accept my fate, or I could fight for him.

I threw back the comforter and made my way to the bathroom, pausing as I passed Riley's room.

Sakura suddenly came to mind and her concerns about Riley self-harming. I hesitated.

Should I knock and check on her?

But how on earth would I approach the subject without betraying Sakura's confidence?

Overcome with unease, I discounted the idea. I would pass Sakura's fears over to Helena tomorrow at work.

I listened for movement, but it was silent. I assumed Riley was out again. It was as if Riley occupied the shadows of my mind. At times, I found myself questioning whether she even used the room or if she was living somewhere else entirely.

I shook my head. I was acting irrationally: Riley was simply a private person.

Closing the bathroom door, I found myself searching for the positive pregnancy test that I had hidden in the bathroom cupboard.

That was only Thursday, and yet, it felt like an eternity ago.

But I couldn't find it. I was wracking my brain to try to recall if I had thrown it out. I was sure I hadn't, but then, so much had happened in the past few days that it wouldn't have surprised me if I had and couldn't remember.

I needed the pregnancy stick to show Jacob. I wanted to try again with him, prepared to look past his indiscretion, and more significantly, his refusal to admit it. I couldn't bear the idea of being on my own. Not now. I needed Jacob. He had known Ava, Issie, Willow and Jaz for the ten years we were together. He understood what they meant to me and how Issie and Jaz's deaths – murders – had the potential to destroy me.

And Willow...

I swallowed back the threatening tears as I recalled her body being hit by the Range Rover. Then finding Issie...

Oh God...

I was so fearful of the fact that I might not come back from this horror. I felt as if I was standing on a precipice staring down into a black abyss that was calling out to me. I needed someone to stop me from letting go and falling. And Jacob was the only person who could pull me back.

If it hadn't been for the pregnancy and wanting to reach out to Jacob with the news, I would have lain in bed, unable to move, held hostage while the horrors of the past days' events plagued my mind.

I planned to turn up at his flat with the positive pregnancy stick. I was offering him a new beginning – for both of us. It was all I had that was keeping me afloat.

I sighed, accepting that I must have thrown the stick away. Not that it mattered. I could buy another one.

I decided to shower and get dressed. I intended to visit Willow before tackling Jacob and the revelation I was pregnant with our child. Her condition remained unchanged, but I just needed to see her. To be close to her.

And Ava? Why haven't you contacted me?

I called Ava after my shower, and when she didn't answer, I left a garbled message, begging her to ring me: that we needed to talk. I just wanted to hear her voice. To know if she understood why this was happening. I still had her parents' number from the times when all of us would get together during the university summer months at their Cornish coastal home. We spent days idling on her parents' yacht or around their outdoor pool without a care in the world. No sense of what the future held.

Oh God... If only we could go back to those halcyon days.

Her father answered, assuring me that Ava was safe. Their doctor had prescribed something to help her sleep after all she had been through, which was why I hadn't heard from her. Concerned for my welfare, he recommended I stay with them for a few days. I could hear the overwhelming desperation in his typically strong voice as he insisted that my presence would be of benefit to Ava. I agreed to consider calling in sick for work in the morning and travelling to Cornwall.

Half an hour later, I was searching through my leather bag that I had left in the kitchen when I had returned from the hospital yesterday morning for my laptop. I planned on distracting myself by marking some scripts while I waited for a text from Charles. He had agreed to let me know when Willow's parents left so I could visit her. I didn't want to see them. I knew that they would have countless questions about what had happened to their daughter. More so, now Issie had been murdered. But I had no answers, only the realisation that Jaz, Ava, Willow and Issie had kept something back from me. Their duplicity hurt. I was still struggling to come to terms with the fact that they had excluded me.

Surely Ava would have told Issie and Willow about the letter sent to Jaz's parents. Of course, she did.

Why didn't you tell me, Issie? Why? Why would you do that to me?

I sighed. I couldn't go there again. I would have to wait until I talked to Ava.

I turned my attention back to the question of where I had left my laptop. I assumed it must still be in my office. I considered going to the English department to collect it but decided against it. Even though it was Sunday, it was highly probable that I would run into someone, and I didn't trust myself not to break down in tears.

My phone suddenly rang. I snatched it up from the kitchen table, willing it to be Jacob. It was Charles.

'Hi,' I greeted. 'How's Willow?'

Charles let out a heavy sigh.

'Charles?' I demanded.

'Something's happened,' he hoarsely replied.

'What? What's happened?'

Silence.

'Charles? Charles? Are you there?'

The line was dead.

What the...?

I called back, but the line was busy. I assumed he had called me from the hospital where the signal was hit and miss.

I tried again. The line was still busy.

I felt as if I couldn't breathe.

I texted:

On my way.

All I could think about was what had happened. Charles sounded so desperate.

Willow? Oh my God... Not you. I've already lost Jaz and Issie... Please, don't be next.

34

'Charles?' I cried as I rushed into the small waiting room.

He raised his weary head and looked at me.

I knew from his grave expression that something terrible had happened.

I closed the door, then turned to him. 'Willow?'

'Her father and mother are with her now,' he lowly answered.

'Oh God,' I muttered, sitting down.

Please, God, don't let her die...

There was a rap at the door before it opened.

I looked up. 'Zain?' I questioned, surprised.

He shot me a sympathetic look.

'What's going on?' I asked, looking from him to Charles.

I could hear the quiver in my voice, despite trying my damnedest to hold it together.

Unable to answer me, Charles shook his head.

'Someone dressed as a nurse managed to get to Willow and...' Zain paused, looking at Charles.

'And?' I prompted, filled with dread.

'And hurt her,' Zain continued.

Charles abruptly stood up to leave. 'I can't go over this again. It's...' He shook his head as his voice broke off.

I watched as his dejected figure left the room.

Zain sat down opposite me and leafed through the file he was holding. He handed me a photograph.

I felt nauseous.

It was a close-up of the letters 'R' and 'S' on Issie's abdomen.

I handed it back to him in disgust. 'I don't understand. Why are you showing me this?'

'A woman pretending to be a nurse did this to Willow,' Zain explained.

'What?' I stared at him, horrified. 'Here? In this hospital?'

He nodded.

Winded, I sat back against the chair. 'That can't be possible...'

He handed me another photograph. 'Do you recognise this woman?'

I studied the grainy colour image of a woman in sunglasses with long, dark brown hair obscuring her features, wearing nursing scrubs with a lanyard ID around her neck. 'This is the woman responsible?'

'Charles has positively identified her. Unfortunately, this is the best image we can get of her,' Zain explained.

'Didn't Charles think it was odd that a nurse was wearing sunglasses?'

'She only wore them when passing the security cameras. It suggests she knew where they were.'

'But why would Charles leave her in the room alone with Willow?'

'He had no reason to doubt her,' Zain stated.

'But—' I began, but Zain cut me off.

'Nurses and doctors are in and out taking readings all the time. She said that she needed to run a few checks. So, Charles left her to make some calls. When he returned, the nurse was gone. He feels bad enough as it is, but this isn't his fault.'

Numb, I shook my head as I tried to absorb the magnitude of what had happened. Someone in nurses' scrubs with an ID lanyard had gained entry into the ICU and had hurt Willow.

She hasn't just hurt Willow; she cut the letters 'R' and 'S' into her skin, Claudia! Fucking hell!

'When did Charles realise what she had done to Willow?'

'Immediately,' answered Zain. 'Blood was seeping through the sheet covering her abdomen. He pulled the sheet back and lifted her bloodstained gown to see the letters cut into her skin.'

'Christ!' I muttered.

I thought of Issie and Jaz and those brutal letters etched in their abdomens as I stared at the CCTV still of the nurse, but it was impossible to make out her features.

'Did Charles get a look at her face?'

'No,' Zain reluctantly admitted. 'He's not slept, apart from the odd hour in the chair by Willow's bedside. He's exhausted mentally and physically. And so, he didn't take any notice of her. He said that doctors and nurses are coming and going all the time, and they've become a blur.'

I stared back down at the photograph. I felt as if I had seen her before, but when, I couldn't say.

'What is it?' Zain asked.

'There's something familiar about her,' I said, frowning. 'But I can't put my finger on it.'

Zain pulled another photograph from the file. 'Could it be this?'

I took the photograph from him and looked at it. It was another CCTV still. But this time it was a car. It took me a moment to understand that I was looking at Ava's Range Rover.

He handed me another image: a close-up of the driver.

Shocked, I shook my head. 'The nurse and the woman driving

Ava's car are the same person. So, she stole Ava's car to set Ava up for Willow's hit-and-run?'

Zain nodded.

I thought back to Friday evening.

There was a piece of the puzzle that suddenly didn't make sense to me. 'But Ava was supposed to be meeting us? So, if this other woman stole Ava's car intending to run Willow down, where was Ava at the time?'

'Ava received a message on Instagram from Willow on Friday afternoon offering to pick her up in a taxi on the way to The Queen Charlotte.'

'That doesn't add up. We were due to meet at 7 p.m.'

'The message stated that you were now meeting at 8.15 p.m. Willow suggested she would collect her at 7.30 p.m. Which suited Ava as she needed to stay late at work.'

'Why would Willow do that? Why get a cab from her place in Kensington, to Ava's house in Fulham, then Fitzrovia? It makes no sense.'

'The message insisted that she had to speak to Ava in confidence about Jaz without you present.'

'Oh...' I mumbled.

It was the confirmation I had been seeking that they were hiding something from me. But the clarity made me feel sick.

I swallowed, trying to dislodge the knot of betrayal at the back of my throat, but failed. I shook my head, unable to understand. What had I done that would make them distrust me?

Hot, prickly tears threatened to undermine me as the answer blindsided me.

The letter... Jaz, Issie, Willow and Ava all believed that you had written that letter to Jaz's parents because the handwriting looked like yours.

How could they think I could do that to Jaz?

'But we don't believe that it was Willow who messaged Ava,' Zain added.

I stared at him as my mind came back to the present.

'Someone managed to infiltrate Willow's Instagram account and reset the passwords. I doubt Willow even realised.'

'So, who the hell is this woman?'

'That's what I am trying to understand,' answered Zain. 'I know I've asked you this before, but can you think of anything that ties Ava, Issie and Willow together?'

Numb, I shook my head.

'And the "R" and the "S" mean nothing to you?' Zain continued.

'Nothing, aside from what Issie whispered to me.'

'Rebecca Spencer?' Zain questioned, frowning.

'Yes.'

'Well, as I explained to you, Rebecca Spencer moved to New York when she was eleven with her mother, and she hasn't been back in the country since.'

The world I had known felt so remote. It was as if I had woken up in a parallel universe and I didn't know how to get back.

I just want it to stop! Please, God. Make it stop.

But what if this wouldn't stop until Willow and Ava were dead?

'Why?' I eventually asked, staring at Zain, hoping he would have the answers. For someone had to have the answers. 'Why Jaz, Issie and now Willow?'

'That's what we're trying to figure out. These are your friends, Claudia, and you have no idea why, if, say she was responsible, this Rebecca Spencer would be doing this.'

'No,' I answered.

'Okay. Let's leave it there for now,' Zain suggested, picking up on my frustration. 'If anything comes to mind, give me a call.'

I wearily nodded.

Then it hit me. I knew why the CCTV still of the nurse looked so familiar, and it had nothing to do with Ava.

'Zain, she was at Jaz's funeral,' I declared. 'That's why she's so familiar. During the burial service, I looked up and beyond the graveyard railings a woman with long dark brown hair and large black designer sunglasses was standing there watching us.'

'Watching the burial?'

'No, watching Issie, Ava, Willow and myself. I thought it was odd that she was on her own and not with the rest of us mourners. Even odder that she was watching us. I was so uncomfortable, I remarked to Issie.'

'What did the woman do?' Zain questioned.

'She continued to watch us until the burial service was over. Then, as everyone started to disperse, she disappeared.'

'Did Issie recognise her?'

'No. Issie suggested it might be someone from Jaz's law firm. But I thought it was odd that she was watching the four of us.'

'And you're certain she is the same woman?'

'Yes.'

Zain's expression disturbed me.

'Why do you look worried?'

'I'm concerned for your safety,' he admitted.

'I don't think it's me she's targeting, Zain. She had her chance when I was at Issie's, and she was still in the property. No one has threatened me in any way. It's Jaz, Issie, Ava and Willow she wants to hurt. But I have no idea why.'

Zain sat back and folded his arms. 'What makes you different?'

'I don't understand.'

'Well, the five of you have been friends since the age of eleven, correct?'

I nodded, wondering what he was getting at.

'Your headmistress, Simone Anstruther, described you as an "exceptional" group of girls who were very popular at the school.'

I nodded.

It then hit me again that Issie and Jaz were gone. That I would never see them again. I broke away from Zain's penetrating gaze.

'Hey, I'm sorry if I upset you. I'm just trying to establish what distinguishes you from the four of them.'

I could feel the wet tears gliding down my cheeks. Embarrassed, I fumbled in my bag for tissues.

'Here,' he said, offering me the box of tissues strategically placed on the small Ikea-style table next to him.

'Thanks,' I mumbled.

I looked at him. 'All I can suggest you do is talk to Ava again. I honestly have no idea who would want to hurt them. Maybe it's someone recently connected to them. I was so busy with work and caught up with Jacob that I didn't see the four of them as often as I should have done. Especially these last few years. I know that Ava kept in regular contact with them.'

I shuddered as an icy chill crept up my spine as I suddenly recalled the woman observing the four of us at the funeral. It felt as if she was studying us – me in particular.

Maybe Zain was right, and I should be worried about my safety.

35

After Zain left, I waited around to see Willow, to later be informed by Charles that they were only allowing next-of-kin visitation rights. After her assault, stricter measures were now in place, including a police officer posted outside her room.

I looked at Charles. He looked dreadful.

'Why don't you go home and get some sleep?' I suggested.

He shakily breathed out as he dragged a hand through his messy blonde hair. 'I can't leave in case something happens. I need to be here.'

I didn't know what to say, so I simply nodded.

'Why did it have to happen the moment her parents decided to go back to their hotel?' he asked.

'It was just one of those things. It's not your fault,' I reassured him.

He looked at me, his eyes plagued with guilt. 'That's not what Willow's father thinks. He made it clear that had he been there, it would never have happened.'

Sadly, I could imagine Willow's father saying something to that effect. After all, in his eyes, Willow would always be his little girl, and as such, no man could ever meet his approval.

'I just thank God that she didn't kill her. I mean, she's the person who killed Issie, right?'

'That's what the police suspect,' I replied.

'But why would someone want to hurt Willow. I mean, this is Willow. The same woman who has been vegan from the age of fifteen because she can't bear the idea of animals suffering. What could she have possibly done that would enrage someone enough to want to...?' He faltered, lost for words.

'I don't know,' I answered, equally at a loss.

'I'm scared,' he suddenly admitted. 'I don't want to lose Willow, but I'm terrified that will happen. I just found her, Claudia.'

'She'll pull through—' I had to believe it, for the alternative was unthinkable.

'You don't understand,' interrupted Charles. 'The medically induced coma is to prevent further injury to Willow's brain, but what it can't do is address pre-existing damage. If it's too severe, then...' He paused, struggling to keep it together.

I breathed in. I hadn't expected this outcome.

Charles was equally struggling with the news.

I touched his arm as I looked up into his glistening eyes. 'Willow will wake up and when she does, you'll be the first person she'll want to see,' I stated.

'She'll be waking up to find those... those horrific letters,' he said, his eyes filled with remorse.

'If anyone can get over this, it's Willow. She'll be okay. Better than okay. I promise you that,' I assured him.

However, it was easy to say, but the reality might be very different. I felt nauseous thinking about when Willow finally woke up and realised that some crazy woman had cut two letters into her abdomen. I couldn't begin to imagine what Willow's reaction would be or how she could live with the initials of someone else carved into her flesh.

I watched as Charles turned, shoulders slumped, and headed back down the hallway to Willow's private room. I couldn't imagine the guilt he felt at what had happened to Willow. But he wasn't responsible. Someone else was, and that person was hellbent on destroying my school friends' lives – including killing them.

Why?

* * *

I knocked on the door of Jacob's basement flat. The need to see him was more powerful than my ego, which demanded that I wait until he returned my call and text. I had bought a pregnancy test kit on the way to his flat, giving me the reason for unexpectedly showing up.

There was no response.

I knocked again.

'Come on!' I muttered.

I wanted him to just hold me. To reassure me that everything was going to be all right. Ultimately, I needed to know that he was all right.

Still, there was no response.

Again, I knocked. Waited.

Disappointment, quickly replaced by anxiety, coursed through me. Accepting that he wasn't there, I turned and headed to the cast-iron stairs that led up to Great Ormond Street.

What if something has happened to him?

I stopped as the thought derailed me.

No... You're becoming hysterical!

But what if he is lying in there, like Issie, and you leave him to die?

My opposing thoughts paralysed me.

I thought of the sealed pregnancy test in my bag. That was the reason I had come here to show Jacob that I was pregnant and tell him he was the father.

I turned and walked back to the door and knocked again, this time with force.

Again, no answer.

I tried the door. It was locked.

'Damn!' I cursed.

I considered what to do. I could sit on the basement steps until Jacob returned, or I could go home and wait for him to call me.

But what if he is lying in there bleeding out?

I recalled that Jacob had a spare key secured under one of the potted plants by the door. I reminded myself that I was his wife and so, technically, I was within my rights to check that he was all right. More so, given what had happened to Willow and Issie, combined with the fact that he hadn't contacted me.

Zain came to mind. I pushed him away. I knew he would accuse me of being paranoid and, worse, acting illegally.

I found the spare key wedged in the Blu Tack. I removed it and, before I changed my mind, unlocked the door.

'Jacob?' I nervously called out as I entered the flat.

Silence.

My mind threw me back to when I'd found Issie. I could hear my blood pounding in my ears with every tentative footstep I took, terrified that I would encounter a similar scene.

I slowly breathed out. I forced myself to look around the minimalist open-plan living space, but nothing had changed. The boxes remained unpacked and stacked against the wall. If it wasn't for Jacob's prized Yamaha GC82C Madagascar rosewood grand concert classical guitar, positioned on a stand next to his treasured vinyl record collection, I would never have known that this was his place.

But, crucially, nothing seemed out of place.

'Jacob?' I repeated.

Again, silence greeted me. Ominous and heavy.

I headed out into the hallway.

'Jacob?' I tremulously cried.

I walked towards the bathroom and pushed the door open and peeked in. It was empty.

Ahead of me was the bedroom. I psyched myself up to walk the final steps to the closed door. My hand was trembling as it reached out for the door handle. I turned it and pushed the door open.

It too was empty.

I breathed out a deep sigh of relief.

He's not here. He's fine, Claudia! Go! Go, before he or someone else catches you here.

I found myself disregarding the thought as I walked over to Jacob's side of the bed. I picked up his pillow and breathed in the heady aroma of Guerlain's Royal Extract II. The smell threw me back to when Jacob and I made love, here in this room, in this bed.

And now you are pregnant and he doesn't know. What if he never finds out?

Tears of panic blurred my eyes as my breath caught at the back of my throat.

He's safe, Claudia! What happened to Issie and Willow won't happen to Jacob.

I shakily breathed out and replaced the pillow.

Wiping the corners of my eyes, I glanced around the bedroom. Typically for Jacob, it was immaculate. No clothes or shoes were lying around, nor were there any magazines or books scattered on the ivory-coloured wool carpet.

I walked over to the built-in wardrobe. If I had expected to find someone else's clothes or shoes inside, I was disappointed, or, rather, I was relieved. Jacob's suits, blazers, shirts, ties, casual shirts and jumpers dominated the space in an unnervingly obsession-driven fashion. I had often mocked his compulsion with our cupboards, wardrobes, drawers, bookshelves, even furnishings, which he arranged in a regimented order. My relaxed attitude was the antithesis to his, and at times, Jacob would infuriate me. And yet, I ironically missed being driven to distraction by his idiosyncrasies.

I glanced down at the countless pristine Tom Ford shoeboxes, again arranged in order. I reached in and pulled out his go-to navy Tom Ford O'Connor wool and silk-blend jacket. I loved him in this blazer. I closed my eyes and luxuriated in the addictive scent that was unique to Jacob, imagining he was here with his arms wrapped around me, whispering that it was all going to be all right. That this nightmare was over. That he would move back home and we would be together and nothing or no one would ever come between us again.

Finally, I tore myself away and hung the blazer back. I then left, locking the door and replacing the spare key so Jacob would never know I had been here. I took out my phone and again checked. There was still nothing from him.

I stared across at Great Ormond Street Children's Hospital.

Then I realised: Jacob must be on call this weekend. That was why I hadn't heard from him. He must be at work.

The compulsion to walk across the road and go into the hospital and find him was overwhelming. But I fought it. I could wait.

We could wait.

* * *

When I got home, there was still nothing from Jacob.

I forced myself to give him some more time before reaching out again. I was trying to keep my dignity, but the fear that something had happened to him replayed on an obsessional loop inside my head. I knew I was being irrational. More so, since I had found nothing in his flat to suggest this was the case.

I tried to think of something else. Anything, to stop myself from calling him.

I picked up my phone, deciding to distract myself with the news. But Issie immediately came to mind. I couldn't bear to watch journalists pick over her life like scavengers while they speculated about her murder.

I had made a point of not reading any news articles or checking Issie's Facebook, Instagram, or Twitter accounts to see whether anyone had posted an update. I couldn't deal with other people's outpourings of grief, especially when they didn't know her that well, if at all. I was all too familiar with the deluge of questions that Jaz's sudden death had elicited on her social media accounts. I struggled to deal with the level of anger and hatred I had towards these virtual 'friends' who'd indulged in excruciating pain comparisons at her loss. Worse were the trolls whose vitriolic and horrifying comments about her sexuality suggested she was better off dead.

If someone had updated Issie's status, there would be statements that I assumed Zain and his team would be keeping an eye on. For whoever was responsible might comment on her post. I forced myself to ignore the burning compulsion to scroll through whatever might be there, searching for someone that I might know – someone who had a grievance with her. However, I could not imagine Issie upsetting anyone.

Issie's final words came back to me: *Rebecca Spencer*.

Zain had said she had moved to the States when she was eleven and hadn't returned to the UK since. Curious, I decided to google her. I scrolled through countless Rebecca Spencers on social media residing in New York City. There were a few that were the same age as me, but whether any of them were her, I couldn't say. I could barely remember what the eleven-year-old Rebecca Spencer looked like, so it was highly doubtful I would recognise her as an adult.

I heavily sighed, realising that it was futile.

Anyway, the police had confirmed that she never returned to the UK. So, how could it be her?

Unless someone was using her name. But why?

I googled Rebecca Spencers in the UK. It was a popular name. I spent ages scrutinising numerous Instagram, Facebook, Twitter and TikTok accounts.

I then remembered Zain mentioning my old headmistress, Simone Anstruther.

Curious, I googled her name. Unsurprisingly, she wasn't on social media. But her name did come up in reference to when she was headmistress of Queen Victoria's School for Girls. There were various newspaper articles about my old boarding school's achievements during her time there, though she finally retired some years back.

I stared at the photographs of her, always with the imposing historic, five-hundred-year-old medieval manor house looming in the background. It was very much a part of her – her identity. She had attended QVS as an eleven-year-old pupil and returned to teach there, finally succeeding as headmistress. She loved that place with every fibre of her body. I couldn't imagine how she filled her time now she was retired. I scrutinised the photographs of her, in which she seemingly never seemed to age from one decade to the next: tall, thin, short blonde hair, no-nonsense features, with a sharp, intelligent glean in her narrow brown eyes.

I felt a pang of sadness looking at my old headmistress. Simone Anstruther had always been kind to me. Perhaps it was because I was one of the few boarders with no home to return to during the holidays. At least, not one in the UK. I wondered what she had made of Rebecca Spencer during her short time under her guidance. I had been hoping to find some contact information, so I could reach out and ask her that exact question, but there was nothing.

Accepting that I had hit a dead end, I got off my bed and headed to the bathroom, deciding to take a long, hot bath. I found myself soaking in my grief. Tears merged with the almond-scented bathwater as the loss of my friends, of what had once been, consumed me.

But Jaz, Issie, Ava and Willow lied to you, and they shut you out. Worse, they believed that you could do something so heinous, so cruel and devastating as to attempt to destroy Jaz's relationship with her parents. What did you do to them to make them think so contemptibly of you?

But I had no idea what I had done wrong.

I turned my thoughts away from them to Jacob, musing over the fact that I still hadn't heard from him. It wasn't like him. Fear had me by the throat like a rabid dog. I couldn't silence the unease that something terrible had happened. My mind was in turmoil, and my body felt in constant fight or flight mode as I kept masochistically revisiting the thought that Jacob's silence meant he was in danger.

I rested my hand on my stomach and thought about the growing life inside me. It was something that I had ached for with Jacob, and now it had happened, the joy I should have felt had been obscured by raging pain and profound sadness. I wondered whether the melancholy that consumed me would be absorbed by this developing foetus becoming part of its very DNA.

I submerged my head under the water in an attempt to silence my mind as it chaotically veered between throwing me back to Issie dying in my arms and Willow being hit by Ava's Range Rover. I lay there looking up at the surface as the burning in my lungs and my thundering heart finally started to drown out my tortured thoughts.

* * *

I pulled on some grey marl lounge bottoms, a baggy white top and piled my thick, damp hair up and headed to my bedroom, where I collapsed onto my bed. I lay on my back, staring at the ceiling as tears glided down the sides of my face. I was angry with myself that I couldn't stop crying.

My phone pinged.

My heart lurched: it was from Jacob. I opened the text message and read it. I breathed out, needing a moment to think before I decided what to do. I checked the time: it was 9.44 p.m.

What the fuck, Jacob?

But I knew I had no choice: he was my husband and the father of my child.

36

I glanced at myself in the rear-view mirror. I looked as anxious as I felt.

Jacob's text message filled my mind:

Drove to Surrey for the day for a hike. Ended up at our clock tower but badly twisted my ankle. Too swollen to put my boot back on. Can you pick me up from there as can't drive back? 1% power left. Hurry. J x

I had immediately called him, but it had cut to voicemail. I'd then texted that I was on my way. He didn't reply, which I'd expected since his phone was out of charge.

I'd thought of calling Zain, but then dismissed the idea. This had nothing to do with what was happening to my friends. Hiking was Jacob's passion, and so, I wasn't surprised he had headed off for the day, or ended up at the clock tower, given its nostalgic connection for us. Part of me was relieved that Jacob had turned to me for help, and not Zain, giving me hope that we would get through this marital impasse.

Whenever he had a problem, Jacob would take off for the day

and hike, and Newlands Corner's breathtaking views of the Surrey Hills and acres of woodland was one of his go-to places. It was also the place where Agatha Christie had dramatically vanished in 1926, to be discovered eleven days later after international coverage and an extensive police hunt, at The Old Swan Hotel in Harrogate. I imagined that Jacob had headed down there with the intention, like the crime author, to escape his marital problems. It explained his radio silence. His unexpected cry for help felt as dramatic to me as Agatha Christie's disappearance.

Consequently, at such a late hour, I was driving to Queen Victoria's School for Girls: my old boarding school. Or, to be precise, the abandoned clock tower above the stone chapel, forgotten about within the fifty acres of woodland surrounding the manor house.

I understood why Jacob would return to the clock tower – *our clock tower*. I had shared with him my childhood, most of which I had spent at boarding school. The clock tower was a place where I would steal off to with Jaz, Issie, Ava and Willow – our secret place – and as we grew older, it became somewhere for us to smoke and drink alcohol.

I had taken Jacob to my old boarding school during our second year together for a school reunion. We had sneaked away so I could show him the stone chapel and clock tower. When we had stumbled upon the dilapidated structure, it had been late evening. I'd been surprised to find that it was just as I last recalled it. No one else had seemingly discovered it or used the furnishings we had left behind within the upper room. Jacob and I had ended up making love in the clock tower room, and before we knew it, deep night had embraced us. That was when, wrapped up in each other's arms, lit only by the hypnotic silvery moonlight, the balmy evening breeze carrying to us the short, repetitive somnolent 'woop' of an owl in a nearby tree, Jacob had found himself seduced by the moment and proposed. He didn't have an engagement ring or champagne; all he had was his all-consuming love for me, as we lay together enveloped by the sounds of nature within the shadows of a clock tower that had been there for centuries.

I was quickly jolted back to the present by the sudden glare of red lights ahead. The driver in front of me had nervously braked for the umpteenth time. Exasperated, I indicated and pulled out into the middle lane of the A3 and sped past them. I checked Google Maps. I was only thirty minutes from my destination. I had the foresight to bring a torch with me to find my way to the clock tower. The last time I had ventured through the woodland surrounding the school premises at night was when I had brought Jacob here eight years ago when he proposed, and we hadn't been back since.

I could feel the resident hornets' nest in the pit of my stomach start to become agitated. I couldn't silence the feeling that something was wrong. Very wrong. That Jacob was seriously hurt. I imagined that Jacob being Jacob, had played down his injuries and that it would be more serious than a twisted ankle.

Thirty minutes passed in a blur as I followed the mesmerising car lights ahead of me. I couldn't even remember leaving the A3 or joining the A24 heading towards Dorking before ending up snaking along a dark, narrow country road. In that time, all I could think about was Issie and Willow. Over and over, visceral images of them flashed through my mind.

Don't! This has nothing to do with what's been happening to your friends.

This is about Jacob.

The knot in my stomach twisted even tighter as I neared the turn-off for Queen Victoria's School for Girls. I pulled in and braked, staring ahead at the grand entrance leading into the extensive school grounds. Shadowy trees closed in on me from either side, adding to my sense of unease. I questioned whether to drive into the private road and park up and then make my way through

the trees to the stone chapel and clock tower. The boarding school
itself was a further half a mile's drive, nestled within the
surrounding woodland. Then I spotted a black vehicle ahead. I
edged forward so my headlights could illuminate the car: as I
suspected, the black Range Rover Sport was Jacob's.

I tucked in behind it, left the headlights on, got out of my car
and walked over to his vehicle. It was empty. I felt the bonnet of the
car. The engine was cold. I turned and searched for any signs of
him. Shivering, I accepted that he must still be at the clock tower. I
headed back to my car, turned the headlights off and grabbed my
jacket. I then opened the first-aid kit, stuffed support bandages and
tape for his injured ankle in my jacket pocket and picked up the
torch. I checked my mobile – my text message remained
unanswered.

I tried calling him. Again, it cut to voicemail.

Damn it, Jacob!

I couldn't stop my body from trembling. I tried to tell myself I
was cold, but in reality, I was scared. Understandably so. I was in
the middle of nowhere, alone and in the dark. I suddenly felt like
the eleven-year-old girl my parents had abandoned at this school
all those years ago.

Deeply breathing in, I aimed the torch on the ground ahead and
started walking. A cacophony of unsettling noises from within the
woodland seemed to encircle me all at once. I continued, brittle
twigs snapping beneath my feet as the nocturnal sounds closed in
on me. I reminded myself that I was trespassing through the habitat
of foxes, fallow deer, tawny owls, hedgehogs and wood mice. And
that I had 'nothing to fear but fear itself,' as Franklin D. Roosevelt
had famously said in his 1933 inaugural address.

An inhuman screech from my right stopped me in my tracks,
contradicting that assumption. I instinctively stabbed the torch
towards the noise, but I couldn't make out anything aside from

formless shapes, dark shadows and distorted and distended, gnarled limbs of looming trees. I assured myself that the unearthly sound would be foxes, who themselves screamed when in fear. Then something darted in front of me.

FUCK!

I dropped the torch in fright. Breathing shallowly, I crouched down to grab it, never taking my eyes off the blackness ahead. Finally locating the torch, I continued on, not wanting to be defeated by a vivid imagination that was catastrophising every unfamiliar sound and movement around me.

Fifteen excruciating minutes later, with much relief, I finally stumbled upon the stone chapel shrouded in darkness. Stones had crumbled and fallen away over the centuries, sneakily concealed by overgrown, wild vegetation as ivy snaked its way over the remains of the chapel, prising its roots deep into the centuries-old building. I shivered, unable to dispel the unease that had descended upon me. The place felt creepy for some reason. I told myself it was because I hadn't been back here for years.

'Jacob?' I called out as I entered, shining the torch down on the stone slabs, slick with bird droppings from over the years. I then threw the beam of light in every direction, between the pillars, searching for him, but to no avail. 'Jacob?' I repeated, heading to the stone staircase at the back of the chapel.

I stabbed the beam of the torch at the stone steps that led upwards. It was then I heard a noise: a shuffle of sorts.

'JACOB?' I yelled up the staircase.

I waited.

Silence.

'JACOB?' I repeated, climbing the treacherous winding stairs.

Nothing.

Finally reaching the top, I shoved open the heavy door that led into the clock tower room.

'Jacob?' I anxiously called out.

I stabbed at the blackness ahead with my torch, illuminating the haunting frosted white glass clock face with its black Roman numerals directly ahead of me, its missing glass plates and elegant black hands positioned forever at thirteen minutes past twelve. The heart of the clock, a cruciform metal framework with its complicated system of gear wheels which sat in the centre of the room, was still, with the metal rod that rotated the clock strokes long since rusted in place.

I suddenly jumped when the beam from the torch hit something – someone –standing by the clock's centuries-old mechanical structure.

'What the...'

The room closed in on me as a suffocating silence descended as I stood there, too shocked to react.

No... It can't be?

I gaped at my lodger.

'Riley?' I mumbled.

She didn't reply.

The hairs on the back of my neck stood up as I stared into the blackness of her eyes.

'Riley? What the fuck is going on?' I demanded, unable to control the tremor in my voice. For there was something very wrong – with her.

I stepped back. My sixth sense was screaming at me to flee.

To turn and run and make sense of why she was there instead of Jacob later.

I took another step back, questioning how fast I could spin around and race down those narrow, cracked and crumbling stone steps without falling. But something swooped down from the rafters past my head, disappearing into the shadows without a trace.

'Argh!' I screamed out, swiping at what I believed to be a bat with the torch.

But as I did so, the torch slipped through my fingers, landing on the old, rotting wooden floorboards. It rolled away from me before stopping, illuminating Riley, dropping to her knees on the floor beside a—

My eyes widened in horror.

A body...

Riley was kneeling next to a body on the floor.

Oh my God... Jacob? JACOB?

37

Frantic, my mind was trying to make sense of the situation. Time was frozen, like the clock hands. I stood transfixed, unable to comprehend what was happening and why. None of it made sense.

Why is Riley here with Jacob? What the hell is going on?

I then realised there was blood ebbing from an ugly four-inch open gash above his swollen right eye.

Oh God... No...

'Have you called an ambulance?' I asked Riley, rushing towards him.

'Don't come any closer!' she hissed.

There was something in her tone that stopped me in my tracks.

'Riley?' I questioned, scared.

'SHUT UP!' she screamed at me.

You need to help him, Claudia! You can't just stand there!

But I couldn't move.

Paralysed, I stared at Jacob's body, processing the white zip ties restraining his hands and feet. Then the dark pool of blood on the floor. It was seeping from the back of his head. Terrified, I studied Jacob's pale, clammy face, unsure whether he was still alive or—

Oh God... Jacob?

'Please,' I beseeched, raising my eyes to meet hers. 'He's seriously injured.'

Riley responded by yanking Jacob's lifeless head, suddenly pressing a serrated knife against his throat, making me panic. I hadn't realised she had a knife.

'RILEY!' I screamed, shocked. 'STOP!'

'Then, you need to do exactly as I tell you.'

'I... I don't understand,' I said, staring into her feverish eyes.

All I could think was that she was mad and I was alone in the middle of nowhere with her.

This is a woman you allowed into your life... into your home. What the fuck, Claudia! What have you done?

My head was reeling as I tried to process what the hell was going on.

Why was this happening? To Jacob? To you?

And who the fuck is she? Who the fuck is Riley Harrison?

Jacob started to moan, his eyes flickering open.

'Jacob, I'm here,' I called out.

'Claudia? Claudia,' he repeated, disorientated. 'I got your text. You weren't here?' he croaked.

I didn't understand what he meant. He was the one who had messaged me to come and pick him up because he had twisted his ankle.

'Argh!' he cried out in pain as Riley yanked his head further back.

'No! Please, Riley. NO!'

She looked up at me.

Oh my God... She's insane.

'What is going on? I... I don't understand,' I begged.

It didn't make any sense. Why was she here? And why was she threatening to hurt Jacob?

'Light those candles with the matches there on the ground in front of you,' Riley instructed.

'Riley? I don't understand. What's this about? I... I... I can fix it. Whatever it is—'

'Light the candles!' she snapped.

I dragged my gaze to Jacob, and then the glinting six-inch knife pressed against his throat. I accepted that I had no choice but to do as she instructed. I would figure out how to get help once I had talked her down – *if that was possible.*

Bewildered, I looked at the box of matches and candles on the ground ahead of me. Numb, I stepped forward and crouched down to light the candles as ordered. There were six in total. I watched as my trembling hand lit the candles, the flickering, hissing flames spilt light out across the floor, illuminating a pen nearby. But my eyes were drawn to the silver aluminium baseball bat lying on the floor by Riley. A dark, slick stain discoloured the shiny metal. It struck me that the baseball bat was the cause of Jacob's head injuries.

But who?

It was a rhetorical question. I was staring at her.

Why?

I made a move to reach for my phone in my pocket. 'This is madness! I'm calling for help!'

Sudden anger flashed across Riley's eyes. 'Don't!' she hissed. 'Or I will kill him.'

Goosebumps covered my body in reaction to her chilling tone. For I knew she was deadly serious.

'Please, Riley. We need to call for help,' I whispered, terrified.

'SHUT UP!' she screamed, spit flying out of her mouth, her eyes ablaze with black rage.

'I don't understand what's happening. I... I...' My voice faltered as the words became lost.

'Don't pretend you don't know!' Riley spat at me as she dug the knife into his flesh, the blood seeping down his neck onto his light-blue shirt.

Jacob let out a gurgling, spluttering sound.

'RILEY. NO!' I screamed out. 'You're hurting him! He's done nothing to you!'

'You're right. He didn't hurt me, but you did!' she fired back.

I shook my head in horror as I stared at her. None of this made sense to me. I let Riley stay in my home: that was all. I hadn't interfered in her life and had kept a respectful distance as she had made it evident that was what she wanted. What had I done to her for this to be happening to me – to Jacob? I willed myself to keep calm while my mind wildly tried to figure out what I could do. However, Riley had the upper hand. She had a knife pressed against Jacob's throat, and she had just shown me that she had no qualms about using it.

'Please. Tell me what it is that you want. Please.'

'I want you to do what you didn't do twenty-two years ago. Here, in this room,' she lowly replied, eyes ablaze with enmity.

I tried to process her words. But they made no sense to me. Blood pounded in my ears, and my heart raced as I stared at her.

She's mad, Claudia!

'I told him all about you and what you made me do! Here!' she said, jerking Jacob's head further back so the knife glinted against the prominent lump of cartilage that was his Adam's apple.

I felt sick as Jacob made a gurgling moan.

I wanted to scream at her: *I don't know what you are talking about! All you are to me is my lodger!*

She suddenly released Jacob's head. I watched as his head lolled forward, confirming he had passed out. The blood seeping from the trauma to his head terrified me.

'Look at me!' she screamed. 'Look at what you did to me, Claudia Harper!'

I shifted my gaze from Jacob to Riley, unsure of what she was about to do. Still gripping the knife, she knelt upright and, pulling her top up, exposed her navel. There was a large gauze dressing taped to her stomach. Shocked, I watched as she ripped it off.

Transfixed, I stared in horror as the torch illuminated her abdomen: etched into her flesh were scars. Pale red, gnarled cuts, some of which had long since healed. I then understood that these were not random marks. They were five rows of capital letters, each one, two inches in height:

JD

WF

AT

IRW

CH

I shook my head, disputing what was going through my mind.

They couldn't be, could they?

Jaz's, Willow's, Ava's, Issie's and my initials? No! How was that possible?

AND WHY?

She had slashed through four of the rows of letters, three of which were still raw and inflamed. However, the first one, 'JD', had healed. I stared in disbelief at the last row 'CH'. It remained untouched.

Sickened, I stepped back, shaking my head at the possibility of what those letters represented – my friends' initials.

And your initials, Claudia! She's cut your initials into her abdomen. What the fuck!

'No...' I weakly mumbled, as terror scorched through me.

'You! You did this to me,' she spat.

'No... I... I don't know what you're talking about.'

'Yes. You do!'

I forced myself to look again at the gruesome initials.

'I... I didn't... I didn't do that to you...' I stuttered, shaking my head.

'YES, YOU DID!' she raged as she looked directly at me.

I stared at her.

'If you don't do as I say, then I'll kill him,' she hissed at me. Suddenly grabbing a fistful of Jacob's hair, she snapped his head back, pressing the tip of the blade into the side of Jacob's neck by his jugular.

She's deranged, Claudia! Do something!

I realised that screaming was futile. We were in the middle of dense woods. There was only one way I could get help. I tried to reach for my iPhone in my jacket to press the side button repeatedly to activate the Emergency SOS. The sound was toggled off, meaning she would be unaware.

'Don't think about it,' warned Riley.

I stopped moving.

'Your phone. Throw it to me.'

As I slowly pulled out my phone, I surreptitiously pressed the side button five times. I then crouched down and slid it across the wooden floor within reaching distance of Riley. The Emergency SOS would automatically call 999. However, the crucial question was how long before they arrived.

She then jerked her head at the floor. 'The craft knife in front of you, pick it up. Now it's your turn to cut my initials, followed by all your friends' initials, into your stomach. To do what you didn't do here, twenty-two years ago.'

I stared down in horror at what I had assumed was an innocuous silver pen with the realisation that this wasn't some cruel, twisted threat – she meant every cutting word.

She wants you to cut into your skin – identical to her. Why?

38

'Riley, please,' I begged, shaking my head. 'I... I can't do this...'

'If you don't, then I kill Jacob,' she threatened. The frenzied glean in her eye told me that she meant it.

I sank to my knees, tears flowing down my cheeks.

'The candles, you need to place them around you in a circle,' she instructed.

Numb, I stared at her. She appeared drawn and haunted, as if whatever hellish thoughts had driven her to this place had now assumed her appearance, her monstrousness eerily accentuated by the flickering candlelight.

'Now!' she commanded, startling me into action.

I slowly, almost ritualistically, spaced the candles out around myself as I tried to figure out how to stop this from going any further.

'Now pick up the craft knife.'

I reached out with a trembling hand and grabbed it.

'Remove your jacket and top,' she ordered.

I took my time removing my jacket, hoping that something would happen to bring this craziness to an end.

Where the hell are the police?

But I knew that by the time they reached us, it would be too late.

'Come on!' she shouted. 'And your top.'

Stalling, I started to slowly drag my arms out of my top.

'I'm serious. Take your top off!'

More tears escaped as I jerkily pulled it over my head with the craft knife clutched in my right hand. For a second, I considered using it to attack Riley. But she had the advantage of holding a serrated knife against Jacob's exposed, taut throat. By the time I reached her, she could have already killed Jacob.

I heard him make a strangled noise as his eyes fluttered open, then closed again.

Oh God, Jacob... Please, please be okay.

I let my top fall to the wooden floor and looked at Riley.

'What now?' I asked with just my bra on. My body was trembling, but it wasn't from the cold, it was the trepidation of what was coming next.

'You use the craft knife to do what you made me do.'

'Riley, I have no idea what you're talking about,' I pleaded.

'Stop saying that!'

'Please, Riley,' I sobbed as the tears fell onto my chest. I felt as if I was in a nightmare, and I was unable to wake up.

'Start calling me by the name you knew!' she spat at me.

I stared at her as if seeing her for the first time.

'No...' I mumbled as the realisation hit. 'You're Rebecca Spencer?' I whispered in horror.

Riley – or whoever she was – watched me as the terror that had blinded me metamorphosed into shock.

'You cut those initials into Issie's stomach?' I questioned, stunned. 'And Jaz, and Willow's?'

She didn't speak, but the positively insensate hatred in her eyes confirmed she was responsible.

'If you mean the eleven-year-old girl, who you forced to cut your initials and those of your friends into my skin, then yes. "The Friends List" is what you called it. It was your idea to have the initiation ceremony here in the clock tower. I so wanted to belong, and you knew that. I would have done anything you asked. Anything You left a note on my bed inviting me here, to this room, to join your club.'

She looked straight at me with accusatory eyes.

Petrified, I shook my head. She wasn't making any sense.

'You arranged it all. The candles, the razor blade. You! And you made me go first, telling me that you would carve my initials with everyone else's onto your skin afterwards. But I had to prove I was worthy of your friendship, and so, you all watched me while I carved your names, crying out in pain, into my stomach. You promised you would all copy me and that the six of us would be tied together forever. But you didn't do it...' Riley faltered as her eyes glazed over. 'I was new here. I knew no one. I lasted three weeks at this school because of what you did to me that Saturday night... If it wasn't for—' She suddenly stopped herself.

I watched the pain flash across her face. Whatever courage I had seeped out of me at the realisation that she actually believed what she was telling me.

I shook my head. 'I... I don't know what you're talking about.'

'YES, YOU DO!' she hysterically screamed. 'And you lied to me! YOU LIED!'

I raised my hands, terrified that my admission would make her kill Jacob. 'I'm... I'm sorry...' I stuttered. 'I... just don't remember.'

I didn't recognise the shy, awkward eleven-year-old, I had briefly met twenty-two years ago. I could barely remember her.

And why would I? She was no one to me back then.

Nor did I recognise the lodger I had invited into my home.

The woman before me was a deranged stranger with delusional allegations.

'Well, maybe carving my initials into your stomach will help you recall what you did to me! Then your friends' initials.'

'Please,' I croaked, fear stealing my voice.

'Your choice. You cut my initials and your friends into your skin, or Jacob dies.'

I tried to swallow back my terror but failed. I knew she meant it.

I looked at Jacob. Not that he could help me. Now unconscious, he was oblivious to the threat to his life or the choice I had to make.

I looked down at my smooth, flat abdomen, unable to contemplate cutting into it, permanently scarring myself with some insane woman's initials. My right hand was shaking so much that I doubted I would be able to hold it steady enough to carve the initials.

'RS?' I mumbled, raising my head to look at her. I barely knew her before she disappeared from school. So why was she doing this? And who had made her cut herself?

I couldn't imagine Issie, Jaz, Willow and Ava being a party to such a cruel, sadistic initiation. There were initiation ceremonies at QVS, but nothing to the extreme described by her.

Tell her she has got it wrong, Claudia! Tell her before it's too late.

She nodded. '"RS" for Rebecca Spencer.'

I thought of Issie and Willow and what she had done to them.

'Please,' I implored.

'You showed me no mercy.'

'I didn't do that to you. I would never force anyone to do that,' I reasoned.

'But you did!' she contemptuously threw back at me. 'You laughed at me as I sat where you are surrounded by candles and covered in blood after mutilating myself. You scorned me, saying I was pathetic! Then you forced the others to join in. They were too scared to argue with you, so they went along with it. They were all scared of you. Not one of them stopped you. Not one. Even when I was sobbing at what you had made me do to myself. Any of them could have prevented it. But they didn't. Instead, your friends watched as I cut their initials into my flesh to remain forever,' she accused.

'I... I...' I stuttered, too horrified by the look in her eyes to formulate words.

'You watched me with glee, enjoying every cut I made with the razor blade.'

Numb, I shook my head.

'Afterwards,' she continued, 'instead of getting help and reporting you, your friends joined you in ridiculing me. You said to me that I would be better off dead after what I'd done.'

I stared at her, trying to absorb what she was telling me.

It couldn't have happened. She's insane, Claudia! And delusional! It couldn't have happened.

The chilling reality dawned on me that if she thought I was the one who had initiated this horrific act, then it wouldn't end with her initials and my school friends' cut into my navel; her ultimate revenge would be to kill me.

She'd killed Issie! She'd left Willow in a critical condition in a medically induced coma. And Jaz...

'Jaz,' I began, shaking my head in disbelief. 'It was you at her funeral? You were watching the four of us at the graveyard?'

Riley didn't reply. Not that she needed to as her expression was confirmation enough that it was her.

I thought back to the woman standing observing myself and the others. 'It was you who knocked Willow down disguised as Ava. How? How did you have the key fob for her Range Rover?'

'I followed all five of you for months. I ascertained your habits. Ava has a favourite coffee place. I bought an identical Gucci handbag to hers and sat down behind her in the coffee shop. Her bag was by her feet, and while she was busy on her phone, I swapped the bags and, finding the key fob, returned her bag, took mine back and left.'

I was stunned.

'And Jaz? She didn't kill herself, did she?'

A dark smile played at the corner of her lips. 'I met Jaz in a bar that she frequented. We got together and dated before she—' Riley stopped. 'Well, you know what happened.'

I couldn't disguise the fact I was surprised. 'You were Jaz's girl-friend? The person that she mentioned to Ava?'

Riley shrugged. 'I assume so.'

I realised that Riley had just played this part to get close to Jaz to begin exacting her revenge.

'I don't understand.'

'The night that she died, I ran her a bath and lit candles in the bathroom. A bottle of Dom Pérignon later, and she started on the vodka in her freezer. Jaz was celebrating making partner at her law firm; I'm sure you must have known that. By the time I eventually persuaded her to get into the bath, she was on the verge of passing out. She made it so easy for me. I cut her wrists without a murmur from her. Then, while she bled to death, I took her phone and deleted every trace of my existence from it.'

'That was you?' I asked, horrified at her cavalier account of Jaz's death. I attempted to swallow, failed. 'When I rang Jaz that night, then messaged her begging her to call me, it was you who read my messages?' I shook my head in disbelief. 'And then you deleted my calls and WhatsApp messages so that when Jaz's parents or the police checked her phone, there would be no trace of my messages that night? It was you who left that suicide note?'

She didn't answer me, but the satisfied gleam in her eye was enough.

'And you somehow copied my handwriting and sent her parents that letter the week before you killed her, outing her?' I stared at her, filled with horror at the magnitude of her crimes.

She held my gaze.

'But...' I dropped my gaze to her body. 'Surely, Jaz would have noticed the initials on your stomach? How did you explain them?'

'She never saw them. I have lived my life making sure no one sees them. And if anyone asks why, I explain that I have an injury from an accident that hasn't healed and needs a permanent dressing in case of infection.'

Then I remembered that Jaz had ghosted me before she died.

'Did you say something to Jaz about me? She stopped answering my messages and calls the weeks before her... her death.'

A smiled played at the corners of her mouth. 'Maybe I did.'

'What did you say?'

She shrugged. 'Does it matter? All that counts is that she believed me.'

'Why did you do it?'

'You know why. Because of what you forced me to do. The five of you destroyed my life!' Her eyes burned with murderous hatred.

'I... I... I wasn't there,' I stuttered. 'I swear on my life that it wasn't me.'

'Then why do I have your initials carved on my stomach? Why do I have your four friends' initials cut into my skin as well?'

I shook my head, unable to answer her. I had no idea why.

'I'll tell you why, because you forced me to do it!' Tears trailed down my cheeks as I accepted that reasoning wouldn't work. Riley wouldn't acknowledge the truth – I wasn't a witness, let alone the perpetrator of the crime she was accusing me of committing against her. My mind was in overdrive as I tried to figure out what had happened here twenty-two years ago. 'Enough stalling! I want you to cut my initials into your skin. Now!'

I weakly nodded, feeling light-headed. I looked at Jacob's sickeningly pale, unresponsive face. One wrong move and the knife would slice through his neck to the carotid artery and jugular vein. If severed, he would rapidly bleed to death. The price of saving Jacob's life was to mutilate my body, but I had no choice: I loved him.

With a trembling hand, I took the lid off the craft knife, exposing the sharp blade. I wiped my blurred eyes with the back of my other hand, accepting my fate. I chewed my bottom lip as the cold tip of the blade touched my skin. I let it rest there as I built up the courage to cut into myself. Below, I could see the raised three-inch scar from my appendectomy.

'Do it!' ordered Riley.

Blinded again by tears, I swiped them away. Wincing, I dug the blade into my flesh. 'Argh!' I cried out, forcing myself to continue downwards, cutting the first part of the 'R' into my skin. Blood oozed out from the incision, making me feel nauseous. I blocked out what I was doing, willing myself to think about Jacob and the baby I was carrying. That I needed to survive, at whatever cost, for the sake of their lives.

Hand shaking, I finished cutting the 'R' as I moaned in pain.

Sobbing, I dropped the craft knife.

'Now the "S",' instructed Riley.

'Please,' I cried. 'I... I need some time...'

'Now!' she forcibly repeated.

I looked at her and then at the tip of the knife delicately poised against Jacob's neck. Filled with dread, I picked the bloodied knife up and steeled myself as I pressed the blade against my flesh, sinking it in to cut out the letter 'S'.

I had no idea how long it had taken me. All I knew was that it felt as if my blood-smeared abdomen was on fire. I raised my eyes and looked straight at her. 'I'm done,' I muttered, letting the craft knife drop from my hand.

'No. Now you have to cut out your friends' initials.'

I can't... I can't do it...

But what will happen if you don't? What will she do to you? To Jacob?

Then everything went black.

39

When I opened my eyes, it was to find Riley leaning over me, violently shaking my shoulders.

'GET UP!' she yelled. 'Get up and finish!'

'Riley?' I mumbled, disorientated.

I realised I must have passed out.

'GET UP!' she spat in my face.

'No,' I whispered. I noted that Riley had dropped the knife she had been holding against Jacob's throat on the floor next to her, tantalisingly just beyond my reach.

'You have to!' she threatened.

'I didn't do that to you,' I hoarsely argued.

'You know you did!'

I was clutching at straws, trying to find something that could prove to her that I wasn't there. Then I remembered one crucial detail. I wore glasses when I was eleven because I was short-sighted.

'Glasses? Was I wearing glasses?' I asked her.

'What?' she replied, caught off guard.

'If it was me, I would have been wearing glasses.'

Startled by my question, she suddenly released her grip on me.

'I was short-sighted and wore glasses. I only started wearing contact lenses in the June of that summer term.'

'I don't believe you!' she stated. 'I've never seen you wearing glasses. Nor are there glasses or any contact lenses cases in the bathroom or your bedroom.'

'My bedroom?' I questioned, startled by this revelation. A coldness crept over me. 'Why were you in my bedroom?'

Riley didn't answer me. I could see the doubt in her eyes as she struggled to recall whether the girl who made her cut those gruesome initials into her flesh was wearing glasses.

'I had laser eye surgery when I was twenty,' I explained, pushing myself up onto my elbows. 'If it had been me, I would have been wearing glasses.'

She didn't answer me, but I could see the realisation in her eyes as they widened at the acknowledgement that whoever forced her to cut herself had perfect eyesight.

'It wasn't me,' I asserted. 'And you know it!'

She grabbed the knife she had dropped and shakily stood up.

'It couldn't have been me,' I repeated, seeing the doubt in her eyes.

She took a couple of steps back as if fearful of my words.

'When did it happen?' I questioned as soon as the thought came to me.

She looked down at me as if I was the crazy one. But I remembered that Rebecca Spencer arrived at Queen Victoria's School for Girls at the start of May, and by the end of May, she had disappeared without a word. But the day she vanished I was absent from school. I wasn't here the night of her initiation. I knew nothing about it – I was critically ill.

She hesitated before asking, 'Why?'

'It's important,' I replied.

She frowned, seemingly trying to figure out if I was trying to trick her.

'When was it?' I firmly asked, holding my nerve.

'Saturday the twenty-second of May!' she spat in disgust. 'How could you not remember?'

Relief coursed through me as tears filled my eyes. She was wrong. She had got it all wrong and I had the evidence to prove it.

'I don't remember because I wasn't here.'

'Stop lying to me! You were here that night!' she contemptuously stated.

I shook my head. 'No. I was rushed into hospital in the early hours of that Saturday morning.'

'No! You were here. You orchestrated all of this! I have your initials cut into my stomach, Claudia Harper. Your initials!'

'I wasn't here,' I continued. 'I was in hospital for six days because my appendix had perforated.'

'It had to be you! There were five of you. You were all friends.'

'It wasn't me!' I insisted. 'Riley, you have to believe me.'

She furiously yanked her sleeves up and stretched out her arms, exposing multiple thick, gnarled scars zigzagging across her wrists and arms.

I gazed in shock. Sakura, my research student, was right.

'Oh God... Riley,' I mumbled, horrified.

'You did this to me!' she accused.

'No...' I muttered.

'You told me I was better off dead and suggested that I use the razor blade to slit my wrists! And that's what I did! I went back to my dormitory, and I ran a hot bath, climbed in, and I did this because I couldn't live with what I had done! It was you, Claudia Harper! YOU!' she yelled.

Did she really try to kill herself at Queen Victoria's School for Girls? Or is she lying?

'Who found you?' I sceptically questioned. I had no reason to believe her. I knew nothing about her, aside from the fact she was a liar. She had lied her way into my home.

Christ, Claudia! She went into your bedroom when you weren't there! What else did she do?

'Madame Barraud,' Riley thickly answered.

'What?' I was surprised. Madame Barraud was our French teacher and a favourite amongst the students. But if Madame Barraud had found her, the other students involved would have been severely punished, if not expelled. So why, if what Riley was claiming was true, didn't that happen?

'Madame Barraud was in the grounds having a cigarette. She saw the bathroom light on and came up to check as no one was supposed to be out of bed. If it hadn't been for Madame Barraud, I would have died. When she asked about the letters cut into my stomach, I told her what you had all forced me to do, and you know what she and the headmistress, who she immediately summoned, did?' Riley asked.

I shook my head.

'They accused me of lying! They covered for you, saying you were in hospital and so couldn't be the ringleader—'

'But that was true,' I interrupted. 'I was in hospital.'

'Your friends denied everything, of course. It was all turned back on to me, the victim. I was demonised and made to look as if I had done this to myself to get you in trouble. They called my mother to arrange for me to be collected immediately and taken for medical treatment. They claimed I was too psychologically unstable to continue at the school. That I was a liar, and an attention-seeker.'

'Riley, I—'

'No!' she interrupted. 'The school protected you! You and your friends. You made me try to take my life, and the school defended you. I tried to kill myself because of what you and your friends did to me. And I was treated as the problem. Not you. ME!'

'I didn't do it,' I stated as I stared into her feverish eyes. 'I didn't do it!'

'Stop lying! You're "CH". No one else at the school had those initials. I checked every graduation yearbook photograph. I followed all five of you through social media. Every photograph you posted. All the school reunions that you attended. Always the five of you. So, you can't pretend it was someone else. There was no one else who was as tall as you with long reddish hair. You orchestrated all of this,' she accused, gesturing at the surroundings. 'You started this in this very clock tower twenty-two years ago.'

I didn't reply. I had no idea how to get out of this situation, but I knew one thing, I wasn't responsible for whatever happened here that night all those years ago. Jacob didn't deserve to die for something I wasn't a party to, and neither did I.

Then it hit me. What if it had happened? At that moment, I understood. Riley Harrison – Rebecca Spencer – had made a mistake. It wasn't me who had been there that evening. But I knew who it might have been.

'What about Lottie?' I suggested, staring at her.

'What?' Riley spluttered, confused.

'Lottie. Lottie Hambleton. She and I were the tallest girls in our year. She also had strawberry blonde hair. She shared the dorm with me, Jaz, Issie, Willow and Ava. It was her, not me.'

'NO! It was you!' screamed Riley as she suddenly rushed at me. 'It was your name that I was told to cut into my skin. CH for Claudia Harper!'

It happened so quickly that I didn't have time to react. I felt a coldness deep in my abdomen. I looked down to see Riley pull the blade of the knife out of my stomach. It was slick with dark blood. I dragged my questioning gaze up to hers. In that moment, I saw in her eyes that she knew I was pregnant.

How? How could she know?

I watched as she pulled her right arm back as she prepared to plunge the blade in again. I realised that she was trying to end my pregnancy.

Some kind of primitive preservation kicked in, overriding the paralysing shock that restrained me. I darted between the clock machinery as she lunged at me again, the knife just missing me.

'NO!' she screamed in frustration.

Heart thundering, and panting, I watched her as she appraised the situation, her eyes wild with murderous rage. Behind me, the clock hands remained perfectly frozen in time.

'Riley, please,' I tried to reason. 'It wasn't me. Lottie Hambleton. It was her!'

'NO! I have your initials on me, not hers!'

I shook my head. 'You have hers. "CH" is Charlotte Hambleton. But she was only ever called Lottie.'

'NO!' she insisted. 'Don't you think I would know?'

'You'd only been here for a few weeks before this happened to you. All you knew was what people told you. Lottie gave you the initial "C" for her name. It meant that if anyone found out, she could argue she didn't do it. No one called her Charlotte. She was only ever known as Lottie. But you wouldn't know that.'

'STOP IT!' she screamed at me. 'You gave me a piece of paper inviting me to the initiation signed, "CH". You!'

'No, I didn't. Lottie did,' I fired back. 'You didn't know any of us. You never spoke to me, or my friends. I doubt you even knew Lottie's name was Charlotte. Did she say she was called Charlotte?' I demanded. 'Did she? Or did she give you my name instead to protect herself since I wasn't here?'

Riley was silent. But I could see the confusion in her eyes.

'You're making all of this up to stall the inevitable. This Lottie or Charlotte Hambleton wasn't in any of the end-of-year graduation photographs. Which means she doesn't exist.'

'No, she wasn't,' I agreed, watching as she stepped towards me.

'Hah! Exactly! You're a liar, Claudia Harper!'

'I'm not. Lottie isn't in the photographs because she had an equestrian accident a week after you left. Our school's equestrian team were competing in a showjumping competition. The wings of one of the jumps spooked her Belgian Warmblood in the arena, and he reared and went back over onto Lottie, crushing her. She broke her neck, and her spinal cord severed,' I recalled, shaking my head. 'The doctors had said she died from acute respiratory and cardiac failure. The paramedics arrived too late to save her.'

'You're lying to me!' Riley cried out.

I could see the distress in her wide eyes as a sliver of doubt had set in.

'I'm not,' I argued. 'Lottie died.'

'No! That's not true! You're lying to me to save yourself!'

'It was a horrific tragedy,' I continued, trying to keep my voice steady.

The shocking accident had completely overshadowed Rebecca Spencer's sudden disappearance. Lottie's tragedy had affected the school terribly; both students and teachers had struggled to come to terms with her death.

'I don't believe you!' Riley spat as she stepped towards me. Closer and closer.

I backed away from her, only to find myself precariously pressed up against the clock face.

'I didn't do it,' I pleaded, my hands instinctively covering my bleeding stomach. 'I would never have made you do that to yourself. And I'm sorry that my friends didn't stop Lottie.'

I knew Charlotte Hambleton, or Lottie as she was otherwise

known, to be an intimidating, forceful girl who used her privileged social status to get what she wanted. I could imagine how challenging it would have been for Jaz, Ava, Issie and Willow to stand up to her, as Riley indicated. I was sure that none of them would willingly have gone along with Lottie's cruel, twisted initiation ceremony.

'You're not sorry because you did it! And so did your friends. Why do you think I wanted you to witness your friends all dying, one by one? Until you were the last one left. Because you were the ringleader. You, Claudia Harper. YOU!' she yelled, running at me with the knife poised, aiming at my stomach.

I dodged to the left to avoid her. But as she reached out for me, something went wrong. I watched in horror as Riley's foot got caught in one of the rotting floorboards. She fell forward, crashing with full force into the clock face. Glass panes exploded with the impact of her body. I tried to grab onto her to stop her fall, but her body brushed past my fingers as she plummeted to the black depths below, her high-pitched screams filling the night air.

In shock, I stared through the shards of broken glass at the grounds far below. But it was too dark to be able to see Riley's broken body.

'Riley?' I whispered.

Silence answered me.

I knew it was unlikely she could survive the fall.

My legs gave way beneath me and I collapsed in a heap on the floor too shocked to move. I then remembered Jacob. I somehow crawled over to him, and held onto him so hard, my body convulsing as I cried uncontrollably. 'I didn't do it, Jacob. I didn't do that to her... I didn't do it...'

But if I was looking for salvation, there was none.

'JACOB?' I howled as his head lolled backwards in my arms. 'Oh

God... NO! Jacob? Please, Jacob. You can't die on me! I'm pregnant! We're pregnant...'

There was no response.

Tears streamed down my cheeks as I rocked him backwards and forwards in my arms. I had already lost Issie and Jaz. I couldn't lose him as well.

Riley Harrison, my lodger, had taken everything from me. But I hadn't committed the atrocious crime she had accused me of, and I didn't believe that my friends could be involved in such a heinous initiation ceremony.

Could it be that they had kept this terrible secret from you?

Horrified, I tried to swallow, but my mouth was too dry. I thought back to Charlotte – Lottie – Hambleton. She had shared our dorm when we started at Queen Victoria's School for Girls, and so, there had been six of us, to begin with, not that I particularly liked Lottie. I found her to be arrogant, vain, entitled and spiteful. But was she that cruel to coerce Rebecca Spencer to cut this Friends List, as she called it, into her flesh?

Shock hit me as it dawned on me there was only one person left alive that could tell me the truth – Ava.

I realised I was trembling. My body was cold – and wet. I looked down at the blood ebbing from my lower abdomen. Fear gripped me. I suddenly felt light-headed at the prospect that the knife could have punctured my uterus.

What if she killed the baby? Oh God... No...

I tightly held on to Jacob, willing him to live.

Please don't take him... Please don't take him... Please....

For without Jacob, I had no one left.

40

MONDAY

I was sat by Jacob's hospital bed, unable to release his left hand. I clung to it, fearing that if I let go, I would lose him. I chewed my bottom lip to stop the tears that threatened to fall. While waiting help in the clock tower, I was terrified that Jacob would die, and nineteen hours later, I still couldn't let go of that terror.

The emergency services had rushed Jacob to Epsom General Hospital in Surrey before transferring him to the National Hospital for Neurology and Neurosurgery in London. It was the UK's largest dedicated neurological and neurosurgical hospital and was part of London College Hospital.

I studied Jacob's chest as it barely moved. He was heavily sedated and looked deathly pale. His right eye was severely swollen and bruised, and stitches sealed the deep four-inch gash above it. The CT scan at Epsom General Hospital had shown a compound depressed fracture at the back of his head. Part of his skull had crushed inwards from the impact of the baseball bat. Jacob's condition had then escalated to a neurosurgical emergency because of the risk of bacterial infection caused by the dislodged bone against the brain, resulting in him being air-lifted here for immediate surgery. During a ten-hour procedure, the pieces of bone pressing inwards were removed and returned to their correct position and a metal mesh inserted to reconnect Jacob's shattered skull together.

I squeezed Jacob's hand, willing him to react. To prove to me that he was going to pull through, but he remained unresponsive. The regular beeping of the machines attached to his body reassured me he was still alive. I held onto the neurosurgeon's prognosis that Jacob should pull through – I had to, as the alternative was unthinkable.

I had also discovered that Willow had been transferred to NHNN this morning as she required another surgery to alleviate further bleeding to her brain. She had undergone a craniotomy to remove blood clots and repair damaged blood vessels. Whether she was going to pull through was highly debatable at this stage.

I could imagine all too well the agony that Charles and Willow's family were going through. More so as Willow remained in a medically induced coma requiring ventilatory support. Both Jacob and Willow had brain traumas caused by the same woman.

The anger I felt at her – Riley – was unbridled. My life, and Jacob's life, was destroyed because of her.

I had no idea whether what she told me was true or not.

She's insane, Claudia... How could it possibly be true?

How could Willow have been there that night in the clock tower, and Jaz, Issie and Ava? Together with Lottie, they had allegedly exhibited an unimaginable level of cruelty against Rebecca Spencer.

It wasn't possible. They couldn't have committed such a heinous act. Not Jaz, Willow, Issie and Ava.

I looked up as Zain walked into the private ICU room holding two drinks.

'Thanks,' I mumbled, giving him a weak smile.

'How are you feeling?' he asked, offering me the coffee.

'Still can't believe it.'

'I mean your injuries?'

'Oh...' I automatically looked down at my abdomen, but my oversized sweatshirt covered the stitches and dressings. 'They've given me something for the pain. But...' I shrugged.

'Are you still...?' Zain faltered, looking awkward as hell.

It dawned on me he was asking about the pregnancy.

'How did you know?' I numbly questioned.

Uncomfortable, he dropped his gaze. 'I read the statements from the officers who attended the scene.'

Everything was a blur. I couldn't even recall talking to the police. My only focus had been on Jacob.

Unable to find the words, I took a sip of coffee instead.

'Shouldn't you be resting?' he asked, pulling up a chair to sit with me.

'I need to be with Jacob,' I simply answered.

Neither of us spoke for what felt like an eternity, both watching Jacob, willing him to be all right.

'Ava's on her way from her parents' place in Cornwall,' Zain quietly stated.

'Oh...'

'She wants to explain what happened that night in the clock tower with Rebecca Spencer or Riley Harrison, as she was later known. She feels terrible. She said they couldn't tell you. They all swore to keep it a secret, believing it was better for you if you didn't know, especially after Lottie died. But the three of them agreed they would tell you everything when they met you for drinks at The Queen Charlotte. Ava had shown Issie and Willow a copy of the letter sent to Jaz, believing it might be from you. She had also received an anonymous letter in the same handwriting, filled with vicious threats to expose her relationship with a married colleague. But Issie could tell it wasn't your handwriting, that someone was trying to impersonate it. That someone was out to get them. Someone from their past who knew their secret.'

'Oh,' I mumbled, struggling to accept that Ava had admitted to Zain that the four of them had been there the night Riley cut herself, tricked by Lottie into believing it was some kind of initiation ceremony.

I shook my head, unable to understand how they could have kept such a heinous secret from me for so long: especially Jaz, my best friend. Worse, how could they have gone along with Lottie's cruel plan?

I felt sickened by Ava's admission. It felt as if I didn't know them. It was as if our friendship was a lie.

'You knew about Ava's affair?' Zain questioned.

'Yes. We all did,' I answered. 'How did Riley know?'

'We recovered photographs from her mobile phone that was evidence she was stalking all five of you; that she had been for a couple of months before moving in with you as a lodger. That was how she knew about Ava's affair.'

I shuddered at the thought.

'But why would Ava think I sent the letter?' I suddenly questioned.

'The handwriting was identical to Jaz's letter; she put two and two together.'

'How could that be?'

'I imagine that Riley went through refuse bins to find something with your writing on.'

'Seriously?' I questioned, horrified.

'That's what people do. They take the rubbish out of the bin and search through, looking for whatever it is they hope to find.'

I suddenly felt overwhelmed with nausea.

It hit me that Riley Harrison – Rebecca Spencer – had targeted me. She had attempted to sabotage my friendships and isolate me because she believed I was the ringleader. She wanted me to watch as she picked them off one by one, finally saving the worst for me. I was now under no illusion that she was planning on making me witness Jacob's death, knowing I was next.

I thought of Jaz, Issie and poor Willow fighting for her life. And the reason why.

They really did that to... To Rebecca Spencer. Something so cruel. Something that haunted her until the end.

Zain watched me as I processed the horrors of my friends' secret.

'That explains the night I saw them at Barrafina in Dean Street. Helena had just left, and I came out of the toilets to find the three of them sitting at the bar...' I faltered. 'They... They didn't expect to see me.'

Numb, I shook my head.

'I suspect that was when Ava shared the letters with them,' Zain explained.

I didn't reply. It hurt so bad knowing that they had kept something of this magnitude from me since the age of eleven. It felt as if Jaz, Issie, Willow and Ava were strangers: for the friends I loved would never have been complicit in such an evil act. They had kept it secret for twenty-two years, which begged the question, what else had they withheld from me?

'It might help knowing how Lottie coerced them all,' Zain suggested.

'I already know what happened. Riley told me.'

'I'm just saying that talking with Ava might help you.'

'How? Will it take away the initials that I carved into my stomach? Or the fact that Jacob nearly died? That he still might...' I faltered, unable to articulate the worst possible scenario presented by Jacob's team of doctors. 'Nor will it bring Jaz or Issie back.'

I was acutely aware that Ava had lost Jaz and Issie too and that I wasn't the only one suffering. Ava wasn't responsible for their deaths, but her actions twenty-two years ago, along with Issie, Jaz and Willow, were the catalyst.

Could I forgive her for this?

I chewed my bottom lip as I watched Jacob.

Maybe... Maybe you could forgive Ava and the others with time, but you would never be able to forget. How could you?

'We found the duplicate key fob for Ava's Range Rover,' Zain stated. 'It was in Riley's apartment along with the wig, Gucci bag and Chanel sunglasses.'

Surprised, I turned to him. 'She had an apartment?'

He nodded. 'A luxury penthouse apartment in Canary Wharf overlooking the Thames.'

'Christ!' I muttered. 'So, it was all a lie. She never needed to rent a room from me.'

'No,' answered Zain. 'The concierge stated that Riley was still using the apartment, that he greeted her every day.'

It now made sense as to why I hardly ever heard her in her room, or saw her.

'Why? Why did she move in with me?'

'It allowed her to get close to you.'

Numb, I slowly shook my head.

'Riley Harrison read your journals,' Zain explained. 'She has countless photos of your entries. I recognised them because of Jacob's name.'

'She photographed my journals?'

I recalled Riley saying that she had been in my bedroom. I now understood that Riley must have discovered my journals, which I kept in a box in my wardrobe and my current one in my bedside cabinet drawer. I couldn't believe that she had gone through them.

Zain nodded. 'That wasn't all we found...' He hesitated. 'We found Darcy's cat collar.'

Startled, I gasped. 'What?'

Zain simply looked at me and waited for me to figure it out.

My mind went into freefall as I struggled to make sense of what it meant. 'I... I left the kitchen bi-folding door open. Darcy got out. So how could Riley have his collar?' I stared at Zain. 'She... She let him out?'

'I assume something like that.'

'Why?' I questioned, feeling sick. 'Why would she take his collar off him? It would mean that no one would know who he belonged to.'

'That's what she intended.'

I sat back, winded. The tears intensified as I then thought about Darcy. I struggled to accept that Riley could hate me so much as to remove Darcy's collar and let him out. Maybe she even took him someplace unfamiliar, so he would never find his way back home. That last glimmer of hope I had held onto of Darcy coming back to me evaporated.

'Why?' I asked.

'To hurt you,' answered Zain.

Hot, angry tears slid down my cheeks.

'Riley had also taken countless photographs of Jacob at work, then out socialising with colleagues,' Zain shared, following my gaze.

I let Zain's words wash over me as I stared at Jacob's damaged face. He was innocent in all of this, guilty through association, as was I.

'I've talked to Jacob's colleagues, and they corroborated his story about the woman Jacob felt compelled to take home because she was so drunk and had no phone or ID on her. They identified her as Riley Harrison.'

'Bex. She was Riley?' I questioned.

Zain nodded.

I took a sip of coffee to try to rid myself of the sickening taste in my mouth.

I realised my hand was trembling. She had even used Bex, an abbreviation of her name, Rebecca. She couldn't have tried harder to flaunt in my face that it was her.

'I've known Jacob since uni, Claudia. Longer than you. And he's never lied to me. Riley planned it. She knew you were away at a two-day conference. She set Jacob up.'

'I know,' I quietly conceded.

'She had to sabotage your marriage in order to move in as your lodger,' Zain explained. 'We also retrieved your laptop from her car.'

'My laptop?' I questioned, surprised.

He nodded. 'Her black Lexus LX570 was parked up on the school grounds. We found documentation on her phone and laptop confirming that the silver Jaguar F-Type R you saw at Issie's cottage was a hire car. The Lexus is registered to her.'

Riley's lies and subterfuge were staggering.

'Are you all right?' Zain asked in response to my silence.

I nodded. 'It's just a lot to take in.'

'I know,' Zain sympathised. 'I imagine Riley has been planning her revenge for years.'

I took another sip of coffee as I gazed back at Jacob.

He had been telling you the truth, Claudia. And you didn't believe him.

Then I remembered the texts he received from an unknown number when I had stayed over at his flat.

'Did she text him asking about her bracelet?'

Zain nodded. 'We found messages on her phone to Jacob asking about meeting up and a bracelet. He had replied that he didn't know who was texting him.'

'I was with him,' I explained. 'We left your party together and... I shrugged. 'But how did she get Jacob's phone number?'

'She no doubt got it from your iPhone.'

There were countless times I had left my phone charging in the kitchen or my bedroom.

'But how would she access it without my six-digit passcode?' I asked.

'Believe it or not, there is a way to access anyone's iPhone without their passcode,' Zain stated.

'How?' I sceptically questioned.

Zain smiled at me. 'I had the same reaction, but it was one of our IT guys who showed me this trick. Give me your phone.'

I picked up my phone and handed it to Zain.

I watched as he held down the home button until Siri appeared.

'Siri, what time is it?' he asked.

I stared at my phone as it displayed the time.

'Click on the image of the clock,' he explained. 'It now brings up the world clock, alarm, stopwatch and timer screen. Click on the time option and select "when timer ends". Now scroll to the top of the ringtone list and select "buy more tones".'

I gasped as it took him to the Apple Store.

'Watch this,' he continued. 'If I click the home button again, it should bring up the main phone screen with full access to your phone, including all your contacts.'

Shocked, I shook my head in disbelief.

Zain handed me my phone back.

'When I couldn't find my laptop, I assumed I had left it at work on Friday, but Riley had taken it – why?'

'You said that Jacob texted you to meet him at the old clock tower.'

I nodded.

'Check your phone.'

'Sorry?'

'Open up the message from Jacob.'

Confused, I did as he instructed.

'Scroll up past Jacob's text message to you,' Zain instructed.

I did.

'Further,' insisted Zain.

'What?' Shocked, I turned to him.

'She sent that from your Apple laptop.'

I stared at my iPhone. I wouldn't have even realised unless I had scrolled up through the texts.

I really need to talk to you.

I recognised the text as I had sent it to Jacob yesterday morning. However, the text had been copied and pasted below another message – one that I hadn't sent. I scanned over all three texts. The original one I had sent, then the message Riley had sent Jacob pretending to be me in between, followed by a copy of my original text. I assumed it was so I wouldn't realise what she had done, as a cursory glance would only show my last text to him. It was utterly Machiavellian.

I really need to talk to you.

Will you meet me at the clock tower at my old boarding school? I'm already here. I came here because of what this place means to us. I'm pregnant and it's yours. My phone is nearly out of battery so don't bother replying. C x

I really need to talk to you.

I was shocked.

'I sent that first message late yesterday morning when I woke up,' I explained to Zain. 'Riley then sent that next text shortly afterwards at 11.55 a.m. asking Jacob to meet me at the clocktower. And she told him I was pregnant?'

Zain nodded. 'Jacob's crazy about you. She knew that. She tried to seduce him that night when he acted as a good Samaritan, and she failed. But she added in the pregnancy revelation to ensure he would turn up.'

I looked at him. His eyes, which were so dark that they appeared black, were filled with sincerity.

'But how did she know what significance the clock tower held for Jacob and me?' I questioned.

'Maybe your journals? Or your engagement announcement online?'

'Oh,' I muttered. 'You're right. I posted that Jacob had proposed to me in the clock tower at my old boarding school. I even added a photo of it. God!'

'Riley Harrison wanted to destroy you. Your career, your marriage and ultimately your life. And she very nearly succeeded,' Zain stated.

I dropped my gaze to my fingers, which were absentmindedly touching Jacob's wedding ring. It struck me that he had never taken it off. I hadn't noticed before. Or maybe I had chosen not to see it?

Why didn't you believe him when he said he hadn't cheated on you?

Why did you let Riley Harrison – Rebecca Spencer – come between you?

Why, Claudia? WHY?

41

We sat in silence for what felt like an eternity watching Jacob, each of us consumed by our thoughts.

'You said my career. That she wanted to destroy it,' I said, turning to Zain.

I had no idea how Riley believed she could sabotage my career. I was aware that she was Helena's research student. But that was all – a student, and crucially, not my student. So, it wasn't as if she could make an allegation against me.

'Earlier, I talked to Dr Ramirez, Riley Harrison's PhD supervisor,' Zain answered. 'She mentioned the two of you were friends.'

I nodded, resisting the compulsion to add that 'were' was the operative word.

'Dr Ramirez is worried about you. She said she's called you but you're not answering.'

I shrugged. I knew that she had called multiple times and left a voice message. Not that I had listened to it. I had too much going on to answer her calls. I planned on calling her back when I knew Jacob was going to be all right.

'She said she's sorry.'

I looked at Zain. 'For what? Riley?'

'She said she accused you of something and that she got it wrong. That she feels bad. Do you know what Dr Ramirez meant?' Zain asked.

I nodded. Not that I was going to tell Zain that my colleague, who was also a close friend, had days ago accused me of having sex with her then-partner in their bathroom at their New Year's Eve party two years back.

'Why do you think she would apologise for Riley?' Zain asked, curious.

'Because it was Helena's idea that I rent the guest room to Riley. She was her new research student and alleged she needed a place for a couple of months.'

Zain cleared his throat. He looked awkward as hell. 'Look, Dr Ramirez said that Riley caused a lot of trouble for you at work.'

I was taken aback. 'I don't understand.'

'She said that there were rumours about you and a...' Embarrassed, Zain cleared his throat again. 'A colleague at work?'

I nodded, feeling my cheeks burn with the admission.

'Well, Dr Ramirez discovered the source of the rumours.'

'She did?'

'It seems that Riley was the person who started them.'

'What?' I stared, open-mouthed, at Zain.

'She talked to a fellow research student by the name of Cassie Williams. Riley told her that you had slept with Dr Novak to get back at your husband because he had cheated on you.'

I slowly breathed out. 'How would she have found out?' Then I realised: 'My journals.'

'She told Cassie that she had overheard you talking to your friend about it,' explained Zain.

'The night Riley moved in. Issie had turned up. I ended up

telling Issie about Ethan. Riley must have overheard our conversation.'

'I suspect so,' Zain said. 'Riley also told Cassie Williams that you were badmouthing your colleagues.'

I was struggling to comprehend Riley's hatred for me. She had set out to destroy every aspect of my life. I had even ended a lecture early because of her. She had thrown me when I saw her in the lecture theatre, more so when she had suddenly disappeared. I assumed that I was suffering from paranoia and was starting to fall apart, believing everyone was whispering about me. But the reality was, my students and colleagues were talking about me because of the rumours Riley had started.

I shook my head again. 'I lost all my work on my laptop. I assumed I had inadvertently wiped all my files, but...' I faltered as it dawned on me that Riley had no doubt accessed it. 'I keep all my passwords on a piece of paper in the study desk in the living room. She could have sabotaged all my lecture and seminar notes to make my professional life even more difficult.'

'I wouldn't be surprised,' answered Zain.

I looked back at Jacob. Rebecca Spencer, aka Riley Harrison, had gone to staggering lengths to enact her revenge on me. Including attempting to kill my husband.

I then realised that the police had said that Rebecca Spencer wasn't in the UK. And yet, she had been here stalking Jaz, Issie, Willow, Ava and myself for months. How was that possible?

'Rebecca Spencer,' I said, turning to Zain. 'You said that she hadn't been back to the UK since her mother relocated, with her, to New York when she was eleven. So, how was she here? Or had she never left?'

'She did move to New York City with her mother, who went on to marry an American property tycoon, Robert William Harrison. He adopted Riley when she was twelve, and she became a naturalised American citizen with an American passport. When Harrison adopted her, she took his surname. At the same time, she legally changed her Christian name. To all intents and purposes she is Riley Harrison. She has been since she was twelve years old.'

'Why change her name at the age of twelve? Doesn't that seem odd to you?'

'There was a reason that her mother relocated to America.'

'Because of what happened to Riley at my boarding school?'

Zain shook his head. 'No. I talked to your old headmistress Simone Anstruther, again. She gave me some new information about Rebecca Spencer. She had been sent to the boarding school so her biological father wouldn't find her. There were fears around her safety where he was concerned. He was convicted of the attempted murder of her mother when she was seven years old witnessed by Rebecca. Her mother sent her to your boarding school when she found out that he was due to be released. He had threatened her that he would take Rebecca from her, and she would never see her again. So, she enrolled her at the school in the assumption she would be safe there.'

I shook my head at the reality. 'Instead, she was coerced into mutilating herself in some depraved initiation ceremony and then attempted to take her own life. And to think that the school's response was to accuse her of lying and have her removed.'

'Remember, she accused you of being the instigator of the initiation ceremony. But you were ill in hospital. Simone Anstruther had no idea it was Charlotte Hambleton. So, she did what she thought was in the best interests of Rebecca Spencer. She recommended her mother remove her from the school and seek medical and psychiatric help. As far as your headmistress was concerned Rebecca Spencer was a traumatised young child and now she was making what were perceived to be wild accusations about you. When Simone Anstruther questioned Ava, Jaz, Issie and Willow they all refuted Rebecca Spencer's claims, saying they were in the dormitory together asleep. It was four against one. Or five, as Lottie Hambleton stated that they never left the dormitory.'

I found myself feeling sorry for Rebecca Spencer.

'So, her mother went to America to escape from her husband?' I asked.

'Ex-husband by then, and yes. She had met Robert William Harrison here in London, and they began dating. When he returned to New York, she followed with her daughter.'

'And her biological father never found her?'

'No. When Robert Harrison and her mother married, Harrison adopted Rebecca, changing both her Christian and surname because of safety concerns. Riley Harrison became an American citizen with a social security number, a passport and later a driver's licence.'

'Rebecca Spencer became Riley Harrison? Why not renew her British passport and have dual nationality? Surely, she could have changed her name with the UK government?'

'At the risk of her biological father finding her?' Zain stated.

I looked at him as I tried to comprehend the fear that had driven her mother to flee to another country to protect her daughter. Then the hatred that had fuelled Riley to return to the UK for retribution despite the fear of her biological father.

'Her accent? There was no trace of an American accent,' I pointed out, surprised.

Zain shrugged. 'I moved to London from Glasgow when I was thirteen and never lost my Glaswegian accent.'

'And Riley was there when her biological father tried to murder her mother when she was seven?'

'Yep.'

'She had one messed-up life. I can't even begin to imagine how you would process that,' I replied.

'Some people don't,' stated Zain.

We sat for a moment as the constant bleeping machines punctuated our thoughts. I stared at Jacob, willing him to wake up. To dispel the crippling fear that he would never recover that consumed me.

'Why now, after all these years?' I asked, breaking the heavy silence. I turned to Zain. 'I mean, why not when she reached eighteen? Why wait?'

'Because her mother died four months ago. Suicide. Her husband, Riley's adoptive father, passed away after a cardiac arrest a month earlier, and she never recovered. Riley had no other family, so, ultimately, nothing to hold her back.'

'That's still one giant leap to make, surely. From loving daughter to murderer,' I pointed out.

Zain nodded. 'The stressor of her adoptive father's sudden death, followed by her mother's suicide, appears to have given her that final impetus to seek revenge. But, obviously, the only person who can answer that is Riley. Or should I say, could have answered that? We'll never really know what drove her to seek the five of you out after twenty-two years.'

I slowly exhaled as I thought about Riley Harrison.

'Riley would have seen those five initials cut into her skin every time she showered. She would never have been able to forget what happened that night at the clock tower.'

I shuddered at the realisation that I now shared the same fate. However, mine was only one initial – RS – those of a dead woman.

A dead woman who had tried to kill me and had killed two of my dearest childhood friends. I considered how easily Riley Harrison had inveigled her way into Jaz's life – then into my own.

'She registered as a PhD student. How was that possible?' I questioned, suddenly remembering.

'She had the money to pay the fees. Also, she was an

international student, so she was a lucrative prospect considering your university's international fees. And she had a BA and MA from Yale. So, she had the entry qualifications.'

'Was she registered at Bristol University before transferring to my department at UCL?'

Zain shook his head.

'So she made it all up?'

'Yes.'

'You said she had a penthouse apartment. How could she afford that?'

'It was originally owned by Robert Harrison – he was an extremely successful property entrepreneur – and Riley inherited everything when her mother died.'

I shook my head. 'She held onto the desire for revenge for twenty-two years. Even though she had a new life, a new name and a new father. She never let go of what happened to her that night in the clock tower,' I muttered.

'Would you?' he asked.

Zain's question caught me off guard. I thought about the Friends List, as Riley had called it, permanently etched on her stomach. Then the scars on her wrist from when she tried to kill herself shortly after the initiation ceremony. It was tragic that her mother had sent her daughter away to protect her, only for the converse to happen.

I didn't answer Zain. I couldn't.

Instead, I watched Jacob, willing him to wake up. To be all right. For us to be all right.

Without him...

I stopped myself. I wiped the tears that had started to fall again.

I didn't know whether I would ever be okay again.

'What will happen to Riley's body?' I asked as the thought came to me.

'When it's released, her body will be flown back to New York City. Her adoptive father's lawyers will be making the arrangements for her burial in the family plot.'

'Is anyone attending the funeral?'

'I can't say for certain, but I doubt it.'

'Oh...' I muttered, overwhelmed by sadness for her despite everything that had happened.

'Look, I need to get going. Will you be all right?'

I nodded.

He gave me a concerned look as he stood up. 'You really should get some sleep.'

'I can't leave Jacob,' I stated. 'I need to be here when he wakes up.'

He nodded.

'Zain?'

He stopped by the doorway and looked back at me.

'Jasper. Was he poisoned? That's what Issie suspected. That was why she didn't meet us at The Queen Charlotte the night...' I stopped myself, unable to repeat what had happened to Willow.

Zain stopped in the doorway and looked back at me. 'We can't conclusively say it was her, but the vet confirmed that Jasper had been poisoned. Issie refused to go home while the vet fought to save Jasper's life.'

I couldn't imagine what Issie must have gone through on Friday evening with Jasper and then Riley turning up to confront her.

'But Jasper's all right?'

Zain smiled. 'Yeah, he's fine.'

Tears started to fall as I thought of Issie. She would want me to look after Jasper. Especially with Darcy gone.

'Where is he?'

'Still at the vets until they find a home for him.'

'His home's with me and Jacob.'

'Sure.' Zain nodded. He turned to leave, then stopped. 'Maybe you'll still find Darcy? It's not unheard of for cats to be returned to their owners months after they disappear.'

'Maybe,' I agreed. But I didn't hold out any hope.

A few seconds later, I heard him talking to someone in the corridor.

I froze when I recognised the voice.

I didn't know if I was ready to talk to her.

Will there ever be a right time, Claudia?

42

Without thinking, I pushed myself up from the chair. I winced as a searing pain scorched through my abdomen. I lifted my sweatshirt to check the dressing. Blood seeped through the gauze from the stapled wound.

I was supposed to remain on hospital bedrest for the first forty eight hours for observation. The fear was a complication from the stab wound, such as an internal infection. However, Jacob's condition took precedence over any concerns over my abdominal injury. The nurses had finally acquiesced to my demand to be allowed to be with him given his critical condition.

The door opened.

'Claudia...' Ava stopped and stared at me, shocked.

But it was Ava whose appearance took me aback. She looked as dreadful as I felt.

Tears started to cascade down Ava's pale skin as she looked from me to Jacob's unresponsive body. 'Oh, Claudia... I am so sorry,' she whispered.

I felt as if I was going to pass out. I stepped backwards and gently lowered my body back into the chair, slowly breathing through the pain.

'Claudia?'

I turned to look at her.

She still was hesitating by the door. 'Can I join you?'

I nodded and looked away.

Ava crept over, as if she was frightened her presence would wake Jacob.

I felt her sit down next to me.

'How?' I found myself asking, unable to bring myself to look at her. For I knew she was crying, as was I. 'How could you do that to her? To Rebecca Spencer?'

'I... I didn't. Lottie forced Rebecca to do it,' she whispered. 'We... We didn't know how to stop her. It was supposed to be a prank, but it all got out of control. Lottie just pushed her and pushed until—'

'Rebecca Spencer was desperate to fit in, Ava. She would have done anything to fit in. And she did.' I sighed.

'God, don't you think I know that? I have gone over that night, again and again, wishing we had never followed Lottie there,' Ava quietly shared. 'Claudia... it was horrific. Lottie wouldn't listen to us. We begged her to stop. That she was going too far. But she wouldn't stop. Not until Rebecca had... had cut herself.'

I heard her give out a strangled sob.

I knew Lottie Hambleton was someone who no one dared say no to.

We both sat in silence, each caught up in our own misery.

'Why didn't any of you tell me what happened that night?' I finally questioned.

'We were going to tell you the night Willow was knocked down,' Ava answered.

'I mean when it happened.'

'You were in hospital,' Ava pointed out.

'Afterwards?'

Ava sighed. 'When Lottie had that terrible accident, we swore we would never talk about it again. Ever. So, we didn't. Not one of us spoke about it until...' Ava stopped.

'The letter arrived?' I questioned, turning to her.

She uneasily nodded.

'Why did you tell Jaz you thought I had written it?'

'The handwriting looked like yours—'

'And you believed I would want to hurt Jaz like that?'

'No... Of course not... But...' Ava looked unsure as to whether she should say it.

'But what?' I demanded. 'Because the handwriting looked like mine, so you both decided I had to have sent it. How could you even think I would write something like that?'

Ava shook her head. 'Remember that terrible argument between you and Jaz when we were on holiday in Italy? The one where she didn't talk to you for days. You argued that she should come out to her parents instead of pretending to be someone she wasn't for fear of upsetting them. You said you would never return to her parents' home until she told them the truth.'

'What?' I spluttered, incredulous. 'Christ! That was... when? Twelve years back when we were all still at uni. You know I apologised to Jaz. I explained that I was being naïve and simply wanted the best life for her.'

I shook my head as I stared at Ava. 'So, the two of you believed I wrote that letter outing her to her parents because of one drunken, silly argument when we were in our early twenties?'

'It was more than just an argument, Claudia. It very nearly ended your friendship.'

I was stunned by this revelation. I hadn't taken the disagreement as seriously as Jaz. But then again, it wasn't my sexual identity or the relationship with my parents at stake. I recalled it began over an offensive homophobic comment her father had made when I had been holidaying with Jaz and her parents, shortly before we flew to Italy to join Ava, Issie and Willow. Jaz quickly silenced me when she realised I was about to challenge her father's statement.

'And because of something years ago, the two of you found me guilty without even asking me first?'

Ava didn't say anything. Not that she needed to, as it was evident that was what they had done. I had always suspected that Ava had been jealous of how close Jaz and I were, but I would never have believed she would try and turn Jaz against me.

And for Jaz to believe that of me...

I could feel the tears threatening to fall.

'And your letter?' I questioned, unable to disguise the hurt in my voice.

'The handwriting was identical. And... there were details in there that only the five of us knew about me.'

'You mean you and Oliver?'

Ava dropped her gaze. 'I'm sorry, Claudia...'

'I would never hurt or threaten you. What made you believe I would do that?'

She shrugged as more tears fell. 'Stupidity? You and Jacob were the perfect couple and... I don't know. Guilt combined with jealousy maybe. You had it all.'

I waited.

'And... I... I hit on Jacob way back in the day, and I know you knew. I... I assumed you had held on to it, and when you found out that Oliver was married with a baby, you decided to take the moral high ground. Maybe it was easier to blame you than think of the alternative, which was that it was Rebecca Spencer. We were all terrified that what happened that night would come back to haunt us. That she would find us and reveal what we had never spoken about since Lottie's death. I'm so...' She faltered. 'I'm so sorry. I should never have treated you the way I did after Jaz's death. Deep down, I knew you hadn't written those letters. But the alternative was just unthinkable.'

I shakily breathed out. Her honesty took me by surprise. I realised then that I was as guilty as Ava of prejudging someone I loved – Jacob.

Of thinking the worst of him rather than the best: for I had accused Jacob of sleeping with another woman and then used his suspected infidelity as a licence to cheat on him.

'I wish you'd told me, Ava.'

'So do I,' she replied, her voice filled with regret.

'At Jaz's funeral, I thought I had done something terrible to have upset you and Jaz. I spent all this time beating myself up when, in fact, the four of you had kept this horrific secret from me for twenty-two years.'

My body was trembling. I slowly breathed out in a bid to slow my heart rate down. More tears slid down my cheeks. I swiped at them with the heel of my hand. I wanted to rage at Ava. If they had told me what they had done to Rebecca Spencer, I might never have ended up here with my husband fighting for his life. But I couldn't get the words out.

I looked at her. I could see the pain in her eyes. The regret and the loss.

'Claudia, I am so, so sorry. If I could undo it all, I would.'

I nodded as tears spilled down my cheeks. 'I know. I know you would. And so would I,' I found myself whispering.

Ava leaned in and hugged me. 'Are we okay?' she mumbled into my hair.

'We will be,' I answered. 'In time.'

'Thank you,' she whispered.

Then I heard a low moan. Jacob?

Ava released me as we turned to look at him.

Shocked, I watched, not daring to believe what I was witnessing. His eyelids were fluttering.

I grabbed his hand. 'Jacob?' I cried out. 'Jacob, I'm here.'

I then felt his hand gently squeeze mine.

I frantically turned to Ava. 'Get help!'

I turned back to Jacob to be certain it wasn't my imagination. His eyes were trying to focus on me as his lips started to silently move.

I realised he was trying to say my name.

'I'm here, Jacob. I'm here with you,' I reassured him as I leaned in close to his face.

He tried to move his head. 'Argh!' he moaned.

'Don't move. Please,' I urged him. 'The doctors will be here in a minute.'

I watched as he tried to focus again. He then tried to swallow but winced in pain.

I picked up the glass with the straw on his bedside cabinet and filled it with water. I put the straw to his dry lips. 'Here. This will help,' I said.

I held it there while he took a drink.

He nodded to let me know he had enough.

'Claudia?' he hoarsely murmured as I replaced the glass on the cabinet.

'I'm here,' I answered, leaning over his face again. 'I'm here.'

'You're crying,' he whispered.

'I'm just happy,' I explained.

He then frowned as his dark eyes filled with apprehension. 'Where is she?'

'She can't hurt us any more,' I gently assured him.

'I thought she was going to make you—'

'Shh...' I soothed. 'It's over.'

'I had no idea. She was Bex, the woman who... who I helped...' He hesitated, confused.

I nodded. 'I know.'

'But you texted me to meet you there?' he questioned, baffled 'How did she know?'

'Bex, as you knew her, was actually Riley, my lodger. She stole my laptop and texted you from it pretending to be me. She then texted me from your phone to meet you at the clock tower after she had attacked you.'

'Oh...' he mumbled as he absorbed this news. A few beats later he murmured, 'Are you all right?'

I smiled at him as tears rolled down my cheeks. 'I'm fine,' whispered as my lips softly brushed his clammy skin. 'I wanted to tell you, that I was...' I hesitated.

He stared up at me with dark eyes filled with apprehension.

'I mean, I still am. I'm pregnant,' I added.

His eyes lit up. 'So it's real?' he questioned in amazement. 'But.. we tried for so long?'

'I know.'

'She didn't hurt you, did she? Or the baby?' he asked, unable to hide the terror in his voice.

'No.' I instinctively touched the dressing on my abdomen. The knife that Riley had plunged into me in an attempt to end my preg nancy had just missed my uterus. I had seen the ultrasound scan and the trace of the tiniest heartbeat imaginable, which confirmed the foetus was viable. I was still pregnant, and Jacob was alive despite Riley Harrison's intentions.

I didn't want to think about what she had taken from me. Or what others – in particular my friends – had taken from her.

couldn't go there. Not yet. I needed time to process everything that had happened before attempting to understand Rebecca Spencer, aka Riley Harrison. Maybe I would never make sense of it. But then, I hadn't witnessed my father attempt to murder my mother at the age of seven or participated in a horrific initiation ceremony at my school in an attempt to be accepted by my peers when I was eleven.

My mother's rejection of me as a child, and my father's complicity was profoundly damaging, but I was still privileged. I hadn't suffered the physical or mental trauma that Riley had endured. Nor had I been targeted or bullied by my peers. So much so, that I tried to end my life. And even then, our headmistress who should have protected Rebecca Spencer failed her. She was expelled from the school as if she were the problem, not the victim of a horrific initiation ceremony. One that should never have been allowed to happen. After her removal from the school, it was as if Rebecca Spencer had never existed. No one talked about her, in particular, Jaz, Ava, Issie and Willow. And now I knew why.

But your so-called friends did this to her! Your friends, Claudia! Including Jaz – your best friend. They hid it from you. How? How could you have not known?

But I hadn't known.

And if you had, what would you have done?

The question tore through me. Would I have protected them? Or would I have reported them at the expense of losing their friendships?

But I knew that I would have stopped the initiation ceremony.

Would you?

I swallowed back the fear that question elicited.

'Hey,' Jacob said. 'you're still crying.'

I wiped at my tears. 'I'm relieved. That's all,' I reassured him.

He gave out a low exhale as he sank back into the pillows.

'I love you,' he murmured.

'I love you,' I whispered.

More tears glided down my face at the acknowledgement that Jacob was going to be all right.

But what about Rebecca Spencer? What about what they did to her? And the consequences of that horrific night... How do you live with that?

43

TWELVE MONTHS LATER

I looked up at Jacob and smiled. My heart ached with joy seeing him holding our daughter.

I reached out and tickled her feet, dangling from the front-facing khaki Ergobaby carrier attached to Jacob. I laughed in response as she kicked and gurgled in delight. The love I felt for both of them threatened at times to destroy me, for I had so much to lose. I reached out for Jacob's hand and held it, needing the reassurance of his touch that this wasn't a dream.

We walked in appreciative silence along the River Frome in Snuff Mills: a wooded park with beautiful walking paths and a community garden – one of our favourite haunts in Bristol. It was the end of May and unseasonably hot. I marvelled at the vibrant, buzzing nature around us, so alive, so filled with the promise of new beginnings. As were we. The three of us had everything we needed and more – so much more.

Jasmine was born four months ago, almost a year after Jaz's death – murder. We both knew when she was born that her name had to be Jasmine. There was no question. And she was Jacob's double, with her big dark, deep brown eyes and dark hair. The paternity test, which I insisted upon after she was born, ruled out any unspoken doubts on his part. *Or mine.*

Jasmine wasn't the only radical change in our lives. We'd moved to St Andrew's in Bristol at the end of last year, buying a fabulous five-bedroomed property with a first-floor veranda on Maurice Road overlooking St Andrew's Park. It was an old, rambling Victorian property, retaining most of its original features and a large back garden, offering us the space we had craved when we had lived in our cosy two-bedroomed house in Kew. Issie's estate had been left to me, as she had no surviving family, and so, with the sale of Kew and Issie's estate, we were in a fortunate position to afford the substantial property in St Andrew's.

It was also a fresh start, away from the memories of Riley Harrison and everything – everyone – I had lost.

And we both loved Bristol. It had a unique magical vibe, and we agreed it was the perfect place to bring up our daughter. Jacob had transferred to Bristol Royal Hospital for Children, one of the leading centres in the UK for children diagnosed with cardiac disease, and I'd secured a post as an associate professor in American literature at Bristol University. My parents shocked us by deciding to move back to the UK when my father retired from the British Embassy in Tokyo at the beginning of the year. My mother, who had always been distant and aloof with me, surprised me with her adoration of Jasmine. Rather than resent my parents' sudden change of heart, I chose to celebrate that Jasmine would have everything I lacked growing up.

As for Willow, she was still recovering. It had been a slow, painful process, but she was a fighter, as I had often reassured Charles during the darkest hours of her recovery. They chose to remain in London, where Willow had bought an art gallery. Her opening exhibition this summer was a tribute to Issie's life, her eclectic paintings and sculptures on display. Willow and Charles were also getting married this summer.

Ava had promised she wouldn't miss their wedding or the opening exhibition. She had relocated to her firm's practice in LA, wanting to put as much distance as physically possible between her and the horror of what had happened to all of us. LA suited Ava. She was thriving out there. Jacob, Jasmine and I were flying out to spend time with her in a few weeks. I wanted her to experience Jasmine while she was still a baby, even though we regularly Face-Timed, and messaged; the same with Willow. The three of us were acutely aware of how precious and arbitrary life could be.

'Did you feed Darcy and Jasper before we left?' I suddenly asked.

Jacob nodded. 'Yes, the boys had breakfast. Not that those two need feeding. You do know they're both obese, right?' Jacob teased.

'Happy is what they are!' I pointed out, smiling.

Zain had been right. Cats do sometimes show up months later. Darcy had returned, half-starved and bedraggled, days before we moved to Bristol. He had somehow found his way back to us. I didn't let myself think about what would have happened if he found his way back home and we had gone: it wasn't worth the pain.

I chose to celebrate the good in life and never talked about the darkness of the past: about what happened to us.

Or what could have happened to us – to my unborn baby. To Jacob.

I understood now why my four school friends chose a pact of silence after that night in the clock tower with Rebecca Spencer and Lottie Hambleton. When something was so dark, so monstrous, why would you speak about it?

I would never understand why Jaz, Issie, Willow and Ava took part in such a heinous act, an initiation that destroyed Rebecca Spencer's life and others. Willow and Ava had tried to explain that they feared Lottie, as we all did back then, but surely, one of them could have stopped it.

Could they, Claudia? Could you have stopped the madness that night?

I shakily breathed out. I still wasn't sure. It was easier to imagine you would do the right thing, but in the moment, who knows?

'Hey, you,' Jacob said, squeezing my hand. 'What are you thinking?'

'Just how lucky I am to have you, Jasmine and the boys,' I replied. 'That's all. I love you, Jacob! And this little one, even though you've been awake since 5 a.m.' I laughed as I kissed Jasmine's precious cheek.

She gurgled again in delight.

How lucky are you, Claudia Harper?

ACKNOWLEDGMENTS

Thanks to my mother and sister for their unwavering support and for being my most valued readers. Thanks always to Francesca, Charlotte, Gabriel-Myles and Ruby. Thanks to Peter Dempsey for all your invaluable and much-appreciated support.

Thanks to Susi Holliday and Ed James for your fabulous advice at the beginning of this journey.

Thanks also to Tom Avitabile.

Thank you to my fantastic literary agent, Annette Crossland.

Thanks to all at Boldwood Books for your brilliance and being such an amazing team. Thank you to both my incredible copy editor, Jade Craddock, and proofreader, Susan Sugden. And, in particular, Caroline Ridding, for being such an exceptional and fabulous editor and for sprinkling her special magic all over this book – thank you.

A final special thank you to my Westie, Issie, for repeatedly trying to share her ball with me while I wrote this book.

ABOUT THE AUTHOR

Danielle Ramsay is the author of the DI Jack Brady crime novels and other dark thrillers. She is a Scot living in the North-East of England.

Sign up to Danielle Ramsay's mailing list here for news, competitions and updates on future books.

Visit Danielle Ramsay's Website:

https://www.danielle-ramsay.com

Follow Danielle Ramsay on social media:

twitter.com/danielleramsay2
facebook.com/Danielle.ramsay.author
instagram.com/danielle.ramsay.author

ALSO BY DANIELLE RAMSAY

The Perfect Husband

My Best Friend's Secret

THE

Murder

LIST

THE MURDER LIST IS A NEWSLETTER DEDICATED TO SPINE-CHILLING FICTION AND GRIPPING PAGE-TURNERS!

SIGN UP TO MAKE SURE YOU'RE ON OUR HIT LIST FOR EXCLUSIVE DEALS, AUTHOR CONTENT, AND COMPETITIONS.

SIGN UP TO OUR NEWSLETTER

BIT.LY/THEMURDERLISTNEWS

Boldwood

Boldwood Books is an award-winning fiction publishing company seeking out the best stories from around the world.

Find out more at www.boldwoodbooks.com

Join our reader community for brilliant books, competitions and offers!

Follow us

@BoldwoodBooks

@TheBoldBookClub

Sign up to our weekly deals newsletter

https://bit.ly/BoldwoodBNewsletter